Mount of Waste

Dayat Suryana

Published by Dayat Suryana, 2025.

This is a work of fiction. Similarities to real people, places, or events are entirely coincidental.

MOUNT OF WASTE

First edition. February 8, 2025.

Copyright © 2025 Dayat Suryana.

ISBN: 979-8230095293

Written by Dayat Suryana.

Also by Dayat Suryana

Adrian
Beyond the Shadow
Echoes of Tomorrow
Out of the Shadow's Reach
The Tapestry of Emotions
Beyond The Shadows: A Journey of Redemption
The Ripple Effect: Awakening
Echoes of the Shadow
Echoes of the Source
Beyond the Shadows: A Journey of Healing
Out of the Circle of Shadows
Breaking the Cycle: Escape from the Architects
Shadow Code
Shadows of the Past
Exit the Shadow Game

Kisah Teladan
Kisah Teladan Jilid 1
Kisah Teladan Jilid 2

Maya
Maya
Maya Series 2
Maya Series 3
Maya Series 4

Standalone
Arka
Jejak Langkah Kolaborasi
Nexus: Shattered Realities
Nexus: Echoes of the Machine
The Quiet After the Storm
Power of Tomorrow
The Dawn of the Forgotten Era
The Trials of Solara
The Last Haven
The Wise King's Wall
The Forgotten Road
Menggapai Surga
Mount of Waste

Table of Contents

Chapter 1: Mount of Waste 1
Chapter 2: The Terrifying Weather 6
Chapter 3: The Eruption of the Mountain of Waste 11
Chapter 4: Panic in the City 16
Chapter 5: The Contaminated Ocean 21
Chapter 6: The Fires That Devoured the City 26
Chapter 7: The Social Impact 31
Chapter 8: The Burned Land 36
Chapter 9: Domino Effect 41
Chapter 10: A Divided World 46
Chapter 11: Life in the Danger Zone 51
Chapter 12: Rediscovering Green Technology 57
Chapter 13: The Rise of New Leadership 63
Bab 14: Global Awareness Movement 68
Chapter 15: The Fortress of Defense 74
Chapter 16: Alpha Research Center 79
Chapter 17: The Shift in Human Mentality 85
Chapter 18: Adventure Amidst the Ruins 91
Chapter 19: Facing New Challenges 96
Chapter 20: The War Against Time 102
Chapter 21: Finding Hope 108
Chapter 22: Limited Resources 114
Chapter 23: The Power of Collaboration 119
Chapter 24: Terror from Nature 125
Chapter 25: The Rise of Technology 130
Chapter 26: Shattered Trust 135
Chapter 27: Mission Beyond the City 141
Chapter 28: Betrayal Amidst the Disaster 150
Chapter 29: Rebuilding Trust 152
Chapter 30: The Rise of a Global Movement 156
Chapter 31: The Race for a Solution 161

Chapter 32: The Connected Network 166
Chapter 33: The New Discovery 171
Chapter 33: A New Discovery 176
Chapter 34: Healing the World 181
Chapter 35: The Meeting of World Leaders 187
Chapter 36: Political Challenges 193
Chapter 37: The Threat from Corporations 199
Chapter 38: Ecosystem Restoration 204
Chapter 39: The Information War 210
Chapter 40: Rising Tensions 216
Chapter 41: Forming a New Alliance 221
Chapter 42: Facing the Energy Crisis 227
Chapter 43: A Breakthrough in Waste Technology 232
Chapter 44: Fighting Hunger 238
Chapter 45: Attack on the Research Center 243
Chapter 46: Introducing Technology on the Ground 248
Chapter 47: The Power of Collective Spirit 253
Chapter 48: Rebuilding the World 259
Chapter 49: Global Uprising 265
Chapter 50: The People's Movement 271
Chapter 51: A New Dawn in the Western World 277
Chapter 52: A Shift in the Eastern World 283
Chapter 53: Digging Deeper 288
Chapter 54: Innovations in Waste Management 294
Chapter 55: Success Amid Despair 300
Chapter 56: Exploring Sustainability 305
Chapter 57: Growing Trust 310
Chapter 58: Fighting the Giants 315
Chapter 59: Revolution in Energy 320
Chapter 60: Challenges in the Remote Regions 325
Chapter 61: Global Dissemination of Technology 331
Chapter 62: Political Tensions 336
Chapter 63: The Fall of the Anti-Development Groups 341

Chapter 64: Technology That Touches Daily Life 347
Chapter 65: Building the Green City 353
Chapter 66: Forging Global Cooperation 359
Chapter 67: Facing an Attack from Within 365
Chapter 68: The Impact on Marine Ecosystems 371
Chapter 69: Collaboration Between Scientists and Activists 377
Chapter 70: Building a Green Economic System 383
Chapter 71: Nurturing the Next Generation 389
Chapter 72: Overcoming the Global Financial Crisis 395
Chapter 73: Spreading Technology in the Third World 401
Chapter 74: The Rise of Terrestrial Ecosystems 407
Chapter 75: Accelerating Global Transformation 413
Chapter 76: The City that Became a Model 419
Chapter 77: Tensions Between Nations 425
Chapter 78: Overcoming Water Scarcity 432
Chapter 79: Coral Reef Restoration 439
Chapter 80: The Zero-Waste Movement 445
Chapter 81: Infrastructure Renewal 451
Chapter 82: Forest Restoration 457
Chapter 83: Global Cultural Shift 466
Chapter 84: Sustainable Economy 472
Chapter 85: The Rise of the Green Generation 478
Chapter 86: Healing the World 484
Chapter 87: Keeping the Awareness Alive 489
Chapter 88: Global Victory 495
Chapter 89: The Final Step 501
Chapter 90: A New Life 507
Chapter 91: A Promising Future 512
Chapter 92: Global Learning 517
Chapter 93: Protecting What Has Been Achieved 523
Chapter 94: New Challenges 529
Chapter 96: A Turning Point 535

Chapter 1: Mount of Waste

The world was suffocating under a thick blanket of discarded materials. A mountain of waste was growing, towering higher than any skyline, casting shadows over cities and forests alike. In every corner of the globe, humanity's negligence and insatiable hunger for consumption had led to the creation of mountains of plastic, metal, and toxic waste. These heaps, once innocuous remnants of daily life, had transformed into monstrous giants. Once pristine beaches were now lines of crumbled plastic bottles and torn wrappers, while fields were buried under electronic junk, old machines, and the ruins of what used to be useful tools. The oceans were clogged with microplastics, their blue depths a memory, now a dull, sickly green. The air, thick with the smell of rotting refuse, hung like a shroud over the planet.

Aldo Clyne, a once-celebrated environmental scientist, stood on the roof of his dilapidated apartment building in what used to be the heart of the city. His eyes scanned the horizon, where the skyline had long been obscured by the immense, rolling mountains of waste that seemed to stretch as far as the eye could see. The air, tainted with the acrid smell of burnt plastic and chemicals, stung his lungs. He coughed, and his fingers instinctively reached for the protective mask hanging loosely around his neck.

The world had changed dramatically in the past few years. Natural disasters had escalated with alarming frequency. Fierce storms, triggered by unpredictable shifts in the atmosphere, ravaged entire cities, while violent earthquakes and eruptions of magma from beneath the Earth's surface rattled the foundations of civilization. Each catastrophe seemed to bring the planet a step closer to its final, irreversible breakdown. But perhaps the most pressing issue was the overwhelming rise of garbage.

When the storm had come, it wasn't just any storm. It had been a disaster like no other, a fierce, almost sentient force that tore through the world, shredding everything in its path. It had scattered mountains of waste far and wide, mixing with the remnants of collapsing buildings and cracked roads. The debris swept across continents, leaving behind scorched lands, ruined towns, and oceans so polluted that the water had become toxic.

For most people, this disaster had felt like the end. The economy had collapsed, governments were no longer functional, and cities were abandoned in favor of makeshift settlements built from the very refuse humanity had discarded. There were no longer any rules, no structure, only the desperate fight to survive in a world that had turned against its own inhabitants. The population had halved in the span of a few short years, and those who remained were constantly battling to find clean air, water, or food.

Aldo, however, could see beyond the immediate chaos. He wasn't just a survivor, he was a man with a mission. The truth was, the storm that had wreaked havoc across the world wasn't a random occurrence. It had been building up for decades, perhaps centuries. The Earth had been pushed too far, and now it was fighting back, attempting to rid itself of the burden of humanity's waste.

For years, Aldo had warned governments and corporations about the dangers of overconsumption, the consequences of disregarding sustainability, and the perils of unchecked industrial growth. His warnings, however, had fallen on deaf ears. Greed, corporate interests, and an ever-growing desire for convenience had blinded the world to the disaster that was already unfolding. And now, with no time left, Aldo found himself at the center of a global crisis that was beyond anything he had ever imagined.

But Aldo wasn't the type to give up. He had spent years working on a solution to this very problem. When the world had first begun to be overwhelmed by waste, he had started researching ways to turn the massive piles of garbage into usable resources. He had designed a machine capable of breaking down complex materials into their base components, converting plastic and metal into reusable substances. He had envisioned a world where waste was no longer a burden but a resource, a world where humanity could live in harmony with the Earth by recycling and reusing everything it consumed.

But his invention had been locked away, buried under layers of bureaucracy and corporate red tape. No one had taken him seriously, not until it was too late. Now, the same invention could be humanity's last hope.

As Aldo stood on the roof, he heard the distant hum of machinery, the grinding sound of another waste-processing plant working overtime to try and deal with the growing mountain of refuse. It was a futile effort. Every day, more trash accumulated than could be processed. There was no escape from the ever-increasing load. There was no way to stop the tide of waste that continued to bury the world.

Aldo turned away from the view and made his way down to the street. Below, the world was a mess of discarded goods, broken buildings, and toxic sludge. People moved like ghosts through the streets, their faces hidden beneath masks, their movements slow and deliberate. The few remaining animals had adapted to the new world, scavenging for food amidst the rubbish.

Aldo's heart ached as he walked. This was the world his generation had created, a world of convenience, excess, and blind consumption. And now, this same world was crumbling.

But in the depths of his despair, Aldo knew there was still a chance to fix it. He wasn't alone in this fight. There were others, people who understood the severity of the situation and were willing to work together. People like Nina.

DAYAT SURYANA

Nina Kavanagh, a tireless environmental activist, had been one of Aldo's closest allies before the storm. She had been outspoken about the dangers of pollution and the need for sustainable practices long before the world's crisis reached its peak. After the storm, Nina had become a leader among the survivors, organizing grassroots efforts to clean up the wastelands and rebuild in ways that were ecologically responsible. She was a beacon of hope, always pushing forward, never giving in to despair.

It was Nina who had contacted Aldo after the storm. She had heard of his work on waste management technology and believed that together they could make a real difference. She had told him that there were still pockets of survivors scattered across the globe, people who were ready to take action, to work together and find a solution. And with her help, Aldo knew they could implement his technology on a large scale, perhaps even reverse some of the damage.

Aldo had agreed to meet Nina, and now he was heading to their rendezvous point, a small community center nestled at the edge of the city. As he walked, he passed a group of scavengers digging through a pile of discarded electronic devices. They were looking for anything that could be repurposed or sold. A few children ran past, playing in the rubble, their faces smeared with dirt. The world was broken, but it was still alive, still fighting.

When Aldo reached the center, he found Nina waiting for him outside. She was as determined as ever, her sharp eyes scanning the horizon, her hands clasped in front of her. Her hair was wild, her clothes torn, but her presence was as strong as ever. She smiled when she saw Aldo.

"You're late," she teased.

"I had to navigate a mountain of trash," Aldo said with a wry grin.

Nina raised an eyebrow. "And?"

MOUNT OF WASTE

Aldo shrugged. "It's getting bigger every day."

Nina's expression darkened. "And that's why we need to act now. People are desperate, Aldo. We can't wait any longer."

"I know," he said, his voice quiet. "But I think we might have a chance. I've been working on something that could change everything."

She stepped closer, her face lit with curiosity. "What is it?"

Aldo pulled a small, weathered notebook from his bag and opened it to a page filled with diagrams and equations. "This," he said, pointing to the complex calculations. "It's a waste-to-resource technology. It can turn trash into usable materials, plastics into fuel, metals into building components. It's still in the prototype phase, but it's something we can work with."

Nina studied the page, her eyes narrowing with thought. "It's ambitious. But if it works..."

"If it works," Aldo interrupted, "it could change the way we think about waste. We can recycle everything, plastic, metal, electronics, everything. We can eliminate the mountains of trash."

Nina nodded, her expression softening. "Then let's make it happen."

Together, they would fight to save the world, one piece of trash at a time.

Chapter 2: The Terrifying Weather

The world had always experienced its share of weather anomalies, but nothing compared to what had begun to unfold. As the mountain of waste continued to grow, so did the intensity and frequency of natural disasters. What had once been rare occurrences, an unexpected storm or an occasional earthquake,bwere now everyday events, each one more violent and unpredictable than the last.

The world was gripped by the forces of nature in ways it had never experienced. Hurricanes, once confined to the tropical regions, now lashed out across continents, their winds and rains destroying everything in their path. Tornadoes appeared in places they had never been seen before, ripping apart buildings and sending debris flying through the air. Earthquakes and volcanic eruptions were becoming commonplace, shaking the ground beneath people's feet and spewing molten lava and ash into the atmosphere. Rivers, once steady and reliable, flooded their banks without warning, washing away entire neighborhoods in a matter of hours.

For Aldo, the scientist who had spent years studying the planet's fragile ecosystem, the changes were not just troubling, they were signs of impending disaster. He had been warning the world for years about the dangers of environmental neglect, about how humanity's wasteful practices were pushing the Earth to its breaking point. And now, with every storm and every disaster, his warnings seemed more like prophecies.

It was the middle of the night when the first truly terrifying storm struck the city. Aldo was awake, as he often was, working on his latest waste-to-resource prototype. The wind howled outside, its gusts rattling the windows and shaking the walls of his small, makeshift lab. He had heard the warning alerts earlier that evening, a rare occurrence, since most weather systems had long since stopped following predictable patterns. But this storm, the meteorologists said, was different. It was no ordinary hurricane or thunderstorm. It was something far worse.

The sky had been a sickly shade of green when the storm began to form. The clouds churned above the city like a vast, dark ocean, pulsating with an unnatural energy. Aldo's eyes had narrowed when he saw it. He had seen similar patterns before, patterns that signaled a major atmospheric disturbance, ones that were often caused by the breakdown of the Earth's natural systems. But this... this was different. This was not just a storm. This was a warning.

He had barely begun to secure the windows when the storm hit. The wind howled with the force of a thousand freight trains, rattling the frame of the building and shaking it to its core. The streets outside were consumed by a wall of water, rising quickly and relentlessly, flooding everything in its path. Lightning cracked through the sky, illuminating the chaos for brief moments before darkness returned.

Aldo stood by the window, watching the tempest rage outside. The storm was unlike anything he had ever seen. There was an intensity to it, a fury that seemed almost intentional. It was as though the Earth itself was retaliating against the damage humanity had inflicted upon it. He knew, deep down, that this was just the beginning.

When the storm finally passed, the city was left in ruins. Buildings had been torn apart, trees uprooted, and streets flooded with debris. The damage was catastrophic, but it wasn't just the destruction that concerned Aldo. It was the pattern, the pattern of storms, earthquakes, and strange weather phenomena that had been occurring more frequently over the past several years. It was no coincidence. The Earth was in the midst of an environmental collapse, and time was running out.

The next morning, Aldo gathered his team at the small, temporary lab they had set up in the heart of the city. Nina Kavanagh, the activist and his closest ally, arrived first, her face as grim as ever. Her hair, once neat and tidy, was now wild and unkempt, a reflection of the chaos that had taken over the world. Her eyes were filled with determination, but there was a deep weariness behind them.

"The storm last night was just the latest," Nina said as she entered the lab. "What's next?"

Aldo sighed, running a hand through his messy hair. "I've been studying the patterns of these storms. And it's not just weather. Earthquakes, volcanic eruptions, they're all becoming more frequent, more intense. I don't think it's a coincidence."

Nina leaned over his shoulder, studying the data on his screen. "What are you saying? You think it's all connected to the waste?"

"I do," Aldo replied, his voice heavy with concern. "The planet is overloaded with waste, garbage, chemicals, plastics, metals. It's all disrupting the natural balance. The Earth is responding to the stress, and it's doing so violently. These storms, the earthquakes, the volcanoes, they're all part of a larger, systemic breakdown."

"But how can we fix it?" Nina asked, her voice tinged with frustration. "We've been trying to stop the pollution for years, but it's only getting worse. The waste keeps piling up."

"We need to act fast," Aldo said, a sense of urgency in his tone. "We can't just focus on cleaning up the waste. We need to find a way to restore the Earth's natural systems, its atmosphere, its oceans, its ecosystems. If we don't, the planet will continue to fight back until there's nothing left."

Nina stared at him for a long moment, her eyes searching his face for answers. "You have a plan?"

Aldo nodded, his fingers flying over the keyboard as he pulled up more data. "I've been working on a waste-to-resource system, something that could turn garbage into usable materials. If we can implement this technology on a global scale, it could reduce the pressure on the planet. We can start with the waste, recycle everything, plastics, metals, even hazardous materials, and convert them into clean energy or building materials. But we need to act quickly. These storms, these disasters, they're just the beginning."

As Aldo spoke, the screen in front of him flashed with new alerts. A massive storm had formed off the coast, one even more powerful than the previous night's. It was moving quickly, with winds reaching speeds of over 200 miles per hour. The forecast predicted it would make landfall within the next 24 hours.

"This is it," Aldo said, his voice tight with tension. "This storm is going to be worse than anything we've seen before."

Nina's jaw tightened. "We have to stop it."

"There's nothing we can do to stop it. The weather systems are beyond our control," Aldo replied. "But we can still fight back. We can mitigate the damage. We can save as many people as possible and start preparing for what's next."

Nina nodded, her resolve hardening. "Then we start now."

As the hours passed and the storm continued to churn toward the city, Aldo and Nina worked furiously, preparing their teams for the worst. They gathered resources, evacuated vulnerable communities, and began implementing their waste-to-resource plans in the hope that it might buy them time. It wasn't a perfect solution, but it was the only one they had.

That night, the storm hit.

It was unlike anything anyone had ever witnessed. The winds were so fierce that they tore entire buildings from their foundations, hurling them across the city like children's toys. The rain fell in torrents, flooding streets and washing away everything in its path. Lightning crackled through the sky in violent bursts, and the air was thick with the stench of burning debris.

As Aldo and Nina worked to guide people to safety, they realized that the storm was only part of a much larger problem. The planet had been pushed beyond its limits, and the consequences were now being felt in real-time. Every storm, every earthquake, every volcanic eruption was a testament to the Earth's suffering. It was as if the planet itself was fighting back, trying to rid itself of the infection that was humanity.

In the aftermath of the storm, the world was left to pick up the pieces. Entire cities lay in ruins, and the cost of the damage was incalculable. But amidst the destruction, there was a glimmer of hope. People had survived. They had banded together in the face of impossible odds, helping each other, finding strength in unity. And in that unity, Aldo saw the possibility of change.

It wasn't too late. Not yet.

But time was running out, and the storms were only going to get worse.

Chapter 3: The Eruption of the Mountain of Waste

The storm had raged for hours, but the worst was yet to come. Dark clouds hung heavy in the sky, swirling in unnatural patterns as if the atmosphere itself had become unhinged. The winds howled, screeching like animals in pain, and lightning cracked across the heavens with an intensity that seemed almost sentient. There was something apocalyptic about this storm, something far more dangerous than any weather event humanity had experienced before. And it wasn't just the fury of the storm that made it so terrifying; it was the way the storm had triggered the collapse of the very thing that had been silently building for decades: the great Mountain of Waste.

The world had seen signs of it in the years leading up to this moment. The garbage had accumulated slowly at first, plastic bottles, cans, electronics, and hazardous materials, all of it piled up in cities, towns, and industrial hubs. But as time passed, and the world continued its reckless consumption, those piles grew larger. The Earth's ecosystems, already stressed by climate change, were now suffocating under the weight of human waste.

And now, the inevitable had occurred. The massive storm, with its unprecedented force, had struck the global waste deposits like a hammer to an anvil. The Mountain of Waste was no longer a distant problem. It was an immediate, catastrophic disaster.

Aldo Clyne, his heart pounding in his chest, stood on the rooftop of his lab once more, staring at the chaos unfolding below. The storm's winds were merciless, uprooting trees, snapping power lines, and shattering the fragile buildings that still stood in the decaying city. But what was most terrifying was the sight of the enormous piles of trash, mountains that had once been immobile and stable, beginning to disintegrate under the storm's fury. With every gust of wind and every flash of lightning, tons of waste began to shift, break apart, and scatter across the land.

"I warned them," Aldo muttered under his breath, his voice barely audible over the howling wind. "I warned them that this day would come."

A massive wave of debris surged down the main street, a torrent of plastic, metal, and electronic scraps. The accumulated waste, which had once seemed harmless, now acted as a destructive force. It slammed into buildings, smashing through windows and tearing apart the fragile walls of what remained of the city. The sound was deafening, like an avalanche of death descending upon them. Aldo could see the streets being buried under tons of waste, turning into a sprawling, uncontrollable river of garbage.

Nina Kavanagh, the activist who had become Aldo's closest ally, appeared beside him on the rooftop, her eyes wide with shock. She had seen devastation before, after all, she had spent years working to clean up the aftermath of the world's carelessness, but even she had not anticipated this level of destruction.

"This is worse than we thought," Nina said, her voice trembling. "The trash is everywhere. It's flooding the streets, it's burying buildings, it's poisoning the air. We can't even breathe out here."

Aldo nodded, his face drawn tight with anxiety. "The storm was the trigger. It's pushing everything into overdrive. The waste was unstable to begin with. And now... now it's everywhere."

Below them, the destruction continued to unfold at an alarming pace. As the mountain of waste collapsed, it spilled out onto the streets like a wave crashing against the shore. The streets that had once been bustling with life were now unrecognizable, completely buried beneath a sea of discarded goods. Some of the debris caught fire, fueled by the high temperatures generated by the storm's lightning strikes. The smoke billowed up into the sky, adding to the toxic cocktail of gases and particles already swirling in the air.

"This isn't just about the waste anymore," Nina said, her voice filled with urgency. "It's about survival. We need to find a way to contain this. We can't let it spread further."

Aldo's mind raced as he processed what she was saying. The global waste crisis was no longer a theoretical problem or a distant threat, it was a full-blown disaster, and it was happening right in front of them. The impact was immediate and devastating. Entire communities were being swallowed by the torrent of trash, and the environment was suffering irreparable damage.

"It's not just about containment anymore, Nina," Aldo said, his voice hardening. "The planet is already broken. We need to stop the bleeding, or we're all going to drown in our own waste."

His words hung in the air between them as they watched the madness unfold below. They could see the flickering lights of emergency responders, trying desperately to navigate through the debris-filled streets, but it was a futile effort. The infrastructure was collapsing. The power grid was down. Communication lines were severed. In the face of such overwhelming destruction, the systems that had once kept society functioning were now powerless.

"Where do we even start?" Nina asked, her expression a mixture of disbelief and determination. "The mountain of waste is everywhere. The cleanup... it's impossible."

"I've been working on something," Aldo replied, his voice steady but filled with a sense of urgency. "My technology. The waste-to-resource system. It's not just a way to recycle, it's a way to break down the waste on a molecular level and convert it into something usable. It can turn this mess into something we can use to rebuild."

"But we need time, Aldo. We don't have time," Nina said, her eyes wide with fear. "The world is already falling apart. The mountains of waste are spreading, and if we don't act fast, it'll be too late."

Aldo was silent for a moment, his mind whirling. He knew she was right. The time for small, incremental changes had passed. The crisis had escalated beyond anyone's control. The Earth had reached a tipping point, and the only thing left to do was to confront the problem head-on.

"We need to take this to the world," Aldo said, his voice firm with resolve. "We need to implement the technology I've been working on, but we need global cooperation. If we can convert the waste into usable materials, we can stop the environmental collapse. We can save what's left of the planet."

"But how do we convince everyone?" Nina asked, her brow furrowing. "The world is in chaos right now. Governments are falling apart. People are fighting just to survive. No one's going to listen."

"We'll make them listen," Aldo replied. "We have no choice. The planet is at war with us, Nina. It's fighting back with everything it's got, and if we don't work together to fix it, we're going to lose."

A thunderous crack of lightning split the sky, followed by a violent rumble of thunder. The earth trembled beneath their feet, and a distant explosion shook the air. Aldo and Nina exchanged a quick, knowing glance. The storm wasn't over yet. The worst was still to come.

They had to act quickly.

The next few days were a blur of frantic activity. Aldo, Nina, and their small group of allies worked around the clock to formulate a plan. They began gathering what little resources remained in the ruined city, tools, equipment, anything they could use to implement Aldo's waste-to-resource technology. The storm had left them with little to work with, but their determination kept them moving forward.

In the midst of the devastation, the reality of what was happening became clear: the planet's fragile systems had failed, and humanity was now on the brink of collapse. The storm that had triggered the eruption of the Mountain of Waste was only a small part of the larger problem. The real threat was the sheer scale of the damage. The environmental crisis wasn't just about waste anymore. It was about survival, about finding a way to rebuild, to restore balance, and to stop the planet's downward spiral.

Aldo knew that if they didn't succeed, the damage would be irreversible. The waste would continue to pile up, poisoning the environment, creating more storms, more disasters. Humanity's negligence had brought them to this point, and now it was time to face the consequences.

But there was hope. The technology Aldo had developed, the waste-to-resource system, could be the key to turning things around. It wasn't a perfect solution, but it was the best chance they had.

As the storm continued to rage outside, Aldo and Nina worked tirelessly to prepare for the next phase of their plan. The clock was ticking, and the world was teetering on the edge of oblivion.

Chapter 4: Panic in the City

The morning after the eruption of the Mountain of Waste, the cities across the globe seemed to pulse with a quiet, yet palpable, sense of dread. The storm had passed, leaving behind a grim, haunting silence. But that silence was soon shattered by the desperate sounds of sirens, cries for help, and the overwhelming cacophony of chaos. The world had not just witnessed a natural disaster; it had watched as its own excesses, its own irresponsibility, exploded into violence, threatening everything humanity had built.

In cities once brimming with life and energy, the streets now felt like warzones. People ran, stumbling through knee-deep mounds of garbage, looking for shelter, trying to escape the relentless onslaught of debris that seemed to fall from the sky in waves. The air was thick with the stench of burning plastic, metals, and chemicals, toxic fumes mixing with the dust and smoke. Visibility was poor, and the very ground beneath them seemed unstable, shifting as massive piles of waste tumbled into the streets, crushing cars, trees, and buildings alike.

In the heart of one such city, the situation was spiraling out of control. Aldo had seen the headlines, read the reports, and witnessed firsthand the devastation that the waste mountain had caused. But the full extent of the disaster, of the chaos that had gripped society, was something he had not fully prepared for. As he watched the scenes unfold on his small, makeshift TV, the images were almost too much to process. People screamed in terror, pushing and shoving one another, trying to escape the carnage and debris. Desperate individuals clawed their way through heaps of trash, some hoping to find shelter, others searching for lost loved ones.

In a way, the eruption of the waste mountain was the final chapter of a story that had been written over years of environmental degradation and neglect. What had once been a distant issue, talk of pollution, climate change, and the dangers of waste, had suddenly become impossible to ignore. Now, the consequences were clear: societies were unprepared for the fallout of their own carelessness.

Nina Kavanagh, ever the activist, had mobilized her team to assist in the relief efforts, but even she was struggling to keep her focus amid the pandemonium. She moved through the streets, rallying people to join in efforts to clear the debris and organize shelters, but the task was insurmountable. In every direction, panic was rising.

As Aldo walked out onto the street, he was immediately struck by the overwhelming sense of fear that hung in the air. People shouted to one another, desperately trying to make sense of what had happened. A group of children, separated from their parents in the chaos, huddled together, their faces streaked with dirt and tears. Their wide eyes reflected the panic that had overtaken the city. The structures around them, buildings once proud and sturdy, had collapsed under the weight of the waste, and what had once been safe, bustling neighborhoods were now buried under tons of debris.

The toxic fog made it difficult to breathe, and yet there was no time to stop. People had become like rats in a maze, running in every direction, seeking shelter, food, water, anything to survive. Those lucky enough to have homes still standing huddled inside, sealing doors and windows in an attempt to shield themselves from the growing environmental disaster outside.

Aldo knew they couldn't keep running from it forever. The world had hit a tipping point, and no matter how hard humanity tried to deny it, the consequences were now undeniable. The waste, like an unstoppable force of nature, had breached all borders. The storm, the collapse of infrastructure, the debris, it was the planet's final warning.

He met Nina near the base of a collapsed skyscraper, her expression tight with determination. Her hair was disheveled, and the dirt and grime streaking across her face only added to the fierce look in her eyes. She looked like she hadn't slept in days, and yet she remained focused on the task at hand.

"It's spreading," Nina said, voice hoarse, her eyes scanning the horizon. "The trash is everywhere, more people are trapped, and it's only getting worse. We can't contain this. We need to get the message out now, Aldo. People have to know what's coming."

Aldo nodded grimly. "The waste is only part of it. It's the systemic breakdown that's the real problem. The infrastructure is failing, the air's toxic, the food supply's been contaminated. The next few days, maybe hours, are going to be critical. We need to act fast."

"Act fast?" Nina's laugh was sharp, bitter. "How? The whole world's falling apart. People are panicking, looting, fighting over resources. There's no system left to rely on."

Aldo turned to her, his eyes filled with resolve. "If we don't take action now, we won't have a future to fight for. I've been working on a solution, Nina, something to convert the waste into usable materials. But we need time, and we need global cooperation. The systems are failing, but we can still start over. We can't fix everything, but we can make sure this doesn't spiral any further."

"I know. But how do we make the world listen when it's already breaking down?" Nina asked, her voice filled with desperation.

Aldo paused, watching as another massive pile of garbage tumbled down the street, knocking over a nearby vehicle and sending a plume of dust and debris into the air. The chaos was overwhelming, and yet there was no time to wallow in helplessness.

MOUNT OF WASTE

"We'll have to force them to listen," Aldo said firmly. "We're not just fighting the waste. We're fighting the world's indifference to this problem. The longer we wait, the worse it's going to get. We need the people, the governments, the organizations, everyone to understand what's at stake."

The moment he said it, Aldo knew it was true. They were no longer just dealing with environmental degradation or waste management. They were fighting for survival.

As nightfall began to descend on the city, the sense of panic reached its zenith. The streets, once filled with the hum of daily life, were now a battlefield. People fought to secure what little they could, a bottle of water, a can of food, a safe place to hide. The sheer scale of the disaster was too vast to comprehend, and yet it was impossible to ignore. Humanity had pushed the planet to its breaking point, and now nature was exacting its toll.

The government had sent in military units to maintain order, but their presence only seemed to heighten the fear. Soldiers clashed with panicked civilians who looted stores for anything they could carry. Gunfire echoed through the streets as tensions escalated. People were desperate, but they were also angry, angry at the government for its inability to prevent the disaster, angry at corporations for contributing to the crisis, and angry at themselves for allowing it to get this far.

Aldo and Nina moved through the streets, doing their best to provide what aid they could, but they were only a small part of a much larger crisis. With the waste spreading like wildfire, there were few places that had remained untouched. The environmental collapse had long since moved beyond simple solutions; it had now become a global emergency.

"It's all falling apart, Aldo," Nina said as they made their way through the chaos. "No one's listening. People are panicking, and they're turning on each other."

"I know," Aldo replied, his voice grim. "But we can't afford to give up. This is why we've been fighting, why we've been warning them. It's now or never."

As they reached a clearing in the middle of a once-thriving commercial district, Aldo took a deep breath. The air was thick with ash and dust, and the smoke from burning debris still lingered in the atmosphere. This was their reality now. The world was teetering on the edge of collapse, and there was no going back.

"We can't stop it all," Aldo said, his voice steady despite the panic around him. "But we can still save what we can. It's not too late to change."

But the question remained: Would the world be able to change before it was too late? Would humanity be able to pull itself back from the brink, or would the waste that had once been a distant problem consume everything in its path?

As the sun set on the horizon, painting the sky with streaks of orange and red, the city plunged into darkness. The power grid had failed. The panic had only just begun.

Chapter 5: The Contaminated Ocean

The storm had torn through everything. It had decimated cities, ravaged ecosystems, and left a trail of destruction that would take decades, if not centuries, to repair. But the true horror of the situation had only begun to unfold. As if the Earth itself had taken its last breath, the storm's fury had not only scattered the mountains of waste across the land but had also cast them into the oceans. Vast, unspeakable volumes of garbage, plastics, metals, chemicals, electronics, had been swept into the waters, tainting the very lifeblood of the planet: the oceans.

It didn't take long before the evidence of the ocean's suffering became apparent.

In the first few days after the storm, the oceans, once a symbol of life and beauty, began to change. The waters that had once shimmered with life were now thick with pollutants, tainted by the garbage that had been cast upon them. The once-clear blue waves had become a dirty, murky brown, the salt air now laced with the acrid stench of burning plastics and chemicals. At first, it was just a few debris patches along the coastlines, drifting in from the storm, but soon the problem grew to catastrophic proportions.

By the end of the week, the marine world had begun to show signs of its demise.

The fish, once abundant and diverse, had begun to die off in horrifying numbers. Entire schools of fish that had once danced through the waters now floated lifeless on the surface, their bodies bloated and discolored from the toxic chemicals that leached from the debris. Coral reefs, those beautiful, fragile ecosystems that had long been the home to millions of species,vwere beginning to bleach and crumble, their vibrant colors fading into ghostly whites as the pollution smothered them.

The impact was far-reaching. For millennia, the oceans had been the foundation of life on Earth, providing sustenance, oxygen, and a balance to the planet's delicate ecosystem. But now, the oceans were choking. The waste that had been dumped into the seas, from plastic bottles to oil and hazardous chemicals, had clogged up the delicate filtration systems of the marine environment. The once-pure waters had become a toxic sludge, a silent killer creeping through the food chain.

In coastal cities, fishermen were among the first to feel the effects of the disaster. Nets once full of fish were now empty or, worse, filled with rotting carcasses. The sea that had provided for them and their communities for generations had become a graveyard. The loss of marine life was devastating, not just to the ecosystem, but to the millions of people who depended on the oceans for their livelihoods. The fishing industry, which had been a pillar of countless economies, was now in freefall.

Aldo had spent his days in a small, makeshift laboratory by the coast, trying to piece together what was happening. He had always understood that the oceans were the planet's great regulator, its vital organ, but now he was witnessing its unraveling in real-time. The data he had collected, the observations he had made, it was all pointing in the same direction. The oceans were dying, and with them, the rest of the world was following suit.

The most alarming development was the growing mass of dead fish that now floated on the surface of the oceans. The smell was unbearable, but it wasn't the smell that horrified Aldo. It was the realization that the problem was not just a regional one, it was a global disaster. The scale of the contamination was unimaginable. Waste had been deposited in every corner of the seas, and the toxic runoff from the land had only added to the burden.

Aldo stood at the edge of the dock, staring at the stretch of blackened water. A few feet away, a group of fishermen in hazmat suits worked to collect the carcasses of dead fish, their movements slow and deliberate as they salvaged what they could. But there was no question, whatever they took from the water would be tainted, beyond repair.

"We're losing everything," a gruff voice interrupted Aldo's thoughts. It was one of the fishermen, an older man whose face was weathered and tired, his eyes dim with the weight of years spent working the sea.

"We were the first to see it," he continued, shaking his head in disbelief. "The fish started dying. Then the reefs... they just vanished. There's nothing left out there, Doc. Nothing. And now, the water's not safe to drink. It's all contaminated."

Aldo didn't respond immediately. He had known the oceans were in trouble, but hearing it from the people who had spent their lives working there, whose very existence had depended on the health of the sea, struck him like a blow to the chest.

"We're running out of time," the fisherman muttered, as if reading Aldo's thoughts. "How long before it spreads to the rest of the world? How long before there's nothing left?"

"I don't know," Aldo replied. His voice was barely a whisper, carried away by the wind. "But we have to find a way to reverse the damage before it's too late."

By the end of the month, the situation had escalated. As the ocean's ecosystems collapsed, the global consequences became undeniable. It wasn't just the loss of fish or the destruction of coral reefs; it was the disruption of the entire marine food chain. Birds that had relied on fish for sustenance began starving, and the larger predators in the ocean, whales, sharks, and seals, were now struggling to find food.

On the shorelines, the once-thriving beach tourism industries were collapsing. Beaches were littered with dead marine life, and the toxic water made it dangerous for humans to even go near the coast. The algae blooms, which had begun to rise in response to the overload of nutrients in the water, were spreading rapidly, turning large sections of the ocean into anoxic dead zones where nothing could survive.

In cities along the coast, panic was setting in. People who had never known life without the sea now found themselves stranded, unable to feed their families. Food prices soared as the catch dwindled to nothing, and the cost of seafood became astronomical. The price of basic resources, especially clean water, skyrocketed. Even the most basic survival tools, water filters, canned goods, basic medicine, became increasingly scarce. Tensions between nations mounted as each country fought for access to dwindling resources.

Aldo had no illusions about the road ahead. The oceans were at the brink of collapse, and the longer the waste and pollution persisted, the less likely it was that any form of recovery could take place. But the idea of giving up was unthinkable.

In the midst of all this destruction, Aldo, Nina, and their team worked around the clock, developing a plan to mitigate the damage. Aldo's technology, designed to convert waste into usable resources, was now more critical than ever. If they could find a way to extract the harmful chemicals and pollutants from the ocean, it could serve as a starting point. They had to purify the water, clean up the beaches, restore the health of the reefs. But time was running out, and every day that passed brought the oceans closer to a point of no return.

As the situation grew more desperate, Aldo reached out to his colleagues in other countries. The oceans were not bound by national borders, and this was a global crisis that demanded a unified response. It wasn't just about waste management anymore; it was about survival. The oceans, once the lifeblood of the planet, were now the final frontier for humanity's efforts to save the Earth.

MOUNT OF WASTE

The world had ignored the oceans for far too long. Now, the oceans were giving humanity its final warning. Would they listen? Would they act in time, or would they allow the oceans to become the tomb of the Earth?

It was a race against time. And Aldo knew, deep down, that if they didn't move quickly, the ocean's destruction would be just the beginning. The planet was fragile, and the delicate balance between humanity and nature had already begun to tip dangerously toward the point of no return.

The news of the ocean's deterioration spread quickly across the world. Social media platforms were flooded with images of the dying marine life, the devastation of coral reefs, and the growing plastic islands in the middle of the oceans. Environmental groups organized protests, demanding that governments take immediate action. The world, once oblivious to the plight of the oceans, was waking up to the reality of what they had done.

But the question remained: Was it too late to reverse the damage?

For Aldo, the answer wasn't clear. What he did know was that the oceans were not just a casualty of human neglect, they were the planet's last hope. If humanity could not heal the oceans, there would be nothing left to save. The time for action was now. And if they didn't act quickly, the world would lose not just the oceans, but everything.

Chapter 6: The Fires That Devoured the City

The crisis was no longer just a question of waste. It was a multi-front war, and each new wave of destruction felt more inevitable than the last. After the oceans began to choke on the waste, the land seemed to fight back in its own way, unleashing a fury that threatened to consume everything in its path. It was as though nature, angered by the decades of human disregard, had finally decided that enough was enough. The storm had already triggered a devastating cascade of events, but the worst was yet to come.

The first sparks were small, unnoticed by many. A trash pile, left to fester in the hot sun, ignited under the blistering heat, feeding on the toxic waste that lay in the streets. Then the fires spread. What started as a minor blaze in a neglected alley quickly escalated, its rapid growth fueled by the endless heaps of discarded plastics, chemicals, and electronics. The streets, once bustling with people and life, became a labyrinth of fire and smoke, twisting and spiraling like a monstrous serpent.

By the time the first sirens wailed across the city, it was too late.

The heat was unbearable. People who had been gathering water, scavenging for food, or trying to rebuild what little they could of their homes, now found themselves trapped in a nightmare of flames. The fires spread with a terrifying speed, licking the sides of buildings, catching trees and cars ablaze, and sparking new fires in the debris scattered across the city. The garbage, the very waste that had been neglected for years, now became the perfect fuel for the inferno.

Inside homes and businesses, the fire quickly became an unstoppable force. Every corner of the city seemed to ignite in an instant, and the toxic fumes from burning plastics filled the air, poisoning everything in its reach. The fires raced along the streets, devouring the landscape with an insatiable hunger. The metallic smell of burning electronics mixed with the sickening stench of burning waste, and the city's once vibrant skyline, now obscured by smoke and fire, seemed to tremble under the weight of the destruction.

Aldo had just returned from the coast, having witnessed firsthand the terrible fate of the oceans. He had barely had time to process what had happened when the news reached him about the fires consuming the city. The air was thick with ash and smoke as he stepped outside, and the sun, blocked out by the plumes of smoke, cast a red hue over everything. The sky, once clear and blue, now resembled a war zone, chaos in the heavens mirrored by chaos below.

"How long before it reaches us?" Nina's voice was raw with worry as she approached Aldo, her face streaked with soot. She had been out in the streets, organizing what little help they could offer, but the scope of the disaster was growing too vast to manage. It was no longer just a local issue, it was a global one.

"It's already here," Aldo muttered, his gaze fixed on the inferno that was rapidly closing in. The fire was not selective; it consumed everything, indifferent to the people, homes, and businesses it obliterated. No building seemed immune, fire leapt from rooftop to rooftop, fueled by the piles of waste that lined the streets. The skyscrapers, once shining symbols of progress, were now towering infernos.

The heat from the flames was unbearable, and people fled in all directions, their eyes wide with fear. The fire had become the perfect storm, born of human negligence, it now consumed entire city blocks in a matter of hours. With no way to contain the flames, and the smoke blurring visibility to almost nothing, there was no place to escape. People raced through streets already choked with debris, some carrying what little they could salvage from their homes, while others ran for their lives, with no hope of returning to anything they once knew.

Aldo and Nina joined a group of survivors who had fled to a nearby building that had somehow remained intact. But even there, they were not safe. The fires were now surrounding them, and they could hear the faint crackling of burning material in the distance. The world had become a tinderbox, and the smallest spark, whether from the heat of the sun or a careless ember, could set it all ablaze.

"Where do we go now?" Nina asked, her voice thick with desperation. "How do we stop this?"

Aldo swallowed hard, looking at the smoke-filled horizon. "We can't stop it now. Not without the right resources, the right help. But we can try to protect those who are left."

As the fire roared through the streets, there was nothing they could do but watch. The damage had already been done. Entire neighborhoods, once full of life, were now reduced to smoldering heaps of ash. Buildings that had stood tall for generations were nothing more than charred skeletons, and the streets, once bustling with commerce and community, were now eerily empty, save for the charred remains of homes and the dead bodies that littered the sidewalks.

The fires, fanned by the volatile fumes from the burning garbage, seemed endless. They crept into residential areas, sparked by the very things humanity had discarded carelessly for decades, plastics, chemicals, and electronic waste. Even the water used to try to contain the flames was rendered useless. The water supply was contaminated, tainted by the very chemicals that had once been confined to landfills and waste treatment plants.

Aldo's mind raced, trying to calculate how long they had before the fire would reach them, but there was no predicting it. This was unlike anything he had ever seen. The destruction was all-consuming, and there were no safe havens.

The next few hours were a blur of frantic efforts to get as many people out as possible. Aldo helped Nina and the rest of the survivors gather whatever supplies they could, water, food, and medical kits. But the task seemed pointless. What good were a few bottles of water when the world itself was drowning in fire? What use was a medical kit when the very air they breathed was toxic?

As night fell, the city was barely recognizable. Flames illuminated the landscape in harsh, flickering light, casting shadows that danced like ghosts across the ruins. The fires burned well into the night, and Aldo knew that the devastation would continue until the fires had consumed every last shred of fuel they could feed on. The city was already lost.

Meanwhile, in the heart of the disaster, global leaders began to convene, desperately trying to piece together a response. But it was too late for bureaucracy. The world had waited too long to act, and now, every decision felt like a bandage on a wound that was already fatal. Aldo, despite his own grief and sense of defeat, was receiving calls from various governments and organizations asking for solutions, for advice on how to stop the fires or at least contain the damage. But how could he answer them?

His mind wandered back to the conversations he had had with Nina and his team. Their innovations in waste management—solutions that were meant to restore balance—had not yet been fully implemented. And now the fires, fueled by the very waste they had hoped to manage, had destroyed any hope of rolling out those solutions on a global scale.

As the city burned, Aldo knew there would be no quick recovery. Not from the waste, not from the fires, not from the ocean's death. The cities, which had once been thriving centers of culture and commerce, had been reduced to ruins. Entire populations were displaced, their lives scattered in the wake of destruction. And though there was no denying the enormity of the crisis, Aldo still held on to one fragile hope, that the world would awaken from its apathy before it was too late.

But it was hard to say if humanity was ready to face the consequences of its actions. Fires that had begun as a result of waste, an aftershock from years of ignorance and disregard, had now become the defining image of an era of collapse. The fires weren't just consuming the city; they were consuming the very soul of the world.

As the dawn broke, casting a faint light over the smoking ruins, Aldo couldn't help but wonder: Could humanity rebuild after this? Or had they finally reached the point of no return?

Chapter 7: The Social Impact

The fires that had torn through the cities had left behind a barren wasteland, a stark reminder of how quickly life could turn to ashes. What was once vibrant urban sprawls now stood as smoldering ruins, their skeletal remains barely visible through the thick haze of smoke that continued to hang in the air. People who had once been accustomed to comfort, security, and routine were now forced into a harsh reality of survival.

The fires had done more than just destroy property. They had dismantled the social fabric that had once held everything together. Families were torn apart, neighborhoods were obliterated, and every system, be it healthcare, food distribution, or law enforcement, had collapsed under the weight of the catastrophe. What followed was something much darker: the breakdown of society itself.

The survivors, those who had managed to escape the infernos, or whose homes had not yet been consumed by the flames, now found themselves in a desperate race for survival. The needs of the hour were clear: food, water, shelter, and security. But those things were in short supply. The world had already been reeling from the waste crisis, and the disaster had only exacerbated the shortage of basic resources. Entire communities were left stranded, isolated from the help they so desperately needed. The remaining infrastructures had collapsed; roads were impassable, utilities were down, and communication lines were severed.

People fled their homes in droves, moving toward what they hoped would be safer areas. But the journey was fraught with danger. The roads were clogged with abandoned vehicles, and long lines of people, some walking, some on bicycles, were scattered across the once-thriving highways. Children cried in their parents' arms, the elderly struggled to keep up, and everyone was gripped by a sense of hopelessness.

In this chaotic mass exodus, people began to lose what little semblance of civility remained. There were stories of looting, violence, and desperation. Entire neighborhoods were overrun by panicked crowds fighting over food and water. People who had once been neighbors now viewed each other as threats. In a world where every resource had become precious, trust was a luxury that no one could afford.

Aldo had witnessed it firsthand. After the fires had ravaged the city, he had joined Nina and their team in an attempt to organize some form of aid distribution for the survivors. But even this, something as fundamental as providing the bare minimum for survival, was nearly impossible. Makeshift camps had sprung up everywhere, on the outskirts of cities, in open fields, and even in the ruins of abandoned buildings. These camps were overcrowded, and the desperation among the people was palpable.

"There's nothing left to give," Nina had said one evening, her voice hoarse from exhaustion. She had been out all day, coordinating efforts to deliver food and medical supplies to the camps. But the distribution was far from enough, and people were beginning to lose patience. "We're barely surviving ourselves. How do we help others when we don't have enough?"

Aldo had no answers. His mind kept racing, running through the ideas he had developed over the years, the waste-to-energy technology, the sustainable systems they had built, but all of it seemed insignificant in the face of the present disaster. The systems that might have prevented this were gone. The solutions they had worked so hard for now seemed like a dream, a fantasy that had faded into the past.

One of the makeshift camps Aldo and Nina visited was located in the ruins of an old park. The survivors there had constructed tents out of whatever materials they could scrounge, from scrap metal to tarps and pieces of wood. The camp was overcrowded, and there was a constant sense of unease. Families huddled together, eyes darting nervously at anyone who passed by. The line for water was a hundred people long, and food was rationed to the point of barely sustaining the people who stood in line. No one was certain how much longer they could hold on.

Aldo moved through the crowd, his heart heavy with guilt and sorrow. He was a scientist, a man who had spent his life searching for ways to fix the world's most pressing environmental problems, yet here he was, powerless. People had died, entire ecosystems had been destroyed, and there seemed to be no way to reverse the damage.

As he walked, a woman approached him. Her face was gaunt, her clothes torn, and her eyes wide with panic.

"Please, help," she begged. "My child... he's sick. I don't know what to do. There's no medicine... nothing to treat him with."

Aldo's heart sank. He had no medical training, no supplies to offer her. His eyes searched the camp for anyone who could help, but it was clear that everyone here was in the same state of need. There were no doctors, no hospitals. There was just a handful of people trying to survive, and everyone was too overwhelmed to help one another.

"We're doing what we can," he said, his voice hollow. "We're trying to get more supplies, more resources. But it's not enough. It's never enough."

The woman's face twisted in agony as she clutched her child to her chest. "We're dying here," she whispered. "Everyone is dying. Please... do something."

Aldo had no answer, no solution. All he could do was stand there, helpless, watching as the weight of the disaster pressed down on the survivors. There was no quick fix for this. No amount of technology or innovation could undo the damage that had been done.

Back at the central shelter, things were only getting worse. The flow of refugees had continued to increase, and soon the area was overrun with people desperate for shelter, food, and water. The line for the few remaining medical supplies stretched for miles, and the medical staff, mostly volunteers who had come from nearby cities, were already overwhelmed.

As the days wore on, Aldo began to notice a growing tension among the people. What had once been a relatively orderly group of survivors had now become a volatile and unpredictable mob. People fought over food, water, and even space to sleep. The basic tenets of human decency began to erode as the situation grew more dire. People who had once been friends now turned on one another, their relationships replaced by fear and suspicion.

"I don't think they'll make it," Nina said one night as they sat in the corner of the shelter, exhausted from a long day of organizing the chaos. "There's too many people. And there's too little left. How long until this turns into something much worse?"

Aldo could only shake his head. He didn't have the answers. But he couldn't stop thinking about the world before the disaster, the cities, the technologies, the systems they had all taken for granted. All of it seemed so distant now, a world that had collapsed under its own weight.

"How long before we lose control?" Nina asked quietly, her voice trembling with the weight of the question.

Aldo didn't know. But he knew that time was running out. The fires had already taken so much. The oceans were dying. And now, the social fabric of humanity was unraveling, thread by thread. The disaster was no longer just about waste or pollution, it was about survival, about whether humanity could hold together long enough to rebuild what had been lost.

MOUNT OF WASTE

As the days stretched on, the tensions grew. The survivors, once hopeful, now faced the grim reality that their world had changed irreparably. The hunger, the thirst, and the loss were beginning to take their toll on the human spirit. People who had once been part of communities were now desperate individuals, willing to do anything to survive.

In the midst of it all, Aldo knew that a new reality was emerging, one where only the strongest, the most ruthless, would survive. And as much as he wanted to believe that humanity could find a way to pull itself together, deep down, he feared that the world was too broken to heal.

Survival had become the only thing that mattered. And in this new world, that meant everything else, the environment, the technology, the solutions, had to be put on hold. The world's focus had shifted from healing the planet to healing itself. But in a place where resources were so scarce and people had so little left to give, the question lingered: could humanity ever heal from the devastation it had wrought?

Chapter 8: The Burned Land

The fires that had ravaged the cities did not die easily. They clung to the earth like an insidious force, consuming everything in their path and leaving behind nothing but scorched earth. As the infernos that had burned for days slowly began to subside, a new, even more terrifying threat emerged. The ground, having been scorched and weakened by the relentless heat, began to shift, as though it were reacting to the devastation.

The ground, once solid beneath their feet, now seemed unstable. Cracks began to appear in the earth, snaking their way across the streets and buildings like the wrinkled skin of an ancient, dying creature. The heat from the fires had caused a distortion in the very structure of the land. What had once been a steady, reliable foundation was now a fragile, uncertain surface.

The first tremors came without warning. They were small, barely perceptible at first, but they were enough to set people on edge. It was as if the earth itself had begun to groan in pain, responding to the devastation of the fires, the earthquakes that followed, and the relentless destruction that seemed to have no end.

Aldo stood in the midst of what had once been a thriving neighborhood, now reduced to rubble. Around him, the heat of the fires still lingered in the air, thick with ash and smoke. The world around him seemed eerily quiet, save for the distant hum of helicopters and the occasional crack of a building collapsing under its own weight. But as he surveyed the scene, he could feel the ground beneath him tremble again, more noticeably this time.

Nina was at his side, her face drawn with exhaustion, her eyes reflecting the same sense of helplessness that had taken root in Aldo's heart. Together, they had worked tirelessly to provide aid, to organize whatever semblance of order they could in the face of the chaos that had engulfed their world. But the ground shifting beneath their feet was something neither of them had prepared for.

"It's getting worse," Nina said quietly, her voice tight with fear. "The ground... It's moving. Is it... is it an aftershock?"

Aldo didn't know how to answer. He had spent his life studying the environment, the cycles of nature, the way the planet worked, but this was different. This was something entirely outside the realm of any disaster he had ever encountered. The land, which had once been a stable foundation, now seemed as fragile as the rest of the world. The earth was reacting to the massive forces that had been unleashed upon it, and there was no predicting what might come next.

The ground trembled again, this time stronger, a deep rumbling that seemed to echo from beneath. Aldo staggered, barely keeping his balance as the earth shifted underfoot. Buildings that had already been weakened by the fires began to groan, their structures cracking and shifting. Some collapsed entirely, their once-proud facades now reduced to heaps of concrete and steel. Others leaned precariously to one side, their foundations eroded by the shifting soil beneath them.

Panic spread quickly among the survivors. People screamed as they scrambled for safety, some running into the streets, others huddling in whatever shelter they could find. The fires, the heat, the contamination, it had all been bad enough. But now, it seemed the very earth was conspiring to make survival even more impossible.

Aldo looked around frantically, trying to assess the situation. The shifting ground was becoming more frequent, and he could see the cracks in the streets growing larger. The once-sturdy buildings around him were now like ticking time bombs, waiting for the next tremor to send them toppling.

"We need to get to higher ground," Aldo shouted over the din of panicked voices and collapsing buildings. "Now!"

Nina grabbed his arm, pulling him in the direction of a nearby hill, away from the unstable ground and crumbling infrastructure. It wasn't much, just a small rise in the landscape, but it was the closest thing to safety they had. They pushed their way through the crowd, their feet stumbling over the uneven ground as the tremors continued.

As they reached the top of the hill, Aldo took a deep breath, trying to steady himself. The city below was a scene of utter devastation. The fires, though diminished, still smoldered in the ruins, and the ground itself seemed to be in a constant state of flux. He watched as the streets cracked open further, and the remnants of buildings tilted dangerously. In some places, entire sections of the ground were collapsing, sinking into deep fissures that seemed to open up without warning.

"We're not safe here, Aldo," Nina said, her voice shaking with the weight of what she was seeing. "This isn't going to stop. The earth is... it's moving, changing. What's happening?"

Aldo's heart pounded in his chest as he struggled to answer. He had no explanation. There were no precedents for this kind of disaster, no data to help him understand what was happening. The fires had been bad enough, but now it seemed like the land itself was reacting to the weight of humanity's mistakes.

"We need to find out what's happening," Aldo said, his voice urgent. "This could be part of a larger shift, something we've triggered. The earth... it's responding to all of this destruction. We've already pushed the environment past its limits."

As the tremors continued, it became clear that what had begun as an isolated catastrophe was rapidly becoming something much more global. The shifting ground wasn't confined to just one city. Reports came in from neighboring regions, from other countries, of similar phenomena: land subsiding, streets cracking open, and entire buildings collapsing under the strain. The world, it seemed, was breaking apart, not just on the surface but beneath as well.

Aldo and Nina continued to watch as the earth beneath them cracked and shifted. The once-stable landscape was now in constant motion, the ground trembling with every passing second. And with each tremor, the city, once a symbol of progress, now reduced to rubble, seemed to sink further into the earth.

It wasn't just the land that was changing. The oceans, already suffocating under the weight of pollution, had begun to react as well. Reports of rising sea levels, massive tidal waves, and the collapse of coastlines were coming in from all corners of the globe. The interconnectedness of the planet, once something humanity had taken for granted, had become its downfall.

Aldo and Nina knew that the disaster had only just begun. The fires, the social unrest, and now the shifting ground, all of it pointed to a single, undeniable truth: the earth could no longer bear the weight of human recklessness.

They had fought to save the planet for years, trying to mitigate the damage, to find solutions to the environmental crisis. But now, as they stood on the edge of the precipice, watching the world crumble around them, they realized that the battle had shifted. It was no longer just about restoring balance or finding ways to manage waste. It was about survival. The planet was in revolt, and humanity was at its mercy.

As the tremors continued to shake the ground beneath them, Aldo felt a deep, gnawing sense of despair. The earth was no longer something they could control, it had become a force beyond their understanding, a force that had grown angry, violent, and unpredictable.

And yet, despite the overwhelming devastation, there was a small part of Aldo that refused to give up. The earth, in all its fury, was still alive. It was responding to the wounds humanity had inflicted upon it, but it was not yet dead. There was still time. But time was running out.

"We have to find a way to survive this," Aldo said quietly, more to himself than to Nina. "We have to keep moving forward. The earth is changing, but so are we. We can't let this be the end."

Nina didn't answer immediately. She stood beside him, her eyes fixed on the shifting ground below, and then nodded, her resolve hardening.

"Then let's find a way," she said, her voice steady. "For everyone."

And so, as the ground continued to shake and crack, they turned away from the hilltop and headed deeper into the unknown, determined to find a way to survive, to rebuild, and to somehow, against all odds, save the world that had once been theirs.

Chapter 9: Domino Effect

The world was in the grips of an unstoppable chain of events, a cascade of destruction that seemed to accelerate with every passing day. The shifting land had set off a domino effect of chaos that rippled across the globe. It was as though the planet had been dealt a fatal blow and was now reeling, trying to find some form of balance amidst the overwhelming devastation.

In the weeks following the first tremors, it became clear that the worst was far from over. The cracks in the earth, which had first appeared in isolated areas, were now spreading across entire continents. Entire cities were swallowed by sinkholes, and others were abandoned as the ground beneath them continued to shift. Infrastructure, which had once been the backbone of modern society, was rapidly deteriorating. Roads cracked open, bridges collapsed, and buildings fell like towers of cards. Every attempt to rebuild was met with another tremor, another shake, another blow to the already fragile systems that remained.

Countries were thrown into turmoil. The strongest economies, those that had once been seen as unshakeable, were crumbling beneath the weight of the disaster. The United States, once a symbol of global stability, was battling against the effects of massive land shifts that had taken out whole regions, while Europe struggled to deal with both flooding from rising seas and the devastation of shifting tectonic plates. China, having long been the industrial powerhouse of the world, now faced the near-total collapse of its manufacturing sector as entire cities were displaced by sudden earthquakes. In every corner of the world, the effects of the crisis were the same: mass migration, widespread famine, and social unrest.

In the midst of this global collapse, nations began to turn against one another. What had once been a time of international cooperation had now devolved into a brutal struggle for survival. The world's greatest powers, who had once sat together in unity at the negotiating tables, now focused solely on their own survival, seeking to secure what little resources remained, no matter the cost.

Aldo and Nina, who had fought so hard to maintain hope, now found themselves in the center of this chaos. The research they had pioneered, waste management technology, sustainable systems, was becoming increasingly irrelevant in the face of such overwhelming global disaster. The technology that had promised to heal the planet now seemed like a faint memory, a dream that had been eclipsed by the desperate need to simply survive.

They had managed to reach a temporary safe zone in the mountainous region of what had once been the United States. The area had been mostly spared from the fires and land shifts, but as they arrived at one of the last remaining refugee camps, Aldo could see the toll that the catastrophe had already taken. The camp was overcrowded, its medical facilities overwhelmed. The once fertile land was now parched and barren. The refugees here, survivors from cities and towns further south, were barely hanging on.

Aldo and Nina had been working day and night to keep the camp running. With the help of a small team of volunteers, they distributed whatever supplies they could scrounge together: clean water, food, and medical aid. But with each passing day, the situation grew more dire. The once-tolerant refugees were now beginning to fight amongst themselves for what little remained. Tensions were high, and the fragile peace that had held for so long was beginning to fracture.

Nina could feel the weight of it all. She had always been a fierce advocate for environmental justice, but she knew now that the world was no longer fighting just for environmental recovery. This was a fight for survival, an existential battle for humanity's very existence. "I don't think we can hold it together much longer," she said, as she glanced over the camp, her eyes scanning the faces of the refugees who now looked more like ghosts than people.

Aldo nodded, his own thoughts heavy. "The longer we wait to rebuild, the more the world unravels. Countries are starting to fall apart. They're fighting over resources like it's the last meal they'll ever eat. And when nations can't cooperate, the result is... chaos."

"Do you think there's still hope for us?" Nina asked, her voice quivering. It wasn't just a question about survival; it was a question about the very future of humanity.

Aldo didn't have an answer. He had never felt so powerless. The domino effect of the disasters, the fires, the land shifts, the famine, the wars, had become a tidal wave, one that no one could stand against. Every solution they had ever worked on, every technological advance, seemed to have been swept away by the destruction. Even the concept of sustainability felt irrelevant now.

On the global stage, the unraveling had already begun. Governments that had once prided themselves on their international leadership were now falling apart at the seams. China, long the world's largest economy, was battling against the effects of widespread land shifts and rising sea levels that threatened to submerge coastal cities. The United States, once the leader of the free world, had descended into a state of chaos, with martial law declared in multiple states and violent clashes breaking out between desperate citizens and law enforcement.

Meanwhile, in Europe, nations that had once banded together in the European Union now found themselves grappling with internal conflict. The refugee crisis, already exacerbated by the initial wave of migration caused by the waste disaster, was now compounded by the shifting ground that had destroyed much of Europe's infrastructure. Food shortages were rampant, and riots were commonplace. Entire countries were on the brink of collapse as their governments failed to address the escalating crisis.

In the midst of this collapse, alliances were tested. The United States and Canada, once close allies, were now at odds over the few remaining resources. Both countries had faced crippling destruction, Canada from massive flooding, and the United States from both the fires and the shifting land, but the pressure to protect their own populations had driven a wedge between them. Russia, already dealing with its own challenges, saw this as an opportunity to expand its influence and began moving forces into Eastern Europe. The world's greatest powers, once intertwined through a web of trade and diplomacy, now saw each other as competitors in a zero-sum game. And in that game, every nation was fighting to protect itself at the expense of everyone else.

The global economy, already fragile from years of environmental strain, was now on the brink of complete collapse. The markets, once the cornerstone of modern civilization, had failed, and global trade had ground to a halt. There was no way to rebuild the infrastructure without resources, resources that were now incredibly scarce and fiercely contested. Nations were hoarding food, water, and medical supplies, locking their borders and restricting aid to their own citizens.

In the midst of this chaos, Aldo and Nina could feel the full weight of the disaster. What had once seemed like a fight to restore balance to the planet now felt like a battle to save whatever humanity remained. The very systems they had once believed in, systems built on cooperation, progress, and shared responsibility, had crumbled under the weight of human greed, neglect, and the environmental collapse that had followed.

"The world isn't just collapsing, Aldo," Nina said, her voice almost a whisper. "It's falling apart at every level. The environment, the economy, the social order... everything. It's all breaking down, piece by piece."

Aldo looked out over the refugees huddled together in makeshift tents, the remnants of what had once been cities reduced to rubble. "We've reached a tipping point," he said softly. "The tipping point where recovery isn't just about managing waste or sustainable development. It's about rebuilding society from the ground up. And it's going to take more than technology or innovation to do it."

Nina nodded, her gaze distant. "But how do we rebuild from here? After everything we've lost... after everything we've done... can we ever fix this?"

Aldo looked down at the ground beneath him, still trembling from the earlier tremor. He didn't have an answer. For the first time in a long while, the hope he had clung to was beginning to fade. The world was slipping through his fingers, and no matter how hard they fought, no matter how hard they tried to rebuild, it seemed as if they were always two steps behind the disaster that was consuming them.

The domino effect was unstoppable now, and the world was falling apart faster than anyone could put it back together.

Chapter 10: A Divided World

The once united front of the global community had shattered into a thousand pieces, each fragment scrambling for survival. The world, in its effort to recover from the cascade of environmental disasters that had nearly annihilated civilization, now found itself standing on the brink of total fragmentation. No longer united by the common goal of rebuilding a shared future, nations turned inward, closing their borders, hoarding resources, and focusing solely on their own survival. The dream of global cooperation that had once been the foundation of international diplomacy was now a distant memory.

The United States, once a leader in the world order, had erected walls around its borders. What had once been a beacon of hope for refugees now became a fortress, its gates tightly shut. A military occupation had been declared in the southern regions, and the country was focused on controlling the limited resources that remained. The fires and shifting tectonic plates had ravaged entire cities, but the government's priorities were clear—protect the homeland at all costs. The rest of the world could fend for itself.

In Europe, the situation was no different. The European Union, once a symbol of collaboration, now lay in ruins. Member states, unable to agree on how to distribute aid or manage the influx of refugees, had pulled away from each other, each country focused on its own recovery. Germany, with its well-organized infrastructure, attempted to rebuild, but internal tensions rose as the country struggled to support both its own population and the millions of displaced people who had nowhere else to turn. France, Italy, Spain, once allies in the battle for global unity, were now acting as individual states, guarding their own borders and scrambling to maintain order within their territories.

MOUNT OF WASTE

Russia, ever opportunistic, had expanded its reach into Eastern Europe. With Europe fractured and NATO weakened, Moscow took advantage of the chaos, deploying troops and securing vital resources, including energy reserves. Russia's isolation from the rest of the world had left it relatively untouched by the initial disasters, but the nation was keenly aware of the dwindling resources and the geopolitical advantage it could gain in such times of instability.

China, too, had withdrawn from the global stage. The massive industrial juggernaut that had once driven the world's economy now found itself grappling with the aftereffects of the environmental catastrophes that had ravaged its coastal cities. Faced with widespread destruction and internal unrest, China focused its efforts on stabilizing its own borders and managing the mass migration of citizens fleeing from the most affected regions. Beijing had declared martial law in several provinces, and the government's crackdown on dissent was swift and brutal. Meanwhile, the once-mighty Chinese economy was in shambles, as factories lay idle, and supply chains collapsed.

India, which had once been seen as a rising power, was now struggling to hold itself together. The southern states were suffering from flooding, while the northern regions were plagued by earthquakes and tremors from the shifting land. The government's resources were stretched thin as it tried to address both the natural disasters and the rising civil unrest. With the global economy in ruins, India found itself isolated, scrambling to secure what resources it could and maintain some semblance of order.

The Middle East, already a region plagued by conflict, now found itself further fractured. The oil-rich nations, once wealthy from their exports, were now facing massive infrastructural damage, and the price of oil had plummeted. Without the global demand for energy, these countries had begun to turn inward, their wealth rendered meaningless in the face of total collapse.

Meanwhile, war-torn regions struggled to cope with the influx of refugees and the breakdown of essential services. Syria, Iraq, and Yemen, already devastated by years of conflict, now faced the added burden of a world that had no resources left to offer.

As nations focused on their own survival, the idea of global cooperation seemed like a distant dream. The United Nations, once a beacon of hope for collective action, had become a shadow of its former self. With no one to lead and no common ground to stand on, the international body had crumbled under the weight of the global crisis. Diplomatic summits were now non-existent, as each nation put up walls, not just physical, but political and ideological as well.

In the refugee camps that had sprung up around the world, the situation was dire. Once-temporary shelters for displaced people had become permanent homes for millions. The camps were overcrowded, unsanitary, and rife with disease. With no global infrastructure to provide aid, local organizations did what they could, but the sheer scale of the disaster overwhelmed them. Resources were scarce, and those who had once been welcome were now seen as a burden. In some areas, violence broke out as people fought for food, water, and shelter.

In the midst of this fractured world, Aldo and Nina found themselves at the center of an increasingly hostile landscape. They had managed to escape the chaos of the collapsed cities and had sought refuge in the mountains, where the land had been less affected by the tremors. But even here, they could feel the ripple effect of the global collapse. The local community was struggling to keep up with the increasing number of refugees who had begun to pour in, fleeing from the larger, more devastated cities. The resources in the mountain villages were limited, and even they had begun to close their borders, unwilling to share what little they had with outsiders.

MOUNT OF WASTE

Aldo, once a scientist driven by the desire to fix the planet, was now grappling with a new and horrifying reality. He had spent his life studying the environment, finding ways to restore balance, but now the planet seemed to be beyond saving. Nations, divided and fractured, were too focused on their own survival to even consider the greater good. The world he had once envisioned, a world where nations worked together to solve the environmental crisis, was slipping further and further away.

Nina, ever the idealist, found herself struggling to hold on to hope. "We can't just let it end like this, Aldo," she said, her voice filled with a quiet desperation. "There has to be something we can do. We can't just watch as the world tears itself apart."

Aldo looked at her, his expression grim. "I don't know what more we can do, Nina. The systems are failing. The global order is collapsing. People aren't thinking about the planet anymore; they're thinking about survival. And that's the problem. If we can't get them to think beyond themselves, there's nothing we can do."

"But we can't give up. We have to find a way," Nina said, her voice pleading. "Maybe it's not about fixing everything all at once. Maybe it's about small steps, about finding those who are still willing to fight for a better world."

Aldo sighed deeply, looking out at the distant mountains. The weight of their situation was crushing. He had always believed in the power of science, in the ability to innovate and change the world. But now, it felt as though the very fabric of society was unraveling faster than any technological advancement could hope to fix.

"We need to find allies," Aldo said after a long pause. "There are still pockets of resistance. Small groups, local leaders who haven't given up hope. But the world is so divided now, Nina. Getting anyone to work together is going to be a battle."

Nina nodded, her eyes burning with determination. "Then we fight that battle. We start with the people who still believe. And we build from there."

As Aldo and Nina worked to gather resources and form alliances in their small, isolated mountain refuge, the world outside continued to fracture. Borders hardened. Nationalism surged. And the hope for a unified global response to the crisis faded into a faint memory. The domino effect of the environmental collapse had turned the world into a battleground for survival, and in its wake, the dream of a united humanity seemed all but impossible.

But despite the overwhelming odds, Aldo and Nina, like many others who had not yet given up, understood one truth: in a world divided by crisis, the fight for unity and survival was the only thing that could save them. Whether or not they could rebuild what had been lost was uncertain, but if there was any chance of salvaging the remnants of their world, it lay in their ability to bridge the divides, to forge connections where none existed, and to rekindle the spark of cooperation that had once burned brightly.

And so, amidst the chaos and despair, they began their search for those willing to rebuild, not just their homes, but the very idea of a world united in purpose. It was a long shot, but for the first time in months, Aldo felt a small glimmer of hope. If they could find enough like-minded people, if they could rekindle the spirit of unity, perhaps the world could rise from the ashes of its division.

Chapter 11: Life in the Danger Zone

The days had blurred into a haze of survival. For the survivors of the disaster, the world had turned into a place of constant danger, where every moment was spent fighting for resources, safety, and hope. Aldo and Nina had managed to escape the chaos of the cities, finding a temporary refuge in the isolated mountain village, but even here, there was no true peace. The natural disasters that had ravaged the earth, shifting tectonic plates, relentless storms, and wildfires, had set the stage for a new world, one in which every day brought new threats.

The village they now called home was surrounded by harsh terrain. The mountains provided some shelter, but the ground beneath them was unstable. Earthquakes, though smaller now, were still frequent, and they had created fissures in the earth that ran deep into the landscape, making it dangerous to move through certain areas. These were not the kind of mountains one could scale easily. The land was jagged, with cliffs and sharp rocks that had once seemed formidable but now felt like barriers between them and the rest of the world.

The survivors here were a mixture of locals and displaced people, refugees from the crumbled cities, the ones who had been able to make it this far, fleeing the infernos and land shifts. Together, they formed a fragile community, held together by necessity rather than any true sense of unity. There was no longer any cohesive social order. People did what they could to survive, relying on a patchwork of old-world knowledge, ingenuity, and whatever resources they could salvage from the wreckage of the old world.

Food was the most precious commodity, but it was scarce. The once fertile lands of the valley were now barren, scorched by the fires that had raged for weeks before the mountains had offered any sort of refuge. The only crops that could grow were those that had adapted to the harsh conditions: tough roots, hardy herbs, and the occasional wild fruit that managed to survive in the sparse forest. But these were not enough to sustain everyone, and the villagers had learned quickly that every meal was a gamble. Rations were tightly controlled, and the slightest shortage could spark riots.

Aldo had worked with some of the more knowledgeable locals to try and cultivate the land, but the efforts were slow and fraught with setbacks. The soil was no longer rich with nutrients; the continuous tremors kept disrupting whatever they tried to grow, and irrigation systems had long since fallen into disrepair. They had no choice but to rely on foraging, hunting, and trading with other nearby villages for what little food they could acquire.

But food wasn't the only problem.

The natural disasters had left the survivors with more than just empty stomachs. The weather, too, had become a constant enemy. Storms were frequent and erratic. There was no predictability to the seasons anymore. Some days, it would rain for hours, causing landslides and making it impossible to move through the mud. Other days, the heat was unbearable, and fires would spark from even the smallest of sparks. And yet, there were still pockets of cold, a reminder that the climate had completely destabilized. It was clear that these extreme conditions weren't going to go away. They would have to adapt.

The Threats That Never Ended

But nature wasn't the only threat that loomed over the survivors. With the world's infrastructure broken, the idea of law and order had disappeared entirely. The chaos had given rise to a new form of danger, human violence.

Without any form of government to enforce peace, the survivors had to rely on each other to create a fragile peace. Trust, once a fundamental aspect of human interaction, had become a rare commodity. People were protective of their food, their homes, and their families, and petty conflicts had the potential to escalate into full-scale violence in a heartbeat.

Aldo and Nina had witnessed it firsthand. A small disagreement over a ration of food between two refugees had escalated quickly, resulting in a fight that drew in others. When no one was around to stop it, it became a brawl that was only quelled when Aldo himself intervened, using the last of his authority as a former scientist to appeal to their better senses. But there was only so much he could do, and he knew that the longer they remained in this situation, the more desperate and violent people would become.

The leaders of the village, a mix of survivors who had emerged as the most resourceful, had created a system of barter and trade. Goods were exchanged, and labor was offered in exchange for food and shelter. But even this was beginning to break down. The villages were starting to hoard supplies, fearing that if they didn't protect their own resources, they would be overrun by outsiders. It was a constant balancing act between survival and solidarity, one that was getting harder to maintain with each passing day.

The Search for Resources

In these difficult conditions, Aldo and Nina had been spending most of their time working with a small group of volunteers to gather resources. They had heard rumors of old warehouses and stores nearby that might still have supplies, medicine, tools, and even canned food. But going to these places was dangerous. The land around them was unstable, and any excursion had to be meticulously planned.

Today, they were preparing for another trip to an old, abandoned city a few hours' walk away. The city had been mostly buried under debris from the landslides, but rumors of hidden warehouses and supplies still drew people to it. It was a gamble, but it was one they had to take. Supplies were running low, and the villagers were growing desperate.

As they packed their bags with what little they had, Nina spoke up, her face etched with concern. "Aldo, do you really think we can find anything out there? Every time we go, we come back with less than we expect."

Aldo paused, glancing around at their team of volunteers. He could see the fatigue in their faces, the hollow eyes that came from days of hard labor and constant uncertainty. He felt it, too. But he couldn't afford to show weakness now. If they didn't keep trying, they would be lost.

"We have to keep looking," he said. "If there's a chance we can find something that will help us survive for another week, we have to take it. We're running out of time."

Nina nodded, but there was no conviction in her eyes. She knew the dangers, knew that the world outside the village was no longer the same. It was wild, unpredictable, and hostile in ways that made every step a risk. And yet, they had no choice but to venture into the unknown once again.

The Trek to the City

The journey to the city was arduous. The ground was unstable, and they had to pick their way through cracked earth, avoiding deep crevices that threatened to swallow them whole. The heat of the sun beat down relentlessly, and the smell of burning vegetation hung in the air from the fires that had ravaged the land days before. They walked cautiously, alert to any signs of danger.

When they finally reached the city, the sight was worse than they had expected. The once-thriving urban center was now a ghost town. The streets were littered with debris, broken glass, collapsed buildings, and the remnants of human life. Cars lay abandoned, their tires deflated, their interiors filled with dust. The city had been shattered, but the real danger was in the air. There were no signs of life, no human presence, but the atmosphere was thick with tension. This place was not just physically unstable; it was psychologically toxic. It was a place where people had lost everything, and Aldo knew that in such places, desperation could drive people to do unspeakable things.

They moved carefully, checking abandoned stores and warehouses, finding little of value. Most of the buildings had been looted long ago, their contents picked clean by others who had come before them. It felt as though the world was being consumed from within, piece by piece, until there was nothing left but memories of what had once been.

As they made their way deeper into the heart of the city, they came across an old medical facility, its doors barely hanging on their hinges. Inside, they found the remnants of what had once been a place of care. Empty shelves, broken equipment, and discarded medical supplies littered the floor. But then, something caught Aldo's eye. In the back of the facility, behind a pile of rubble, there was a storage room. And inside that room, they found something that had long been thought lost, medicine. Some antibiotics, bandages, and pain relievers, small things, but things that could save lives.

Aldo felt a sense of relief wash over him. They hadn't found much, but they had found something.

As they packed up the supplies, ready to head back to the village, Nina looked at him with a glimmer of hope in her eyes. "This is good, Aldo. It's not much, but it's something. Maybe there's still a chance for us."

Aldo nodded, but the weight of their situation pressed down on him. He had seen too much to believe that the worst was behind them. The world was still a place of danger, of uncertainty, and the fight for survival would only grow harder from here.

But for now, this small victory was enough. The road ahead was long, but at least they had something to fight for, a small glimmer of hope in a world that had nearly forgotten what it meant to hope.

Chapter 12: Rediscovering Green Technology

The world had been brought to its knees by the catastrophic storm and the ensuing destruction. Cities lay in ruins, the environment had been decimated, and people struggled daily to survive in a landscape that seemed to defy recovery. Amidst the devastation, however, there was a glimmer of hope, a small beacon in the form of a groundbreaking innovation that could shift the tide. It was not in the hands of governments or corporations but in the hands of a handful of scientists who had managed to hold on to the very knowledge that could rebuild the world, green technology.

Aldo, alongside his team of environmental scientists, had always been a firm believer that humanity could reverse its damage to the Earth, but the recent disasters had left him questioning everything. The sheer magnitude of the global environmental collapse seemed insurmountable. But deep within the heart of the crisis, Aldo saw a small possibility, a way forward through the very waste that had brought the world to the brink of ruin.

The Beginning of the Plan

Aldo had been working tirelessly with his colleagues, Dr. Maya, an expert in renewable energy, and Reza, a mechanical engineer,vto develop sustainable methods of waste management and energy production. After the storm and the widespread scattering of debris, the mountains of garbage became more than a nuisance; they were a direct threat to the planet. The pollution of the oceans, the air, and the land were not only causing irreversible damage to ecosystems, but they were also suffocating human existence. It was clear that something had to be done, and quickly.

In the middle of the chaos, Aldo had an idea. "What if we could harness the energy within the waste itself? Not just to dispose of it, but to use it to power everything, houses, cities, even entire countries," he suggested one evening, his voice laced with urgency.

Maya looked at him with a mixture of skepticism and curiosity. "You're talking about turning trash into power?" she asked.

"Exactly," Aldo said, his eyes lighting up with the possibility. "We've been recycling, but what if we could go beyond that? What if we could use the waste to create the energy we need to power our recovery? Bioenergy, solar power, waste-to-energy conversion, it's all possible. We just have to figure out how to make it scalable."

Reza, always the practical one, raised an eyebrow. "It's ambitious, Aldo. But how are we going to do it? The resources we need to create this technology are scattered, and the infrastructure is gone. We don't have much to work with."

Aldo shook his head, his gaze unwavering. "We may not have the infrastructure, but we still have the knowledge. And we have the waste. The solution is already here, right in front of us. We just need to figure out how to use it."

The team knew that this wasn't going to be easy. The resources to create advanced green technology were few and far between, and most of the tools they would need had been destroyed in the storms or buried under mountains of debris. But Aldo was determined. If they could harness the energy from waste, whether it was through converting plastic into fuel, turning organic waste into biogas, or using waste to generate electricity, they could not only solve the problem of waste management but also create a new, sustainable energy source.

Rebuilding from the Ground Up

The first challenge was finding the right materials. Aldo, Maya, and Reza scavenged what was left of the old world's infrastructure. There were pieces of solar panels, old wind turbines, and scraps of electronics that could be repurposed. It was a painstaking process.

MOUNT OF WASTE

Every day, they would dig through the wreckage, searching for anything that might be useful in their quest to build a sustainable solution. It wasn't just about finding the right components, it was about surviving long enough to make their idea a reality.

In the midst of this chaos, Aldo's team began to focus on the waste itself. The plastic that was piling up in the streets, the electronic waste that littered the cities, and the food scraps that were rotting in the abandoned settlements, all of these materials could be used, but they needed to be processed in new ways. Traditional waste management techniques were outdated, inefficient, and increasingly ineffective in the face of the disaster.

They started experimenting with waste-to-energy technology. Aldo's knowledge of environmental systems led him to a breakthrough. He discovered a way to convert plastic waste into a form of crude oil through a process called pyrolysis. In simple terms, they would heat the plastic to extremely high temperatures in the absence of oxygen, breaking it down into usable fuel. This fuel could then be used to power engines, generators, and even provide electricity to nearby villages.

At the same time, Maya and Reza worked on a biogas system that could be fed with organic waste. They built a digester that could convert food scraps and other organic materials into methane gas. This biogas could be used to generate electricity or provide heat for cooking and warming shelter during the cold months. It was a small step forward, but it was a step in the right direction. They could already see the first fruits of their labor, small systems that could provide energy for a few households, but the long-term goal was much larger.

However, they faced many obstacles. The technical challenges were formidable. Waste-to-energy systems required high temperatures, specialized equipment, and precise control of the reaction conditions. Many of the materials they needed to create these systems simply weren't available. They had to improvise, using whatever scraps they could find, old motors, wires, and damaged machinery.

But Aldo remained optimistic. "We've got this," he said, rallying his team. "Every failure is just a step closer to success."

The Green Energy Breakthrough

After months of tireless work, Aldo's team managed to build their first small-scale waste-to-energy plant. It was a humble facility, crude and makeshift, but it worked. Plastic waste was converted into fuel, and organic waste produced biogas that powered a small generator. The team was ecstatic. They had done it. They had proven that it was possible to turn waste into energy, even in the midst of global collapse.

The next step was to scale up their technology. They needed to build a larger facility that could process the vast amounts of waste piling up in the streets and convert it into usable energy. This would require more advanced infrastructure, which was in short supply. But Aldo was relentless in his pursuit. He convinced other survivors to join the cause, appealing to their desire to restore the Earth. Slowly but surely, the team expanded, gathering more resources and skilled workers to help build the necessary infrastructure.

Soon, they had created a prototype for a larger, more efficient waste-to-energy plant. The design involved a combination of pyrolysis and biogas production, as well as small-scale solar panels that could be used to power the facility itself. They even incorporated wind turbines, taking advantage of the constant high winds that had been a consequence of the climate instability. The facility could generate a significant amount of energy, enough to power entire villages, maybe even small cities.

With this success came a newfound sense of hope. People had begun to take notice of the technology Aldo and his team were developing. Word spread, and neighboring villages sent representatives to learn from them, eager to adopt the green technology and begin their own recovery efforts. Aldo's work was no longer just a theory, it was a tangible solution to the environmental and energy crisis that the world now faced.

The Ripple Effect

As the technology gained traction, Aldo and his team began to expand their efforts. They worked with international groups to share their findings, hoping that their small-scale success could become a global movement. Countries, devastated by the environmental disasters, saw the potential of this new green technology and began investing in similar systems.

However, the road ahead was still fraught with challenges. Resources were limited, and many nations were still struggling to rebuild their basic infrastructure. But the hope of a sustainable future, powered by the waste that had once destroyed the world, was now a beacon for global recovery.

Aldo knew that this was just the beginning. They had a long way to go, but for the first time since the storm, there was a sense that humanity might have a fighting chance. With innovation, resilience, and determination, they could heal the Earth, restore balance, and create a new, sustainable world.

It was a long road ahead, but Aldo believed in the power of human ingenuity. He had seen what people could do when faced with the direst of circumstances. And now, with the rediscovery of green technology, he knew that humanity had the power to rise from the ashes and reclaim their place as stewards of the Earth.

The battle was far from over, but the seeds of recovery had been planted. The world might be broken, but it was not beyond saving. The future of the planet, and of humanity, lay in the hands of those who dared to believe in the impossible.

And for the first time in a long while, Aldo was sure of one thing: they could save the Earth, if only they kept pushing forward.

Chapter 13: The Rise of New Leadership

The world had fractured into isolated pockets of survival. It had been months since the storm, the mountains of trash had caused irreparable destruction to ecosystems, communities, and entire nations. Cities lay in ruin, governments were struggling to maintain order, and the people were left fighting not just for survival, but for hope. Amidst the disarray, the first true spark of unity began to take shape.

It wasn't born out of a political system or a global summit, there was no organization left to lead the charge. The solution, Aldo realized, had to come from the people. He, Nina, and the small but passionate group of survivors and scientists working with them began laying the groundwork for something larger: a global movement that transcended borders, ideologies, and fragmented nations. It was the only way forward.

Aldo's Vision

Aldo had seen the potential of what his team had accomplished. They had successfully developed small-scale waste-to-energy systems that were starting to make a tangible difference. In isolated villages, entire communities were now powered by the very waste that had once threatened to destroy them. But he knew this solution couldn't be implemented on a global scale unless the world united. The scope of the crisis was far too great for any one nation or organization to handle alone.

Aldo had always believed that unity, cooperation, and innovation were the keys to solving humanity's most pressing problems, but the current crisis demanded more than just technical solutions. It required leadership.

That leadership, Aldo realized, had to come from someone who was able to navigate the complex web of fractured politics, ideological divides, and the mistrust that had festered between nations. He was that person, or at least, he would be if he could get enough people to listen.

"Aldo, we need to be strategic," Nina told him one night, as they reviewed their plans in the remnants of an old research facility that had become their temporary headquarters. "We can't keep operating as a small group of scientists and activists. We need to get the attention of global leaders and rally people from every corner of the world."

Aldo nodded, feeling the weight of Nina's words. He knew that rallying people from diverse nations would be a monumental task. But it was not impossible.

"We have the technology. We have the blueprint for a new, sustainable future. Now, it's time to show the world that we are the solution. Not governments, not corporations. Us. The people who have been living through this disaster and are now finding a way to make things right."

Nina smiled, her determination mirrored in Aldo's own. She had been an activist long before the storm, fighting for environmental justice and social equity. Now, as the world descended into chaos, she had become one of the strongest voices for hope. Together, Aldo and Nina became the face of the movement. The hope of a united Earth was now resting on their shoulders.

Building the Movement

Aldo and Nina spent weeks gathering representatives from all over the world, scientists, survivors, local leaders, and activists. Using the small-scale systems they had built, they began to demonstrate that waste could be transformed into energy, that communities could be self-sufficient, and that recovery was not only possible, but necessary.

Through a network of encrypted communication channels, they shared their successes. It wasn't easy, many nations were still struggling to keep order within their borders, but there was a growing realization among the survivors that the future couldn't be rebuilt with isolationist policies. Something had to change.

"We need to show them that cooperation is not a choice. It's the only way forward," Nina said during one of their meetings. "The global community needs to be rebuilt on the foundation of sustainability, and we need to lead by example."

Their message began to gain traction. Slowly, leaders from various nations started reaching out to Aldo and Nina, intrigued by the results of the waste-to-energy systems that had been implemented in a few regions. While governments were still in disarray, their citizens were calling for action, for leadership that was pragmatic, forward-thinking, and rooted in science.

It wasn't long before Aldo's voice was heard on the global stage. He began addressing international audiences, via satellite, through the remaining media networks, and through digital platforms. In these speeches, Aldo made the case for a new kind of leadership, one that wasn't tied to national borders or the interests of the powerful elite, but one that was committed to the survival of the planet.

"We are at a crossroads," Aldo said in his first address to the world. "We have spent decades exploiting the Earth and ignoring the warning signs of the coming disaster. But now, we are facing the consequences. If we don't act now, we risk losing everything. But there is hope. Together, we can rebuild. We can use what we've destroyed to fuel a new, sustainable world."

The response was overwhelming. Thousands of people took to the streets in support of Aldo's vision, and soon a coalition of global leaders, desperate to save their nations from collapse, began to listen. It wasn't just about technology, it was about the message of unity, shared responsibility, and the necessity of putting the planet's health above all else.

The Global Alliance

In the face of growing pressure from the people, the fractured governments began to respond. A summit was organized, and representatives from dozens of nations gathered in a neutral zone, one of the few places in the world still somewhat intact. The stakes were higher than ever.

Aldo, Nina, and their team of scientists, environmentalists, and innovators were invited to present their findings. For the first time since the global disaster began, there was a real conversation about cooperation. The leaders who once closed their borders were now willing to listen. The idea of a "New Earth Alliance" took shape, an alliance that would work together to address the waste crisis, climate change, and the global recovery.

The summit was not without its challenges. Old tensions between nations remained, and some leaders were reluctant to relinquish their power in favor of a global solution. But Aldo's charisma and his unwavering belief in the importance of cooperation began to sway even the most skeptical. He understood that leadership didn't mean just speaking, it meant listening, finding common ground, and building trust.

Nina, who had worked with Aldo from the beginning, played a pivotal role in bridging the gap between different factions. She advocated for a bottom-up approach, where local communities would be empowered to adopt sustainable practices, while governments provided the necessary resources and infrastructure. The vision was one of shared responsibility, where both global leadership and local action were seen as equally important.

A New Kind of Leadership

MOUNT OF WASTE

As the summit drew to a close, the world began to take its first steps toward global cooperation. The New Earth Alliance was formed, with Aldo at its helm as the first Secretary-General. This was not a position of traditional political power; instead, it was a role that focused on collaboration, innovation, and sustainability. The Alliance's primary goal was to implement large-scale waste-to-energy systems and create sustainable energy solutions for all nations.

"We are not here to take control of the world," Aldo said in his acceptance speech. "We are here to help guide the world to a future where we live in harmony with the planet. The task before us is immense, but it is not impossible. Together, we will find solutions. Together, we will restore what has been broken."

It was a message that resonated deeply with people from all walks of life. The Alliance wasn't just about fixing the environment, it was about healing the wounds that had divided humanity for centuries. It was about recognizing that the challenges of the past were not isolated problems, but interconnected ones that could only be solved through collective action.

With the formation of the New Earth Alliance, hope began to take root. The first steps of a global transformation had been taken. Aldo and Nina, two people who had come from different worlds but shared a singular vision, now stood at the forefront of a movement that was rewriting the future.

The journey ahead would not be easy. The challenges were immense, and the road to recovery was long. But with Aldo's leadership and Nina's unwavering belief in the power of the people, the world had begun to move toward a new era, an era where humanity no longer saw itself as separate from the Earth, but as its caretakers.

The rise of new leadership had begun. And with it, the possibility of a brighter future.

Bab 14: Global Awareness Movement

The collapse of the old world and the birth of a new Earth Alliance had sparked a glimmer of hope. Aldo, Nina, and their team had managed to unite the fractured nations, but the real challenge was yet to come. It wasn't enough to simply build new waste management technologies or pass international policies, there had to be a radical shift in the way people viewed their relationship with the planet. The fight against the global waste crisis required a transformation of consciousness.

The movement for a cleaner, sustainable world had to come from the ground up. It needed to be driven by the people themselves. And so, the Global Awareness Movement (GAM) was born, a worldwide initiative to not only address the immediate waste crisis but also to educate and inspire individuals to change their everyday habits.

The Campaign Begins

The first steps in the campaign were digital. Using the remains of the old communications infrastructure, Aldo and Nina's team launched a series of online platforms dedicated to spreading knowledge about waste management, recycling, and sustainable living. They created educational content, engaging videos, and interactive courses that could be accessed by anyone, anywhere in the world.

"I know it seems impossible," Aldo said in one of his first broadcast messages, "but we can make a difference. Every piece of plastic you don't use, every item you recycle, is a step closer to restoring our Earth. This is not just about survival, it's about dignity, respect, and giving future generations a chance."

The message resonated with many. Social media platforms exploded with hashtags like #WasteLessLiveMore and #EarthAllianceAction. Celebrities, influencers, and grassroots activists alike shared the message of reducing waste and rethinking consumption. People who had once been unaware of the scale of the crisis now became vocal advocates for change.

But the true power of the movement came when it reached beyond the digital realm. Aldo knew that awareness alone wouldn't be enough. They needed to create tangible actions, to involve people in the process of change.

A New Culture of Consumption

Nina spearheaded the initiative to transform everyday consumer behavior. She worked alongside local leaders, activists, and environmental groups to implement large-scale community programs. These programs focused on the importance of reducing, reusing, and recycling, both in urban areas and rural communities.

The initial focus was on single-use plastics—the demon of the waste crisis. Plastic bags, straws, and bottles were among the biggest contributors to the environmental disaster. And yet, they were so ingrained in daily life that many people had stopped thinking twice about their usage.

"We need to make people realize that every single-use plastic item they use has a lasting impact," Nina said during one of her community outreach sessions in a small town. "It doesn't just disappear. It takes hundreds, even thousands, of years to break down, and in the meantime, it's poisoning our oceans, killing wildlife, and overwhelming our landfills."

In towns and cities across the globe, plastic-free campaigns were launched. Local governments worked together to enforce bans on single-use plastics, and shops began offering reusable alternatives. Aldo's team designed and distributed easy-to-use composting kits, and small businesses transitioned to eco-friendly packaging. It was a challenging, slow process, but people slowly started to change.

The real turning point, however, came when individuals began taking ownership of the movement. A small business in India, for example, launched a campaign encouraging people to bring their own bags and containers when shopping. What started as a small gesture gained momentum. Soon, the movement spread to neighboring communities and then to cities across the country.

Social media played a crucial role in this transition. The #PlasticFreeChallenge quickly gained traction, where people posted videos showing how they were eliminating plastic from their daily lives. People shared their tips on how to shop sustainably, how to repurpose items, and how to make their own zero-waste products.

The movement was no longer just a series of campaigns, it was a culture. People began to see the value of living waste-free, and many started to adopt new practices out of a sense of personal responsibility and pride. Composting became a household norm. People began to repair broken items instead of throwing them away. Upcycling was no longer just a trendy buzzword, but a lifestyle.

The Schools' Role in Awakening the Future

The next major step in the campaign involved reaching out to the younger generation, the ones who would carry the movement forward. Aldo and Nina knew that lasting change would only occur if environmental education became a cornerstone of every child's upbringing.

With the help of environmental experts, they worked with schools worldwide to develop a curriculum that would teach students not just the science of waste management, but also the importance of living in harmony with the planet. The program included hands-on projects such as creating community gardens, building small composting systems, and organizing waste-reduction challenges within schools.

MOUNT OF WASTE

Nina traveled to several countries, visiting schools and communities, inspiring students to lead the charge in their families and neighborhoods. She was amazed at how quickly the younger generation embraced the idea of sustainability. It became cool to be eco-conscious, and soon, schools were competing to see who could reduce waste the most.

In a small town in Kenya, a group of schoolchildren turned a local trash dump into a community garden. They used the organic waste they collected to fertilize the soil, growing vegetables that not only fed their families but were sold at local markets to raise funds for environmental causes. It was a small, grassroots project, but its impact was profound, it proved that small efforts could result in large-scale change.

Global Policy and Corporate Responsibility

While grassroots movements were essential, global policy was equally critical. Aldo and Nina knew that the world's largest polluters needed to be held accountable. Governments, corporations, and industries had to transition to more sustainable practices, and this would only happen through tough regulation and policy changes.

The Earth Alliance, under Aldo's leadership, worked tirelessly to enact policies that reduced carbon emissions, banned harmful chemicals, and established rigorous standards for recycling. Aldo also worked with global industries to develop new standards for packaging, urging them to adopt biodegradable or reusable alternatives.

Global corporations, many of which had once resisted such changes due to cost concerns, slowly started to embrace the movement. There was increasing pressure from the public and from governments to hold them accountable for their role in the waste crisis. Several multinational companies agreed to reduce their plastic output and invest in renewable energy.

By working together with international leaders, Aldo and Nina were able to bring about legislative change. They pushed for the establishment of a global waste management fund, which would be used to help underdeveloped nations build their waste management infrastructure and fight pollution. They introduced stricter regulations on industrial waste, pushing for accountability at every level of production.

The Ripple Effect

As the months went by, the movement began to gain momentum. The world was slowly changing, but it wasn't just the large-scale changes that made an impact, it was the small, everyday actions of millions of individuals. Aldo often remarked that the true measure of success was not in the large headlines, but in the small moments, the individual choices that people made every day.

The transformation of society was evident in countless small ways. In Buenos Aires, Argentina, a neighborhood had adopted a "zero-waste" approach, where residents not only separated their recycling but actively reduced consumption and organized regular clean-up events. In Tokyo, Japan, a group of high school students used their spare time to build a local waste-to-energy plant, with the help of Aldo's technology.

People began to realize that living sustainably didn't require major sacrifices, it was about making mindful decisions. The days of mass consumption were over, and a new age of mindful living was dawning.

A New Era

The Global Awareness Movement had set in motion a transformation that no one could have predicted. It wasn't just about the planet's survival anymore, it was about the survival of humanity's connection to the Earth. People had begun to see that they were not separate from the environment; they were a part of it.

MOUNT OF WASTE

Aldo and Nina stood together one evening on a balcony, overlooking a city that had been rebuilt from the rubble. The streets were cleaner, the air fresher, and the sky clearer. The world was still far from perfect, but the momentum of change was undeniable.

"We've come a long way," Nina said, her voice filled with hope.

Aldo nodded, his gaze fixed on the horizon. "This is just the beginning."

The battle against the waste crisis was far from over, but the world had awakened. And with that awakening, a new era had begun, one where humanity, at long last, learned to live in harmony with the Earth.

And together, they would rebuild.

Chapter 15: The Fortress of Defense

The spread of the disaster had altered the face of the world, and the cities that survived the immediate effects of the great catastrophe now stood on the brink of further destruction. The scattered waste, uncontrolled fires, and the threat of environmental degradation had made it clear that the remaining cities would have to build a new kind of fortress to protect themselves. These weren't traditional fortresses made of stone or high walls, but rather, fortresses based on sustainability, utilizing technology and collective efforts to survive. In this chapter, we witness how the remaining communities in this post-disaster world come together to face the threats of scattered waste and the ever-growing risk of fire that threatens their existence.

An Inevitable Decision

Amid the ruins of what was once a bustling city, Aldo and his team made a critical decision. If they were to survive in a world that was becoming increasingly hostile, they had to create a fortress of defense that would protect them not just from waste scattering, but also from the fires that were spreading uncontrollably. This fortress would not only be physical but also a system combining technology, sustainable natural resources, and social strength to ensure survival.

The cities that remained knew they could no longer rely on conventional methods to survive. They needed a system that could protect them from threats not just from outside, but also from within, the increasing strain of limited resources, food shortages, and mounting social tensions. In the first meeting between Aldo, Nina, and the remaining leaders of the cities, they agreed that building a fortress was the only way forward, a fortress founded on global collaboration and the use of green technologies.

MOUNT OF WASTE

Aldo spoke to the leaders and citizens present at the meeting, "We have to build a fortress, not just to protect ourselves from the waste that continues to threaten us, but from the fires that could destroy what we've managed to salvage. And we must do it together. No one can do this alone."

Building the Fortress with Limited Resources

The construction of the fortress was no easy task. The remaining cities had to use whatever they had. Concrete and steel, once abundant in the construction of skyscrapers, were now scarce commodities. Instead, they began developing new materials that were more environmentally friendly, using recycled plastics to create walls and barriers. The waste that had scattered across the land now became the very building blocks they needed to construct a structure that could provide protection.

One of the cities that began constructing a fortress was a coastal city known as Neotropolis. Neotropolis had survived largely due to its advances in renewable energy systems and more effective waste management practices. However, the threats of fire and scattered waste were still the biggest dangers they faced.

In Neotropolis, Aldo visited the city's recovery center where they had started assembling their first defense walls. Walls made from recycled plastic, processed and tightly compacted, now surrounded the city's main district, offering protection against future waste disruptions.

"This is the material we have," Aldo explained as he showed his team how recycled plastic could be used to build sturdy barriers. "But we need to make sure these walls allow airflow, so they don't trap too much heat and ignite fires."

The natural ventilation system integrated into each wall was a breakthrough that allowed the waste used to create the barrier not only to act as protection against further waste but also to provide passive cooling. This was the core idea behind the fortress: not just protecting from physical threats, but using technology to mitigate the conditions that could escalate the disaster.

Social Defense System

However, building physical fortifications was only one part of the survival effort. Aldo and Nina understood that the security and stability of the city would not only depend on walls and structures. Social security became just as important as physical defense to ensure that the population could live in peace and order despite the crisis.

With dwindling resources, social tensions began to rise. Scarcity of food, water, and energy became the primary causes of conflict among the people. To address this, Aldo decided to form small groups responsible for managing resources equitably. Each group was tasked with handling a specific sector of the defense fortress, some managed clean water, others produced food, and some kept watch over the perimeter.

Nina, with her experience in social activism, spearheaded efforts to create a fair and transparent monitoring system where every individual had a voice in decision-making. She held regular meetings with citizens to discuss the issues they were facing and brainstorm solutions together. Her goal was to ensure that no group felt isolated or left behind.

"In this new world, we can't just rely on physical strength. We need to build social bonds that are strong enough not to break," Nina said in their first meeting. "We're all in this together, and only by working together can we survive."

Fire Defense and Waste Protection Systems

One of the biggest challenges in building the fortress was preventing the wildfires that could decimate entire cities. With waste scattered around the city and weather conditions worsening, fires became an ever-present threat. To combat this, Aldo's team developed fire protection systems based on innovative technologies.

In Neotropolis, they installed automatic fire suppression systems that used eco-friendly materials and renewable energy to operate efficiently. These systems were supported by air purifiers that filtered harmful particles from the air to prevent fires from spreading. Outside the fortress, they also constructed fire-resistant walls using hydrogen technology to reduce temperatures and prevent fires from reaching the city.

However, these systems were far from perfect. Some of the more remote areas of the city lacked sufficient protection. In those areas, the residents had to rely on older methods they had learned through experience, ways to combat fires manually using simple tools, while still ensuring the waste didn't pile up in their territories.

Preparing for the Future

Life inside these fortresses was not without its challenges. Citizens had to remain vigilant, always prepared to act quickly in the event of a fire or when a storm hit. But there was hope. A new spirit of cooperation and innovation was rising from the ashes of destruction, as people realized they could rebuild a better world, one based on sustainability.

Like the cities that remained standing, so too did the hope for the world. If these cities could survive in a new way, if they could rise from the ruins of the past by building a fortress of defense rooted in sustainability, then perhaps the world still had a chance to recover.

Aldo looked ahead, at the city that was slowly coming back to life. "This is the beginning of a new era. We're not just surviving; we're rebuilding a better world, a world that's founded on cooperation, innovation, and sustainability."

With determination in their hearts, these fortresses became a symbol of hope for those still fighting. A reminder that, even though the world had fallen apart, humanity had the power to rise again and create a future that was green and secure for the generations to come.

These fortresses were not just buildings but concepts. A symbol of sustainability that could inspire the world to rebuild from the ground up, with hope and determination to not only survive but to protect the planet for future generations.

Chapter 16: Alpha Research Center

The world was crumbling. The cities that still stood were in ruins, and the global effort to reverse the damage seemed like an impossible dream. However, in the midst of chaos, there was one glimmer of hope. Aldo and his team had located a haven, a place where they could develop the necessary technologies to combat the global crisis. The Alpha Research Center, hidden deep within a once-forgotten part of the world, was now their last refuge, their last chance to save the planet.

A New Beginning

The Alpha Research Center was an imposing complex, designed to house the world's brightest minds in various scientific fields. It was an old facility, once a high-tech research hub funded by international organizations for projects related to sustainability and clean energy. However, it had been abandoned for years, forgotten by the rest of the world as the crisis deepened.

Now, Aldo and his team, including Nina, had arrived in the vast and remote facility. They saw it as their last opportunity to make a difference. Here, they could focus without the constant fear of fires or waste storms, without the distractions of a collapsing world. The center was equipped with old machinery, computers, and tools that had the potential to be restored and re-purposed for their new mission.

"Aldo, this is it. This is where we can finally make a difference," Nina said, her voice filled with a mix of exhaustion and hope.

Aldo nodded, surveying the vast, empty halls. "This place may be abandoned, but we can bring it back to life. We have no other choice."

The First Days at Alpha

The first few days at the Alpha Research Center were a whirlwind. The team worked tirelessly to organize the space and begin assessing the technology they had inherited. It was evident that, while much of the equipment was outdated, there were still vital tools that could be used to develop sustainable waste management systems, clean energy sources, and fire-resistant technologies. They needed to understand the full scope of the facility's resources and capabilities.

The old computers in the control room hummed back to life, their flickering screens displaying data that had not been accessed in years. Aldo and his team found ancient research papers detailing projects on waste-to-energy systems, carbon capture technologies, and methods of creating biodegradable materials from plastics.

"We can use this," Aldo said, pointing to a dusty file that seemed to contain blueprints for a waste-to-energy converter. "These ideas were years ahead of their time. If we can adapt them to our current situation, we could develop a sustainable system to help the cities."

The team immediately set to work. They divided into groups to focus on the most pressing issues: reducing waste, developing renewable energy sources, and creating fire-resistant materials. The center also had a fully equipped laboratory for environmental testing, allowing them to study new materials and processes that could revolutionize waste management.

Nina, having been a leader in grassroots movements, took charge of the social aspect of the operation. She began organizing meetings with survivors, local leaders, and activists, urging them to support the scientific efforts of the team. She knew that public support was crucial for the success of their mission.

"We need more than just science to solve this problem," she told Aldo one evening as they reviewed their progress. "We need the people to be on our side, to understand that these technologies can change their lives."

Developing the Waste-to-Energy System

MOUNT OF WASTE

The first breakthrough came when Aldo's team successfully adapted a prototype waste-to-energy converter that had been abandoned years ago. By applying modern modifications, they were able to create a system that could safely process the mountains of waste while simultaneously generating clean energy. The technology was simple, yet elegant. It used a chemical reaction to break down organic waste into biofuel, which could then be used to power the center and, eventually, entire cities.

"We're getting there," Aldo said, smiling as he watched the first batch of waste being converted into usable energy. "This could change everything. If we can scale this up, we'll have a solution for the waste problem."

Nina stood nearby, observing the process. "This is incredible, Aldo. But we need to take this to the world. If people see that waste can be transformed into energy, they'll be more willing to participate in the cleanup effort."

The breakthrough was monumental. It offered hope that the waste that had once caused destruction could now be harnessed as a resource. The Alpha Research Center became a beacon of progress, attracting the attention of both local communities and the few remaining governments who had not yet collapsed under the weight of the disaster.

Fire-Resistant Materials

The second challenge was fire. The spread of flames from burning waste had devastated entire regions, and the risk of further fires was a constant threat. In the heart of the Alpha Research Center, Aldo's team began experimenting with fire-resistant materials that could be used to build fortifications and protect vital infrastructure.

Using the waste-to-energy system as a foundation, they developed a fireproof material made from recycled plastics combined with non-combustible elements. The resulting composite was durable and capable of withstanding extreme heat. The team built a series of prototypes and tested them in controlled fires. The results were promising. The material not only resisted fires but also had the potential to be used in construction projects to rebuild the cities.

"We need to make sure this can be scaled for entire cities," Aldo said, studying the material under the microscope. "This could protect people from the flames that have been consuming everything."

The development of fire-resistant materials was another step toward survival. With a means to protect homes and public buildings, the cities could rebuild in ways that would minimize future destruction.

Clean Energy from Waste

Another significant development came in the form of renewable energy. The waste-to-energy system, while powerful, was only part of the solution. The team worked on perfecting solar panels, wind turbines, and even algae-based biofuels. Using the resources they had, Aldo's team was able to design more efficient solar panels using recycled materials that had been left in the aftermath of the disaster.

"Solar power is going to be crucial in the coming months," Aldo explained as he looked at the designs. "We need a self-sustaining network, and the more we can rely on solar energy, the better."

With renewable energy sources, they could power not only the research center but also the surrounding communities. The Alpha Research Center had become the testing ground for a new way of living, one that used the earth's natural resources efficiently, while minimizing waste and pollution.

Spreading the Word

As the technology developed, Nina's efforts to engage the global community began to gain traction. She worked with the remaining media outlets, organizing virtual town halls and conferences to share their progress with the world. The message was clear: the crisis was not over, but with cooperation and innovation, humanity could still save the planet.

"We have to show them that we're not giving up," Nina said during one of their meetings. "We have to remind them that they can make a difference too."

Slowly but surely, the world began to listen. Communities in the neighboring cities started to adopt the technologies developed at Alpha. People began cleaning up the waste, rebuilding their homes with fire-resistant materials, and utilizing renewable energy sources to power their cities.

A New Dawn

With each passing day, Aldo and his team made progress. The Alpha Research Center had become a symbol of hope and innovation, a place where the impossible seemed possible. As they worked to perfect their solutions, they also worked to inspire others, showing them that they could rebuild the world in a way that respected the planet and its resources.

As the first large-scale waste-to-energy system came online, Aldo looked at the monitor displaying the energy output. It was a small victory, but it was a victory nonetheless. It meant that the technology was working, that they had the tools to address the crisis that had once seemed insurmountable.

"We're not just surviving anymore," Aldo said, his voice filled with resolve. "We're rebuilding. And this time, we'll build a world that works with the Earth, not against it."

The Alpha Research Center had become the last hope for humanity, a place where science, innovation, and resilience could bring the planet back from the brink of collapse. And Aldo, Nina, and their team had become the vanguard of a movement that would redefine humanity's relationship with the Earth, one breakthrough at a time.

Chapter 17: The Shift in Human Mentality

The air had thickened with smoke, the smell of burning plastic and scorched earth still lingering in the atmosphere. Yet, for the first time in years, there was something else in the air, something that could not be measured in pollutants or toxins. It was hope, a slow but tangible shift in the way people thought about the world and their place in it.

The chaos that had unfolded in the years before had changed something deep within humanity's psyche. The constant barrage of disasters, the floods, fires, and storms, had taught people an invaluable lesson. The earth could no longer be treated as an infinite resource. Every piece of trash, every ounce of pollution, and every decision to consume without considering the consequences now held a deeper meaning.

As the global efforts to rebuild progressed, a new pattern emerged, one that Aldo and his team had hoped for but never expected to see so soon. A wave of change began to ripple through societies around the world. People, once indifferent to their role in environmental destruction, were now stepping forward to embrace responsibility. They were taking small steps, but they were steps in the right direction.

A New Philosophy

It started in small communities, far away from the major cities that had been consumed by the raging fires and flooding. The survivors, having endured the worst of the disaster, realized they could no longer live in the same way. Local leaders began to promote new philosophies on waste, consumption, and sustainability. The message was simple: if humanity was going to survive, it needed to live in harmony with nature.

Sophie, a local leader in a small coastal town that had been spared from the worst of the waste storms, was one of the first to advocate for this shift in mindset. She had witnessed the devastating effects of waste pollution firsthand, the once-pristine beaches now littered with plastic and hazardous materials. The ocean, once the lifeblood of the community, had become a graveyard for marine life.

"We can't keep going the way we were," Sophie said at a public meeting one evening. "We need to stop thinking that the earth is here to serve us. We are the ones who need to serve it."

Her words resonated deeply with the people in her town. They had seen their fishing industry collapse, and they had watched the devastation unfold in surrounding cities. They knew they needed to change, and Sophie's message sparked the beginning of a widespread mental shift.

Slowly, more and more communities began to follow suit. People began to reduce their consumption of single-use plastics. They started composting their food waste, recycling more rigorously, and learning to repurpose materials instead of throwing them away. New, eco-friendly industries emerged, providing sustainable alternatives to the products that had once contributed to the crisis. From biodegradable packaging to zero-waste shops, these changes spread like wildfire.

Aldo's Vision Realized

Aldo had always believed that science alone would not be enough to fix the environmental crisis. He knew that technological advancements were crucial, but he also understood that the root of the problem lay in humanity's approach to the planet. For years, he had been advocating for a collective consciousness—a shift in how people viewed the earth, their resources, and their own role in the destruction.

MOUNT OF WASTE

Now, watching the changes unfold, Aldo felt a sense of vindication. The work they had done at the Alpha Research Center had set the stage for these transformations. The renewable energy systems they had created, the waste-to-energy converters, and the fire-resistant materials had all contributed to the idea that change was possible. But it was the broader societal change, the shift in how people thought about the environment, that was the true victory.

"I didn't think it would happen this fast," Aldo remarked to Nina one evening as they reviewed the progress in the town of Greendale, where they had first implemented their waste management technology.

Nina smiled. "It's amazing, isn't it? People are finally seeing that this isn't just a solution to the waste crisis. It's a way to live better, to live in a way that respects the planet."

In Greendale, the community had embraced a zero-waste lifestyle. They had set up communal composting systems, created urban gardens, and adopted renewable energy sources for their homes. The local government had even begun implementing policies to reduce waste and promote sustainable practices. The shift in mentality was tangible. People were no longer just trying to survive; they were actively working to thrive in a way that didn't harm the earth.

Education and Awareness

As more towns and cities began to adopt sustainable practices, the focus turned to education. Schools, once focused solely on traditional subjects, began to integrate environmental awareness into their curricula. Children were taught from an early age about the importance of reducing waste, conserving resources, and living in harmony with the earth.

Aldo knew that this was where the real change would happen. The next generation would be the ones to carry the torch forward.

If they were raised with a deep understanding of sustainability, the planet would stand a better chance of recovery.

"We need to reach the children," Aldo said to Nina as they discussed their outreach strategy. "They're the ones who will shape the future. If they understand the importance of sustainability, it won't just be a trend, it will be a way of life."

Nina agreed. "And we need to make sure that everyone, no matter their age or background, has access to this knowledge. It's about creating a culture of environmental responsibility."

Schools across the globe began to adopt programs that emphasized environmental stewardship. In some places, children were encouraged to design projects around waste reduction, renewable energy, and sustainable living. In others, students participated in community cleanups or worked to restore local ecosystems. The impact was profound. As these children grew up, they would carry with them the lessons they had learned, creating a future where sustainable practices were the norm, not the exception.

Changing the Corporate World

It wasn't just individuals and small communities that were starting to shift their mindset. Corporations, too, were being forced to adapt to the new world. The once-dominant industries that had thrived on mass consumption and wasteful practices were now being challenged by new regulations and consumer demand for sustainable products.

Companies that had once relied on plastic packaging were now searching for alternatives. The fashion industry, notorious for its waste and pollution, was moving toward more sustainable materials and practices. Even tech giants, which had been responsible for massive amounts of e-waste, were now investing in circular economies and renewable energy sources.

MOUNT OF WASTE

"We can't ignore this anymore," said a CEO of a major electronics company during a global summit on sustainability. "Consumers want products that are sustainable, and they want to know that companies are doing their part to help the planet. If we don't adapt, we risk becoming irrelevant."

The rise of conscious consumerism had transformed the business landscape. People were no longer willing to accept products that came at the expense of the earth. Companies that once thrived on mass production and wasteful practices now had to find ways to operate that didn't harm the planet.

A Global Network

As the shift in mentality spread, the world began to see a more unified approach to environmental sustainability. Aldo, Nina, and their team continued to lead the charge, but they were no longer alone. Global coalitions began to form, uniting governments, businesses, and individuals in the fight to restore the planet.

The United Nations held its first global summit on sustainability in the wake of the disaster. It was a summit not just about policies and agreements but about sharing knowledge, innovations, and ideas for a sustainable future. Nations that had once been at odds now cooperated in efforts to reduce their carbon footprints, protect natural resources, and ensure that future generations would not face the same environmental collapse that had nearly destroyed the world.

The Rebirth of a Planet

Years passed, and the earth began to heal. The mountains of waste that had once threatened to engulf everything were now being transformed into resources, energy, building materials, and even food. Cities that had once been filled with smog and pollution were now powered by clean energy, their air crisp and clear. The oceans, while still scarred, began to recover, with marine life slowly returning as ecosystems were rebuilt.

Humanity, for the first time in history, had learned to live within its means. The environmental catastrophe that had once seemed insurmountable was now a distant memory, a lesson learned through suffering and survival. The world had been given a second chance, and it was determined not to waste it.

As Aldo stood on the balcony of the Alpha Research Center, watching the sun rise over the rejuvenated landscape, he felt a deep sense of peace. The work was far from over, but the shift in mentality had set the world on a new path. The fight to protect the earth was not a battle that could be won overnight, but it was one that could, and would, be won through perseverance, collaboration, and a deep respect for the planet.

"We've come a long way," Aldo said softly to Nina, who stood beside him, gazing at the horizon.

"We have," she agreed, her voice filled with quiet pride. "But the real work starts now. We've changed the way people think, but we need to make sure they never forget the lessons of the past."

And as the first light of day illuminated the earth, it was clear that humanity had learned those lessons. They had begun the long, difficult journey toward a future where the planet was not a resource to be exploited, but a partner to be respected.

The earth was healing. And humanity was, too.

Chapter 18: Adventure Amidst the Ruins

The world had been broken, torn apart by its own excesses, and yet, amid the ashes of civilization, there was something stirring, a fragile hope. Aldo, Nina, and their team were no longer just observers of the crisis. They had become its active participants, seeking solutions and providing guidance wherever it was needed most. But there was still so much to do, so many places that had been devastated, so many lives that needed rebuilding. Their journey was far from over.

A Dangerous Expedition

The devastation left in the wake of the waste storm was unlike anything Aldo had ever imagined. Whole cities had been swallowed by mountains of debris, their once-proud skylines reduced to heaps of broken concrete and twisted metal. Rivers, clogged with plastics and toxic waste, wound through desolate landscapes. Some places were nothing more than smoldering ruins, the fires still burning beneath the surface, while others were consumed by stagnation and decay.

As Aldo, Nina, and their group prepared for their journey, they knew the risks. The expedition would take them into the heart of these ruined cities, places where the human spirit had been tested in ways they couldn't yet fully comprehend. The roads were treacherous, covered with rubble, and many areas were still dangerous due to ongoing fires or unstable ground. Yet, there was no time to waste. The team had to see the situation firsthand to understand the full scale of the catastrophe, and to offer solutions where they could.

With a small convoy of armored vehicles carrying supplies and equipment, they set out on the first leg of their journey, heading toward what had once been the bustling metropolis of Libera City.

Libera, now a ghost town, had once been a shining example of urban development, but it was now a symbol of everything that had gone wrong. The storm's fury had torn through the city with unmatched intensity, spreading debris across vast distances and leaving behind a wasteland where thriving neighborhoods once stood.

"Are we ready for this?" Nina asked, her voice heavy with the weight of uncertainty. They had come a long way, but the task ahead seemed insurmountable.

"We have no choice," Aldo replied, his gaze fixed on the horizon, where the faint outline of the city loomed in the distance. "The world needs to see the truth. Only by confronting the full scale of the disaster will we be able to convince people that change is not optional. It's essential."

Libera City: The Desolate Landscape

Arriving in Libera City felt like stepping into a warzone. The streets were choked with debris, and entire neighborhoods had been flattened. Buildings that had once gleamed with modernity were now mere skeletons of their former selves. The air was thick with dust, and a faint smell of burning lingered in the atmosphere. There were no signs of life here—no children playing in the streets, no cars rushing by, no bustling markets. It was as though civilization had never existed.

Aldo and his team moved carefully through the wreckage, observing the destruction. It was worse than he had imagined. Buildings that were once full of life had been reduced to rubble, and streets were littered with plastics, metals, and other waste. The once-thriving city was now a graveyard, a testament to human negligence.

"We need to get to the center of the city," Aldo said, his voice determined despite the bleakness of the scene. "This is where the largest accumulation of waste was, and it's where the worst of the damage occurred."

As they navigated through the ruins, they encountered remnants of the old world. An overturned car here, a toppled lamp post there, and the occasional glimpse of a once-beautiful park, now smothered in plastic waste. The shock of seeing it all laid bare in such a raw, unfiltered way hit Aldo harder than he had anticipated.

"This place used to be alive," Nina muttered, her eyes scanning the devastation. "Now it's a tomb."

"There's still hope," Aldo replied, trying to sound more confident than he felt. "We just need to show people that we can rebuild, better, and more sustainably. But we can't do that by ignoring the past. We have to face the full extent of the damage."

Spreading the Message

In the weeks that followed, Aldo, Nina, and their team continued their journey through the ruins. Each new city they visited presented its own unique challenges. In some places, fires were still smoldering beneath the surface, making it impossible to search certain areas. In others, the ground was unstable, shifting and cracking underfoot due to the heat from the fires below. But despite the risks, they pushed on, determined to get their message out.

At each stop, Aldo and Nina held public meetings with the survivors, those few who had managed to hold on in the face of the disaster. They spoke about the importance of waste management, of reducing consumption, and of shifting to renewable energy. They shared their vision for a world where humanity didn't simply survive, but thrived in harmony with the earth.

The reactions were mixed. Some people were skeptical, their spirits too broken by the devastation to believe in change. They had lost everything, their homes, their businesses, their loved ones, and the idea of starting over seemed almost impossible.

But there were others who listened closely, their faces filled with quiet hope. These were the people who had seen the destruction firsthand, and they were determined not to let it define them. They were ready to rebuild, but they needed the tools, the knowledge, and the support to do so.

"That's the key," Nina said one evening, as they sat around a campfire after another long day of traveling. "It's not just about having the technology, it's about having the support. These people need to know that they're not alone in this. They need to feel that we're in this together."

"I agree," Aldo said, his gaze drifting toward the horizon. "But it's also about education. The more people understand how we got here, the more likely they'll be to take responsibility for their actions in the future."

A Rising Tide of Change

As the weeks turned into months, Aldo and his team continued their journey. With each city they visited, they planted the seeds of change. People began to listen, to rethink their relationship with the earth. In some cities, they set up recycling programs, and in others, they helped establish small-scale renewable energy systems. It wasn't enough to reverse the damage, but it was a start.

One city they visited, once a major industrial hub, had suffered immensely from the collapse of the global supply chain. Factories that had once produced goods in massive quantities now stood empty, their smokestacks silent. But amid the destruction, there was a glimmer of innovation. A group of local engineers had started experimenting with new ways to convert waste into energy, using the same technology Aldo and Nina had developed at the Alpha Research Center.

"This is what we need," Aldo said, watching the group work. "Local solutions, tailored to the unique challenges of each place."

Nina smiled. "Exactly. It's not just about imposing a solution from the top down. It's about empowering people to take control of their own future."

The Road Ahead

After months of traveling, Aldo and his team returned to the Alpha Research Center. The journey had been grueling, but it had been worth it. They had seen the worst of the disaster and had shared their vision for a better future with the people who needed it most. They had witnessed firsthand the resilience of humanity, the willingness of people to change, and the power of collective action.

But the battle was far from over. There were still countless cities and communities that had yet to be reached, and the full scale of the environmental disaster was still unfolding. Aldo knew that their work was just beginning. But as he stood on the balcony of the center, looking out over the landscape, he couldn't help but feel a sense of pride. The world was not beyond saving, not yet. But it would take all of humanity working together, with unwavering determination, to turn things around.

The road ahead was long, but it was a road filled with promise. If humanity could come together, if it could adapt and change, there was hope. There was always hope.

Chapter 19: Facing New Challenges

The world had descended into chaos, but even amid the ruins, there was still a flicker of hope, a hope that Aldo, Nina, and their team clung to as they continued their journey. They had seen devastation and despair, but they had also witnessed humanity's determination to rebuild and evolve. However, their path was not without obstacles. As they ventured further into the disaster zones, the challenges they faced grew more complex and dangerous. The world was no longer just a place of natural calamities; it had become a battleground for the remnants of human society.

A Fractured World

The cities they visited were increasingly desolate. Whole regions had collapsed under the weight of the environmental disaster, with governments unable to maintain order or provide basic services. People had turned against each other, driven by the scarcity of resources. Where once there had been cooperation, there was now competition. Some cities had fallen under the control of violent militias, while others had devolved into anarchy. The worst part was that these groups were not just interested in survival, they were driven by the desire to control what little was left.

Aldo and his team knew they had to be cautious. Their mission was clear: to spread the message of hope, to teach people how to manage waste, reduce consumption, and restore the Earth. But as they made their way through increasingly dangerous territory, they were forced to reckon with the darker side of human nature.

"We're entering new territory," Nina said as they neared the edge of a once-thriving industrial city, now abandoned and overtaken by lawlessness. "We need to be prepared for anything."

MOUNT OF WASTE

Aldo nodded, his expression grim. "The world has changed. People are desperate. And when people are desperate, they do things they wouldn't otherwise."

The city ahead of them was eerily silent, but Aldo and Nina knew that silence was not a sign of safety. In the months following the storm, survival instincts had overridden civility, and people who once lived side by side now fought over the scraps of a broken world. While many had banded together to rebuild, others had fractured into small, aggressive factions, each seeking to claim control over what little was left.

A Deadly Encounter

As Aldo's convoy made its way through the city's ruins, the group encountered their first real threat. They had stopped at a makeshift camp just outside the city to assess the damage and talk to a few survivors when a loud shout broke the stillness.

"Get down!" shouted Marcus, the team's security expert, as he immediately drew his weapon. Aldo and Nina crouched low behind the cover of a crumbled wall, while the rest of the team scrambled for safety.

A group of heavily armed men appeared from behind a collapsed building, their faces hardened by months of survival. They were a part of a local militia, one of many that had formed in the wake of the disaster, preying on weaker survivors and scavenging what they could.

"What do you want?" Aldo called out, trying to remain calm but aware of the dangerous situation they were in.

One of the men sneered, stepping forward. "What do we want? We want what's ours. And that means whatever you've got, your food, your supplies, your equipment."

Nina, her face set in a defiant expression, stood up slowly, speaking with the calm authority she had learned over the years.

"You don't have to do this. We're not here to take from you. We've come to help."

The militia leader laughed harshly. "Help? In a world like this, there's no help. Only power. And you're standing on my territory. So hand over everything, and maybe we'll let you leave in one piece."

The situation was tense. Aldo's mind raced, calculating the best course of action. These men were not interested in dialogue; they only understood one language. The reality of the new world they inhabited had become painfully clear, survival came first, and everything else, including trust and cooperation, was secondary.

Just as the militia leader raised his weapon, ready to escalate the situation, a loud explosion shook the ground, followed by the unmistakable sound of gunfire. The militia men froze, confused by the sudden attack. It wasn't long before they were engulfed in a firefight with a rival faction, who had obviously been tracking them.

"We need to move, now!" Marcus shouted.

Without hesitation, the group packed up quickly and began retreating toward their convoy. It was clear that the encounter was a reminder of just how fragile their mission had become. The world was no longer a place where idealism could survive without a strong defense. There were too many dangers lurking, and not everyone was ready to embrace the changes that Aldo and Nina were preaching.

Navigating the Political Landscape

After narrowly escaping the attack, the group retreated to a safer location to regroup. They had been fortunate, but the reality of the situation weighed heavily on Aldo's mind. These militias were just one manifestation of a much larger problem. In the wake of the disaster, the world had fractured into competing factions, some simply trying to survive, others trying to establish control.

MOUNT OF WASTE

It was a dangerous environment for anyone seeking to rebuild, let alone bring people together.

"We need to rethink our approach," Aldo said, looking at Nina. "We can't just go into places like this with our message and expect it to be well-received. We need allies. We need to understand the power structures here."

Nina nodded, her face etched with concern. "I think we've underestimated how desperate people have become. The world isn't just broken, it's in a constant state of conflict now. We have to be careful who we trust."

The following days were spent learning more about the political landscape of the region. They spoke to survivors who had joined various factions, as well as independent groups who had formed in the wake of the collapse. It was clear that many of these groups were not interested in peace or collaboration. They were interested in survival, and survival alone.

But even amidst the chaos, Aldo saw glimpses of the change he sought. A small community on the outskirts of the city had managed to form a cooperative, working together to repurpose waste into valuable resources. They had set up a basic waste management system, processing plastic waste into biodegradable materials. The cooperative was small but growing, and it was an example of what was possible even in a world so torn apart by conflict.

"Maybe this is how we can reach them," Aldo said, his mind racing with possibilities. "We can't change everything overnight. But if we can show them that working together can provide tangible results, like food, energy, and safety, maybe we can build the alliances we need to succeed."

Nina agreed. "The people here may not trust us, but they trust what they can see, what they can use. If we can show them that our solutions work, they'll listen. Eventually."

The Road to Unity

As they continued their journey, the group became more strategic in their efforts to spread their message. They began to focus on smaller, more isolated communities, places that hadn't yet fallen under the control of militias or other factions. These communities were often more open to new ideas, having been left to their own devices as governments collapsed.

Aldo and Nina's team spent weeks traveling from one village to the next, showing survivors how to process waste, grow food sustainably, and build small-scale renewable energy systems. They encountered resistance, of course, many people were wary of outsiders, especially those who had no immediate answers to the larger political struggles they were facing. But Aldo was relentless. He knew that the only way to overcome the skepticism was to prove that the solutions worked.

Gradually, their efforts began to pay off. People started to see the benefits of waste management and sustainable living. The small groups they had helped began to grow, and soon, they were able to share their successes with other communities. Word of their work spread, and while there were still many obstacles to overcome, the first glimmers of unity began to emerge.

A World Divided, But Not Defeated

The journey was far from over, and the challenges would only grow greater. The militias were not the only threat; the continued environmental degradation, the lack of infrastructure, and the fractured political landscape all posed significant risks. But Aldo, Nina, and their team were no longer just outsiders trying to change the world. They had become part of it, working within its complexities, learning from its mistakes, and offering solutions where they could.

As they prepared for the next stage of their journey, Aldo took a moment to reflect on what they had accomplished so far. They had faced down militias, helped rebuild communities, and spread a message of hope to places that had long since lost it. And though the road ahead would be fraught with challenges, he knew that their mission had only just begun.

"We're making a difference," Aldo said, his voice resolute. "One step at a time."

Nina nodded, her eyes shining with determination. "We have to. The world needs us."

And with that, they continued forward, facing the new challenges that lay ahead, but never losing sight of the hope they carried with them. The world might have been broken, but as long as there was still hope, there was still a chance to rebuild.

Chapter 20: The War Against Time

The weight of urgency pressed down on Aldo's shoulders as he stood at the window of their temporary headquarters, gazing out at the fractured landscape. His mind raced with thoughts of the planet's impending collapse, the fragile threads of survival stretching thinner each day. Time was not a luxury they could afford anymore. It was slipping away like sand through their fingers.

The Earth was deteriorating at an alarming rate, and though they had made some progress, Aldo and his team knew it wasn't enough. The damage was vast, the climate was deteriorating, and the effects of their ever-growing waste crisis were far-reaching. Every hour that passed meant more lives lost, more ecosystems destroyed, and more potential solutions slipping further out of reach.

Aldo turned to Nina, who had just returned from a meeting with one of their newly formed alliances. Her face was set, her eyes reflecting the same determination that had driven them from the start. But even she, with all her resilience, couldn't ignore the mounting tension in the air.

"We don't have much time left," Nina said, her voice calm yet heavy with the weight of their shared understanding. "The world is on the brink. If we don't accelerate our efforts, it may be too late."

Aldo nodded. "I know. The science is clear. The systems we've put in place, while effective on a small scale, need to be adopted worldwide. And quickly. The environment won't wait for us to catch up."

The Stakes Have Never Been Higher

The global situation had escalated beyond what anyone could have predicted. With the collapse of traditional power structures and the rise of militias and rogue states, international cooperation had all but ceased. Countries, once interconnected, were now

MOUNT OF WASTE

islands of isolation, focused solely on their own survival. The shared responsibility for managing the Earth's fate seemed like an impossible dream. Yet Aldo, Nina, and their team were still fighting for that dream.

"We need to think bigger," Aldo said, pacing the room. "These small-scale efforts are just the start. We have a solution that can help, but it requires global implementation. We need to get governments, corporations, and the public to act now, or we will lose everything."

Nina sat at the table, reviewing data on her tablet. "I've been speaking with various groups, some are on board, but many are still hesitant. The political instability and the fractured world make it nearly impossible to get the necessary backing for such a sweeping change."

The challenge was not only technical but deeply political. There were still many who denied the urgency of the crisis, believing that the Earth could heal on its own without radical action. Others, driven by fear or greed, saw Aldo's solutions as a threat to their power, and actively worked to suppress them.

"The longer we wait," Aldo muttered, "the more entrenched these factions become. It's a race against time."

They had made progress with some nations. A handful of smaller states had implemented Aldo's waste management systems, and they had witnessed remarkable improvements in waste reduction and energy generation. But these successes were isolated, and the scale of the crisis had long surpassed what any one country could manage alone. They needed global coordination, a unified effort to roll out the technology that could save the planet before it was too late.

Reaching the Unreachable

One of the team's biggest challenges was communication. After the storm, most communication networks had been destroyed, and what remained was fragmented and unreliable. Even when they were able to get in touch with governments or international bodies, their voices were often ignored or dismissed. It was hard for world leaders to hear the message of hope when they were consumed by their own survival.

Aldo and his team had already seen the failure of traditional diplomacy. They realized that if they wanted to succeed, they would have to forge a new path, one that involved not just governments, but the people. Ordinary citizens, empowered with the right knowledge and tools, could help accelerate the transition toward a sustainable world.

"We need to focus on grassroots movements," Nina suggested. "People are the key. If we can inspire the masses to take action, we can create pressure on governments to follow suit. We need to ignite a global awakening."

Aldo agreed. The power of social movements had never been clearer. History had shown that when enough people united for a cause, they could change the course of history. It was no longer about waiting for the politicians or corporations to act, it was about rallying the public to demand change.

"Let's start with the people. Let them drive the change," Aldo said, his voice filled with conviction.

A Global Campaign

The next few weeks were a blur of planning, organizing, and executing. The team launched a global campaign to spread the message of sustainable living and waste management. They used every tool at their disposal—from radio broadcasts and social media to underground networks that had sprung up in the absence of government oversight. They broadcasted messages of hope, offering concrete solutions to the environmental crisis that was tearing the planet apart. The goal was clear: to create a groundswell of support for radical action, to turn the tide before it was too late.

MOUNT OF WASTE

"We have to reach as many people as possible, and fast," Nina said. "This isn't just about raising awareness. We need action."

They distributed thousands of pamphlets detailing how individuals could reduce their waste, how communities could start implementing Aldo's waste management systems, and how people could demand that their governments take decisive action. They set up training workshops and online courses to teach people how to set up small-scale recycling operations, renewable energy systems, and sustainable farming practices.

The response was overwhelming. Across the globe, people began to take notice. A new movement was rising, a movement focused on saving the Earth, not just for today, but for future generations. Social media exploded with viral hashtags calling for a worldwide ban on single-use plastics and greater investment in green technologies. Citizens from every corner of the world began sharing their stories of how they had implemented sustainable practices in their own lives.

"I can see the change happening," Aldo said one evening, watching as the global movement gained momentum. "But we need to keep pushing. We can't afford to slow down."

The Collapse of the Old Order

The growing movement began to put unprecedented pressure on governments and corporations. International organizations that had once been at odds with each other were now forced to acknowledge the urgency of the situation. Under mounting pressure from their populations, several large nations began to negotiate for a new kind of global agreement, one that prioritized the planet's survival over political rivalry.

Aldo, Nina, and the team worked tirelessly to provide the solutions needed to implement a worldwide waste management and renewable energy initiative. They formed alliances with environmental organizations, corporate leaders who were willing to embrace sustainable practices, and even former political adversaries who had seen the writing on the wall. The momentum was building, and though there were still powerful forces fighting against them, the tide was beginning to turn.

But there were still those who were unwilling to let go of the old ways. Large corporations with vested interests in maintaining the status quo fought tooth and nail to preserve their power. They spread misinformation, undermined the movement, and tried to sow division. In many places, the public was still divided. Some resisted change, unwilling to believe that the Earth was truly on the brink of destruction.

The battle was far from won, but Aldo's team remained undeterred. They knew that in this war against time, every victory, no matter how small, was crucial.

The Final Countdown

With each passing day, the pressure increased. The signs of environmental collapse were everywhere, rising temperatures, extreme weather, and ecosystems on the brink of collapse. There was no more time for delay. Aldo and his team knew that the next few months would be crucial. If they failed to unite the world behind a common cause, if they couldn't convince enough people to take action, then the Earth would fall into irreversible ruin.

The solution was clear, the need for action urgent. But the world still teetered on the edge, and every day that passed brought humanity closer to the precipice.

"We're fighting against a ticking clock," Aldo said one night as they prepared for another round of negotiations with global leaders. "But we can still win. We have the solutions. We just need the will to make them happen."

The battle wasn't over, and the war against time was far from won. But as Aldo and Nina looked out over the horizon, they knew that there was still hope. The fight was long, and the road ahead was fraught with obstacles, but they had seen the power of unity. They had seen what was possible when people came together for a common cause.

And as long as there was still time, they would keep fighting.

A Ray of Hope

In the final moments of this chapter, as Aldo and his team stood together, ready for the next phase of their mission, one thing was certain: they would not give up. They could not afford to. For in their hands lay the future of the Earth. And if they succeeded, they would not just be saving the planet, they would be saving humanity itself.

The war against time had only just begun.

Chapter 21: Finding Hope

Aldo and Nina trudged through the remnants of a once-thriving city, their faces set with determination, but the weight of exhaustion was evident in their every step. It had been weeks since they'd started their journey, and the planet seemed to grow more desperate by the day. Every corner they turned revealed more devastation. The cities that had once been hubs of life were now silent ghost towns, ravaged by the storm, the fire, and the ongoing struggle for survival.

The political system was in disarray, and international cooperation had all but evaporated. The global crisis was getting worse, not better, and Aldo and his team were running out of time. However, despite the overwhelming sense of failure that loomed over them, Aldo refused to give up. If anything, the devastation fueled his resolve to find a solution.

The Search for Something Different

The journey was dangerous, taking them through territories where survival had become a matter of ingenuity and sheer willpower. Cities had become battlegrounds, with fractured societies competing for resources. But Aldo wasn't looking for battles or military solutions, he was looking for the heart of what could save them: sustainable practices, people who had found a way to live in harmony with the land, and communities that had not just survived but thrived in the aftermath.

The team had come across several small groups living in isolation, but most were struggling just to make it through another day. But it was during one of their travels through the rural outskirts of a long-abandoned region that they stumbled upon something that gave them a flicker of hope.

It was a community of just under a hundred people, a small village nestled between the remnants of old cities and the wilderness. It was far from perfect, yet there was something different about it, something that spoke to the possibilities of rebuilding.

The Community of Waste Management

As Aldo and Nina entered the village, they were immediately struck by how organized it was. The streets were clean, and there was a sense of calm, even amid the chaos. It wasn't much, but it was a sign of life, a rare glimpse of the resilience of humanity. The air, for the first time in a long while, felt cleaner. There were gardens where food was grown in a sustainable manner, buildings made of recycled materials, and, most striking of all, an intricate waste management system that seemed to be at the heart of it all.

At first glance, Aldo couldn't quite understand how such a small community had managed to create a functioning system for waste disposal and resource management in the middle of a collapsing world. But as they moved deeper into the village, it became clear. The villagers had discovered ways to recycle and repurpose materials using simple technology, methods that Aldo and his team had only dreamed of bringing to scale.

The community used what they had, working with minimal resources, relying on a mix of ingenuity and practical knowledge. They had built a waste-to-energy system that not only dealt with the mountain of garbage but also generated the power they needed to run their homes. They used a combination of composting, mechanical shredders, and fermentation processes to break down organic waste, while plastics and metals were meticulously sorted and repurposed into materials that could be used for construction or tools.

But it wasn't just about waste management. This community had learned how to live sustainably in every aspect of their lives. Solar panels lined rooftops, water was collected from rain and filtered using simple but effective methods, and nearly every item used in daily life was reused or repurposed.

A Glimmer of Hope

Aldo couldn't contain his amazement. "I've seen nothing like this since the disaster," he said, his voice tinged with awe. "This is the answer. This is exactly what we've been looking for."

Nina looked around, her face lit with a mixture of wonder and disbelief. "It's incredible. They've managed to survive the crisis, and they're thriving. They're not just dealing with the waste. They're turning it into something valuable."

The village leader, a middle-aged woman named Emilia, welcomed them with open arms. She had heard of Aldo's work and the solutions he had proposed to save the planet. Yet, unlike many of the others Aldo had encountered, Emilia didn't need to be convinced. Her community had already embraced these principles out of necessity, and now, it was their way of life.

"We didn't have a choice," Emilia explained as she sat with Aldo and Nina in a small gathering space made of salvaged materials. "When the storms started, when the cities burned, we knew we had to do something. We didn't have the luxury of waiting for someone else to fix the problem. We had to fix it ourselves."

It wasn't just the practical knowledge that amazed Aldo, it was the spirit of cooperation that permeated the village. Despite the hardships, they had come together to build something sustainable. They had created a community in which everyone played a part, where waste wasn't just a byproduct but a resource. The people here understood that their survival depended on their ability to adapt, to innovate, and to work together.

Learning from the Past

As Aldo spent more time in the village, he began to see how much their way of life could be adapted on a larger scale. They were living proof that a different approach was possible. It wasn't just about the technology; it was about a mindset shift, a deep understanding of the earth's cycles and a commitment to living within its means.

"We used to be wasteful," Emilia continued, "just like the cities that burned. We consumed without thinking about the long-term consequences. But when we were left with nothing, we had to change. And we realized that we could still live, but we had to be smarter, more conscious of how we used the planet's resources."

Aldo and Nina exchanged a glance. This was the solution they had been searching for: a community that had learned from their mistakes, a community that understood sustainability at a level most governments and corporations had long ignored.

"We can scale this up," Aldo said, a spark of excitement in his eyes. "If we could implement something like this globally, using technology and knowledge from communities like this, we could stop the cycle of destruction. We could reverse the damage we've done."

A Global Model

Over the next few days, Aldo, Nina, and their team worked closely with Emilia and the village. They learned everything they could about their waste management techniques, their methods of renewable energy generation, and their agricultural practices. Aldo documented every detail, every small innovation that had allowed this community to thrive in the face of catastrophe.

But it wasn't just the technical aspects that Aldo found valuable, it was the mindset. Emilia had spoken of how they had learned to value cooperation over competition, community over individualism. They didn't just work together to solve problems; they had created a culture of responsibility, where each person knew that their actions impacted the whole. They shared resources, they shared knowledge, and they shared hope.

"This," Aldo said, his voice filled with resolve, "is what the world needs. We can show them that there is a way out of this mess. We can replicate this on a global scale."

A Vision for the Future

Before leaving, Aldo made a promise to Emilia and her people. "We will take your example to the world. We'll use this as the foundation for the global campaign we've been fighting for. What you've done here can be the blueprint for the future."

Emilia smiled, a sense of quiet pride in her eyes. "We're just doing what we have to. But if it helps others, if it helps the planet, then I'll be glad to share everything we know."

Aldo and Nina left the village with a renewed sense of purpose. They knew that the task ahead was monumental, but for the first time in a long while, they felt the faintest glimmer of hope. They had found a model for survival, a shining example of what was possible if humanity came together, adapted, and learned from the past.

A New Beginning

As they walked back to their headquarters, Aldo's mind was racing with possibilities. The technology, the systems, the community-driven approach, it all had the potential to transform the world. The challenge now was to convince the rest of the planet to follow this path.

"We have the solution," Aldo said quietly to Nina. "Now we just have to make the world believe it."

Nina nodded, her eyes filled with determination. "We will. We've seen it with our own eyes. Now it's time to show everyone else."

Together, they had found hope in a world teetering on the edge of destruction. And with that hope, they would fight harder than ever to bring about the change the planet so desperately needed.

MOUNT OF WASTE

The war against time was still raging, but now Aldo and his team knew that with the right knowledge, the right spirit, and the right technology, there was still time to save the Earth.

Chapter 22: Limited Resources

Aldo gazed out across the desolate landscape, a silent witness to the ever-encroaching threat that loomed over them. It had been weeks since they left the small village, months, perhaps, on their mission to bring hope to the world. But the further they ventured into the wasteland, the more apparent it became that the Earth was running out of time. The world they had known was unraveling, and survival had become a grim and constant struggle.

The situation was dire.

Despite all their efforts to spread the message of sustainability, despite the groundbreaking innovations they had uncovered, they were faced with a simple, undeniable truth: the resources they had come to rely on—water, food, and energy, were rapidly depleting. What had once seemed like an insurmountable task was now becoming a race against time. Aldo had always been a scientist of great optimism, but even he could not ignore the grim reality of the present moment.

A World of Scarcity

They had reached what was once a thriving agricultural zone on the outskirts of what was now a half-ruined metropolis. It was here that they hoped to find some respite, perhaps crops they could harvest, or clean water they could collect, but what they encountered instead was nothing more than dried-up soil and abandoned farms, the land as barren as the air itself.

"We're running out of time, Aldo," Nina said, her voice strained as she scanned the horizon. "I don't think there's anything left here."

Aldo sighed heavily, his mind racing. He had known the situation was deteriorating rapidly, but seeing it firsthand was something entirely different. They had relied on old methods of survival, but now even those methods seemed outdated, irrelevant.

MOUNT OF WASTE

What good was sustainable technology if there was no water to power it? What use was waste management when the waste was being consumed by the very elements themselves?

"It's not just here, Nina," Aldo replied quietly. "It's everywhere. The resources we need to survive, the water, the food, are disappearing faster than we can find new sources. The planet is running out of fuel, and we've spent years waiting for someone else to solve the problem. Now, we have to be the ones to do it."

Nina nodded solemnly. She had seen it too, the lack of resources, the collapse of ecosystems, the breakdown of supply chains. Everything was interconnected. The rising temperatures, the melting ice caps, the shifting tectonic plates, all were the consequences of generations of neglect and overconsumption. Now, humanity was paying the price, and the cost was only going to climb.

The Struggle for Water

The first crisis they faced was water. The scarcity of clean drinking water had become a pressing issue, one that weighed heavily on Aldo's shoulders. The wasteful practices of previous generations, combined with the disastrous storms and shifting earth, had rendered much of the world's water sources either polluted or inaccessible.

"What's left?" Aldo asked, crouching beside a small stream that had once been a reliable source of water for the region. But it now ran with thick sludge, a result of the toxic chemicals that had leached into the water system from the ruined cities nearby.

Nina inspected the water. "There's nothing left. This used to be clean, pure water. Now..." She shook her head. "This is undrinkable."

Aldo grimaced and looked at the sky, which had been overcast for days. There was no sign of rain on the horizon, and the little fresh water that remained was locked deep beneath the earth's surface, inaccessible to most of the world.

The team had already set up a filtration system designed to purify any water they came across, but the amount of clean water was barely enough to sustain them. They couldn't afford to waste a single drop.

"We need to move on," Aldo said after a long pause, determination in his voice. "If we stay here, we'll be trapped. We need to find a place where we can gather water, before it's all gone."

Nina agreed, and they began to pack up. But even as they moved on, Aldo couldn't shake the gnawing feeling in his stomach. If this region was devoid of clean water, how many others were in the same situation?

The Search for Food

The next obstacle was food. With no crops to harvest and the land in ruins, finding sufficient nourishment was becoming increasingly difficult. The communities they had visited had managed to sustain themselves through small-scale farming and innovative agricultural techniques, but those methods required fertile soil, soil that was in short supply.

As they journeyed, Aldo tried to maintain hope. His team had developed strategies for growing food in small, controlled environments, utilizing recycled materials and waste for composting. But these systems were slow and limited in scope. They could feed only small groups at a time. The global population was too vast to rely solely on these methods, especially with the ever-increasing number of refugees and displaced persons.

They arrived at an abandoned farm that had once been part of a larger agricultural project, hoping to scavenge what was left. The crops were withered and the soil cracked, a visual reminder of how much they had lost in such a short period of time.

MOUNT OF WASTE

"There's nothing here," Nina muttered, frustration seeping into her voice. "It's all gone."

Aldo surveyed the land, his heart heavy with the realization that even their carefully crafted systems were inadequate. What could they do when the very foundation of their survival, food, was slipping out of reach?

"We can't give up now," Aldo said, his voice firmer than he felt. "We still have resources. We still have knowledge. There has to be a way."

But deep down, Aldo knew that there were no easy answers. They were in a race against the very survival of humanity.

The Harsh Reality of Limited Resources

As the days passed, the team found themselves increasingly relying on the most basic forms of survival, rationing food, conserving water, and searching for any small scraps of sustenance they could find. Every night, they camped in makeshift shelters, using what little was left to protect themselves from the elements. Every morning, they awoke to face the crushing reality of the world around them.

The air was thick with dust and the smell of decay. There was no sign of recovery in sight. Every city they visited had fallen into disarray, its infrastructure either decimated by storms or overrun by scavengers. Aldo's hopes of bringing about meaningful change seemed increasingly remote.

But there was still one thing that kept him going: his team. Despite the odds, despite the overwhelming nature of their journey, they still believed in the possibility of change. Every member of the team, from the tech experts to the field scientists, was committed to finding a solution. They had come too far to quit now.

The Global Crisis Becomes Personal

The shortage of resources was no longer just a theoretical problem. It was personal. Every decision they made now had life-or-death consequences. Every drop of water they collected, every morsel of food they salvaged, became precious.

Aldo watched as his team members carefully rationed their supplies. Each person was becoming thinner, their faces worn with the strain of their arduous journey. They were all painfully aware that their current way of life, living on borrowed time, could not last forever.

Despite everything, Aldo remained resolute. If humanity was to survive, they would have to adapt in ways they hadn't even imagined yet. They would have to push the limits of innovation, survival, and hope.

The Final Push

As the days grew shorter and the air grew colder, Aldo and his team made a pact: they would find a way, no matter the cost. The resources available to them were limited, but their knowledge, their resolve, and their unity were not.

"We'll keep pushing forward," Aldo said one evening as they huddled around a fire. "We have to."

And so, despite the limited resources, despite the exhaustion, despite the world crumbling around them, they moved forward. The road ahead was uncertain, but Aldo knew that if they could hold on long enough, if they could continue to fight for a better future, there might still be a way out of the darkness.

With each step, they were not just fighting for survival. They were fighting for a world that still had the potential to heal, a world where hope was not yet lost.

The battle against time, against resources, and against the forces of nature itself had only just begun. But Aldo and his team were ready. They had no choice but to be.

Chapter 23: The Power of Collaboration

The sun hung low in the sky, casting a muted orange glow over the barren landscape. Aldo sat hunched over a makeshift desk in the corner of their temporary headquarters, his eyes scanning the vast sea of data that lay before him. Despite the growing urgency of the crisis, he felt an increasing weight on his shoulders. The Earth was dying. The resources that had once sustained life on this planet were now running out faster than anyone had anticipated. But even more pressing was the growing realization that time was no longer on their side.

"We need to act now," Aldo muttered under his breath, staring at the screen. "But how do we convince the world to unite before it's too late?"

The Challenge of Global Cooperation

The idea had been growing in Aldo's mind for weeks—since the moment he first saw the widespread devastation. He had come to the conclusion that solving the environmental crisis was not something any one nation, no matter how powerful or advanced, could do alone. The Earth's problems were global, interconnected, and transcended political borders. The only way forward was through global cooperation.

But there was one glaring problem: convincing the nations of the world to collaborate.

"We can't just rely on isolated efforts," Aldo had said to Nina one evening as they discussed the matter. "The scale of the crisis requires a unified front, a global effort. If we work together, pooling our resources and knowledge, we can reverse the damage done and begin rebuilding. But if we continue to act in isolation, we're doomed."

Nina, ever the realist, had nodded slowly. "I agree with you. But the problem isn't just about convincing people, it's about getting governments to set aside their own interests long enough to make real change. They've been at each other's throats for years. After the storm, after the economic collapse, many countries are more concerned with their own survival than with the survival of the planet."

Aldo had known she was right. In the aftermath of the storm, global instability had reached an all-time high. Nations had retreated into themselves, closing borders, restricting trade, and hoarding resources. They were struggling to recover from the widespread devastation, and their focus was inward, not outward. The idea of a global alliance to address a crisis as vast and complex as the environmental one seemed like an impossible dream.

The Proposal

But Aldo wasn't one to give up. He drafted a proposal, an ambitious plan to bring the world together in the face of catastrophe. He called it the "Global Waste and Resource Restoration Initiative." It outlined a framework for the shared management of waste, the recovery of ecosystems, and the implementation of sustainable technologies across the globe. His proposal was clear: the environmental collapse was not just an ecological issue, but a global security issue. The interconnectedness of nature and human society meant that no nation could survive in isolation.

Aldo knew that to have any chance of success, he needed the backing of influential leaders. He reached out to the heads of governments and international organizations, requesting meetings, hoping to gather support for his vision. It wasn't easy. Each meeting was a challenge in itself, as resistance to the idea came in many forms: skepticism, political infighting, and nationalistic pride.

MOUNT OF WASTE

One of the first leaders to respond was Chancellor Li of the Republic of China. Li had always been pragmatic, focused on long-term survival strategies, but his country had also been ravaged by the storm, and his people were suffering. During a video conference with Aldo, he leaned forward, his eyes intense.

"We understand the gravity of the situation, Aldo," Chancellor Li said. "But we have to consider the implications of such a global initiative. How do we protect our sovereignty while sharing resources with the world? What guarantee do we have that our contributions won't be exploited by others?"

Aldo was ready for this question. "Chancellor, I'm not asking you to sacrifice your sovereignty. What I'm proposing is an international framework for mutual benefit, one that ensures that resources are distributed equitably. We can create a system of checks and balances that ensures no nation is taken advantage of. But to do that, we need to work together. If we don't, the planet will collapse, and no one will be left standing."

Li paused, clearly considering the implications. "I will think about it. But the world is fractured right now, and trust is in short supply. Convincing others will be a monumental task."

Aldo's heart sank, but he pressed on, knowing that this was just the beginning of a long and arduous process.

Resistance and Doubts

Aldo faced resistance from every corner of the world. In the European Union, political infighting made it nearly impossible to reach a consensus. The United States, still reeling from its own devastation, seemed more focused on rebuilding its military strength than addressing the environmental crisis. India, dealing with the aftermath of severe flooding, was reluctant to commit to global initiatives while its own people were struggling to survive.

At one point, Aldo received a response from the President of Brazil, who had been in denial about the true scale of the environmental disaster. In a letter, the President wrote: "We are facing our own problems here. While your initiative is admirable, it is not our priority. The people of Brazil are suffering, and we must focus on our recovery before we can think of global solutions."

It was a harsh reality. Aldo understood the sentiment, every country was fighting its own battles. But the refusal to acknowledge the interconnected nature of the crisis only deepened the divide. Without cooperation, the chances of solving the environmental catastrophe were slim.

A Turning Point

In the midst of these challenges, Aldo received an unexpected message: the leader of a small, remote island nation in the Pacific, once considered insignificant on the world stage, had expressed an interest in his proposal. The island nation of Kiribati, one of the most vulnerable countries to climate change, was struggling to survive. Their entire way of life had been threatened by rising sea levels, and their agricultural systems were collapsing.

The president of Kiribati, President Titia, was well aware of the global struggles but had a unique perspective. In a video call with Aldo, she spoke with raw emotion.

"We have lost so much," President Titia said, her voice calm but tinged with sorrow. "We've lost our land, our homes, our culture. But we understand the reality. We cannot survive alone. The world must act as one, before it's too late."

Aldo was taken aback by her words. "President Titia, your country has been devastated. Yet you still believe in collaboration?"

"We have no choice but to believe," she said, her face resolute. "If we wait for others to act first, we will be gone before they realize what's at stake. We must lead by example, Aldo. We will support your initiative."

Her words were like a beacon of hope. She was the first leader to openly support Aldo's vision without hesitation. And her support had a profound impact. Within weeks, other smaller nations, those most at risk, began to rally around the proposal, understanding that their survival depended on a united front. They saw that the collapse of one country could have cascading effects on the entire global system.

The Turning Tide

Despite the resistance from some of the world's largest and most powerful nations, Aldo began to see a shift. As more nations signed on to the initiative, the pressure mounted on those who were still holding out. The longer they waited, the more isolated they would become. The world was changing, rapidly, and those who refused to act would be left behind.

The turning point came when a series of powerful storms hit the United States, devastating cities along the East Coast. The destruction was unprecedented. The government, already strained by internal turmoil, had no choice but to acknowledge the reality of the crisis. Under pressure from the people and global organizations, the United States finally agreed to participate in the Global Waste and Resource Restoration Initiative.

This decision set off a chain reaction. With the support of the United States, other major nations began to reconsider their positions. Within a matter of months, the once fragmented world began to coalesce. The shift in political power had finally created the momentum needed to initiate meaningful collaboration.

The Power of Collaboration

Aldo and his team stood on the balcony of their headquarters, overlooking the now-bustling center of their new initiative. Countries that had once been divided by politics, economics, and history were now working together. The global task force was officially established, and countries were beginning to share resources, technologies, and knowledge.

"We've come a long way," Nina said, her voice tinged with exhaustion but also with pride. "But the real work is just beginning."

Aldo nodded. "This is just the start. We've learned that we can't solve this on our own. The world must act as one. Only together can we fix the damage we've caused, and rebuild a future worth living for."

And for the first time in months, Aldo allowed himself a moment of hope. The world was broken, but the power of collaboration had given them a chance. It wasn't too late, not yet. Together, they would fight for a better future.

Chapter 24: Terror from Nature

The sky had darkened early that day, an ominous sign of the brewing storm. Even before the first rumble of thunder echoed across the horizon, the world seemed to hold its breath, as if sensing the oncoming terror. Aldo, Nina, and the rest of their team stood near the edge of their makeshift camp, watching the shifting clouds and listening to the distant howls of the wind. They had grown used to the unpredictability of the climate, but this was different. The air was heavy, almost suffocating, as if nature itself was ready to strike.

It was the beginning of the end.

The First Tremors

A low, guttural rumble broke the silence. At first, it was subtle, just a tremor that seemed to make the ground shiver beneath their feet. But as the seconds ticked by, the rumble grew louder, more pronounced. It became clear that something far worse was coming.

Aldo felt his heart race. His years of studying environmental systems told him that what was about to happen was not just a freak occurrence; it was a consequence of the ongoing ecological devastation. The instability of the planet was reaching its tipping point. As more tectonic plates shifted in response to the extreme heat generated by the storm, it was only a matter of time before the earth would shake in fury.

"Get inside the shelter!" Aldo shouted, his voice barely audible over the growing sound of the tremors. "Now!"

The team scrambled into their designated safety zones, but the ground was already beginning to crack open. Large fissures appeared, snaking through the camp with terrifying speed. Buildings that had been hastily erected in the wake of the previous disasters crumbled as the earth beneath them cracked apart. The harsh groan of the earth seemed to echo across the landscape as if the planet itself was protesting.

"Hold on!" Aldo shouted, grabbing Nina's arm as they ducked into the shelter. The rest of the team followed suit, barely escaping the collapsing ground above them. For a moment, all was still. Then the first shockwave hit.

It was like nothing they had ever experienced before.

The Earth Shakes

The ground beneath them buckled violently, sending Aldo and the others sprawling to the floor. The walls of the shelter rattled as if they were made of paper. Outside, the sound of cracking rock and splitting earth filled the air. For a long, terrifying moment, it felt as though the entire planet was coming apart.

Aldo held his breath, trying to steady himself, his heart racing as the vibrations intensified. The walls of the shelter creaked, groaned, and then, with a deafening crack, a portion of the roof collapsed inward, sending a plume of dust and debris into the air.

"Nina!" Aldo cried, reaching out to her as she staggered to her feet. She was already covered in dust, but she was alive. He helped her to a more stable corner of the shelter.

"We need to move, Aldo!" she shouted over the deafening noise. "This is getting worse!"

Aldo nodded grimly. The tremors were only the beginning. The earth had only just begun to reveal its fury. The team had no choice but to leave the relative safety of their shelter and move to higher ground. But the question remained: how far could they go before the planet itself became too unstable to survive?

The Aftershock

Minutes later, they emerged into the chaos of the outside world. The landscape had been transformed. The once-familiar surroundings of their camp were now a nightmare of collapsed buildings, shattered roads, and jagged chasms that cut through the earth like open wounds. The sky above was a dark, swirling mass of clouds, and the winds howled with an almost feral intensity.

Another tremor struck, stronger than the last.

"Run!" Aldo shouted, grabbing Nina's hand and pulling her along. The others followed, but it was clear that the ground was becoming increasingly unstable. Their only hope was to reach higher ground, somewhere that might offer them a modicum of safety. The nearby mountains, once a peaceful symbol of the Earth's enduring power, now loomed over them like a jagged, hostile beast.

As they ran, Aldo couldn't help but feel a sense of dread deep in his gut. This wasn't just a natural disaster. It was the culmination of everything they had fought against. The storm, the shifting tectonic plates, the escalating climate crises, everything was now coming to a head. The Earth was angry, and there was no stopping it.

A World in Crisis

The team climbed through the debris-littered streets, avoiding fissures and cracks that threatened to swallow them whole. As they neared the base of the mountains, Aldo glanced at the horizon. The landscape stretched out before him, a vast wasteland that had once been teeming with life. Now, it was an open grave, a monument to humanity's failure to protect the world.

"We can't outrun this," Nina said, her voice strained. "What if it keeps getting worse? What if the planet collapses entirely?"

Aldo stopped in his tracks, staring at her for a moment. He could see the fear in her eyes, the uncertainty that had taken root in her soul. But he also saw the fire that had always driven her. They had come this far, and they couldn't give up now.

"We won't give up," he said firmly. "We've fought too hard to survive. We can still make a difference, if we can just hold on long enough."

But even as he spoke, another massive tremor hit. The ground beneath their feet shifted violently, and Aldo lost his footing. He tumbled to the ground, narrowly avoiding a large boulder that crashed just inches from where he had been standing.

"Keep moving!" Aldo shouted, pushing himself back to his feet. "We can't stop now!"

But just as they began to move again, the earth seemed to open up beneath them. A massive chasm formed in the earth, stretching wide enough to split the group in two. Aldo, Nina, and the others on one side; the rest of the team on the other.

"No!" Nina cried, reaching out to the others. But it was too late. The team on the other side of the chasm was lost in the ensuing chaos, swallowed by the deep crevice in the Earth.

Struggling for Survival

The seconds felt like hours as Aldo and Nina stood there, watching helplessly as their companions disappeared into the abyss. The ground continued to shake, and large chunks of rock began to plummet from the sky. They had to act fast, or they too would be caught in the deadly tremors.

"We can't stay here," Aldo said, his voice hard with resolve. "We need to get to the top of the mountain. It's the only chance we have."

With their hearts heavy, they climbed the mountain, the earth continuing to tremble beneath their feet. Every step felt like a battle against the very planet itself. As they ascended, the tremors became more frequent, each one making the ground shake more violently. They had no way of knowing how long they could hold out before the mountains themselves were torn apart.

But Aldo refused to let fear take over. If this was the end, he would face it on his terms. His mission had always been clear: to find a way to save the Earth and its people. But now, as the world around him crumbled, he understood the true depth of the challenge. It wasn't just about saving the planet, it was about survival. And survival meant facing the terror that nature was unleashing on them.

A World in Ruin

Hours passed, and finally, they reached the top of the mountain. From their vantage point, they could see the devastation below, cities reduced to rubble, the earth cracked open, fires raging in the distance, and oceans that had risen far beyond their shores.

But the storm was not over. Aldo knew that, just like the Earth, they too had been broken. The fight was no longer just about saving the world, it was about finding a way to survive in the chaos that remained.

The Earth was angry. And in its fury, it had shown them just how fragile their existence truly was. But Aldo refused to give in. He and Nina would continue to fight. They would survive. For the world. For the future.

There was no turning back now. The fight for survival had become a battle not just against nature—but against time itself.

Chapter 25: The Rise of Technology

The sun was beginning to set, casting an orange glow over the horizon. The world was still reeling from the aftershocks of the recent disasters. The Earth had trembled violently, oceans had risen, fires had spread like wildfire, and people were still struggling to adapt. But even in the midst of this devastation, there was a glimmer of hope. It came not from the land, but from the minds of those like Aldo, who had refused to give in.

Aldo and his team had spent countless sleepless nights working in their makeshift lab, their only light coming from flickering solar-powered lamps and their only sustenance from rationed meals. The breakthrough they had been hoping for had finally arrived: a new technology capable of transforming the mountains of waste that now covered the Earth into a valuable resource.

This technology was not just a band-aid for the crisis, it was a game-changer. It could turn waste, the very thing that had nearly destroyed the planet, into fuel. This fuel could power generators, provide heat, and even drive vehicles. It wasn't just a temporary solution. It was the key to reawakening the dying world.

But despite the promising results from their lab experiments, Aldo knew that the real test would come in the field. The stakes were higher than ever. If the technology failed, there would be no second chances. The planet couldn't afford another failure.

A Breakthrough in the Lab

The team had gathered in the small, cramped lab, their faces lit by the dim light of old monitors. Aldo stood at the center of it all, holding a vial of the fuel they had created. It was a thick, viscous liquid, black as tar, with an oily sheen that caught the light. This fuel had been synthesized by breaking down the complex compounds found in waste, using a process of pyrolysis and chemical reactions to produce a usable form of energy.

MOUNT OF WASTE

"Is it ready?" Nina asked, her voice laced with a mix of excitement and nervousness.

Aldo nodded. "It's ready. This is the fuel that can power our future."

"Is it stable?" she pressed, looking at the vial in his hand.

"We've tested it under controlled conditions, and it works," Aldo replied, carefully placing the vial down on the workbench. "But we need to see how it performs in real-world conditions. If it works as expected, it could change everything. But if it fails..."

He didn't need to finish the sentence. They all understood the gravity of the situation. This wasn't just about advancing technology, it was about survival.

The team stood in silence for a moment, the weight of their discovery hanging in the air. Then, Aldo turned toward the others.

"We've got one shot at this," he said. "Let's take it."

Preparing for the Test

They had chosen a nearby city, what was left of it, to test the technology. It was a place where the streets were buried under a thick layer of trash and debris, where the buildings were half-destroyed, and where no one had dared to return. The perfect test site.

The team packed their equipment and set off. The journey was difficult, as the roads had long since become impassable. But they persevered, navigating through the wreckage, knowing that the future of the Earth rested on their shoulders.

When they arrived, the city was eerily quiet. The silence was broken only by the distant rumble of thunder and the occasional creak of collapsing structures. The air was thick with the stench of rotting waste, a reminder of how far the world had fallen.

Aldo and his team set up camp in the heart of the city, near a massive pile of discarded plastics, metals, and electronics. The plan was simple: they would feed the waste into the newly developed machine, which would convert it into fuel. The machine had been designed to run on minimal energy, drawing power from the very fuel it created. It was a closed-loop system, capable of self-sustaining its operations as long as there was waste to process.

The team worked quickly to connect the machine to a small generator, which would serve as the initial power source. Aldo stood beside the machine, watching as his team carefully fed waste into the system. This was it, the moment of truth.

"Are you ready?" Nina asked, standing beside him.

Aldo nodded, his heart racing. "Let's do it."

With a turn of the dial, the machine hummed to life. At first, nothing happened. But then, a soft whirring sound filled the air as the waste began to be broken down by the machine's internal systems. The heat from the process caused the pile of garbage to emit a faint glow, a sign that the fuel was beginning to form.

Minutes passed. It felt like hours. But then, the machine gave a low, steady hum, and a thick, black liquid began to drip from the output valve.

"It's working," Aldo breathed, his voice filled with a mix of relief and disbelief.

Nina smiled. "We've done it."

But they weren't done yet. Now came the real test: would the fuel actually be usable?

Testing the Fuel

The team had brought along a few old vehicles that had been left behind in the city, discarded remnants of the world before the disaster. They weren't much, but they would serve their purpose. Aldo approached one of the vehicles, an old electric truck that had long since been out of service. He opened the fuel compartment and poured the black liquid into the tank, watching as the fuel filled the empty space.

For a moment, everything seemed to freeze. Was this really happening? Was this the solution they had been searching for?

Nina stood beside him, her face tense with anticipation. "If this works..."

"It has to work," Aldo replied, his voice steady. "For the future."

He climbed into the driver's seat of the truck and turned the key. The engine sputtered to life, coughing and sputtering as it came to life. The hum of the engine grew louder, stronger. The truck roared to life.

"It's working!" Nina shouted, her voice filled with excitement. "It's actually working!"

Aldo grinned, his heart swelling with pride. They had done it. They had created something that could change the world.

The truck accelerated down the deserted streets, the sound of its engine echoing in the empty city. For the first time in what felt like forever, there was a sense of movement, of progress. Aldo could see the future unfolding before him, a future where waste could be turned into fuel, where energy could be harvested from the debris of a broken world.

The Risks Ahead

But even as Aldo reveled in the success of the test, he knew that this was just the beginning. The technology was still in its infancy, and there were risks they hadn't yet accounted for. The waste they were using to create the fuel was diverse, plastics, metals, chemicals, and there was no way to know what kind of impact this new fuel would have on the environment in the long term.

"We've made a breakthrough," Nina said, her voice tinged with caution. "But we need to test it further. We don't know what this could do to the atmosphere, the soil... the oceans."

Aldo nodded. "I know. We'll keep testing, keep refining the process. But for now, this is a start. It's a solution."

They returned to their camp, where the machine continued to churn out fuel from the waste. They had a long road ahead of them, but for the first time in a long while, there was hope. They had proven that technology could save the Earth, but only if they were careful.

Looking Toward the Future

As the sun set, casting a warm glow over the ruined city, Aldo stood in silence, looking at the machine and the truck that now stood as a symbol of the future. He knew there was still so much to do. The technology was untested, the risks were unknown, and the world was still in the throes of collapse.

But for the first time in what felt like forever, Aldo had a glimmer of hope. The Earth could still be saved—but only if humanity was willing to fight for it.

"This is just the beginning," he whispered to himself, watching the flames of the dying sun flicker in the distance. "We can still turn things around. We have to."

And with that thought, the journey toward redemption began anew.

Chapter 26: Shattered Trust

The firelight flickered in the camp as the group sat around the small circle, their faces grim. The past few days had been a whirlwind of progress and setbacks. While Aldo's breakthrough with the new waste-to-fuel technology had provided a glimmer of hope, doubts had begun to creep into the minds of those who had once followed him without question.

Aldo sat on a weathered log, his fingers running through his hair as he stared at the fire. The flames danced, but they didn't bring him warmth. Despite their victory in the city, the tension among the survivors was palpable. They had made incredible progress, but now it seemed that the fragile bonds of unity were beginning to fray.

Nina, sitting next to him, noticed the heavy silence that had settled over the group. It wasn't just the fire that flickered. The trust among the survivors seemed to be fading, and Aldo knew it.

"How are we going to fix this?" she asked softly, her voice laced with concern.

Aldo didn't answer immediately. His eyes were focused on the flames, but his mind was elsewhere. He could feel the shift. It had started subtly, little comments, sharp looks, overheard murmurs. It had started with the survivors who had always been the most skeptical. Some questioned whether Aldo and his team had the right to lead. Others wondered if they were even capable of pulling off such an ambitious plan. And then there were those who simply doubted the very technology they had worked so hard to develop.

"What are they saying?" Aldo asked quietly.

Nina's gaze drifted to the other side of the camp, where a small group of survivors huddled in a tight circle. Their heads were low, their words too soft for Aldo to catch. But Nina knew. She had heard the whispers, the uncertainty in their voices, the underlying mistrust.

"They're saying we're moving too fast," Nina replied. "That maybe we don't know what we're doing. Some are asking if the fuel is really safe. If it's going to make things worse instead of better."

Aldo sighed, his shoulders slumping. The weight of the responsibility had never felt heavier. He had known that this path would not be easy, that there would be skeptics and critics. But he had never imagined how quickly the seeds of doubt would spread.

Seeds of Doubt

It wasn't long before the murmurs turned into open confrontations. A day after their successful test of the waste-to-fuel technology, a heated argument erupted in the camp.

"You're playing with fire, Aldo!" Mark, a former engineer who had joined their cause, shouted as he stood in front of the makeshift campfire. His face was red with anger, his hands clenched into fists. "We don't know what this fuel is going to do! We're turning the very thing that's destroying the planet into something we're going to use in our homes and vehicles? This is madness!"

Aldo stood his ground, his expression unwavering. "Mark, we've tested it. It works. It's the only option we have right now."

"You don't get it, do you?" Mark snapped, pointing a finger at him. "We've seen how everything's been falling apart. The oceans are dying, the air's toxic, and now you want to turn trash into fuel? What if this just makes things worse? What if we're causing irreparable damage to the planet by using this stuff?"

"Mark," Nina said, stepping forward to calm the situation, her voice firm but gentle. "We're all scared. But we can't afford to let fear guide us. Aldo's been working on this for months. He's sure it will work. We have to take a leap of faith."

MOUNT OF WASTE

Mark glared at her. "Faith? This isn't about faith, Nina. This is about survival. If we make the wrong choice, we could be sealing our doom."

The tension in the air was thick, and Aldo felt it like a physical weight pressing on his chest. He had always believed that the technology he had developed would be the key to saving humanity, but now, as the doubts grew louder, he wasn't sure if even his own team believed in him anymore.

The Rift Widens

Over the following days, the rift between Aldo's team and the skeptics grew. Mark wasn't the only one questioning the plans. Others voiced their concerns, and even the once-unified group of survivors began to fracture into factions. Some supported Aldo, believing in the technology and the possibility of a future free from the clutches of waste. Others, however, felt that the risks were too high, and that they needed to rethink their approach. The discussions were no longer civil, and the trust that had once been their strongest asset was now shattered.

Aldo and Nina worked tirelessly to ease the tensions, but the wounds were deep. Every day, there was more division. Some members of the group began hoarding resources, questioning the leadership, and even talking about striking out on their own. The unity they had fought so hard to build was slipping through their fingers, like sand.

One night, as the group gathered around the campfire, the fracture became undeniable. A woman named Lila, a mother of two who had been quiet up until that point, stood up and spoke her mind.

"We're all just waiting for Aldo to pull us out of this mess, aren't we?" she said, her voice tinged with bitterness. "But what if he's wrong? What if this technology is just a distraction? Maybe it's time we stop waiting for miracles and start taking control ourselves."

The words hit Aldo like a blow to the chest. He had always believed that they were all in this together, but now it seemed that even those closest to him were beginning to question everything. His stomach twisted as he looked around at the faces of the people he had once trusted, now staring back at him with suspicion and doubt.

"We don't have all the answers," Aldo replied quietly, his voice trembling with frustration. "But if we don't try, we'll never know. Do you want to go back to the old ways? The ways that got us into this mess in the first place?"

Lila didn't respond immediately. She just shook her head, as if lost in thought, before walking away from the circle.

Regaining Trust

That night, Aldo lay awake in his tent, the weight of the situation pressing down on him. He had always been the one to lead, the one who had the answers, but now, it felt as though the answers were slipping away from him. He couldn't help but wonder if he had pushed too hard, too fast. He had never expected his own people to turn against him.

It was then that Nina came to sit beside him. She didn't say anything at first. She just sat in silence, offering him her presence. After a while, she spoke.

"Don't give up, Aldo. You've come too far. We've come too far. This is just one of the many challenges we're going to face. But if we want to save the world, we have to do it together."

Aldo looked at her, his eyes weary. "I don't know if I can. They don't trust me anymore."

"They're scared," Nina replied. "And they're right to be. The world is falling apart. But if we want to rebuild, we need to rebuild the trust, too. It's not just about the technology. It's about bringing everyone together."

Aldo nodded, his mind racing. He knew Nina was right. He had to show the survivors that they were in this together. He had to rebuild the trust, one person at a time. It wouldn't be easy, but it was the only way forward.

Rebuilding Unity

The next day, Aldo called a meeting. It wasn't an easy decision. He knew that the fractures in the group were deep, but he also knew that they had no chance of survival if they couldn't work together. He needed to face the doubts head-on, confront the fear, and remind everyone why they had come together in the first place.

He stood in front of the group, his voice steady. "I know that many of you are scared. I know that you don't trust me right now. And I understand why. But I want you to remember something. We've always been in this together. We've always been a family. And now, more than ever, we need to believe in each other."

"I know the technology I've developed isn't perfect. I know it's risky. But if we don't try, if we don't take this chance, then what's left for us? What's left for our children? We're running out of time."

He paused, letting his words sink in. "I'm not asking for blind faith. I'm asking for us to trust each other again. To work together. Because if we don't, there's nothing left to fight for."

The group sat in silence for a long moment. Then, one by one, the skeptics began to speak. Mark, though still hesitant, finally spoke up.

"I don't know if I believe this will work, Aldo," he said, his voice softer than before. "But I believe in you. I believe in us. We'll figure this out together."

The others nodded in agreement. It wasn't an easy reconciliation, but it was a start. Aldo could feel the walls between them begin to crack.

In that moment, Aldo realized that rebuilding trust wasn't about proving the technology's worth, it was about proving that they were still united, still capable of fighting for a future.

And that, he knew, was the first step toward saving the Earth.

Chapter 27: Mission Beyond the City

Aldo stood on the edge of the city, gazing at the sprawling ruins before him. The sun was low in the sky, casting long shadows over the broken buildings and streets littered with debris. The city, once a bustling hub of innovation and culture, was now little more than a wasteland, an eerie reminder of how quickly everything could collapse. The overwhelming smell of smoke still lingered in the air, mixed with the acrid scent of burning plastic and decaying organic matter.

Nina stood beside him, her face grim. "This is worse than we imagined."

"Yeah," Aldo replied softly, his eyes scanning the horizon. "But we need to go in. We need those materials if we're going to keep the project going. If we're going to make this work, we can't afford to wait any longer."

The team was assembled, ready to head out on a mission that had become more dangerous with every passing day. They needed raw materials, scrap metal, broken electronics, and any leftover infrastructure, that could be repurposed for their waste-to-fuel technology. The area they were headed to was one of the hardest-hit regions. The city had been decimated by the storm, and no one knew what remained.

"Are we ready?" Aldo asked, turning to his team.

"Ready as we'll ever be," Nina answered, adjusting her pack. Her eyes reflected a mixture of fear and determination.

The journey ahead was uncertain, and the risks were high. The group had been surviving on limited resources, and while they had made some progress with their technology, they needed more, materials that were only available in areas outside their safe zones. But venturing into these devastated regions meant facing not only the harsh environmental conditions but also the growing threat of other survivors, many of whom were desperate and armed, willing to do whatever it took to claim whatever was left of the world's resources.

Aldo nodded. "Let's move out."

The Road Less Traveled

The group set off early the next morning. The once-paved roads were now overgrown with weeds and littered with wreckage from collapsed buildings and overturned vehicles. The city's outskirts were eerily quiet, save for the occasional gust of wind that sent debris scattering across their path. The sense of isolation was palpable. In a world that had been connected by technology and commerce, now it felt as though everything had been torn apart, leaving nothing but remnants of a forgotten civilization.

As they moved deeper into the ruins, the damage became more evident. The streets were blocked with piles of rubble, buildings that had once stood tall now reduced to skeletal remains. In the distance, a large fire still smoldered, a reminder of how quickly the world had fallen into chaos. The smell of burning plastic mixed with the faint scent of decay in the air, making it difficult to breathe. But they pushed on.

"We need to stay focused," Aldo said, his voice firm. "The materials we need are further in. We can't afford to get distracted."

Nina nodded, scanning the area around them. "We're not the only ones out here. There could be others. People who want what we have. We need to keep our guard up."

As the group moved forward, they kept their weapons close. It wasn't just the environment that posed a threat, it was the survivors, many of whom had turned to violence in order to survive. The world had grown unforgiving, and it was no longer just the storm or the waste threatening humanity. It was the people, too.

The Encounter

MOUNT OF WASTE

It wasn't long before the group came across their first sign of life beyond their own camp. A small group of survivors appeared from behind a ruined building, their faces gaunt and weary. They were dressed in makeshift clothing, scraps of fabric stitched together with thread and wire. Their eyes, however, were sharp, watching the group closely, their hands resting on weapons that looked hastily crafted.

Aldo and his team stopped, instinctively falling into a defensive stance. They hadn't anticipated meeting anyone so soon, especially not in this area.

"Who are you?" one of the survivors asked, his voice rough, as if unused to speech. He was holding a crowbar, which he pointed toward them with a mixture of suspicion and caution.

"We're just passing through," Aldo said carefully, raising his hands in a non-threatening gesture. "We're looking for materials. We need to gather what we can to help save what's left of the world."

The man's eyes narrowed, but his grip on the crowbar relaxed slightly. "Save the world?" He laughed bitterly. "You think you're the only ones trying to do that? The world's already gone. We're just trying to stay alive."

Nina stepped forward, her tone steady but firm. "We know things look bleak. But we're working on a solution. A way to turn waste into fuel, to give us another chance."

The survivor studied them, his eyes flicking to the rest of the group. Then, after a long pause, he spoke again. "We've seen people like you before. Promises of saving the world. But nothing ever changes. Why should we believe you?"

Aldo felt the sting of those words, but he didn't back down. "Because we have a plan. It's not a miracle. It's not a quick fix. But if we all work together, we can turn this around. The world might be broken, but that doesn't mean we can't try to rebuild it."

There was a long silence as the group of survivors debated among themselves. Finally, the man with the crowbar nodded slowly, lowering it.

"Alright," he said. "You can pass. But we need something in return."

Aldo raised an eyebrow. "What do you want?"

"Food. Water. Something to help us survive," the man said bluntly. "And don't think we'll just let you walk out of here with whatever you find. You take what you need, but we'll take a share."

Nina stepped forward, eyeing the man warily. "We can't just give away what little we have. We need it for our own survival."

The survivor's expression hardened. "Then we can't let you through."

Aldo took a deep breath, feeling the tension in the air. It was a delicate situation, too much confrontation could turn the encounter violent, but too much compromise could leave them vulnerable. He had no choice but to negotiate.

"Alright," he said finally, his voice calm but resolute. "We'll share what we can. But we need to make sure we get what we came for. No tricks. No violence."

The man grunted, his face hardening, but he stepped aside. "Fine. But don't get any funny ideas. You take what you need, and we'll make sure you get out of here safely. For now."

With a tense nod, Aldo signaled to his team to move forward.

Gathering Supplies

The group made their way through the wreckage, gathering what they could. Broken electronics, scrap metal, wires, anything that could be repurposed for their waste-to-fuel technology. Aldo knew the clock was ticking. The longer they stayed in this dangerous area, the more likely it was that other survivors would discover their presence. They needed to move quickly.

MOUNT OF WASTE

But as they scavenged, something unexpected happened. The group of survivors who had initially been hostile began to help. One by one, they joined in the search, offering pieces of scrap metal or tools they had salvaged from the ruins. It wasn't much, but it was something. And slowly, the walls between them began to come down.

Aldo caught Nina's eye as they worked side by side. "Maybe there's still hope for us," he said quietly, his voice filled with a tentative optimism.

Nina smiled, though it was tinged with caution. "Maybe. But it's going to take more than just us to fix this."

Aldo nodded. "We can't do it alone. But together, we have a chance."

Leaving with Hope

As the sun began to set, the group finished collecting the materials they needed. The survivor group, once skeptical, had come through, sharing what they could without asking for anything in return. It wasn't perfect, but it was progress. They were leaving with supplies and, perhaps more importantly, a sense of solidarity, a small but significant victory in a world that had lost so much.

"Thank you," Aldo said to the leader of the survivors, his voice sincere. "You've helped more than you know."

The man nodded, his expression softened. "Just don't make promises you can't keep, alright? We've had enough of that."

Aldo smiled. "We're doing our best. We're not giving up."

As they made their way back to their camp, the team was quiet, each person lost in their thoughts. The road ahead was still uncertain, filled with danger and hardship, but for the first time in a long while, Aldo felt a glimmer of hope.

Maybe, just maybe, they were on the right path.

And perhaps the world could still be saved, if only they could keep moving forward, together.

Aldo pushed forward, his thoughts racing. The path ahead was uncertain, clouded by the weight of betrayal, but he couldn't afford to falter. Not now. The world was teetering on the edge of collapse, and the technology he and his team had developed was the only hope for a future. Every step, every decision mattered more than ever.

As Aldo and Mark walked through the shattered remnants of what used to be a thriving city, the sounds of distant explosions echoed in the background. The world outside the walls of the warehouse had descended into chaos, and the tension in the air was palpable. The crisis that had been years in the making had finally reached its breaking point. Aldo couldn't help but wonder if Nina's betrayal was just the beginning—what if there were others who felt the same way, willing to sacrifice the future for power or control?

The streets were dark, the only light coming from the occasional flickering fires that still burned from the destruction left by the storms and subsequent chaos. The once-bustling city had been reduced to rubble. Buildings, now hollow and broken, loomed like silent witnesses to the disaster that had unfolded. Aldo clenched his fists, the frustration of the situation threatening to overwhelm him. It had all seemed so simple when they first started, fix the waste crisis, restore balance, and give humanity a chance at survival.

But Nina's actions had shattered that illusion. Now, the battle wasn't just for the environment, it was for the control of the very technology that could turn the tide.

"We can't go back there, Aldo," Mark said quietly, breaking the silence. His voice was strained, as if the weight of the betrayal was too much for him to bear as well. "She's already got people in place. We can't risk the technology falling into the wrong hands."

Aldo nodded grimly. "I know. But we can't just let her destroy everything we've worked for. We need to act quickly. If we get to the main compound, we can try to salvage what's left."

Mark hesitated. "But the compound... it's too exposed now. The people she's working with, they'll be there already. It's too risky."

Aldo met his gaze, determination setting in. "We have no other choice. We have to take that risk. If we don't, Nina and her people will have what we need, and they'll use it for their own gain. We've seen what happens when people like her get control of this kind of power."

Mark reluctantly agreed, and the two of them set off toward the compound. The journey was treacherous, the landscape littered with debris from the storm and the fires that still raged in the distance. The once-vibrant cities they had traveled through were now ghost towns, the remnants of humanity's greed and apathy scattered in their wake. Aldo couldn't help but think about the people who had been left behind, those who had been unable to adapt to the changing world. How many more would suffer if they failed now?

As they approached the compound, Aldo could feel the weight of the decision pressing down on him. This was no longer just a fight for the planet, it was a fight for the future. And the cost of failure had never been so high.

They reached the compound just before dawn. The area was eerily quiet, the only sounds the distant crackle of flames and the howling wind. Aldo and Mark moved cautiously, knowing that the element of surprise was their best advantage. If Nina's collaborators had already infiltrated the compound, they would need to act fast.

Inside the compound, Aldo's heart sank as he saw the state of the lab. The equipment, the data they had worked so hard to gather, everything was in disarray. Some of the machines had been destroyed, while others appeared to have been tampered with. It was clear that Nina had been here, and the damage she had caused was far worse than Aldo had imagined.

"We need to find the main server," Aldo said urgently. "That's where everything is stored. If we can get it back online, we can salvage the data and the research. It's our only hope."

Mark nodded, but his expression was grim. "Aldo, do you really think we can do this? After everything that's happened?"

Aldo paused, taking a deep breath. "We have no choice. If we don't, everything we've done will be for nothing. We have to believe we can make it through this."

The two of them made their way through the ruined lab, carefully searching for the server. As they rounded a corner, Aldo froze. There, standing in front of the control panel, was Nina. Her back was to them, her fingers moving swiftly over the keys. She was clearly working to erase any trace of the technology, trying to wipe out everything they had worked for.

"Nina!" Aldo called out, his voice firm but filled with disbelief. "What are you doing? Stop!"

Nina didn't turn around immediately. She continued typing, as if Aldo's voice meant nothing. Then, slowly, she straightened up and turned to face him. The look in her eyes was cold, calculating.

"I'm saving us, Aldo," she said, her voice almost too calm. "You're so caught up in your ideals, you can't see the bigger picture. The world is beyond saving. This technology, this power, it was never meant to be in your hands. It's mine now."

Aldo's mind raced. He couldn't let her do this. Not when they were so close. "You're wrong, Nina," he said, his voice low but firm. "This isn't about power. This is about survival. We can still save the planet. We can still fix this."

Nina scoffed. "You think you can fix it? Look around you, Aldo. The world is already dead. You're just too blind to see it. The only thing left is to control what's left."

MOUNT OF WASTE

Aldo's heart sank as he realized the truth, Nina had abandoned everything they had worked for. She had embraced the very mindset that had led to the destruction of the planet in the first place. She was willing to exploit the very technology that could save them, using it to further her own agenda.

But Aldo wasn't going to let her win. Not now. Not when they had come so far.

With a single motion, Aldo lunged forward, slamming his hand onto the control panel. Sparks flew as he disabled the system, cutting off Nina's access to the data. She reacted instantly, grabbing a nearby wrench and swinging it toward Aldo.

The two struggled, their bodies clashing as the sound of metal on metal echoed through the room. But Aldo was determined. He couldn't let her take everything from them. With one final push, he knocked the wrench out of her hand and sent her sprawling to the floor.

"Nina, it's over," Aldo said, breathing heavily. "This isn't the way. You're not going to win."

She glared up at him, her chest rising and falling rapidly with anger and exhaustion. "You think you've won? You think you can stop me? You're nothing. The world is mine to control, and nothing you do can change that."

Aldo stood over her, his heart heavy but resolute. "You're wrong. The world belongs to everyone, Nina. And as long as we're alive, we'll fight for it."

With that, Aldo turned and began to gather the last pieces of the technology they needed. They couldn't afford to waste any more time. There was still hope, but it was running out fast. And he wasn't about to let Nina's betrayal be the end of it all.

As he and Mark made their way out of the compound, Aldo felt a sense of resolve settle within him. The fight wasn't over. Not yet.

Chapter 28: Betrayal Amidst the Disaster

Aldo's team had been working tirelessly, dedicating themselves to finding a solution for the global waste crisis. The technology they had developed was the world's last hope, and they knew time was running out. But as they got closer to their goal, a devastating truth began to unfold.

One of Aldo's most trusted team members, Ethan, had been secretly collaborating with a powerful faction that sought to take control of the groundbreaking technology for their own selfish interests. This betrayal hit hard, not only because it came from within but because it threatened the very survival of the planet. Ethan had secretly sabotaged key elements of their research, leaking critical information to the group that wanted to monopolize the technology and use it for personal gain.

The implications were grave. If Aldo and his team couldn't recover from this betrayal, all their progress could be erased. The technology they had worked so hard to develop could be used to exploit the remaining resources, leaving the world in an even worse state than it was before.

As tensions ran high within the group, Aldo had to make quick decisions. He needed to confront Ethan, figure out how deep the betrayal went, and ensure that the technology didn't fall into the wrong hands. But as Aldo investigated further, he realized that the scope of the betrayal was far more significant than he had imagined. The group Ethan was involved with had infiltrated other key parts of the organization, and they were already laying the groundwork for a dangerous power grab.

The chapter explores the emotional turmoil that Aldo faces as he grapples with the reality of the situation. He had always believed in the integrity of his team, but now, that trust was shattered. His sense of urgency intensified as he realized that the future of the planet was no longer just about saving the environment, it was about protecting humanity from a new kind of tyranny.

As Aldo takes decisive steps to recover the stolen research and regain control of the technology, he faces a race against time. His team's unity is tested like never before, and the lines between friend and foe begin to blur. In this chapter, Aldo discovers that betrayal can sometimes come from the places you least expect, and that trust is a fragile thing when the stakes are this high.

Chapter 29: Rebuilding Trust

The aftershock of Ethan's betrayal reverberated through the team, leaving a fissure in the once-unified group. For days, Aldo could hardly concentrate, weighed down by the lingering suspicion that had taken root among his team members. The technology they had developed, their last hope for survival, was now at risk, not just from external forces but from within. Trust, the foundation of any collaborative effort, had been broken, and Aldo knew that he needed to act fast to salvage what was left of his mission, and the future of the Earth.

The Opening Struggle: A Fragile Unity

The chapter opens with a scene in the makeshift base. Aldo gathers his team, each member looking weary and guarded. There is an unmistakable tension in the air, eyes that avoid one another, uncomfortable silences, and lingering questions of loyalty. It's clear that the group's unity has been shattered, and while they had once been a tight-knit, resilient team, they are now fractured, unsure of whom to trust.

Aldo stands at the front, determined but visibly fatigued. He knows that this moment requires more than just technical expertise, it calls for emotional healing, understanding, and, most importantly, an acknowledgment of the pain and betrayal they have endured. As he speaks to the group, Aldo's voice is firm yet empathetic, trying to bridge the gap that has widened since Ethan's treachery.

"We've lost more than just a teammate," Aldo begins, "we've lost a part of ourselves. But if we don't rebuild trust, if we don't face this head-on, we'll never make it through this. We've come too far, and the Earth doesn't have the luxury of waiting for us to figure it out."

Navigating Conflict: The Internal Divide

One by one, the team members express their feelings, anger, hurt, fear. Marla, the technician who had always been Aldo's confidant, is particularly vocal. "How can we trust each other now? How do we know this won't happen again? Ethan's betrayal was just the beginning of a much bigger issue," she argues, her voice quivering with frustration. "There are factions out there that want this technology, and we can't let ourselves be divided."

Meanwhile, Lucas, a scientist who had worked alongside Aldo for years, is more cautious. He acknowledges that the betrayal has rocked their foundation, but he believes that they can overcome it. "We've always been a team. One mistake doesn't mean it's over. We need to trust in the work we've done together."

The conflict within the group intensifies. Aldo finds himself at the center of it, trying to mediate the growing tensions. His leadership is now being questioned, and his personal responsibility weighs heavily on him. He knows that rebuilding trust won't happen overnight, but the urgency of their mission leaves little room for hesitation. The group has to come together, or they'll lose everything.

Aldo's Personal Struggle: A Crisis of Confidence

As the chapter progresses, Aldo grapples with his own feelings of guilt and doubt. He wonders if he's the one responsible for Ethan's betrayal, if he had missed the signs, failed to notice the cracks in their team dynamic. He begins to question his own ability to lead, wondering whether the mission can survive without Ethan, and if his actions, even with the best of intentions, had inadvertently pushed Ethan toward treason.

He finds himself seeking solitude in the corner of their base, wrestling with these thoughts. Nina, ever the steadfast supporter, approaches him, noticing his inner turmoil. She reminds him of what they've accomplished and the importance of not losing sight of the bigger picture. "You can't blame yourself for what happened.

People make choices, they always do. But you didn't make this decision, Aldo. We can still make a difference, but we need to pull ourselves back together."

Her words offer some comfort, but the weight of the situation remains. Aldo knows that trust cannot simply be rebuilt with words alone, it must be earned, through actions that prove the team's commitment to the cause. He resolves to lead by example, showing the team that, despite everything, they can still come together to save the planet.

A Moment of Reconciliation: Small Steps Forward

The turning point comes when Aldo, Lucas, and Marla work late into the night to secure the next phase of their research. They recognize that the technology they've developed could change everything if it reaches the right people. As the hours pass, the group works seamlessly together, their earlier tension beginning to subside. They are no longer just individuals with a shared goal, they are a team, rediscovering the strength of collaboration.

The next morning, Aldo calls another meeting, not to lecture but to listen. He opens the floor for everyone to express their concerns, their ideas, and their fears. For the first time since Ethan's betrayal, the team begins to talk openly, each member acknowledging the pain and mistrust that had built up but also reaffirming their commitment to the mission.

Lucas steps forward, extending a hand to Aldo. "We can rebuild this," he says. "We'll need to work harder than ever, but we can make it through."

Marla follows suit, offering a hesitant but genuine apology to Aldo. "I didn't mean to make things harder. I'm just scared we're running out of time."

Aldo nods, acknowledging the pain that they all carry. "We all are. But together, we're stronger. And that's how we'll save this world, by working together, by trusting each other."

MOUNT OF WASTE

Moving Forward: The Path to Recovery

By the end of the chapter, Aldo and his team begin to regain some semblance of unity. While the scars of Ethan's betrayal remain, they've taken the first steps toward healing. Aldo knows the road ahead will be difficult. Trust is fragile, and they'll face many more obstacles. But in this moment, he sees a flicker of hope, a sign that even in the face of disaster, humanity can come together and rebuild.

The chapter closes with Aldo looking out over the horizon, the weight of his responsibilities pressing down on him. But as he surveys the wreckage of the world, he realizes that the real battle isn't just against the external forces threatening their survival; it's also about rebuilding the trust that binds them together.

Chapter 30: The Rise of a Global Movement

The Spark of a Global Awakening

The chapter opens with a dramatic shift: the movement Aldo and Nina have been tirelessly advocating for begins to catch fire across the globe. The international community, once fractured and suspicious, is now starting to acknowledge the urgency of the crisis. Nations that had previously been reluctant to cooperate in the face of environmental disaster are beginning to recognize the potential of Aldo's solutions. The tides are slowly turning, and what once seemed like an impossible mission is now gaining momentum.

The narrative shifts between the different regions of the world where people are beginning to organize and embrace the message that Aldo and Nina have pushed forward. The movement is not just about technology, it is about a fundamental shift in the way people perceive their relationship with the environment, with waste, and with each other.

The First Major International Summit

One of the key turning points of this chapter is the international summit convened to address the escalating environmental crisis. Aldo and Nina are invited to speak, along with a select group of global leaders, environmental activists, and scientists. The summit is set in a city that has been heavily impacted by the garbage storm, symbolizing the desperate need for action.

In the speech that opens the summit, Aldo lays out the stark realities of the crisis: "We are at the edge of the abyss," he tells the audience, his voice calm yet urgent. "The systems we have built are failing. But it is not too late to rebuild. We have the tools. We have the knowledge. What we need now is the will to act."

MOUNT OF WASTE

The speech resonates with many of the leaders present, but not everyone is convinced. Some of the world's most powerful nations remain hesitant, driven by political interests, economic concerns, and an ingrained resistance to change. Aldo's message is bold, but it faces resistance from factions that have long profited from the status quo. Tension runs high as debates erupt in the halls of the summit.

However, there are signs of hope. Several smaller nations, especially those in the Pacific and Africa, stand up in support of Aldo's ideas, recognizing that their very survival depends on finding solutions to the crisis. These nations pledge to implement the new waste management technology and adopt more sustainable practices. Their voices serve as powerful examples for others, calling attention to the disproportionate impact of the environmental crisis on developing nations.

Nina's Role in Mobilizing the Masses

While Aldo works within the summit's political framework, Nina takes her campaign directly to the people. She becomes the face of a grassroots movement, traveling to cities and rural areas alike, meeting with everyday citizens, organizing rallies, and hosting public forums to spread the message about waste reduction and sustainability.

Her efforts spark a wave of enthusiasm. People of all ages join the cause, young students, environmental organizations, and concerned citizens eager to make a difference. Nina's dynamic speeches and infectious passion bring new energy to the movement, inspiring communities around the world to take action.

In one scene, Nina visits a coastal city that has been devastated by the storm. The once-vibrant area, now littered with trash and debris, is a poignant reminder of the damage humanity has inflicted on the planet. But instead of despair, Nina rallies the locals to clean up the streets, demonstrating how small acts of collective effort can create real change. "We can't wait for governments to fix this," she tells the crowd. "We have to start right here, right now. Every piece of trash we pick up is one less that will poison our oceans, one less that will destroy our homes."

The Surge of Media Attention

As the summit continues, global media outlets begin covering the developments surrounding the movement. The hashtag #ReclaimTheEarth starts trending worldwide. News anchors and social media influencers alike pick up the story, broadcasting Aldo and Nina's efforts to millions of people across the globe. What had once been a niche environmental cause is now a mainstream topic, driving conversations in living rooms, classrooms, and boardrooms alike.

Documentaries are made, articles published, and viral campaigns launched, all centered on the urgency of waste management and the need for international cooperation. People everywhere are challenged to reconsider their consumer habits, to reduce, reuse, and recycle. Schools introduce educational programs, while businesses are pressured to adopt more sustainable practices. Governments, meanwhile, face mounting public pressure to take decisive action.

One particularly touching scene unfolds as a group of schoolchildren, inspired by the movement, begins collecting plastic waste from their local beaches. Their teacher, an environmental activist, encourages them to create art from the collected materials—transforming the debris into powerful symbols of hope and resilience.

Global Collaboration and Innovation

As the movement gains strength, Aldo's innovative technology becomes the centerpiece of a new collaborative effort between countries. What began as a small research project at the Alfa

MOUNT OF WASTE

Research Center is now being adopted by multiple nations, each adapting the technology to fit their specific environmental needs.

A scene in the chapter shows an international team of scientists, engineers, and waste management experts working together in a high-tech facility. The technology has evolved from Aldo's initial concept into a more refined, scalable solution capable of transforming waste into usable energy. Each participating country contributes its own unique resources and expertise, working together to build a global network of sustainable waste management.

Meanwhile, global leaders begin meeting more frequently to address the logistics of implementing these technologies worldwide. Funding is allocated, trade agreements are established to share resources, and partnerships between governments, corporations, and non-governmental organizations (NGOs) are forged.

However, the challenges are far from over. While the movement has gained significant traction, the complex nature of the crisis demands even more innovative solutions. The energy created from waste is one part of the solution, but large-scale environmental restoration, the rebuilding of ecosystems, and a complete transformation of consumer behavior remain monumental tasks.

Growing Resistance and Challenges

As the global movement begins to take shape, resistance does not disappear. Powerful corporations that have benefited from the status quo, particularly those in the plastic industry, fight back. They lobby governments to slow down or halt the adoption of the new technology, fearing it will upend their profits.

In response, Aldo and Nina intensify their efforts to expose the destructive practices of these corporations, revealing how they have prioritized profits over the planet. Public outrage grows as more evidence is uncovered, leading to boycotts and protests in major cities. People demand accountability from companies that have long been complicit in the environmental degradation.

One of the key moments in the chapter is when Aldo, in a televised debate, faces off against a corporate CEO who denies the severity of the environmental crisis. The debate serves as a powerful turning point, with Aldo delivering a passionate and data-backed argument for why these companies must change their practices, or face legal and economic repercussions.

The Hopeful Horizon

The chapter closes with a sense of cautious optimism. Though the movement has gained significant momentum, Aldo and Nina know that the fight is far from over. There are still many hurdles to overcome, and there will undoubtedly be setbacks along the way. But as they look out over a newly formed global coalition, they realize that a paradigm shift is already underway. The world is waking up.

"We've started something that can't be stopped," Nina says, a smile on her face as she looks out at a group of volunteers cleaning up a park. "This is just the beginning."

Aldo nods, his eyes filled with resolve. "The real work starts now. But we can do it. Together."

Chapter 31: The Race for a Solution

The Pressure Mounts

The world is in crisis, and Aldo knows that every passing day without a viable solution to the waste disaster brings humanity closer to irreversible collapse. His team at the Alfa Research Center has made significant strides in developing waste-to-energy technologies, but with the scope of the environmental disaster continuing to worsen, time is running out.

Inside the dimly lit laboratory, the team works tirelessly around the clock. Aldo's face, marked by exhaustion but filled with determination, reflects the urgency of their mission. "We have no room for failure," Aldo mutters, looking over the complicated equations on the whiteboard. "Every second counts. The systems we have built cannot survive another collapse."

Nina, standing beside him, gives him a reassuring look. She's been at the forefront of pushing the global movement, but now, in the lab with the team, she feels the weight of the task more than ever. "Aldo, we're almost there," she says, her voice filled with hope, despite the chaos outside. "We just need to fine-tune a few more things, and this technology could be the game-changer."

Aldo nods, though a sense of foreboding lingers. The team's work has been promising, but they are facing increasingly difficult challenges. The waste piling up worldwide is more toxic and diverse than they anticipated, making it hard to extract usable energy. Additionally, the resources required to maintain their machines are running low, and the technological infrastructure they need is strained by the scarcity of materials.

"We need more than just theory. We need practical applications," Aldo says, his hands shaking slightly from fatigue as he flips through research papers. His mind races, calculating the effects of their potential failure. If they don't succeed soon, the planet will suffer even more devastating consequences.

The Struggles of Innovation

The lab is a maze of equipment, test tubes, monitors, and schematics, all scattered across the space where the team is trying to optimize the waste-to-energy process. Dr. Mei, one of Aldo's most trusted scientists, is knee-deep in the technical aspect, adjusting the machines that will break down plastic waste into usable fuel.

"Adjusting the catalytic process is the key here," Dr. Mei explains to the group, her fingers moving quickly over the touchscreens. "If we can refine this, it will increase our energy yield by at least thirty percent."

Aldo watches closely, knowing that the smallest improvement could make a difference in saving millions of lives. "We need the system to be scalable, if it's not adaptable to every type of waste, it won't matter. This can't be limited to just one country or one region."

Nina steps forward, her enthusiasm sparking new energy in the room. "Think about it. If we get this right, it could be implemented everywhere. Imagine a world where the waste doesn't accumulate, it powers our cities, it fuels transportation, it even grows our food."

The room buzzes with the excitement of the possibility, but Aldo's face is set in hard lines. He knows that while the dream is there, the reality of their situation is grim.

"There's no time for imagination," Aldo says bluntly. "We need results now. We need this process to be flawless, no errors. Not for the people who are suffering, and not for the planet that is already on the brink."

Despite their best efforts, every test run shows imperfections. The energy yields are inconsistent, and the waste-to-energy conversion is not as efficient as they need it to be. Some materials, especially those that have been subjected to heat or chemical exposure during the disaster, are practically impossible to break down.

As days turn into weeks, the pressure weighs even heavier on the team. Supplies are dwindling. Power shortages cause intermittent disruptions. Communication with the outside world is harder than ever. The collapse of infrastructure in many parts of the world means that the team can no longer rely on the usual channels for acquiring the materials they need. Worse, they're starting to see the deterioration of the world's ecosystems firsthand, wildfires rage, cities flood, and the oceans are nearly impassable due to pollution.

"We have to push through this," Aldo says, rallying his team once more. "We're not just working for a solution, we're working for survival."

The Human Cost of Progress

One evening, the team gathers to assess their progress. Exhaustion is taking its toll on everyone, especially Nina, who has been managing the political side of the movement and overseeing outreach to countries that had once been hesitant to adopt the technology.

"Nina, how are the discussions with the world leaders going?" Aldo asks, though his voice carries the weight of doubt. Despite the movement's momentum, not all countries are on board with the waste-to-energy solutions. Resistance remains strong in wealthier countries with entrenched industries, and political infighting makes negotiations nearly impossible.

Nina slumps into a chair, rubbing her eyes. "It's complicated. Some are on board, but the others still view this as a threat to their economies. They want solutions, but they don't want to make the hard decisions. It's the same old story, profits over people."

Aldo's frustration is palpable. "Then they're condemning the people who need us most. We don't have time for politics. We need a global commitment, now."

Outside the lab, the world is falling apart faster than anyone can imagine. Cities once thriving are now reduced to ruins, and famine, disease, and conflict are spreading faster than their ability to respond. Every night, the team is forced to come to terms with the grim reality: their work is the last hope for saving the planet, but it might be too late.

One late-night scene highlights the strain on their health and spirits. Dr. Mei, having worked for days without rest, collapses from exhaustion. Her body is drained from the constant stress of trying to perfect the technology. Aldo and Nina take a moment to breathe, feeling the burden of everything they're trying to accomplish.

"We can't fail now," Aldo murmurs as he kneels beside Dr. Mei, checking her vitals. "We have to keep going."

Nina nods, but her eyes reveal the fear she tries so hard to mask. "But what if we do fail, Aldo? What if we don't have enough time to finish this?"

Aldo looks at her, his gaze steady, unwavering. "Then we'll go down fighting. But we won't stop."

An Unexpected Breakthrough

The breakthrough comes when the team revisits their approach to recycling mixed waste, including dangerous chemicals and complex plastics. A radical new idea, one they had briefly dismissed due to its complexity, comes to the forefront. They decide to focus on a hybrid system, combining bioengineering with nanotechnology to break down harmful substances.

In a rush of excitement, they test the idea. The first results are promising: the waste is breaking down more efficiently, and the energy conversion rate is the highest it has been yet. But there are still risks. The technology is untested at scale and comes with potential dangers. They need to run several tests before they can fully deploy the system in affected areas.

Aldo watches anxiously as the data streams across the screens. After what feels like an eternity, the results stabilize. "This could work," Aldo says softly, not allowing himself to feel too hopeful just yet. "But we'll need a full-scale trial. We'll need the resources and support to make it happen."

The stakes are higher than ever, and with their resources running thin, Aldo knows that they're on the edge of success, or complete disaster. Still, for the first time in a long while, he allows himself a moment of hope. Perhaps, just perhaps, they're on the verge of turning the tide.

Chapter 32: The Connected Network

Building Bridges Across the Divide

As the world teeters on the edge of environmental collapse, one thing becomes undeniably clear to Aldo and his team: communication is key. In a world increasingly fragmented by political and environmental disasters, building a network that can share information, spread solutions, and coordinate relief is paramount. With nations still in disarray and borders closed, the idea of a connected, global communication network seems almost impossible. But Aldo and Nina know that if the world is to survive, it is not just the technology that will save it, it is the ability to unite, to inform, and to inspire action on a scale never before seen.

"This has to be more than just a communication system," Aldo says, standing in the new command center of the Alfa Research Center. The walls are covered in large screens showing real-time data from around the world: satellite images of climate shifts, the movement of waste in the oceans, and the status of their new waste-to-energy technology as it begins to be tested in various regions.

"We're not just talking about sending emails or tweets," Nina adds, her eyes scanning the map of the world that is now divided by crumbling countries and fragile alliances. "This has to be a platform that can share knowledge, foster cooperation, and most importantly, coordinate efforts for a unified solution. Information is our greatest resource right now."

The idea for a global communication network has been brewing for weeks, but today, it begins to take shape. Despite the dire circumstances and limited resources, Aldo knows that there is no time to waste. The destruction caused by the waste storm and the continued environmental degradation have fractured the world into isolated zones. Countries are locked in a battle for survival,

MOUNT OF WASTE

and borders, physical, political, and digital, have never been more pronounced. However, if humanity is to overcome the global waste crisis, they must be able to communicate across these barriers. They need a new kind of network.

A System of Global Cooperation

The concept Aldo and Nina have in mind is nothing short of revolutionary. It's not enough to build a communication network with satellites and fiber optics. They need something that can reach even the most remote and devastated regions of the world. They need a system that can bypass traditional communication infrastructure, something decentralized, perhaps even peer-to-peer, that can connect survivors in real time.

"There are some regions where the internet simply doesn't exist anymore," says Dr. Mei, one of Aldo's closest colleagues. "The destruction has taken out much of the global communication infrastructure. But if we can create a low-bandwidth system, something that can operate off the grid and transmit over short distances..."

"Exactly," Aldo interrupts, his mind racing. "We need to establish a system of local hubs, then create secure communication lines between them, forming a chain that stretches across the globe."

Nina, already thinking ahead, starts outlining a plan. "We'll need to work with the survivors. They've already started building their own networks, even if it's rudimentary. If we can provide them with the tools and knowledge to link their hubs, they'll be able to transmit vital information, how to recycle, where resources are located, which areas are safe to travel through, and what technologies are working."

"Not just technologies," Aldo adds. "We'll also need to share stories, solutions, success stories from communities that are already using our technology. These stories will inspire others, show them that change is possible. They'll create a sense of hope, of unity."

Overcoming the Obstacles

The plan is bold, but the road ahead is filled with obstacles. The first hurdle is security. Aldo knows that while they need to build this network to share information, they also need to protect it. In this fractured world, not everyone will have noble intentions. In fact, some groups have been hunting for the technology Aldo and his team have developed, hoping to use it for their own gain. There are already stories of rogue militias and power-hungry leaders who are trying to seize the remnants of society's resources, including the waste-to-energy systems.

"This has to be a secure network," says Nina, her voice firm. "We can't afford to let our technology fall into the wrong hands. We need encryption, data protection, and firewalls that can keep the worst out. This network will be a beacon of hope, and we can't let it be hijacked by those who want to exploit it."

"We're not just dealing with the environment here," Aldo adds. "We're dealing with the social fabric of the world. Trust is something we need to rebuild. If people don't believe in the system, they won't use it."

Finding Partners in Unexpected Places

Despite the tension, progress begins to unfold as they work with local survivors, engineers, and scientists around the world. In the midst of the devastation, there are sparks of ingenuity. In cities once cut off by floods, communities are coming together, rebuilding makeshift solutions from the wreckage.

In a remote part of the world, a former tech engineer, once skeptical of global cooperation, now takes it upon himself to connect his village to the network. "We don't have much," he admits over a rudimentary communication device, "but we can start small. If we can just connect with the people downriver, we

MOUNT OF WASTE

can share information on water purification, how to build new energy generators from the waste around us. It's not much, but it's a start."

Elsewhere, in the devastated areas of Eastern Europe, survivors have built their own hubs out of salvaged materials. They may not have the latest technology, but they are determined to be part of the global solution.

"The human spirit hasn't been destroyed," Nina says, smiling as she views the incoming data streams from these communities. "We may have lost so much, but we've gained something we didn't have before, collaboration. People are realizing that their survival depends on the survival of others. That's the key to this network."

A New Hope

As the communication network spreads, it becomes apparent that the world, while still divided, is starting to unite. The network is proving to be more than just a tool for survival, it's a platform for innovation, collaboration, and education. New solutions emerge as the knowledge shared through the network sparks creative thinking in even the most remote areas.

In one part of Africa, a group of survivors begins experimenting with a new kind of solar-powered waste converter, a breakthrough that could make waste management in arid regions much easier. The news spreads through the network, reaching Aldo's team within hours. The excitement is contagious.

"We're doing it, Aldo," Nina says. "This is exactly what we needed. People are sharing their ideas, their innovations. We're not just talking about waste anymore. We're talking about a new world."

Aldo looks at the screen, showing the network's global reach, the maps lighting up with every new hub that connects. He feels a surge of hope, something he hasn't felt in years. For the first time in months, it's not just about surviving, it's about thriving. The race against time isn't over, but the world is starting to move in the right direction.

"We can do this," Aldo whispers, more to himself than anyone else.

And as the communication network continues to grow, linking every survivor, every innovator, every community, Aldo's words take on new meaning. Perhaps, just perhaps, there is still a chance to heal the planet. The road ahead will be long, and the obstacles enormous, but Aldo now knows that humanity's greatest strength lies not in technology alone, but in the power of connection.

Chapter 33: The New Discovery

A Shift in Perspective

The Alfa Research Center had become a beacon of hope in the midst of chaos. Inside its reinforced walls, scientists, engineers, and environmentalists worked tirelessly to find solutions to the many problems that the global waste crisis had caused. The world was in ruins, with once-thriving cities reduced to rubble, and the earth's resources dwindling. But Aldo and his team had never been more determined. The need to rebuild was urgent, but they faced an enormous challenge: How could they restore the world when so much of it had been polluted, when the very materials they needed to rebuild were the ones that had caused the destruction in the first place?

That's when a breakthrough occurred, a discovery so simple, yet revolutionary, it could change the future of the planet forever.

It started with a simple experiment. They were testing new methods to repurpose waste, particularly plastic, which had become one of the greatest environmental threats. The oceans were choked with it, landfills piled high with it, and yet Aldo and his team had managed to make a startling observation. With the right processes, plastic didn't need to be discarded, it could be converted into something new. Something useful. Something sustainable.

"We've been thinking about this the wrong way," Aldo muttered, staring at a small pile of shredded plastic. His mind raced as he turned the idea over in his head. The breakthrough wasn't a high-tech, advanced gadget. It was a rethinking of how they used the material that was everywhere and yet everywhere was a problem.

They began experimenting with creating a new form of construction material from plastic waste. By melting down and chemically treating the plastic, they could turn it into sturdy, durable bricks that could be used for building homes, roads, and infrastructure.

"This could change everything," Aldo said, his voice filled with a rare excitement. "We've been focusing on reducing waste, but now... we can turn it into something that helps us rebuild."

Transforming Plastic into Construction Materials

The research team worked around the clock, refining the process. What they had discovered was that plastic, when properly treated and combined with certain additives, could form a resilient material that could be molded into bricks, tiles, and other essential construction components. The possibilities seemed endless.

As the first test batches of plastic bricks came out of the oven, Aldo's heart pounded with anticipation. He held one in his hands, examining its weight, texture, and integrity. They had used various combinations of plastic waste: bottles, bags, containers, anything that could be recycled into something new. The results were astonishing. The bricks were just as sturdy as those made from traditional materials like cement or clay.

"We're on the verge of something big," Aldo said, eyes wide with disbelief. "This material could be used to rebuild cities... not just here, but everywhere. Imagine... cities rising from the debris of waste. Literally."

The team began to test the bricks in different conditions, heat, cold, pressure, and water resistance. They passed every test. These plastic bricks were durable, sustainable, and, most importantly, they were made from the waste that had been choking the planet for decades.

Nina was the first to see the potential for widespread use. "We're not just saving the planet from waste. We're building a new kind of future, one that can grow from the very destruction we've caused. These bricks could be the foundation of every rebuilt city, every new community. We don't have to keep relying on concrete or steel, materials that are expensive and difficult to produce. This is something everyone can use."

Scaling Up

Aldo, Nina, and the team immediately realized that their discovery needed to be scaled up. The demand for construction materials in the aftermath of the waste crisis was monumental. Cities around the world needed to be rebuilt, and with traditional methods either unavailable or too expensive, they had to find ways to mass-produce these plastic-based building materials.

But scaling up their efforts wouldn't be easy. The logistics of gathering and processing plastic waste were daunting. They would need immense quantities of plastic from all over the world. As the team worked on the process to scale it, they began to realize that it wasn't just a technological problem, it was a global issue. They would need to organize collection networks, distribution systems, and educational initiatives to show communities how to use this new material.

The network Aldo had started creating for communication and collaboration would become crucial in this phase. It wasn't enough to just have a few laboratories working on the plastic bricks. They needed to get the message out to the survivors in every region, to teach them how to build with the new material, and to mobilize the global effort to collect plastic.

In one of the first mass trials, teams across different regions of the world began to gather plastic waste, sorting through it, cleaning it, and then sending it to local facilities for processing. The first plastic brick-building projects began in isolated communities, where survivors had little more than scavenged materials to build shelters. In these small but growing outposts, the plastic bricks provided a lifeline. They were easy to produce, cheap, and, most importantly, sustainable.

"We've only just begun," Nina said, watching the first buildings constructed from the new material rising from the rubble. "The real work starts now."

The Ripple Effect

As news of the discovery spread, survivors around the world began to understand that the answer to their rebuilding efforts lay in their own waste. Aldo's new material became a symbol of hope, and every community that adopted it felt as though they were part of a global solution. The connection between waste and construction didn't just transform the physical landscape, it transformed the mindset of millions of people.

In Africa, survivors had long been accustomed to dealing with limited resources. The introduction of plastic bricks brought a new sense of possibility. With a lack of access to traditional construction materials, many had given up hope of ever having a proper home. But now, they were building new houses from their own waste.

In South America, communities that had been devastated by the storms began using the plastic bricks to create disaster-resistant shelters. With each successful structure, confidence grew. People saw that their world was not as irreparably damaged as they had feared. The solution was in their hands, they just needed to see the potential in the waste around them.

And as more nations and regions joined the effort, the full impact of the discovery began to take shape. This new material could be used for everything from schools to hospitals, from roads to public spaces. Plastic was no longer just a problem; it had become the foundation for rebuilding the world.

Rebuilding from the Ground Up

The significance of Aldo's discovery cannot be overstated. By transforming plastic waste into usable construction materials, they were not only helping to restore the environment, they were creating a new economy based on sustainability. The cost of rebuilding the world was immense, but it was now within reach.

Aldo knew that the success of this project depended on more than just the material itself. They would need to encourage cooperation, share knowledge, and continue the fight against the underlying causes of the global waste crisis. But this was a starting point, a new foundation on which to build the future.

In the months that followed, more and more cities adopted the plastic brick technology. As the world began to slowly rebuild, Aldo couldn't help but feel a sense of accomplishment. The road ahead was still uncertain, but this discovery, this moment of ingenuity, had given humanity something precious: a second chance.

The mountains of waste that had once seemed insurmountable were now being turned into the very bricks that could rebuild the planet.

Chapter 33: A New Discovery

Aldo stood at the edge of the laboratory, staring out into the barren landscape. The horizon, once dotted with lush greenery, now sprawled with debris, mountains of waste that stretched for miles. His heart ached every time he looked out at the destruction, but it was also a reminder of why he kept pushing forward. The world needed change, and he was determined to be the one to ignite that spark.

For weeks now, Aldo and his team of scientists, engineers, and environmental experts had been working tirelessly to develop a solution. Their goal was clear: to find a sustainable way to deal with the world's overwhelming waste problem, one that could reverse some of the damage done by decades of human neglect. In a world teetering on the brink of collapse, every minute mattered.

Nina, standing next to him, glanced at the data displayed on the screen in front of them. The numbers were staggering, but they were also promising. They had found something. A breakthrough.

"How long until we can test it?" she asked, her voice filled with urgency. She had always been a fighter, and now more than ever, she was determined to see the world rise from the ashes of its past mistakes.

Aldo didn't immediately answer. Instead, he ran a hand through his disheveled hair, thinking. The discovery had come unexpectedly, a combination of late nights, countless failed experiments, and a stroke of pure luck. It wasn't just the answer to the crisis, it was something far more significant.

"Within the week," Aldo replied, his voice tinged with both excitement and caution. "We need to run some more simulations to be sure, but the early results are looking very promising."

Nina nodded, her eyes scanning the data with practiced precision. "You're sure this will work?"

MOUNT OF WASTE

Aldo hesitated for a moment before answering. "If everything goes as planned, it could change everything. It's a new way to use plastic waste, not just recycle it, but transform it into something that could be used to rebuild what we've lost."

Plastic, once thought to be an insurmountable problem, had become the focal point of their efforts. In the wake of the global disaster, plastic waste had become one of the deadliest pollutants, its accumulation in the oceans, soil, and air suffocating life. Recycling had always been seen as the ultimate solution, but traditional methods were insufficient to handle the sheer volume of waste.

That was where Aldo's team had made their breakthrough. They had discovered a way to break down plastic on a molecular level, transforming it into a highly durable, lightweight material suitable for construction. It wasn't just another form of plastic, this material was far more versatile, able to withstand extreme weather conditions and even the seismic shifts caused by the ongoing tectonic instability.

Nina took a deep breath. "If this works, we could rebuild entire cities. The waste could be used to create the very structures that will house the survivors."

Aldo nodded, his mind already racing through the possibilities. Entire neighborhoods, devastated by the storm and subsequent fires, could be rebuilt using materials that had once been considered waste. The need for raw materials like steel, wood, and concrete could be reduced, lowering emissions and resource depletion. Not only would it provide a solution to the waste crisis, but it would also create a sustainable and scalable method of rebuilding civilization in a way that didn't further harm the planet.

The world had been waiting for something like this. A true breakthrough.

"We need to make sure it's safe," Aldo continued. "We've run preliminary tests on small-scale prototypes, but now we need to move to the next stage. If we're going to put this into the hands of governments and organizations, it has to be foolproof."

"Understood," Nina said, already pulling up a set of project timelines and materials on her tablet. "I'll organize the teams. We need to get the word out to the international recovery coalition. If this can scale quickly, we might be able to stop the worst of the environmental damage before it's too late."

Aldo turned back to the lab's large windows, watching as the sun dipped below the horizon, casting a shadow over the vast expanse of garbage that now stretched across the earth. It was easy to feel defeated when faced with the enormity of the problem. But tonight, something was different. For the first time in a long while, hope glimmered on the horizon.

"We don't have much time," Aldo said, his voice firm. "We need to make this happen before the waste mountain grows even bigger."

The storm that had first triggered the global disaster was still fresh in the minds of everyone. Winds that tore through entire cities, lightning that set forests ablaze, and floods that swallowed everything in their path. The destruction had been catastrophic, but in many ways, it had also been a wake-up call, a warning that they could no longer ignore the fragile balance of the planet.

The mounting pressure was palpable, but Aldo knew that this discovery, if successful, could be the key to turning the tide. A world where garbage could be transformed into building blocks, literally and figuratively. It wasn't just about saving the planet anymore; it was about rebuilding it in a way that didn't repeat the mistakes of the past.

"We need to get this right," Aldo muttered to himself, more as a reminder than anything else.

MOUNT OF WASTE

"I'll make sure we do," Nina said with a determined smile. "We'll make sure the world knows what we've found."

The next few days were a blur of activity. Teams of scientists worked around the clock to refine their process, analyzing data, and conducting tests to ensure that the material was both durable and safe for large-scale construction. They worked with engineers to design the first prototype buildings that would utilize the new plastic-based material. Meanwhile, Nina contacted the international recovery coalition, sharing the news of their breakthrough and convincing the global leaders to back the initiative.

The response was overwhelming. Countries across the globe, once fragmented and hesitant to collaborate, began to see the potential of Aldo's discovery. If this new material could be scaled efficiently, it could offer a lifeline to the millions of displaced people who had nowhere to go after the disasters.

But even with the optimism surrounding the project, Aldo couldn't shake the nagging feeling that they were only at the beginning. There was still much to do, logistics, production, distribution, and ensuring the material could be deployed on a global scale.

As he sat in the conference room with Nina and the other members of his team, Aldo felt the weight of the task ahead of them. But there was something else, too, a flicker of hope that, despite the odds, humanity could find its way back from the brink.

"This is only the beginning," Aldo said, looking around the room. "But we have a chance. A real chance."

Nina smiled. "And we're not going to waste it."

The journey ahead would be difficult, filled with challenges and setbacks. But for the first time in years, Aldo felt something he hadn't allowed himself to feel in a long while: hope. It was fragile, yes, but it was there. And it was enough to push them forward.

As they prepared to present their findings to the world, Aldo couldn't help but think back to the moment when everything had seemed lost. When the Earth seemed doomed to suffocate under its own waste, when the storms raged and the seas rose, swallowing entire islands.

But now, they had a solution. They had a way to not only manage the waste, but to use it to rebuild, to create a sustainable future. The mountain of garbage no longer felt like a symbol of destruction; it was a challenge, a challenge they were ready to face.

The world might have been on the brink of collapse, but Aldo and his team were ready to take the first step toward saving it.

Chapter 34: Healing the World

The air had a new scent, one that was free of the acrid tang of burning plastic and the staleness of polluted air. For the first time in what felt like forever, the world seemed to breathe again. It wasn't a complete transformation, but the change was undeniable. The cities, once buried under mountains of refuse, were beginning to show the first signs of recovery. Aldo stood on the rooftop of a newly reconstructed building in what was once a thriving metropolis, now barely recognizable after the storm and the subsequent collapse. He inhaled deeply, feeling the weight of the moment.

It was happening. The impossible was becoming reality.

The material they had developed, constructed from recycled plastic waste, was now being used to rebuild the shattered cities, and the results were beyond what they had hoped for. The buildings were not only structurally sound but also designed to be energy-efficient, leveraging the latest green technologies. They were living buildings, capable of adjusting their temperature based on the seasons, equipped with solar panels, and, most importantly, made of materials that would decompose safely over time if they ever needed to be replaced. In the midst of the chaos, Aldo had managed to help start a new era of construction, an era where sustainability wasn't just a concept but a tangible, everyday reality.

Nina joined him on the rooftop, looking out over the sprawling city. The skyline had been altered, no longer filled with crumbling towers and charred remains, but with sleek, modern buildings covered in vines, designed with nature in mind. She smiled, her face softening as she took in the sight.

"Look at this," she said, her voice filled with awe. "It's like we're watching a new world being born."

Aldo nodded, feeling the weight of her words. It wasn't just about rebuilding the cities, it was about rebuilding trust in the possibility of a better future. The cities being rebuilt now weren't replicas of the old ones, but entirely new structures designed to coexist with nature, instead of exploiting it. They had learned from the mistakes of the past, and now, they were using those lessons to create a world that was more harmonious, more resilient.

But the process hadn't been easy. Rebuilding wasn't just about laying down new foundations; it was about changing minds, convincing people that this was the future they needed. It was about pushing governments to prioritize long-term solutions over short-term gains. It had meant overcoming the doubts of skeptics and the resistance of those who still clung to outdated ways of thinking.

"Do you think we're making enough of an impact?" Aldo asked, his gaze narrowing slightly as he observed the construction crews below. "The mountain of waste still looms, and not all of it is being used in the way it should. There's still so much more to do."

Nina placed a hand on his shoulder. "We're just getting started, Aldo. Yes, the challenges are enormous, but look at what we've already done. There are whole cities starting to rise from the rubble, and they're doing it with sustainable materials. We're proving that it can be done. We're proving that change is possible."

Aldo exhaled, releasing a breath he hadn't even realized he'd been holding. She was right. The progress they had made in just a few months was staggering. What had once seemed like a distant dream, cities rebuilt from the waste that had destroyed them, was now becoming the new standard. Aldo knew the road ahead would still be long, but the first steps had been taken. The ripple effect had already begun.

The scene in the downtown area was bustling with activity. Construction crews were hard at work, assembling the new structures using the plastic-based material that had been transformed into something entirely new. Aldo and Nina had spent the past few weeks traveling between cities, overseeing the progress and ensuring that the new methods were being implemented correctly.

As they walked through the streets of the city, they passed what had once been a charred wasteland. The buildings that had stood here before were now nothing more than a memory, replaced by towering structures that blended seamlessly with the environment. The walls of the buildings were covered in vertical gardens, each one designed to help filter the air and absorb carbon dioxide. The roofs were covered in solar panels, and there were green spaces everywhere, public parks, gardens, and recreational areas.

"This is incredible," Nina said, her eyes wide as she looked around. "You can feel the difference, can't you? The energy here is… different."

Aldo smiled, his heart swelling with pride. "It's not just the buildings. It's the people. They're starting to understand. They're starting to see that sustainability isn't just an ideal, it's the only way forward."

They stopped in front of one of the newly constructed buildings. It was sleek and modern, but with an organic twist. The exterior was a mix of dark gray panels and light-colored plastic material, giving it a futuristic yet grounded look. Aldo reached out and touched one of the walls, feeling its cool surface. It was hard to believe that this had once been discarded plastic waste.

"Imagine this," he said. "What we're seeing now is just the beginning. We've proven that it can work, but what happens when we scale it? When entire countries, or even continents, are using this technology? The possibilities are endless."

Nina nodded, her eyes sparkling with excitement. "We've already seen the first fruits of our labor, but now, it's time to take this to the next level. We need to scale it globally. Every city, every country, should be using this new material. The more we produce, the more waste we can manage. And the more we manage, the closer we get to reversing the damage we've done."

Aldo's gaze turned inward, thinking. It wasn't enough to rebuild. They had to ensure that these new cities were self-sustaining, that the materials they were using wouldn't become just another cycle of waste. It was about ensuring that humanity wasn't just rebuilding in a way that mimicked the old world, but in a way that was truly in harmony with the planet.

Days turned into weeks, and the momentum continued to grow. Other cities began to take notice of the success of the rebuilding efforts, and soon, countries from all over the world were reaching out to Aldo and his team for help. Aldo had become a symbol of hope, a symbol of the possibility of recovery. His name was now known not just in scientific circles but across the globe.

However, with the success came new challenges. The infrastructure for producing the new material had to be rapidly expanded, and not everyone was on board with the new approach. Some industries, still clinging to traditional methods of construction, feared the shift in the market. They saw it as a threat to their profits, and they would do anything to slow the progress.

But Aldo was undeterred. He knew that the future depended on collaboration, not competition. He had witnessed firsthand the power of global cooperation, and he was determined to keep pushing forward.

One morning, a video call came through from an international summit. Aldo and Nina were sitting in the meeting room, preparing for another round of negotiations with world leaders.

"Do you think they'll agree?" Nina asked, her voice tinged with doubt. "Some of the nations we're dealing with still don't fully grasp the urgency of the situation. They've been hesitant to invest in the kind of change we need."

Aldo looked at her, his face serious. "They don't have a choice. They either adapt or become irrelevant. We've proven the potential of our solution. They'll see the value, or they'll be left behind."

When the call connected, Aldo was greeted by a sea of faces. Leaders from every corner of the globe had gathered in this virtual space, ready to discuss the future. Aldo took a deep breath, steeling himself for the conversation ahead.

"Thank you for meeting with us today," Aldo began, his voice calm but filled with conviction. "I know that many of you are facing immense pressure, and I understand that change is difficult. But what we are proposing isn't just a solution for today's waste crisis, it's a blueprint for a new way of life. We have the opportunity to not only fix the damage we've done but to create a sustainable future for the next generations."

There was a pause, and then one of the leaders from the Global Sustainability Initiative spoke up. "We've seen the results, Aldo. The cities you've rebuilt are proof that your technology works. But we have questions about scalability and the economic impact of such a widespread change. How do we ensure that this process doesn't cause further disruption?"

Aldo smiled. "The disruption is inevitable, but the question isn't whether we will disrupt the old system, it's whether we will allow that system to collapse without having something better in place to take its place. Our solution isn't just about replacing what was lost; it's about evolving, adapting, and learning from our past mistakes."

The room fell silent, and for the first time, Aldo saw a shift in the faces around him. They were listening. They were ready to hear the truth.

"We have the chance to heal this planet," Aldo continued, his voice steady. "It won't happen overnight, but it will happen if we all commit to this journey. Together."

As the summit continued, Aldo felt a renewed sense of purpose. The world was changing, and they were the ones leading that change. The future wasn't set in stone, but it was now within their grasp.

The work ahead was monumental, but for the first time in years, Aldo believed that the world could be healed, one building, one city, one life at a time. The mountain of waste was no longer an insurmountable obstacle. It was a challenge, a challenge they were on the brink of overcoming.

And with that thought, Aldo allowed himself a rare moment of hope. The world, once broken, was slowly beginning to mend.

Chapter 35: The Meeting of World Leaders

The day of the summit had arrived, and the tension in the air was palpable. The world's fate seemed to rest on the decisions made within the next few hours. Aldo and Nina sat in the sleek, modern conference room of the United Nations headquarters, the walls lined with high-definition screens displaying live updates from cities across the globe. Each screen showed a different corner of the world where Aldo's revolutionary waste-to-material technology was being implemented, from Tokyo to Cape Town, from New York to Rio de Janeiro. The progress was visible, but it wasn't enough. Not yet.

Today wasn't about showcasing what they had already accomplished, it was about convincing the world's leaders to commit to the future. And that meant more than just adopting Aldo's solution. It meant changing the global economic system, rethinking how nations interacted with the environment, and, most importantly, prioritizing the health of the planet over profits.

"Are you ready for this?" Nina asked, her voice low as she adjusted the collar of her jacket.

Aldo gave her a brief, yet reassuring, smile. "I don't think we have a choice. The world is watching us."

He wasn't sure who he was trying to reassure more, Nina or himself. This wasn't just another presentation or research report. This was their chance to make history. If they failed here, if the global leaders didn't back their proposal, then the fragile momentum they had built over the past few months would come crashing down. The vision of a cleaner, more sustainable world would remain just that, a vision.

They both stood and made their way toward the stage, where the world's leaders, representatives, and dignitaries were seated. The stage was grand, with a circular layout to signify equality and cooperation. At the front, a massive holographic globe hovered, displaying real-time data on the state of the planet, rising sea levels, deforestation rates, carbon emissions, and, of course, the staggering amount of waste that continued to accumulate across the globe.

Aldo took his seat beside Nina, scanning the room. The leaders of the world's most powerful nations were present, from the United States to China, from Russia to Brazil. They were flanked by representatives from international organizations, environmental NGOs, and business leaders who held the keys to the economic future. There was a palpable sense of urgency in the room, but also skepticism. Aldo could see it in their eyes, the doubts, the questions, the resistance to change.

A voice rang out across the room, cutting through the murmur of conversation. The President of the United Nations, a stoic woman from Norway named Ingrid Solberg, stepped to the podium.

"Ladies and gentlemen," she began, her voice firm and commanding, "today we are gathered not just to discuss the state of our planet, but to chart the course for its future. The work of the last several decades has brought us to this point, this moment where we must make choices that will shape the lives of generations to come. We are at a crossroads, and the path we take today will define the world our children inherit."

She paused, allowing the weight of her words to settle over the room.

"Today, we will hear from Dr. Aldo Ramirez and Nina Liu, whose groundbreaking research and solutions have shown us a path forward. A path that promises not only to tackle the global waste crisis but to build a new, sustainable future. The floor is yours, Dr. Ramirez, Ms. Liu."

Aldo stood, taking a deep breath as he approached the podium. Nina gave him a reassuring nod, her eyes filled with the same quiet determination that had been driving him all along. As he took the microphone, the room fell silent. He could feel the weight of the moment, the eyes of the world on him. He could almost hear the heartbeat of the planet itself in the silence.

"Thank you, President Solberg," Aldo began, his voice steady. "Distinguished guests, world leaders, and friends. It is an honor to be here today, not just as a scientist, but as a representative of the countless people who have worked alongside me to create a solution to the global crisis we face. A crisis that has, in many ways, been of our own making."

He paused, letting his words resonate.

"We stand at the edge of a precipice. The evidence is clear: our planet is overwhelmed by waste, by pollution, and by the destruction of its ecosystems. The oceans are choking on plastic, the forests are being razed, and the very air we breathe is poisoned by carbon emissions. And the worst part is, we've known about it for decades, yet we have failed to act in time."

Aldo's gaze swept across the room, meeting the eyes of the leaders in the front row. There was no turning back now.

"But it doesn't have to be this way," he continued, his voice gaining strength. "In the last year, my team and I have developed a groundbreaking technology that can not only deal with the waste crisis but also offer a sustainable solution to rebuild the very cities that have been devastated by natural disasters. This technology turns plastic waste into a new building material, one that is not only durable and resilient but also environmentally friendly. It is a material that can be used to create self-sustaining cities, powered by renewable energy, designed to work in harmony with nature, not against it."

Aldo paused again, allowing the room to process the weight of his words. He could see the skepticism, but there was something else now, curiosity.

"This technology isn't just about rebuilding cities," Aldo said, his voice softening. "It's about restoring the balance between humanity and the Earth. It's about shifting from a mindset of consumption to one of stewardship. It's about recognizing that we are not separate from the planet, we are part of it. And if we continue to treat it as something to exploit, we will destroy ourselves in the process."

The room was still, the silence thick with the gravity of his message. He could feel the tension, but also the collective hope that this could be the beginning of something monumental.

"We are not asking for a handout," Aldo said, his tone resolute. "We are not asking for charity. We are asking for partnership. We need the commitment of governments, businesses, and individuals to support the widespread adoption of this technology. We need the political will to pass laws that prioritize sustainability, to fund research into new materials and energy solutions, and to create the infrastructure needed to scale these efforts. And, most importantly, we need to recognize that this is not just an environmental issue, it is a survival issue."

Aldo turned slightly to his side, where Nina stood by, her face illuminated by the soft glow of the overhead lights. She stepped forward, her eyes filled with a quiet intensity.

"The future is not a given," Nina said, her voice steady but impassioned. "It is something we create with every action we take. And right now, our actions are driving us toward a precipice. But it doesn't have to be that way. We have the power to choose a different path. We have the technology, we have the knowledge, and we have the urgency. All we need is the will to act."

She paused, meeting the eyes of the room's leaders one by one.

"This is our chance to write a different story. A story where we look back in twenty years and say, 'This was the moment we decided to change the course of history.'"

There was a murmur of agreement from several of the representatives in the room. Some nodded thoughtfully, others exchanged glances. But Aldo knew that the hardest part was just beginning. Changing the hearts and minds of world leaders was no small task, especially when so much of the current economic system was built on unsustainable practices.

The President of the United States was the first to speak, his voice measured but firm.

"Dr. Ramirez, Ms. Liu, your technology is impressive, no doubt. But the challenges you've outlined are massive. There are economic systems, industries, and entire sectors that would have to be completely restructured. How can we be sure that this is the solution we need? That it won't create new problems in the process?"

Aldo nodded, fully expecting this question. It was the kind of resistance they had faced before, fear of change, fear of the unknown.

"We understand the scale of the challenge," Aldo said. "But the truth is, we are already facing the consequences of not acting. The costs of inaction are much higher than the costs of transition. We are not asking to dismantle the global economy, we are asking to shift it. To align it with the principles of sustainability. And as for the implementation, we have already begun seeing the positive impacts on the cities that have adopted this technology. The energy savings, the reduced pollution, and the revitalization of communities are all tangible benefits."

A silence settled over the room again. It wasn't an answer that immediately convinced everyone, but it was a step forward. The conversation had shifted from skepticism to dialogue.

Another leader, this one from India, raised a hand. "How do you propose we address the global disparities? Not all nations have the resources or infrastructure to implement this technology on the same scale."

Nina responded, her voice calm yet assertive, "We recognize that every nation is different, and we don't expect every country to implement this in the same way. But the technology we've developed is scalable. It can be adapted to different contexts, from large cities to smaller communities. What's needed is a global effort, a partnership between wealthy nations and those still struggling to recover. We are not just talking about technology; we are talking about creating new economic opportunities, new industries, and new jobs for people who need them most."

The discussions continued, with leaders debating logistics, funding, and the feasibility of implementing such an ambitious plan. The questions were tough, but Aldo and Nina had anticipated them. What mattered most was that the conversation was happening. It wasn't about convincing every leader in the room today, it was about getting them to see the possibility of a different future. A future where they weren't just discussing problems, but actively solving them.

As the summit continued into the evening, Aldo and Nina felt a flicker of hope. It was small, perhaps, but it was there. The world's leaders had heard their message. And for the first time, it seemed that they were ready to act.

The road ahead was long and uncertain, but the most crucial step had been taken.

And it was up to them to keep moving forward.

Chapter 36: Political Challenges

The weeks that followed the global summit were a whirlwind of media appearances, interviews, and endless negotiations. While Aldo and Nina had managed to capture the world's attention with their groundbreaking technology and their impassioned plea for a sustainable future, the reality of political friction soon became apparent. The excitement and hope that had bloomed in the conference room quickly started to dissipate in the face of entrenched national interests, economic pressures, and ideological divides.

Aldo stood at the window of his office, watching as the city of Geneva stretched out before him. The bustling streets, the gleaming skyscrapers, and the constant hum of activity felt surreal compared to the weight on his shoulders. This wasn't just about technology or science anymore, it was about navigating the labyrinthine world of geopolitics, where progress often seemed like an illusion.

The challenge was bigger than anything he had ever faced. Aldo had spent his career fighting for the planet, for the environment, but now, he was realizing how deeply politics and power dynamics were intertwined with every solution he had hoped to implement. They were up against global forces much stronger than they had anticipated, and in many ways, they were fighting an uphill battle.

The door to his office creaked open, and Nina entered. She was dressed in a simple yet professional blazer, her expression as tense as his own. The faint lines beneath her eyes told the story of countless sleepless nights spent in strategy meetings, drafting speeches, and lobbying for support.

"They're stalling," she said flatly, dropping a thick dossier onto the desk in front of him. "This is what we're up against now."

Aldo opened the file and skimmed through the reports, documents filled with references to political gridlock, multinational corporations using their influence to block any meaningful environmental regulations, and various governments resisting any policies that might hurt their short-term economic interests. Some countries, including a few of the major powers in Asia and the Americas, had already voiced opposition to the widespread adoption of the technology, citing its potential disruption of established industries, especially in the manufacturing and fossil fuel sectors.

"The fossil fuel lobby is more powerful than I ever imagined," Aldo muttered, running a hand through his hair. "They've always had a hold on the global economy, but now they're using every tool they have to slow us down. They know that if we succeed, their days are numbered."

Nina nodded. "It's not just the fossil fuel industry. There's the mining sector too, the plastics manufacturers, and even agricultural interests. They're all mobilizing to prevent any kind of significant change. They've been running ads in the media, lobbying at the UN, and even planting seeds of doubt in the minds of the public."

"We've seen some of that already," Aldo replied. "We know that misinformation is one of their primary weapons. But what about the political leaders? What are we hearing from them?"

Nina sighed, clearly frustrated. "It's the same story over and over. A few leaders support us in principle, but when it comes to actually pushing through policies or allocating funding for the transition, they freeze up. They're worried about the economic fallout. They're worried about losing their grip on power."

Aldo closed his eyes for a moment. The political landscape was complex and hostile, but they couldn't afford to give up. They had come so far, millions of people were already benefiting from their technology, and entire communities were beginning to rebuild using their sustainable materials. Yet here they were, facing a much greater challenge than they had anticipated.

"We need to shift the narrative," Aldo said, his voice firm with renewed resolve. "We've already shown that our technology works. We've got the evidence on the ground. Now we need to show the world that this isn't just an environmental issue, it's an economic one, too. We need to get the message out that this is the future. A future that creates jobs, stimulates new industries, and reduces costs in the long run."

Nina leaned over the desk, pointing at a specific section of the report. "There's something here that could help us do that. A few countries, like India and Brazil, are already seeing the economic benefits of adopting our technology. They're using it not just to rebuild their cities, but to create new jobs in the green energy and construction sectors. We can use that as a model to show other nations that transitioning to a sustainable economy isn't just good for the planet, it's good for business, too."

Aldo thought for a moment, then nodded. "Yes. That's the angle we need. We can't let them paint this as a threat to the global economy. Instead, we need to show that it's an opportunity, one that offers solutions to both environmental and economic crises. If we can get the right people in the room to see it that way, we might finally have a chance."

As they strategized, Aldo and Nina were well aware of the delicate balancing act that lay ahead. For all the progress they had made on the ground, the political situation was moving in the opposite direction. In the corridors of power, the forces of resistance were regrouping, and they were determined to keep things as they were.

The next few days were a blur of meetings and conference calls, as Aldo's team worked tirelessly to forge new alliances and strengthen their existing partnerships. It was clear that they needed to expand their influence beyond environmental circles if they were to make a real difference. So, they began to reach out to business leaders, investors, and policy advocates, people who could push the agenda forward and help overcome the political hurdles standing in their way.

But even as Aldo's team worked tirelessly, there were moments when the weight of it all felt suffocating. During a particularly tense call with one of the key UN representatives, Aldo could feel the frustration boiling within him. The representative, a well-known diplomat from the European Union, had been polite but evasive, offering nothing concrete in terms of support for the global rollout of their technology.

"We can't afford to wait any longer," Aldo had said, his voice tight with urgency. "The planet can't afford to wait. We've demonstrated that this technology works. We've seen the results. What more do we need to prove?"

"I understand your urgency, Dr. Ramirez," the diplomat replied, "but you must understand the political realities we face. There are interests at play here that go beyond the environment. The geopolitical situation is unstable, and the economic landscape is fragile. Implementing your technology on a global scale is a massive undertaking that requires careful consideration and time."

Aldo gritted his teeth. He had heard this argument too many times already. Time was a luxury they didn't have. The planet was dying, and political games were standing in the way of the only real solution.

After hanging up, Aldo felt a wave of exhaustion wash over him. He looked at Nina, who had been listening quietly, her face etched with a mixture of concern and determination.

"It's like we're up against an invisible wall," he muttered. "They keep moving the goalposts. Every time we make progress, they throw up another obstacle."

MOUNT OF WASTE

Nina placed a hand on his shoulder. "I know. But we can't give up. Not now. We've come this far, and we've got something that can change the world. We've already proven that."

Her words were a reminder that they weren't alone in this battle. They had a team, a movement, and a cause that went far beyond their personal ambitions. It was easy to get discouraged when facing powerful political forces, but Nina was right, they couldn't afford to give in. They had to keep pushing, keep fighting, even when it seemed impossible.

The next few weeks were filled with more high-stakes meetings, public relations campaigns, and political maneuvering. There were small victories, pockets of progress in countries like Kenya, India, and Mexico, where local governments were adopting their technology and starting to see real benefits. But those wins felt like drops in an ocean of resistance.

It was clear that the challenge was bigger than Aldo and Nina had ever imagined. They were up against global forces that had a stake in maintaining the status quo, forces that would stop at nothing to block any efforts to disrupt their profit-driven systems.

But Aldo was not one to back down. He had seen firsthand the power of human resilience and ingenuity. He had witnessed the transformation of communities, the rebuilding of cities, and the renewed hope in people's eyes when they realized that a better future was possible.

"We have to keep fighting," Aldo said to Nina one evening, his resolve hardening. "We can't let them win."

Nina nodded. "We won't. We'll find a way."

It wasn't just a matter of technology anymore. It was a matter of belief. Aldo and his team had already proven that their solution worked. Now, they just had to convince the world's leaders that the future they envisioned wasn't a threat, it was a lifeline. The political challenges they faced were steep, but they had no choice but to rise above them, to push forward against the tide of resistance.

The world was waiting. And Aldo and Nina were determined to see it saved.

Chapter 37: The Threat from Corporations

It had been a week since the high-level meeting at the United Nations, and Aldo's optimism had begun to fade. The media had seized on the summit, but despite the initial excitement, the momentum they had built was starting to sputter. The corporations who had so much to lose from the widespread adoption of Aldo's waste-to-material technology were not sitting idly by, they were fighting back, using every weapon in their vast arsenals to undermine their efforts.

Aldo had been expecting resistance, but the scale and intensity of it had taken him by surprise. From social media smear campaigns to corporate lobbyists spreading misinformation, it was clear that the most powerful industries in the world had mobilized against them. They were using every tool they had, public relations firms, think tanks, and political connections, to block the transition to a sustainable future.

Nina entered his office, holding a stack of documents. Her face was set in grim determination, a reflection of the storm that was gathering on the horizon.

"We need to talk," she said, her voice tight. "They're stepping up their game. It's not just about blocking us politically anymore, they're playing dirty."

Aldo frowned, rubbing his temple. "What now?"

Nina set the papers down on the desk with a sharp thud. "I just got off the phone with Sofia. You remember her, the journalist we've been working with in the U.S. Well, she's uncovered something big. There's a coordinated effort among some of the world's biggest corporations, energy giants, chemical manufacturers, and even some of the largest construction firms.

They're not just lobbying anymore. They're actively trying to sabotage our work."

Aldo leaned forward, his gaze fixed on the documents. "Sabotage?"

Nina nodded. "It's not just about slowing us down. These companies are using a variety of tactics, spreading false reports about our technology's safety, launching aggressive lawsuits, and worst of all, undermining our supply chain."

Aldo's pulse quickened. He had suspected something like this might happen, but to hear it confirmed was a blow. Their technology was a threat to industries that had profited from unsustainable practices for decades. It wasn't just about economics; it was about control. If Aldo's waste-to-material technology became widespread, it could potentially disrupt entire sectors of the global economy, energy, construction, plastics, and even waste management itself. This kind of power was too much for these industries to give up without a fight.

"Tell me more," Aldo said, his voice steady despite the rising panic inside him.

Nina pulled up a chair and sat across from him. "First off, the chemical industry has been spreading rumors that our technology isn't as safe as we claim. They've been claiming that the material we produce is prone to corrosion, that it leaches harmful chemicals into the environment when exposed to heat. And they're paying off independent researchers to publish false studies to back up these claims."

"Are they really buying the science?" Aldo asked, incredulous. "We've done the tests. Our material is safer than most traditional construction materials."

Nina's eyes narrowed. "That's not stopping them. They've got money and influence, Aldo. The average person doesn't know the difference between a peer-reviewed study and an advertorial published in a 'reputable' science magazine. And these false reports are being picked up by media outlets with massive reach."

Aldo clenched his fists, his mind racing. He knew the truth. He knew that their technology was safe. It had been tested in the harshest environments, extreme temperatures, heavy storms, and even saltwater exposure. But what did that matter when the forces they were up against were manipulating public perception with fake data?

Nina continued. "And it's not just misinformation. They're infiltrating the supply chain. A few key suppliers for our raw materials have suddenly been 'bought out' by large corporations with ties to the fossil fuel and chemical industries. They're refusing to cooperate with us, making it nearly impossible for us to scale production."

Aldo's mind raced. He had anticipated some level of corporate resistance, but to have these companies deliberately sabotage their ability to build on their progress, it was a direct attack on everything they had worked for.

"They can't just block us like this," Aldo said, his voice laced with determination. "We've got the support of people. We've got the data. The technology is out there, it works."

Nina met his gaze with a mixture of understanding and concern. "I know. But they don't need to block us completely. All they need to do is stall us long enough to make people lose faith. To make them question whether this is really the answer. They're going to play the long game."

Aldo stood up abruptly, pacing around the room. He felt trapped. The technology was ready to change the world, yet these corporate forces were doing everything they could to keep it from reaching the masses. They had the financial power, the political connections, and the media influence to undermine everything. How could they fight that?

"We need to expose them," Aldo said suddenly, his voice resolute. "We need to get ahead of this before it spirals out of control."

Nina nodded. "That's exactly what Sofia's working on. She's trying to get the evidence we need to expose this corporate conspiracy. But we need to be careful. If we go public with this too soon, we'll be walking right into their hands. They'll twist it and use it against us."

Aldo thought for a moment. It was a delicate situation. They couldn't afford to alienate the public or attract the attention of the wrong people. But they also couldn't sit idly by while these corporations undermined everything they had fought for.

"We can't keep playing by their rules," Aldo said finally. "If we're going to win this, we need to outsmart them. We need to build a coalition of activists, workers, and politicians who can stand up to this kind of corporate manipulation."

Nina's eyes brightened. "You're right. If we can build a movement that's not just about the technology but about the values it represents, about challenging these giant corporations and their stranglehold on the world's resources, we'll have a much stronger position."

Aldo stopped pacing and turned to face her. "But we can't do this alone. We need allies. People in power who aren't afraid to stand up to the corporatocracy."

"I've already started reaching out," Nina said. "There are groups, environmental organizations, labor unions, and even some progressive business leaders, who are fed up with this system. They're starting to see the need for change. But we need to act quickly."

Aldo felt a spark of hope. They had a chance, not just to save their technology but to shift the entire global conversation. The issue wasn't just about the environment, it was about breaking free from the stranglehold of corporations that put profit over people, over the planet.

"Okay," Aldo said, a new resolve hardening in his chest. "We're going to fight back. We're going to make sure the world knows what these companies are doing. We'll take this fight to the people."

Nina smiled, her eyes alight with determination. "I knew you'd say that. Let's take them down."

The next few days were a whirlwind of meetings, calls, and strategy sessions. Aldo and Nina were determined to keep the momentum going, even in the face of the mounting corporate resistance. They had no illusions, it would be a long, hard battle. But they were no longer fighting alone. The coalition they were building began to grow, with more and more organizations, activists, and progressive businesses joining their cause. The narrative was shifting. People were starting to see the truth, that these powerful corporations weren't just blocking their technology; they were blocking progress, blocking a better future for everyone.

And with each passing day, Aldo could feel the energy building, the resistance growing. The battle was far from over, but for the first time in weeks, he felt the weight of the world lift from his shoulders, just a little. It wasn't just about technology. It wasn't just about saving the planet.

It was about taking back control.

And they were ready to fight for it.

Chapter 38: Ecosystem Restoration

The world had already felt the crushing weight of environmental devastation, oceans choked with plastic, rivers clogged with industrial runoff, forests razed for profit, and the land buried beneath mountains of waste. For decades, the signs of the planet's suffering had been ignored, dismissed as inevitable consequences of human progress. But now, as Aldo and his team stood on the precipice of a new dawn, armed with their groundbreaking waste-to-material technology, the time had come not just to stem the tide of destruction but to begin the long, arduous process of healing the Earth itself.

Aldo gazed out at the vast expanse of the Pacific Ocean from his temporary office in a coastal research facility. The waves were restless today, battering against the jagged cliffs with fierce determination. But beneath the surface, there was a quieter desperation, an oceanic ecosystem struggling to stay afloat, suffocated by the plastic waste that was slowly killing it.

"Nina," Aldo said, breaking the silence. "Do you ever wonder how we can truly reverse the damage?"

Nina, seated across from him, met his gaze with a thoughtful look. "Every day," she replied, "but that's what we're working towards, isn't it? Not just the technology, but the whole restoration. There's no point in rebuilding cities if the oceans are dying or the forests are gone. We can't fix one part of the planet and leave the rest to rot."

Aldo nodded. "Exactly. The technology we've created is just one piece of the puzzle. We can take the waste and turn it into something useful. But we need to address the root cause of the destruction, pollution, deforestation, overexploitation of resources, and restore what's been lost."

MOUNT OF WASTE

Nina leaned back in her chair, her expression contemplative. "You're right. It's about more than just cleaning up. We need to make sure that when we restore the ecosystems, they're able to thrive on their own, without relying on us to prop them up. It's about rebuilding the balance."

The balance of nature had been shattered, and they knew that it wouldn't be enough to simply remove the plastic from the ocean or plant a few trees in the barren soil. The process of ecological recovery would take time, effort, and collaboration from scientists, activists, and local communities around the world.

In the weeks that followed, Aldo and Nina coordinated a global initiative focused on ecosystem restoration. It wasn't just a matter of clearing out the waste, they had to bring back the biodiversity that had been lost, revitalize the soil, and restore the health of the oceans. This was going to be their greatest challenge yet: the effort to heal the Earth on a global scale.

They assembled a team of scientists from various fields, marine biologists, soil experts, forest conservationists, and climate specialists. Each of them brought a unique set of skills and knowledge to the table, and together, they mapped out a plan for restoration that would span continents.

The first priority was the ocean.

Aldo and Nina traveled to the Pacific to meet with marine biologists who had been working on methods to remove plastic waste from the ocean. The situation was dire, the ocean currents had spread the waste across vast distances, creating enormous "garbage patches" that were slowly killing marine life. In many areas, sea turtles, fish, and whales had become entangled in the plastic, suffocating or starving from ingesting it.

One of the most promising innovations was an autonomous system developed by a team of engineers that used floating devices to collect plastic debris from the water's surface. But the real challenge lay beneath the surface. The marine ecosystem was more complex than they had anticipated, coral reefs, which were once thriving ecosystems, were dying at an alarming rate due to ocean acidification and plastic contamination.

"It's not just about cleaning up," said Dr. Mira Santos, a marine biologist who had been working on the front lines of ocean restoration for years. "We need to bring back the coral reefs. Without them, entire ecosystems will collapse. And we have to reverse the acidification caused by CO_2 emissions."

Aldo and Nina listened intently as Dr. Santos explained the importance of coral reefs in sustaining marine life. The reefs were home to a vast number of species, and their destruction had caused a domino effect throughout the ocean. Fish populations were dwindling, and many species were on the brink of extinction. In some areas, whole marine food webs had been decimated.

But the team wasn't without hope. "We've been working on a technique that uses algae-based carbon capture," Dr. Santos explained. "If we can neutralize the acidification in targeted areas, we can give the reefs a chance to regenerate."

Aldo's mind began to race with ideas. "We could incorporate our waste-to-material technology into this. If we can use our material to build artificial reefs, we could give the coral a foundation to grow on, while also using the material to filter out pollutants."

The team agreed to test this concept, combining Aldo's technology with Dr. Santos's algae-based carbon capture. It would be a long process, but the idea of rebuilding the ocean's ecosystems had taken root. With the right combination of technology and natural processes, they might have a chance to revive the coral reefs and, in turn, the rest of the marine life that depended on them.

The second focus of the restoration efforts was the soil.

MOUNT OF WASTE

In many parts of the world, land had been overexploited, polluted by industrial waste, or ravaged by deforestation. In some regions, the soil had become so degraded that it could no longer support plant life. Aldo and his team worked with soil scientists who had developed methods to restore soil health through a combination of natural fertilizers and sustainable farming practices.

One of the key components of this initiative was the creation of "soil regeneration hubs", community-based centers where local farmers could learn about and adopt sustainable agricultural techniques. These hubs would not only provide training but also distribute materials like compost, biochar, and soil conditioners to help restore the health of the land.

Nina was instrumental in connecting with local communities and activists who had been working for years to raise awareness about soil degradation. They needed to demonstrate that restoring soil health wasn't just about environmental conservation, it was also about food security.

"In many rural communities, people are struggling to grow enough food to survive," Nina said during a meeting with a group of activists. "If we don't restore the soil, we're not just destroying the planet, we're jeopardizing our own future."

The activists agreed, and together, they developed a plan to establish sustainable farming networks in areas where the soil had been most affected. They worked to create a model for land restoration that included both indigenous knowledge and modern scientific techniques, a hybrid approach that respected the wisdom of local communities while utilizing the latest innovations in ecological restoration.

The third piece of the puzzle was the forests.

Aldo and Nina traveled to the Amazon rainforest, which had been ravaged by illegal logging, mining, and deforestation. The destruction of these vital ecosystems was one of the most pressing crises facing the planet. Forests didn't just provide oxygen, they were essential for regulating the Earth's climate, absorbing carbon dioxide, and supporting countless species of flora and fauna.

When they arrived, they were greeted by Dr. Lucas Pereira, an ecologist who had been leading efforts to restore the Amazon for years. His team had been replanting trees, but the challenges were immense. Deforestation had left vast areas of the forest vulnerable to erosion and flooding, and the biodiversity that had once flourished was now in peril.

"There's no way to simply 'replant' the forest," Dr. Pereira explained. "The soil has been so degraded that it's not conducive to regrowth. We need to restore the entire ecosystem, including the water cycle and the soil."

Aldo and Nina discussed how they could integrate their technology into this restoration process. By using their biodegradable materials to create natural barriers against erosion and planting specific species of trees that could revitalize the soil, they could help accelerate the recovery process. The team also worked on developing a drone-based system that could deliver seeds to areas that were difficult to access, allowing for the large-scale reforestation of remote regions.

Through collaboration with local indigenous groups, who had long understood the importance of the rainforest, they were able to weave traditional knowledge with cutting-edge technology. These communities had lived in harmony with the forest for generations, and they understood the delicate balance that needed to be restored.

As the restoration efforts progressed, Aldo felt a sense of optimism slowly returning. The task was enormous, and the challenges were manifold, but they were beginning to see results. The first artificial reefs were showing signs of coral regrowth. The soil regeneration hubs were starting to produce healthier crops. In the Amazon, the first trees were beginning to take root again.

But Aldo knew that this was just the beginning. The road ahead would be long and fraught with setbacks. The scale of the planet's environmental wounds was almost too large to comprehend. But for the first time, there was hope.

For the first time, the Earth was beginning to heal.

Chapter 39: The Information War

The battle for the planet's future had shifted. After months of relentless work, with the support of activists, scientists, and local communities, Aldo's team had made significant strides in restoring the oceans, land, and forests. The global movement was growing stronger, and their technology, designed to convert waste into sustainable construction materials, was beginning to take root across the globe. Cities that had once been drowning in pollution were finding new life through their innovations.

But now, something far more insidious was emerging, an unseen enemy. It wasn't just the corporate lobbyists or the politicians who had been undermining their efforts anymore. The real battle was shifting to the digital realm, where truth was being blurred and reality was being distorted.

Aldo sat in his office, the weight of a mountain pressing down on his shoulders. He had just finished a video call with Nina, who had been at the frontlines of their campaign for months. Her voice was filled with frustration as she briefed him on the latest developments.

"You're not going to believe this, Aldo," Nina said. "There's been a surge in misinformation campaigns, spreading like wildfire across social media, news outlets, everywhere. They've got bots flooding online forums, using paid influencers to smear our name. They're calling us eco-terrorists, and now they're claiming that our technology causes more pollution than it solves."

Aldo's heart sank. He knew they had enemies, but he hadn't anticipated the scope of this new threat. He leaned forward in his chair, running a hand through his hair.

"Eco-terrorists? How are they getting away with this?" Aldo asked, his voice tinged with disbelief.

Nina's tone was grim. "They've got resources, money, networks, and access to media. And it's not just a few people. It's organized. There's a whole network of media outlets, pundits, and online figures who are being paid to push this narrative. They're planting fake studies, using deepfake videos, and flooding the airwaves with confusion. The more we try to set the record straight, the louder they get."

Aldo let out a frustrated breath. He had always known that the road to environmental recovery would be fraught with challenges, but this was something new. These attacks weren't just about politics or economics, they were about information, about controlling the narrative.

"This is a full-scale information war," Aldo muttered. "And we're on the front lines."

Nina's voice softened. "They want to distract people from the real issues, Aldo. If they can confuse the public, if they can make us look like the villains, they'll keep the status quo. And the status quo is exactly what these corporations need to keep profiting."

Aldo's mind raced as he processed the scale of the challenge. The battle wasn't just about creating a sustainable world anymore, it was about controlling the flow of information. It was about ensuring that the truth would prevail over the falsehoods being spread by the powerful forces fighting to maintain their stranglehold over the world.

"We need to fight back," Aldo said, determination hardening his voice. "We can't just let them control the narrative. We need to expose them for what they are and give people the truth."

Nina agreed. "We've been working with journalists, but now it's time to go bigger. We need to rally our supporters, get the truth out there in a way that cuts through the noise. We can't let them control the conversation anymore."

The next few days were a blur of activity. Aldo and Nina assembled their team of activists, journalists, and digital strategists to develop a counteroffensive. It was clear that the misinformation campaign was being pushed by a coalition of powerful corporate interests, all of whom stood to lose if Aldo's technology took hold. The spread of fake studies, doctored images, and misleading narratives was only the tip of the iceberg.

They needed to act fast. The digital landscape was rapidly shifting, and each day that passed without a response made it harder to undo the damage being done. They couldn't just counter the lies, they needed to take the initiative and expose the machine behind the misinformation.

Aldo's first step was to reach out to Sofia, the investigative journalist who had been following their work for months. Sofia had already proven to be invaluable in their efforts, uncovering the corporate sabotage and spreading the truth about their technology.

"I need you to dig deeper," Aldo said during their call. "We know that these attacks aren't just coming from random trolls. There's a coordinated effort behind all of this. I need you to uncover who's funding these campaigns and how deep this goes. If we can expose the puppeteers behind the curtain, we can turn the tide."

Sofia, her eyes filled with determination, nodded. "I've been tracking the money trails. I'll get to the bottom of this. We'll expose them, Aldo. We'll show the world who's behind all this chaos."

Meanwhile, Nina worked closely with their digital strategy team to launch a counter-campaign. They couldn't just respond to each individual attack, they needed to create a massive, unified movement that would drown out the lies and give people the truth.

"It's not just about defending ourselves," Nina explained to the team. "We need to go on the offensive. We have to flood social media, news outlets, and forums with the truth. We need to show people the real science behind what we're doing, the impact of our technology, and how it's changing lives."

The team brainstormed creative ways to engage with their audience, creating viral campaigns that showcased the real-world benefits of their technology. They released videos featuring testimonials from cities that had successfully implemented their waste-to-material solutions, showing the tangible impact it had on the environment and local communities. They also began working with climate scientists to debunk the fake studies that were being circulated, presenting their own peer-reviewed data and real-life evidence of their success.

The information war wasn't just happening online. The media landscape was also shifting. As their counteroffensive grew, so did the pushback from the corporate-backed media outlets. Talk shows, news networks, and influencers who had been in the pocket of large corporations began to air segments that twisted the truth, misrepresented their findings, and outright lied about their intentions.

Aldo knew that they needed to take control of the narrative, not just in the digital space but in the traditional media as well. He and Nina arranged an exclusive interview with a major international news outlet, where they could present the truth in front of millions of viewers.

The interview was set. The world would be watching.

On the day of the broadcast, Aldo and Nina sat side by side in front of a large studio camera. The interviewer, a seasoned anchor, introduced them as the innovators behind the revolutionary waste-to-material technology that had the potential to change the world.

"Mr. Aldo, Ms. Nina," the interviewer began, "there's been a lot of controversy surrounding your technology. Some are claiming that your work is dangerous, that it's causing more harm than good. What do you say to those accusations?"

Aldo, his hands steady despite the pressure, leaned into the microphone. "What we're doing is the future of the planet. We're transforming waste, plastic, metal, and other harmful materials, into sustainable, eco-friendly construction materials. Our technology is not only safe but has been thoroughly tested by independent scientists. The attacks you're hearing are coming from those who are invested in maintaining the status quo, those who profit from pollution and environmental degradation. They want to keep the world stuck in the past, where they control the resources, the land, and the air we breathe."

Nina added, her voice unwavering, "The evidence is clear. The data shows that our technology reduces carbon emissions, cleans up the oceans, and helps restore damaged ecosystems. The real threat isn't from us, it's from those who have been polluting the planet for decades and who now want to stop progress."

The interviewer nodded, clearly impressed by their calm and assured responses. "But there are concerns about your corporate backers, your financial ties. Some argue that this is just another corporate agenda masked as environmentalism. How do you respond?"

Aldo's gaze remained steady. "Our work is not about corporate profits. It's about creating a sustainable future for everyone, whether you're a billionaire or someone living in a small coastal town. This isn't just about technology; it's about changing the way we live, the way we relate to the planet. We're building a movement for the people, not for profit."

Nina looked directly into the camera. "And the truth will always find its way through the lies. We've already seen the difference we can make. And we're just getting started."

The interview aired to a massive audience, and the impact was immediate. Social media buzzed with renewed support for Aldo's team. People rallied to the cause, sharing the truth and amplifying their message. The misinformation began to lose traction, as more and more people saw through the lies and stood with them in the fight for a better future.

The tide was turning, but Aldo knew that this war was far from over. There would be more battles ahead, more lies to expose, more media outlets to challenge, more forces to reckon with. But for the first time in weeks, he felt a sense of optimism. They were fighting not just for the planet, but for the truth. And as long as they had that, they would win.

Chapter 40: Rising Tensions

The days were growing darker. The global response to Aldo and his team's technology had been a mix of support and backlash, but now, the conflict had reached a boiling point. The information war had not only riled up the corporations and their allies but had also stirred governments and powerful economic stakeholders who were now beginning to show more aggressive responses.

Aldo sat in his office, the usual hum of activity around him subdued. His once hopeful outlook had shifted to one of cautious resolve. He knew that the road ahead would not be easy, and the forces against them were growing stronger by the day. What had started as a few corporate lobbying groups trying to silence them had quickly escalated into a much larger, more dangerous confrontation.

"We've received intel," Nina's voice crackled through the phone line, snapping Aldo back to the present. "Some of the larger nations are starting to put pressure on governments that are adopting our technology. I've been tracking this for a while, and it's starting to get serious. These governments are being threatened with trade sanctions and economic blackmail."

Aldo's heart sank. "Sanctions? Blackmail?"

"Exactly. There's no other way to describe it. Several countries, especially those with large fossil fuel and waste management industries, are working behind the scenes to intimidate and isolate nations that are moving forward with our solution," Nina explained, her tone tinged with worry. "Some governments are already reversing their agreements with us."

Aldo felt a tightening in his chest. Their technology had begun to change the global dialogue on waste and environmental recovery, and in doing so, it had inadvertently struck at the heart of some of the world's most entrenched economic systems. The corporate behemoths that had profited for decades from pollution and waste management were no longer merely opposing them, they were actively undermining them at every turn.

"Which countries are we talking about?" Aldo asked, trying to make sense of the situation. He'd always known that the environmental revolution would face resistance, but this felt different, more coordinated, more urgent.

"China, India, and the United States are leading the charge," Nina replied. "They're directly pressuring developing nations, especially those in Africa and South America, that have begun to implement our waste-to-material technology. Some of these governments are being offered trade incentives to abandon their partnerships with us. Others are being warned about potential tariffs and economic blockades."

Aldo ran a hand through his hair. It wasn't just corporate interests that they were up against anymore, it was entire governments willing to sacrifice progress for their own economic stability. These countries, built on the back of pollution and unchecked industrial growth, were seeing their stranglehold on global resources slipping. They weren't about to let a sustainable future take that from them.

"We have to find a way to counter this," Aldo said, his voice grim. "We can't allow them to crush progress just because it doesn't serve their interests."

"I know," Nina agreed. "We've been trying to build alliances with smaller nations, those that don't have the same economic ties to the industrial giants. But it's getting harder. The pressure's building."

Over the next few weeks, tensions escalated rapidly. The global stage was set for a showdown, and Aldo's team found themselves at the center of it all. The pressure wasn't just coming from the outside, it was beginning to hit closer to home.

Aldo received an invitation to meet with representatives from several nations, some of which had been at the forefront of adopting his technology. It was supposed to be a diplomatic summit, a chance for governments to discuss sustainable solutions and global cooperation. But Aldo knew better. The invitation felt more like a trap than an opportunity.

When he arrived at the summit, he was greeted with a cold reception. The representatives from the larger, more powerful nations were already in the room, their expressions tight, their eyes filled with suspicion. Aldo could feel the weight of their gaze as he sat down across from them.

"We've invited you here to discuss your technology, Mr. Aldo," one of the representatives from the United States said, his tone neutral but icy. "But we must be clear, we are concerned. Your so-called 'revolutionary solution' is causing disruption. It's undermining global trade. It's threatening industries that are vital to our economies."

Aldo's eyes narrowed. He'd expected something like this, but hearing it out loud still stung.

"My technology is not causing disruption," Aldo said, his voice steady. "It's providing a solution to a crisis that has been decades in the making. It's reducing waste, cleaning the oceans, and creating sustainable materials for construction. It's saving lives, not destroying economies."

"Economies built on industries that have provided jobs and growth for generations," another representative from China interjected. "You're asking us to turn our backs on those industries. How do you expect nations to make this transition without crippling their economies? What's your plan for those who will lose their livelihoods?"

Aldo knew that the loss of jobs in certain industries was a legitimate concern. But he also knew that the status quo was no longer tenable. He wasn't here to protect the old way of doing things. He was here to fight for a future that didn't depend on the exploitation of the planet.

"Transitioning away from unsustainable practices will require investment and planning," Aldo said, his voice firm. "But I assure you, it can be done. The alternative is far worse. We're facing a global environmental crisis. We can't keep building our future on a foundation of pollution and exploitation. We need to think about long-term survival, not just short-term profit."

The room fell silent, the tension palpable. The representatives exchanged glances, and Aldo could sense the growing unease in the room. But he didn't back down. He had worked too hard for this moment, and he knew that they had to stand their ground, no matter how difficult it became.

"You've made your point, Mr. Aldo," the representative from the U.S. said after a long pause. "But we'll need more than just promises to convince our leaders and the global community. We need assurances. And we need you to understand the consequences of your actions. This isn't just about saving the planet. It's about maintaining global order."

Aldo's eyes flashed with anger, but he kept his composure. "You talk about global order, but what good is an order built on exploitation? What good is it if the planet is dead? If the oceans are too polluted to sustain life? If the air is poisoned? We cannot afford to wait any longer. This is about survival, not just economics."

The representatives fell silent again, their expressions hardened. Aldo could feel the weight of their power in that room, but he also knew that their time was running out. They were standing on the wrong side of history.

Back at the research facility, Aldo's team was also feeling the strain of the rising tensions. The global markets were reacting to the pressure. Stock prices for companies that had adopted Aldo's technology were starting to plummet. Some nations were reversing their decisions to implement the waste-to-material solutions, bowing to the economic pressure exerted by the larger nations.

Nina walked into Aldo's office, her face tight with frustration. "We've lost two more countries. The pressure is too much. They're saying that they can't afford to antagonize their trading partners, and some of them are already facing internal unrest. It's as if the world is turning its back on progress."

Aldo stood up, pacing in agitation. "We can't let this happen. These governments are compromising their future for short-term stability. We need to make them understand that their economies are built on sand. The sooner they realize that, the better. We need to take this to the people."

Nina nodded. "We've already got protests happening in several countries, but it's not enough. We need a global movement. We need the masses to rise up and demand a new way forward."

Aldo's mind raced. They had to find a way to unite the people, to show them that this wasn't just about technology, it was about survival, about saving their homes, their futures. They needed to ignite a fire that could no longer be put out.

"Get in touch with Sofia," Aldo said, his voice steady once more. "It's time we take this fight to the streets. If we can rally enough support, we can put pressure on the leaders. They can't afford to ignore the people."

The world was on the verge of collapse. As tensions mounted and the global stage prepared for an all-out clash between progress and the forces of greed, Aldo knew one thing for certain: there was no turning back now. The stakes had never been higher, and the fight for the future of the planet had become a battle for humanity's very survival. The world's fate rested in their hands, and they were ready to face whatever came next.

Chapter 41: Forming a New Alliance

The battle was far from over. The world was on the precipice of a new era, one where the old systems of exploitation and short-term profit were being challenged by the rising tide of change. Aldo and Nina had been through countless trials, corporate sabotage, political pressure, global resistance, but now, they were facing the most crucial step in their mission: building a new alliance, one based not on economic power, but on shared responsibility for the planet's future.

The recent summit had been a wake-up call. Aldo had known from the beginning that the road to success would be fraught with opposition. But what he hadn't anticipated was the scale of the pushback from the established powers. The larger nations,vthose with entrenched economic interests in pollution, waste management, and fossil fuels,cwere determined to keep the status quo. They had used every tool at their disposal: media manipulation, economic threats, and diplomatic isolation.

Despite the odds, Aldo and Nina refused to back down. They had seen the results of their efforts, cities were being rebuilt with sustainable materials, ecosystems were beginning to recover, and small nations were thriving. The change was happening, but it was clear that they needed a united front to overcome the remaining obstacles. It was time to forge alliances with those who shared their vision, and together, they would fight for a future that could no longer be ignored.

Aldo stood in front of a large map of the world, his fingers tracing the outlines of countries that had expressed an interest in joining their cause. It wasn't just about adopting the waste-to-material technology; it was about creating a network of nations that would stand together in the face of the corporate giants and the political resistance. Countries that understood the urgent need for systemic change, countries that were willing to put the future of the planet above short-term profits.

Nina entered the room, her face alight with determination. "I've been in touch with Sofia. She's managed to secure commitments from several smaller countries in Africa and Southeast Asia. They're ready to move forward with the technology, but they need assurances that they won't be left to fend for themselves. They want a coalition, a united front of nations that will support each other."

Aldo nodded, a small smile tugging at the corner of his mouth. "That's a step in the right direction. But we need more. We need countries that have the power to influence the global stage, nations with economic and political clout. Without them, this won't be enough."

Nina's expression grew serious. "I agree. But that's the challenge, isn't it? The larger nations are either too entrenched in their old ways or too afraid of what the future might bring. It's going to take more than just technology to change their minds. We need to show them that this is about survival, not just economics."

Aldo paused, his mind racing. They had made progress, but the clock was ticking. The longer they waited, the harder it would be to overcome the opposition. They needed to act fast, and they needed to act boldly.

A few days later, Aldo and Nina were sitting at a conference table in a small, nondescript building in Geneva, Switzerland. The air was thick with tension as representatives from a handful of countries filed into the room. These nations, many of them small and often overlooked on the world stage, had shown the most promise in supporting Aldo's cause. Now, they had come together to form a new coalition, a united front that would work together to build a sustainable future for the planet.

MOUNT OF WASTE

Aldo stood at the head of the table, his heart pounding in his chest. This was the moment he had been working toward for so long. These countries had something to lose, and they understood the stakes. It was time to convince them that they could no longer wait for the larger powers to act. The future of the planet was in their hands.

"We stand at a crossroads," Aldo began, his voice steady but filled with urgency. "We are facing an environmental crisis unlike anything humanity has ever seen. The consequences of inaction are already being felt across the globe, rising sea levels, catastrophic weather events, polluted oceans, and destroyed ecosystems. These are not distant threats. They are happening right now, and they are the result of decades of negligence."

He paused, letting the weight of his words sink in. The representatives around the table nodded, their faces a mixture of concern and resolve.

"But there is hope," Aldo continued, his voice growing stronger. "We have a solution. A technology that can reduce waste, clean the oceans, and create sustainable materials for construction. This is not a pipe dream. It is already being implemented in several countries, and the results speak for themselves. We can rebuild our cities, restore our ecosystems, and create a new, sustainable economy."

Nina stepped forward, her eyes scanning the room. "But we cannot do this alone. We need to build a coalition, an alliance of nations that will stand together in the face of resistance from the corporate giants and the political powers that have kept us in this destructive cycle for far too long."

Aldo's gaze swept across the room, meeting the eyes of the representatives. "This is our chance to change the course of history. To show the world that it is possible to build a future where the environment and the economy are not at odds, but work together for the benefit of all."

The room was silent for a moment as the representatives exchanged glances. Aldo could sense the hesitation in the air. They were ready to act, but the risks were high. Aligning themselves with Aldo and Nina would not only mean defying the world's most powerful nations, but it would also mean standing up to the entrenched forces of greed and corruption.

Finally, a voice broke the silence. "You're right," said the representative from Costa Rica. "We cannot wait any longer. We've already seen the effects of climate change in our own country. Droughts, floods, and wildfires have become more frequent and more severe. Our people are suffering, and we cannot afford to ignore the science any longer. We will support this alliance."

One by one, the other representatives voiced their support. The representative from Senegal spoke passionately about the destruction of coastal communities due to rising sea levels. The representative from Vietnam shared the struggles of farmers facing increasingly unpredictable weather patterns. And the representative from Chile spoke about the devastation of the Amazon rainforest and the urgent need for reforestation.

As the support for the alliance grew, Aldo felt a sense of hope wash over him. These nations, though small, had the power to make a real difference. And together, they could change the course of the future.

In the days that followed, the alliance began to take shape. The member nations worked together to draft a set of guiding principles that would govern their collective efforts. They would share knowledge, technology, and resources, and work together to implement sustainable waste management systems, reduce pollution, and rebuild damaged ecosystems. The goal was to create

MOUNT OF WASTE

a network of nations that would not only support each other in their efforts but also serve as a model for the rest of the world.

Aldo and Nina traveled from country to country, meeting with leaders and officials to finalize the agreements and build momentum. Everywhere they went, they found more countries willing to join the coalition. Some were hesitant at first, but once they saw the progress being made by the smaller nations that had already adopted the technology, they began to understand the potential.

But as the alliance grew, so did the pressure from the opposing forces. Corporate lobbyists and political leaders from the world's largest nations began to intensify their efforts to stop the coalition. They used every tool at their disposal: economic threats, media campaigns, and diplomatic maneuvering. They tried to discredit Aldo and Nina's work, painting them as radicals or idealists who didn't understand the complexities of the global economy.

But Aldo and Nina knew they couldn't back down. The future of the planet was at stake, and they had no choice but to keep fighting.

As the alliance continued to gain strength, it became clear that this was more than just a diplomatic effort—it was a movement. The people of the member nations began to rally behind the cause, demanding that their governments take action. Protests erupted in cities around the world, as citizens called for a new approach to waste, pollution, and environmental destruction.

The global stage was shifting, and the balance of power was slowly starting to tip. The old guard, the corporate giants and their political allies, were beginning to feel the pressure. They could no longer ignore the demands for change.

In the midst of this growing movement, Aldo and Nina knew that they had only one chance to make a lasting impact. The next steps would be critical. They needed to keep pushing forward, rallying more nations to their cause, and showing the world that a sustainable future was not only possible, it was the only path forward.

As the summit came to a close and the new alliance began to take shape, Aldo looked around the room at the representatives of the nations who had pledged their support. They were standing together, united by a common purpose. For the first time in a long while, Aldo felt a surge of hope.

The fight was far from over, but with each passing day, they were one step closer to securing a future where humanity and the planet could coexist in harmony. And that was a future worth fighting for.

Chapter 42: Facing the Energy Crisis

The world's energy crisis had reached a tipping point. Fossil fuels, once the lifeblood of global industry, were now a liability. Oil reserves were running dry, coal mines had become death traps for both workers and the planet, and natural gas was no longer the clean alternative it once seemed to be. With every passing day, the air quality worsened, and the temperatures climbed higher. The energy that powered cities, fueled industries, and kept the global economy running had become a ticking time bomb.

Aldo stood in his lab, staring at the array of monitors that displayed data from the latest tests on his renewable energy project. The results were promising, but the stakes were higher than ever. The world depended on them to find a solution to the energy crisis, and fast. He knew the clock was ticking. The impact of the global waste catastrophe and the political resistance to environmental reform had left the world vulnerable, but the energy crisis could break it completely. Entire economies could collapse if a solution wasn't found soon.

Nina entered the room, her face etched with concern. "How's it going?" she asked, her voice tinged with anxiety.

"Better than expected," Aldo replied, his tone measured. He gestured to the large screen in front of him. "We've got a breakthrough. If we can fine-tune this, it might just be the answer to the energy crisis."

Nina leaned in, examining the data. "What exactly are we looking at here?"

"This," Aldo said, his finger tracing the display, "is a new method of harnessing solar energy. Not just the traditional photovoltaic cells, but a more efficient system. We've been experimenting with quantum dots, small nanoparticles that can absorb light across a broader spectrum. The efficiency is staggering.

If we can scale this technology, we can create solar panels that can generate energy even under the dimmest conditions."

"That's incredible," Nina said, her eyes lighting up. "This could change everything."

"It could," Aldo agreed. "But it's not just about efficiency. This system can be integrated into any surface, rooftops, roadways, even the sides of buildings. We're looking at a completely decentralized energy grid that doesn't rely on fossil fuels or central power plants. This could give countries the energy independence they desperately need."

"But is it ready for implementation?" Nina asked, the urgency in her voice matching Aldo's own sense of pressure.

"Not yet. There are still some kinks to work out," Aldo said, his voice trailing off. He was aware of the enormity of what they were trying to achieve. The energy crisis was global, and the solutions needed to be scalable, practical, and affordable. It wasn't just about creating the technology, it was about making sure the world could actually use it.

Days turned into weeks, and Aldo's team worked tirelessly to refine the new energy system. They encountered setbacks, but each failure brought them closer to a breakthrough. The process was grueling, but Aldo remained focused. The world was watching, and failure wasn't an option.

Meanwhile, the energy crisis was escalating. Blackouts had become routine in some of the world's largest cities, and countries were beginning to experience civil unrest as people grew increasingly desperate for reliable power. The political landscape was shifting, with leaders scrambling to find solutions, but many were still clinging to outdated energy models. Coal and natural gas were dying industries, but they weren't going down without a fight. Powerful corporations, who had invested heavily in fossil fuels, lobbied fiercely to prevent the transition to renewable energy.

MOUNT OF WASTE

They knew that once the world shifted to sustainable energy, their dominance would evaporate.

Aldo and Nina had seen this resistance before. It wasn't just about energy, it was about power, control, and profits. But they also knew that change was inevitable. The question was not whether the world would transition to renewable energy, but how long it would take, and how many would suffer in the process.

On a cold, gray morning, Aldo received a call from a government representative in Kenya. The representative, a woman named Amina, had heard about Aldo's work and was interested in integrating the new solar technology into Kenya's energy infrastructure. Kenya, like many nations, had been struggling with unreliable power. The country had abundant sunlight, but the traditional solar panels had been expensive and inefficient. Amina saw the potential in Aldo's new system. It could be the solution that would elevate Kenya to a new level of energy independence.

Aldo didn't hesitate. "We're ready to partner with you," he said, excited by the prospect of the technology being deployed in a country that was hungry for change. "We'll need to conduct tests and evaluate the grid system, but we can begin the transition right away."

Amina expressed her gratitude, but she also cautioned that the political climate in Kenya was volatile. The opposition party was pushing hard for continued reliance on fossil fuels, and any move away from those sources would be met with fierce resistance. Nevertheless, she was determined to move forward.

"The future of Kenya, and perhaps the entire continent, depends on this," Amina said. "We cannot afford to wait."

Aldo and Nina boarded a flight to Nairobi, Kenya, the next day. They were accompanied by a small team of engineers, scientists, and diplomats who had helped them shape the project.

When they arrived, they were greeted with warmth and optimism, but they also understood the challenges ahead.

Kenya had made strides in renewable energy in recent years, but it still relied heavily on imported fossil fuels. The government had set ambitious targets to move toward a greener future, but old habits and entrenched interests were slow to change. Now, they had a real chance to leapfrog over the traditional energy grid and embrace something revolutionary. It was a risk, but it was a risk worth taking.

Aldo was introduced to the president of Kenya, a pragmatic leader who was skeptical but open-minded. "We've tried to go green before," the president said. "But the technology never lived up to the promises. I need to know that this will work, on a large scale. Our people are counting on us to provide reliable, affordable power."

Aldo understood the president's hesitance. The failure of previous attempts weighed heavily on the government's credibility. But Aldo was confident. "This is different. The technology we've developed isn't just more efficient, it's adaptable. It can be deployed in cities, rural areas, even remote villages. And it's cost-effective."

Nina added, "We've already conducted tests in other regions, and the results are beyond promising. We can provide the resources, the expertise, and the training to make this a success. The people of Kenya, and the world—deserve a future where energy is abundant and sustainable."

The president remained silent for a moment, weighing the options. Finally, he spoke. "I'm willing to take a chance. Let's do it. But we'll need full support from the international community."

It was a breakthrough moment. Kenya was ready to lead the charge in renewable energy, and Aldo and Nina knew that if they could make it work here, they could take the model global.

MOUNT OF WASTE

As Aldo and his team worked alongside Kenyan engineers and policymakers, the first solar panels using the new technology were installed in rural villages and urban areas. Within weeks, the results were clear. Energy production had increased significantly, and the decentralized energy grid allowed for greater flexibility and distribution. Kenya's energy costs dropped, and the country became a shining example of how innovation could drive sustainable growth.

But as Aldo celebrated the success in Kenya, the world around him was in turmoil. The political situation in several major countries was deteriorating. Governments that had relied on fossil fuels were finding it difficult to make the transition to renewable energy. The global economy was faltering, and energy scarcity was becoming a reality. The larger nations, particularly in the West, were pushing back against the renewable energy revolution, fearing it would hurt their economies and industries. Corporate giants, who had built their empires on oil, gas, and coal, launched aggressive campaigns to discredit Aldo's work and prevent the spread of renewable energy technologies.

It was clear that Aldo and Nina had entered a new phase of their struggle. The fight for the future of energy wasn't just a matter of technology, it was a battle for political and economic power. They needed to find a way to ensure that the world's energy transition wasn't stalled by the interests of the few.

As Aldo stared out over the horizon in Nairobi, he realized that the energy crisis was a reflection of a larger battle. It wasn't just about energy, it was about the kind of world humanity would build for itself. Would it be a world of scarcity, greed, and conflict, or a world of abundance, sustainability, and cooperation?

And he knew that whatever the answer was, they had to fight for it.

Chapter 43: A Breakthrough in Waste Technology

The world had reached a tipping point. For years, humanity had turned a blind eye to the environmental cost of overconsumption, and the planet was paying the price. Cities choked on waste, oceans filled with plastic, and landfills grew at an alarming rate, seeping toxic substances into the earth. The waste crisis was no longer just an eyesore, it was a ticking time bomb that threatened to destroy the delicate balance of the planet.

Aldo and his team had fought tirelessly to find solutions, but even the most innovative technologies had not been enough to reverse the damage. Renewable energy was crucial, and their solar advancements were promising, but the key to truly solving the crisis lay in tackling the root cause: the staggering amount of waste humans generated every day. If they could harness waste as a resource, they could solve two problems at once, reducing the waste burden on the planet while generating clean, sustainable energy.

It was in this context that Aldo's revolutionary new invention came to life.

For months, Aldo had been working on a secret project in his lab, surrounded by piles of discarded plastic, metal, and organic matter. His mind was focused on one question: How could he create a machine that could take the endless mountains of waste and convert it into something useful? Something that could not only power the world but also close the loop on waste management, turning trash into treasure.

His idea was simple in theory but complex in execution: a machine that could break down waste at a molecular level, converting it into clean energy with minimal environmental impact. He had spent countless hours studying the principles of

MOUNT OF WASTE

thermodynamics, plasma arc technology, and waste-to-energy processes. He had drawn inspiration from everything, from the combustion engines that powered early industrial machines to the natural processes of decomposition in the earth's ecosystems. But his goal was to take these concepts and push them to the limits of efficiency and sustainability.

The breakthrough came when Aldo discovered a way to combine plasma arc technology with a new catalytic process. Plasma arcs, which were capable of reaching temperatures of over 10,000 degrees Celsius, could break down waste materials at an atomic level, turning them into basic components like hydrogen, carbon monoxide, and carbon dioxide. However, these gases were often dangerous or useless in their raw form.

Aldo's innovation lay in a catalyst he had developed that could transform these byproducts into clean energy. Using a specially designed filtration system, the gases would be separated and refined, with only the cleanest components retained for energy production. The result was a machine that could take nearly any form of waste, plastic, paper, organic matter, even hazardous materials, and convert it into usable energy with near-zero emissions.

The day Aldo first tested the prototype was one of the most intense moments of his career. His team gathered in the lab, waiting for the machine to roar to life. The machine, which Aldo had affectionately called "The Recycler," stood in the center of the room, a towering structure made of reinforced steel, piping, and advanced circuitry. It looked like a fusion of a giant furnace and a power plant, a beast that would either make history or become a monument to failure.

"Are we ready?" Nina asked, her voice filled with a mix of anticipation and nerves.

Aldo nodded. "Let's see if it works."

He pressed the button, and the Recycler's internal systems powered up. A low hum filled the room as the plasma arc ignited, and a brilliant blue light flickered from within the core of the machine. The waste, bags of plastic, metal scraps, food waste, was fed into the system, its components quickly breaking down as the plasma arc did its work.

For a moment, everything went silent. The team held their breath, watching as the machine's systems displayed data on the screen. Then, the moment they had all been waiting for arrived: the Recycler's output began to rise. The system was producing energy.

"We're getting energy," Aldo said in disbelief, his voice trembling with excitement. "It's working."

The data confirmed it. The machine was not only converting waste into usable energy, but it was doing so with an efficiency that far exceeded anything they had anticipated. The energy being generated was clean, sustainable, and most importantly, renewable. The Recycler was the answer they had been searching for, a revolutionary technology that could change the course of human history.

The next few weeks were a blur of excitement and preparation. Aldo and his team fine-tuned the Recycler, optimizing its efficiency and scaling up its capabilities. They conducted tests with different types of waste, plastic, metal, glass, food waste, and even hazardous materials, and the results were consistently impressive. The machine worked on every type of waste, generating clean energy with minimal emissions. The Recycler wasn't just a solution to the waste crisis, it was also a game-changer in the global energy market.

As word of Aldo's invention spread, governments, corporations, and environmental organizations began to take notice. It wasn't long before Aldo was invited to present the Recycler at an international summit on environmental technology, held in Berlin. This was the moment he had been waiting for: the

MOUNT OF WASTE

chance to showcase his invention on the global stage and convince the world that this technology could solve the planet's most pressing problems.

At the summit, Aldo stood before a room full of world leaders, scientists, and industry experts. The tension was palpable. The energy crisis was at its peak, and the world was desperate for solutions. As Aldo took the stage, he could feel the weight of the moment. This wasn't just about presenting a new technology, it was about presenting a vision for a better future.

"Ladies and gentlemen," Aldo began, his voice steady but filled with passion. "What we have here is more than just a machine. It's a lifeline for our planet. The Recycler is a new approach to waste management and energy production. It can take the mountains of waste that we've created over the years, plastic, metal, organic matter, and turn them into clean, renewable energy. It's efficient, scalable, and sustainable. And most importantly, it can be implemented globally."

He paused, allowing the weight of his words to sink in. "We are facing an unprecedented crisis. Our oceans are choked with plastic, our landfills are overflowing, and our energy systems are on the brink of collapse. If we don't act now, the consequences will be catastrophic. But the Recycler offers us hope. It's a solution that can address both our waste problem and our energy crisis at the same time."

Aldo's presentation was met with a mix of skepticism and curiosity. Some of the world's largest energy corporations viewed the Recycler as a threat to their business models. They had invested billions in fossil fuels, and the idea of a clean, waste-to-energy system posed a direct challenge to their profits. But Aldo wasn't deterred. He knew that the world's future depended on making this technology a reality.

After the summit, Aldo and Nina traveled the globe, meeting with leaders, scientists, and activists who were eager to adopt the Recycler. Countries in Africa, Asia, and Latin America, many of which had been hit hardest by the waste crisis, were especially eager to embrace the technology. In Kenya, where Aldo had first made a mark with his renewable energy innovations, the government committed to implementing the Recycler nationwide, turning the country into a leader in waste-to-energy technology.

But even as the Recycler gained traction around the world, Aldo faced opposition from powerful industries that had a vested interest in maintaining the status quo. Corporations that had long profited from waste management, landfills, and energy production lobbied hard against the new technology, using their influence to delay its widespread adoption. They feared that the Recycler would disrupt their business models, and they weren't willing to let go of their power so easily.

Aldo and Nina were undeterred. They knew that the Recycler represented the future of the planet. The world needed to shift away from unsustainable practices, and they were determined to make that happen.

In the months that followed, the Recycler's success spread like wildfire. Cities around the world began to implement the technology, transforming their waste into clean energy. Landfills shrank, pollution levels dropped, and energy costs fell dramatically. The Recycler wasn't just a breakthrough, it was a revolution, changing the way humanity interacted with its environment.

The battle wasn't over. There were still powerful forces trying to stop the progress, and the world's political and economic systems were slow to adapt. But Aldo and Nina were determined to keep pushing forward. The Recycler had proven that the impossible was possible. It was a symbol of what humanity could achieve when it worked together to create a better future.

MOUNT OF WASTE

As Aldo looked out over the skyline of a city powered by the Recycler, he felt a sense of hope that he had never known before. The planet was healing, and the future was brighter than ever. The road ahead would be long and challenging, but for the first time in years, Aldo felt confident that humanity was on the right path.

The Recycler was just the beginning. And together, they would continue to fight for a sustainable, thriving world.

Chapter 44: Fighting Hunger

The world, scarred by the relentless storm and the subsequent collapse of its ecosystems, had entered a dark age of scarcity. Climate change, shifting tectonic plates, and a global waste crisis had decimated agricultural productivity. Soil became poisoned with plastics, toxic chemicals, and ash from the cities that had burned. Ocean currents, once a lifeline for millions of people, were now filled with trash, and fisheries were in decline. Food became a luxury few could afford. Hunger, once a distant issue for the wealthiest parts of the world, was now a pressing reality for billions.

As the years passed since the catastrophic event, Aldo and his team had been focused on combating the waste crisis, but they knew that without addressing the growing hunger problem, their efforts would be futile. A world where people starved to death, surrounded by a mountain of waste and pollution, was one that could never be sustainable. They needed to tackle the dual problems of food scarcity and environmental collapse.

Aldo had already proven that waste could be converted into energy, but now he faced an even greater challenge: food. How could they use the mountains of organic waste to solve a problem as dire as global hunger? The answer lay in the intersection of biotechnology, agriculture, and waste management. If Aldo could develop a way to transform organic waste into nutritious food, it would be a game-changer.

He assembled a team of environmental scientists, biotechnologists, and agricultural experts to tackle the problem. They spent long days brainstorming and experimenting in their lab. After months of testing and refining, they came up with a radical idea: bioengineered food production using organic waste as the base material.

MOUNT OF WASTE

The concept was simple, yet profound. Aldo's team would use organic waste, food scraps, plant debris, and other biodegradable materials, as the foundation for growing food. They would develop a biotechnology solution that could turn waste into nutrient-rich soil, which in turn could support the growth of high-protein, fast-growing crops. These crops could be cultivated in controlled environments, making it possible to grow food where traditional agriculture had failed.

The team's first breakthrough came with a special strain of fungi, which could break down organic waste in a way that allowed it to be transformed into nutrient-rich soil. The fungi acted as an efficient decomposer, breaking down plant matter, food scraps, and even waste from animal products, converting them into valuable organic matter. The result was a rich, fertile substance capable of supporting crop growth. This process not only dealt with waste but also produced a byproduct that could be used for food production.

"We've cracked it," said Dr. Maria Chavez, a biologist who had been working alongside Aldo on the project. "This is it. We can take the organic waste and convert it into nutrient-rich soil for growing food."

But Aldo knew that just turning organic waste into fertile soil wasn't enough. They needed to find a way to grow food quickly and sustainably in the conditions the world was facing. Traditional farming methods were no longer viable in most parts of the world. Crops required too much water, and the soil was too contaminated to support them. So they turned their attention to a more radical approach: vertical farming combined with biotechnological innovation.

In vertical farming, crops were grown in stacked layers, minimizing the use of land while maximizing the amount of food that could be produced in a small space. This method also reduced water consumption, as the water used for the plants was recirculated and purified, making it a far more sustainable solution than traditional farming. But Aldo and his team wanted to go further. They wanted to combine the process of growing food with their innovative approach to waste.

The answer came when they began experimenting with algae. Algae, particularly species like spirulina, had long been recognized as a high-protein, highly nutritious food source. It could be grown quickly, in small spaces, and with minimal water. But growing algae was an energy-intensive process that required specialized facilities and conditions. Aldo saw an opportunity to combine the algae's rapid growth potential with the nutrient-rich soil they had created from organic waste.

By feeding the waste-derived soil to algae in controlled, vertical tanks, they were able to grow the algae in a more energy-efficient manner. This process resulted in algae that was not only high in protein but also rich in other essential nutrients, including vitamins, minerals, and fatty acids. It was the perfect solution to the world's food crisis: a highly nutritious, sustainable, and fast-growing food source that could be cultivated anywhere.

The next challenge was scaling the solution. While the team's laboratory had successfully grown small amounts of algae, they knew that to make a real impact on global hunger, they needed to build large-scale, decentralized production systems that could be deployed around the world. Aldo turned to his network of engineers and architects to design modular, self-sustaining farms that could operate in urban environments and areas where traditional agriculture was no longer possible. These farms would rely on renewable energy sources, like solar and wind power, to reduce their environmental impact and ensure long-term sustainability.

The modular farms were designed to be portable and scalable. They could be shipped to regions in need and set up quickly, without the need for large tracts of arable land. Each farm would consist of multiple vertical tanks filled with algae, surrounded by small-scale agricultural beds where crops could be grown using the nutrient-rich soil created from organic waste. The algae tanks would serve as both a food source and a means of producing biofuels for energy.

As the first pilot project began to take shape in Kenya, the team knew they had something potentially world-changing on their hands. The farm, designed to be self-sufficient and scalable, was constructed in a barren region once ravaged by drought and food scarcity. It was the perfect testing ground for this new approach to food production.

The farm's success exceeded even Aldo's expectations. After just a few weeks, the algae tanks began to produce enough nutritious algae to feed hundreds of people. The soil, enriched with organic waste, supported the growth of fast-growing crops like spinach, kale, and beans. Within months, the farm had transformed a desert landscape into a thriving food production center. Local communities, once plagued by hunger, were now able to grow their own food and feed their families.

Word of the success in Kenya quickly spread, and soon, other regions hit by food insecurity reached out for help. Aldo's team worked tirelessly to establish more farms in Africa, Asia, and Latin America, areas that had been hardest hit by the global food crisis. Each farm was tailored to the unique needs of its environment, taking into account local waste streams and renewable energy resources.

The impact was immediate and profound. The algae farms provided an essential source of nutrition for communities, and the innovative food production system empowered local farmers to regain control of their food security. By using organic waste as a resource, they not only addressed hunger but also helped to reduce the massive piles of waste that continued to accumulate in cities around the world.

As the months went by, the success of the algae-based farms became a beacon of hope in a world that had long since lost its way. The technology was replicated in cities and rural areas alike. Nations began to embrace it as a key part of their environmental and agricultural strategies, understanding that food security could no longer rely on traditional farming alone.

But Aldo knew that the work was far from over. While the algae farms were making a significant impact, the world still faced a massive challenge. As populations continued to grow, so did the demand for food. Aldo believed that the only way to ensure a sustainable future was to continue innovating and scaling these systems, transforming waste into nourishment, not just for today, but for generations to come.

"We've only just begun," Aldo said one evening, gazing out at the vibrant farm in Kenya. "We've proven it's possible. Now, we need to take this technology to every corner of the planet."

His resolve was unwavering. There was still much to be done, much to fight for. But for the first time in a long while, Aldo felt like the future was within reach. Through innovation, collaboration, and determination, they could fight hunger, heal the planet, and create a future where no one was left to starve in a world overflowing with waste.

And that, to him, was a future worth fighting for.

Chapter 45: Attack on the Research Center

The world had been changing, slowly, painfully, but undeniably. Aldo and his team had made remarkable progress in addressing the critical challenges of waste, food security, and environmental collapse. Their innovations were beginning to take root in cities and regions that had once been deemed uninhabitable. But as always, progress came at a cost. The very forces that sought to preserve the status quo, the old powers, entrenched industries, and the corporate giants whose profits were linked to polluting practices, would not go down without a fight.

It had been an unusually quiet morning at Research Center Alpha. The air was crisp, and Aldo sat in his office, looking out at the landscape. Outside, the sunlight filtered through the layers of vertical farms they had built, farms that stood as symbols of hope for a world on the brink of ecological collapse. Inside the lab, scientists were busy refining the latest version of their algae-to-nutrient technology, while engineers worked on scaling the waste-to-energy systems that had begun to change the dynamics of the global power grid.

But as Aldo took a moment of peace, an unexpected call came through his secure line. It was Nina, her voice panicked.

"Aldo, you need to get to the lab. Now," she urged.

He stood up immediately. "What happened?"

"They're here," Nina said, the words barely audible through the phone's crackling connection. "A group of armed men, they've broken in."

Aldo's heart skipped a beat. He knew what this was about. There had been whispers of attacks, of radical groups organizing to sabotage the research that Aldo and his team were spearheading.

The corporations whose interests were threatened by their advancements had made it clear that they would not allow such innovations to disrupt their profits. But Aldo never imagined it would escalate this far.

Within minutes, he was rushing through the facility's corridors, passing rooms filled with researchers who had no idea what was happening outside. He reached the lab, where Nina and the rest of the core team had gathered, barricading themselves inside.

The air was thick with tension.

"They've cut the power to the main gate," Nina said, pacing. "We've secured the research but, "

Before she could finish her sentence, a deafening explosion echoed from outside the facility, sending tremors through the walls. The glass windows shook violently as another blast followed. Aldo instinctively ducked, his mind racing.

"They're trying to get in," he said grimly. "But we can't let them destroy this place. It's our last chance."

The room was silent for a moment as the reality of the situation sank in. The center, which had become a beacon of hope for a dying planet, was now under attack. Aldo turned to his team.

"I've been preparing for this possibility. We have to protect the research," he said, his voice calm but firm. "Nina, start the data backup. We need to ensure that every piece of research, every blueprint, every breakthrough we've made is stored safely offsite. You know the protocol."

Nina nodded, her fingers moving quickly over her console as she initiated the emergency data backup procedure. Aldo turned to the others.

"We can't let them destroy our work," he repeated. "Our research isn't just information, it's a lifeline for humanity. Let's hold them off."

MOUNT OF WASTE

The team split into smaller groups. Some worked on reinforcing the barricades, while others prepared to defend the most valuable sections of the center. Aldo, however, had a different task in mind. He needed to confront the threat head-on. There was no time to wait for law enforcement or military intervention. He had to act fast, using every ounce of ingenuity his team had worked so hard to develop.

"Listen," Aldo said, addressing his team once more. "We have one advantage, this facility is designed to be self-sustaining. We can control the power grid, the water supply, and even the communications network. If we can turn the tide in their favor, we can make the attackers regret ever setting foot in here."

Nina's voice crackled through the comms, "I've initiated the backup, Aldo. It's working. But you should know, they've breached the first gate. They're coming in fast."

Aldo's mind worked at lightning speed. He ran to the control panel, activating the facility's defense mechanisms. They had developed automated systems to secure the perimeter in the event of an emergency, including high-powered floodlights, sound-based deterrents, and thick steel doors that could be locked remotely.

He knew these systems wouldn't be enough to stop determined attackers, but they could slow them down. Every second counted.

Outside, the distant rumble of more explosions echoed in the air. The attackers were relentless, and Aldo knew that every moment they spent on the offensive brought them closer to the heart of the research center. But he wasn't about to let that happen.

"We need to send a message," Aldo muttered to himself as he prepared his next move. He turned to a small team of engineers who had been tasked with developing a new communication system to spread their research globally.

"Aldo?" one of the engineers asked, his voice filled with uncertainty. "What are we going to do?"

"We're going to broadcast live," Aldo said, a determined glint in his eyes. "We're going to show the world what's happening here. We have nothing to hide."

The engineer's eyes widened. "You want to stream this?"

"Exactly," Aldo replied. "If these corporate-backed groups want to destroy us, let them know that the world is watching."

The team set up the equipment, connecting the center's emergency communication system to a satellite uplink. Within minutes, they were broadcasting live to millions of people around the world.

"People need to know what's at stake," Aldo said, his voice steady but urgent as the camera zoomed in on his face. "We've created something that can save this planet, waste-to-energy technology, algae farms, sustainable food production systems. All of this is being attacked because it threatens the profits of the powerful few."

He paused, his eyes scanning the room where the team continued to work tirelessly to protect the facility.

"The people attacking us want to keep the world dependent on polluting, unsustainable practices. They'll stop at nothing to preserve their control over energy, food, and resources. But they cannot stop what we've started. This is bigger than any one company, bigger than any one person. This is about the future of our planet, and we will fight for it."

His voice grew stronger with each word. "To those of you watching, I say this: stand with us. Stand with the Earth. We will not back down."

The live broadcast sent shockwaves across the globe. The message resonated with millions who had been following Aldo's work from the beginning. Support poured in from activists, environmentalists, and ordinary citizens who believed in the mission. But the battle was far from over.

MOUNT OF WASTE

The attackers were now inside the compound, and Aldo's team was forced to retreat further into the heart of the facility. They had set up a secure server room that housed the most critical data, and it was their last line of defense. Aldo, Nina, and the others rushed to the room, locking the door behind them.

"We can hold them here," Nina said, her face tense. "But we can't keep this up for long."

Aldo glanced at the server racks that filled the room. "We don't need long. The backup is safe, and the world knows the truth now. They won't be able to destroy this."

As they fortified their position, the team monitored the security feeds, watching as the attackers advanced deeper into the compound. But Aldo's confidence didn't waver. The world was watching, and every move they made was being broadcasted. The attackers knew it too. With each passing moment, the pressure on them increased.

Eventually, the sound of boots pounding against the hallways grew faint. The attackers had reached the core, but it seemed they had underestimated the resolve of Aldo and his team. Soon, the room grew quiet. A sense of calm began to settle over them as they continued to defend the facility.

Aldo's eyes narrowed. This fight was not over—but they had won the first battle. "We've survived the storm," Aldo said quietly to Nina. "Now, let's finish what we started."

And they would.

Chapter 46: Introducing Technology on the Ground

The early morning sun cast a golden hue over the barren landscape. A thick layer of dust hung in the air, remnants of a world that had once thrived and now seemed to be teetering on the edge of destruction. The once-bustling city of Hafford was now a shell of its former self. Buildings lay in ruins, and the streets were littered with the remnants of the past, a constant reminder of the devastating storm that had ravaged the planet.

Aldo stood on the edge of the city, surveying the damage. But his eyes were not filled with despair. Instead, they shone with determination. It was here, amidst the rubble and the ruin, that the first trial of their revolutionary waste management technology would take place. Here, they would prove that innovation could rebuild what had been lost.

Beside him stood Nina, her face marked by the stress of the ongoing struggle but resolute. She had been by his side from the beginning, pushing for solutions, tirelessly working to make their dream a reality. This was their moment to make a tangible difference in the world.

"You ready for this?" Nina asked, her voice laced with a mixture of anticipation and anxiety.

Aldo nodded, his mind racing through the plans that had been months in the making. "We've come a long way, Nina. This is it. If we can make this work here, it will change everything."

The team was already at work, setting up their equipment. They had brought with them the technology they had spent years perfecting, machines capable of converting waste into usable energy and sustainable building materials. It wasn't just about cleaning up the environment; it was about giving people the tools to rebuild their lives in a way that was environmentally responsible and sustainable.

Aldo's voice carried across the busy site as he addressed his team. "We're not just fixing a problem; we're creating a new way of living. Let's make sure this works. For the people here, and for the future."

Hafford had been chosen as the first city for their test because it was one of the most devastated areas in the aftermath of the storm. Entire neighborhoods had been buried under mountains of debris, and the population had been struggling to survive. Many had fled, but those who remained were desperate for a way to rebuild their community.

The technology they had brought could process the vast quantities of waste that had accumulated, plastic, metal, paper, and organic refuse, and turn it into clean energy or reusable materials. There were no longer any excuses for leaving cities like Hafford to rot in the aftermath of the disaster. Aldo was determined that his team would not let this opportunity slip away.

As they began setting up the machines, Aldo felt a wave of uncertainty. The scale of the task ahead was immense. The global system of waste management had been broken long before the storm had struck. And now, in the wake of that cataclysm, the challenge of rebuilding was daunting. But this was not just about technology. This was about people. It was about giving them hope again.

Soon, the machines were humming to life. A team of local volunteers, most of them from the surviving communities, had gathered to watch the process unfold. These people had witnessed firsthand the devastating effects of the storm, and many of them had been living in makeshift shelters for months. Some had lost family members, others had seen their homes reduced to ash. Yet, they came with an unshakable belief that something could be done to save their city.

The process was straightforward. First, waste was collected from the piles of rubble that littered the streets. The team used a combination of robotics and manual labor to sort and break down the debris into smaller, manageable pieces. This was the most labor-intensive part of the process, but it was essential to ensure that only the materials that could be repurposed were used. Non-recyclable waste, such as toxic chemicals, was separated and disposed of safely.

Next, the materials were fed into the core of the waste-processing machine, a massive device that Aldo had designed. The machine was equipped with advanced pyrolysis technology, which broke down the waste at extremely high temperatures, converting it into biofuel and other usable forms of energy. Simultaneously, any organic waste was processed into compost, which could be used to enrich the soil that had been depleted by years of environmental degradation.

As the machine roared to life, the first batch of waste was processed. Aldo's heart raced as he watched the system in action. The biofuel tank began to fill with clean energy, and the compost started to pile up, ready to be distributed to local farms. The waste that had once been a burden to the community was now being transformed into something useful, something life-giving.

Nina, watching from the control station, looked over at Aldo with a proud smile. "It's working," she said, her voice filled with relief.

Aldo nodded, but his mind was already racing ahead. This was just the beginning. The real challenge lay in how to scale this technology to other cities, to entire countries, and ultimately, to the world. But he couldn't help but feel a sense of accomplishment. For the first time in a long while, the future didn't look as bleak as it once had.

But even as they celebrated the success of the first test, Aldo knew there were hurdles to overcome. The road to recovery would not be easy. The world had grown accustomed to a certain way of doing things, and changing that mindset would require more than just technology, it would require a shift in how people thought about waste, consumption, and the environment.

As the days passed, Aldo and his team continued to work closely with the local community. They showed the residents how to use the compost to grow food, how to power their homes with the biofuel produced by the waste-processing machine, and how to build with the sustainable materials they had created. Slowly, the city began to come back to life. Small shops reopened, people began to rebuild their homes, and the once-desolate streets started to show signs of vitality.

One afternoon, as Aldo was walking through the streets of Hafford, a young mother approached him. She was holding her child in her arms, her face lined with exhaustion, but there was something else in her eyes, hope.

"Thank you," she said, her voice soft but filled with emotion. "We didn't know how we were going to survive. But now... now we have a chance."

Aldo smiled, feeling a lump form in his throat. This was why he had fought so hard, why he had pushed through the endless setbacks and struggles. For moments like this.

But as he looked around, he knew that Hafford was only the beginning. The technology that had worked here could work in other cities, other countries. If they could replicate their success in Hafford on a global scale, they could begin to reverse the damage that had been done to the planet. They could heal the Earth, one city at a time.

That evening, Aldo gathered his team for a debriefing session. The results of their first test had exceeded expectations, but they had to plan their next steps carefully. They could not afford to make mistakes. The world was watching, and the stakes had never been higher.

"We've shown that it works," Aldo said, looking at each of his team members. "Now we need to scale it. We need to take what we've learned here and apply it to other cities, other communities. We need to prove that this is the future, one where waste is no longer a burden, but a resource."

The team nodded in agreement. There was a renewed sense of purpose in the room. They had made a breakthrough, but the journey was far from over.

Aldo paused, looking out the window at the city they had helped to revive. "This is just the beginning. If we can make this work here, we can make it work everywhere."

And with that, the real work began.

As they continued to implement their technology across the world, Aldo and his team knew that the battle for the planet's future was far from over. But for the first time in years, they could see a path forward, a path where innovation, cooperation, and determination could pave the way for a new, sustainable future. And no matter how difficult the road ahead, they would not give up. The Earth depended on it.

Chapter 47: The Power of Collective Spirit

The winds had begun to shift. It wasn't just the change in the atmosphere but a shift within the hearts of the people. There was something almost palpable in the air as Aldo walked through the streets of Hafford, where once there had been hopelessness, now there was something else, unity. The community, which had once been fragmented by despair, was now bound together by a shared purpose, a single goal: survival, renewal, and a future where they no longer relied on the systems that had caused their downfall.

It was early morning, and the first rays of light stretched across the horizon, casting a soft glow on the newly rebuilt structures, many of them made from the sustainable materials that Aldo and his team had pioneered. The streets, once littered with debris and destruction, were now bustling with activity. People were gathering, working together to create something new, something sustainable.

Aldo could see the change in the way they looked at the world. It wasn't just about survival anymore. It was about something deeper, something far more powerful. It was the realization that they were no longer helpless victims of a broken system, but active participants in its reconstruction.

"You can see it, can't you?" Nina's voice broke through his thoughts. She had been walking beside him for a while, and her eyes reflected the same sense of accomplishment that he felt, though she was always focused on the next challenge.

Aldo nodded. "I can feel it. The people here, they're not just rebuilding their homes. They're rebuilding their sense of self. Their faith in the future. We've given them the tools, but they've taken it and made it their own."

They watched as a group of local farmers gathered around a machine that Aldo and his team had set up to turn organic waste into compost. The farmers, some of whom had never even seen a machine like it before, were now exchanging ideas, learning how to better use the compost to enrich their soil and boost crop yields. There was an excitement in their voices, a joy that Aldo hadn't heard in years.

"That's the power of collective spirit," Nina said softly. "They're not just using the technology. They're shaping it to fit their needs, making it part of their daily lives."

Aldo watched the farmers with a sense of pride. This was not just a technological breakthrough; this was a cultural shift. They were no longer just passive recipients of aid. They were active participants in the renewal of their city, their community, their world. The boundaries between the people and the technology had blurred. It had become a part of their identity.

He could see the same shift happening elsewhere. The women who had once been forced to rely on foreign aid now ran local markets that were powered by the energy generated from the recycled waste. The children, who had spent their early years in makeshift shelters, were now learning how to create and build with sustainable materials, their innocence replaced by a sense of purpose that few could have imagined just months ago.

Aldo and Nina had always known that the key to lasting change lay not in technology alone, but in the human spirit, the collective will to adapt, to survive, and to make the world better for future generations. And they were witnessing it now, in real time, unfolding before their eyes.

"I never thought I'd see something like this," Nina said, her voice thick with emotion. "It's not just the technology, it's the people. They're changing the way they think about the world.

MOUNT OF WASTE

They're not just accepting what's been handed to them, they're creating something better."

Aldo took a deep breath, looking out over the city. It wasn't perfect, but it was alive again. The smell of freshly tilled soil mixed with the faint hum of wind turbines in the distance, generating clean energy for the community. People were building homes from the new materials they had produced, homes that were not only structurally sound but environmentally responsible. The waste that had once threatened to swallow them was now being repurposed, used to power the city, to grow food, to create livelihoods.

"We can't stop here," Aldo said quietly. "This is just one city. We need to scale this. We need to spread this spirit of unity, this power of collaboration, across the globe."

Nina smiled. "We will. One community at a time."

They continued to walk through the streets, meeting with locals, answering questions, and helping to guide them as they implemented new techniques. Everywhere they went, they were met with open arms. People were no longer just waiting for someone to save them. They were rolling up their sleeves and getting to work. The once-cynical attitudes had been replaced by a sense of shared responsibility.

In one corner of the city, Aldo saw a group of young people working together to construct a new playground made entirely from repurposed plastic waste. The idea had been proposed by one of the local teenagers, and with guidance from Aldo's team, it had become a reality. The once-hollow streets now echoed with the laughter of children who were experiencing a world that was different from the one they had been born into. A world where waste didn't exist to destroy their future, but to build a better one.

Aldo approached the group of teenagers, his heart swelling with pride. "You did this?" he asked, his voice filled with admiration.

The girl who had spearheaded the project nodded enthusiastically. "We did. We had some help from the machines, but it was our idea. We're going to make this city a place where we don't have to worry about what's going to happen to our world. We're going to fix it ourselves."

Her words struck Aldo deeply. This was it, the essence of the change they had been fighting for. It wasn't about rescuing a generation, it was about empowering it to rescue itself. The technology was a tool, but the true force behind it was the determination of the people who now wielded it.

Later that afternoon, Aldo gathered the community leaders in a local meeting hall. These were the people who had been at the forefront of the recovery effort, teachers, farmers, shopkeepers, and engineers. They had all contributed in different ways, but now they needed to come together to formalize their next steps.

As Aldo looked around the room, he could see the same spark in their eyes that he had seen in the teenagers earlier. They were no longer just passive recipients of change. They were the change.

"I know we've come a long way," Aldo began, his voice steady but full of conviction. "But this is just the beginning. We've shown that it's possible to turn things around, to create something better. But it's not enough to do it here, in Hafford. We need to spread this. We need to build a network of communities, all working together to change the way we live, the way we interact with the Earth."

He paused, allowing his words to settle in. "You're the ones who have made this possible. The people here have rebuilt this city. They've shown the world that it's possible to create a sustainable, resilient future. Now it's up to us to make sure that this spirit of unity spreads beyond these walls."

MOUNT OF WASTE

The room was silent for a moment, and then one of the older leaders, a woman named Miriam who had been a key figure in the recovery effort, stood up.

"We're ready," she said, her voice filled with determination. "We've seen the change, and we know what needs to be done. We've been working together, and we'll continue working together. We'll spread the word, share what we've learned, and teach others to do the same."

Her words were met with nods of agreement. The community was no longer just a collection of individuals, it was a force. And together, they could take on the world.

Over the next few weeks, Aldo and his team worked with the community leaders to establish a sustainable model for recovery, one that could be replicated in cities across the globe. They began developing educational programs, providing training in sustainable farming, energy production, and waste management. The spirit of collaboration that had taken root in Hafford began to spread, as neighboring towns and cities saw the success of the project and began to reach out for help.

By the end of the month, Aldo's team had trained dozens of local leaders, who in turn began organizing their own communities to implement the same sustainable practices. The ripple effect was beginning.

And as Aldo and Nina stood together, watching yet another group of volunteers prepare to distribute compost to local farms, Aldo felt a deep sense of fulfillment. This wasn't just about technology; it was about building a movement, a movement that transcended borders and governments. A movement rooted in the power of collective spirit, where every individual had a role to play, and together, they could rebuild the world.

The storm had come and gone, but now, in the wake of that destruction, a new world was being born, one where unity, innovation, and resilience would be the cornerstones of the future. And Aldo knew that this was only the beginning.

Chapter 48: Rebuilding the World

The dawn of a new era had arrived.

Aldo sat at the head of the table in a newly established command center, surrounded by a team of experts, activists, and leaders from all corners of the world. The center, located in what was once a decimated urban area, was now a symbol of hope, a headquarters for their vision of rebuilding a greener and more sustainable world. Outside the windows, the city hummed with life, the streets lined with solar panels, vertical gardens, and small-scale waste-to-energy plants. It was a city transformed, a prototype for what was to come.

"This is it," Aldo said, his voice calm yet filled with determination. "This is where we begin to shape the future. Where we take the lessons we've learned from the past and ensure they're not forgotten. We have one chance to get this right, and this time, we're doing it together."

Nina, standing beside him, glanced around the room at the diverse faces, people from all walks of life, united in their mission. They had all been affected by the global crisis in some way. Some had lost loved ones to the storm, some had seen their communities torn apart, but all of them shared the same goal: to rebuild the world, not just for survival, but for a future that was more harmonious with the Earth.

"We're not just rebuilding cities or economies," Nina spoke up, her voice strong, echoing Aldo's words. "We're rebuilding trust. We're rebuilding the relationship between humanity and nature. And it starts here, with each and every one of us."

The group nodded in agreement, as they began to outline the first steps of their ambitious plan. But this wouldn't be easy. The challenges they faced were not only technological; they were political, social, and deeply entrenched in the fabric of society. For decades, the world had grown accustomed to waste, pollution, and unsustainable growth. To change that mindset, on a global scale, would require a monumental effort.

Aldo pulled up a digital map on the screen in front of him, showing the world's most affected areas: regions ravaged by floods, droughts, and rising sea levels. "We need to target these regions first," he said. "The recovery efforts must start where the damage is most severe. From there, we can create a blueprint for the rest of the world."

But the map also revealed something more promising: small pockets of recovery. Cities that had implemented sustainable practices, rural communities that were thriving off of renewable energy, and places where waste had been repurposed into useful resources. These were the models they could use to inspire others, to show that a better world was possible if people worked together.

"We need to ensure that the recovery is inclusive," said a new voice at the table. It was Hassan, an economist from the Middle East who had worked with Aldo's team on the financial implications of their projects. "We can't just focus on the wealthy nations or the powerful corporations. We need to involve every community, from the smallest villages to the largest cities. Otherwise, we risk leaving entire populations behind."

Aldo smiled, grateful for Hassan's insight. "Exactly. We've seen it happen before, when crises arise, the poorest suffer the most. But when solutions come, they often bypass them. This time, we make sure everyone is part of the solution."

Aldo had always believed in the power of collaboration, but what they were discussing now was something on an entirely different scale. The plan they were creating would require not just the cooperation of governments, but of citizens, corporations, scientists, and activists. It would require the mobilization of resources on a global scale, and above all, it would require time and patience. There was no turning back from the path they had chosen, but every step forward would be a challenge.

Nina, standing by Aldo's side, added, "We can't just focus on rebuilding physical infrastructure. We also need to rebuild systems. The economic system, the political system, the education system. Everything needs to change if we're going to create a sustainable world. We need to shift away from short-term profit and focus on long-term well-being."

As the discussion continued, Aldo's mind raced with possibilities. They had already seen what was possible in the smaller cities and communities they had worked with. He had witnessed people rising above their circumstances, overcoming obstacles that had once seemed insurmountable. They had learned to use the technology Aldo's team had developed, to repurpose waste, and to create self-sustaining communities.

But this was bigger. Much bigger. Aldo's dream wasn't just for pockets of success, it was for a global transformation. A world where renewable energy was the norm, where waste was seen as a resource, and where environmental protection was central to every decision made.

"We need to focus on four key areas," Aldo said, outlining the plan on the digital board. "First: waste management. We need to continue refining the technologies that can turn waste into usable resources. From energy production to construction materials, we can repurpose what was once discarded. Second: agriculture. We've seen that organic waste can be transformed into food. We can scale that and feed the world, without the need for harmful pesticides and fertilizers."

"Third: energy," Nina added. "Renewable sources like solar, wind, and hydro are key to reducing dependence on fossil fuels. We need to make these technologies accessible to everyone, everywhere. And finally: education. We need to teach future generations how to live sustainably and to respect the Earth."

Their eyes met across the table, and in that brief moment, Aldo saw the weight of what they were undertaking. They weren't just building a new world—they were crafting a new paradigm, one that would ripple across generations.

Over the next few months, the team worked tirelessly to bring their plan to life. They created task forces to address each of the four key areas, working closely with local leaders, experts, and organizations around the world. They began designing a global network of sustainable cities, built on the principles of waste reduction, renewable energy, and ecological balance. These cities would be models for the future, places where innovation and sustainability thrived hand in hand.

One of the first steps was to convene a global summit, bringing together world leaders, scientists, and activists to discuss the path forward. Aldo and Nina knew that this summit would be a pivotal moment in the history of the planet. It would be their chance to present their vision on the world stage, to convince governments to invest in green infrastructure, to fund renewable energy projects, and to adopt policies that prioritized long-term environmental health over short-term profit.

But Aldo knew that the challenges they faced went beyond technology or policy. They would need to shift the way people thought about the world. The battle was not just against corporate interests or political corruption, it was against the ingrained habits of humanity itself. People had become so used to their unsustainable lifestyles that it would take an effort of monumental proportions to convince them to change.

That's when Aldo turned to an idea he had been mulling over for some time. If they were going to change the world, they needed to do more than just present facts, they needed to inspire. And to do that, they would need a new kind of storytelling.

"We need to create a global campaign," Aldo said to his team. "Not just about the science and the technology, but about the people. About the stories of individuals and communities who are already embracing this new way of life. We need to show the world that this isn't just an abstract concept, it's happening right now, and it's working."

Nina nodded, her eyes lighting up at the idea. "We'll tell the stories of those who are making a difference, and show how they're transforming their communities. We need to make this movement personal. People need to feel connected to it."

And so, the team set to work, gathering stories from every corner of the world. They featured communities in Africa that were transforming deserts into fertile farmland, cities in Asia that had transitioned to 100% renewable energy, and families in South America that were living off the waste they produced. These stories would be the heart of the campaign, showing the world that sustainability was not a distant dream, it was already happening, in real time.

As the summit approached, Aldo and his team prepared to present their vision to the world. They had worked hard to craft a plan that was not just feasible, but necessary. It was a blueprint for the future, a future where the Earth was respected, where waste was no longer a burden, and where the well-being of all life was prioritized over profits.

The world was watching. And it was time for Aldo, Nina, and their team to show them that it was possible to rebuild the world, piece by piece, with unity, innovation, and a commitment to sustainability.

DAYAT SURYANA

The journey was far from over. But Aldo knew that they had taken the first step, together. And together, they would rebuild the world.

Chapter 49: Global Uprising

The storm had been brewing for years, but now it was here.

Aldo stared at the screen in disbelief, his pulse quickening as the news flashed in front of him. In cities across the world, protests had erupted into violent uprisings. The people who had once been hopeful were now filled with anger, their dreams shattered by the rapid changes they couldn't keep up with. The movement that had once inspired millions had now become a battleground between progress and resistance.

"Global Uprising: Protests Sweep Across Nations," the headline read. Images of burning barricades, tear gas clouds, and thousands of demonstrators flooded the screen.

Nina walked into the room, her face pale as she read over Aldo's shoulder. She clenched her fists, frustration and fear seizing her all at once.

"It was only a matter of time, I suppose," Nina said quietly. "Not everyone is going to embrace change this fast. But I didn't expect this, people are desperate. And desperation breeds chaos."

Aldo leaned back in his chair, taking in the gravity of the situation. The changes they had worked so hard to bring about were undeniable: cities were being rebuilt with sustainable practices, renewable energy was slowly becoming the global standard, and the waste-to-energy systems they had pioneered were showing promise. Yet, as the world began to shift toward a new, greener future, it was clear that not everyone was ready to move forward.

In the aftermath of the global disaster, entire industries had collapsed. Fossil fuel giants, agricultural monopolies, and global manufacturing companies had seen their profits plummet, and in their wake, millions of workers had lost their jobs. As governments scrambled to address the environmental collapse, many of these displaced workers had turned to radical groups for support. These groups, some fueled by nationalism, others by fear of losing their livelihoods, had now mobilized into a force determined to undo the progress that had been made.

"We knew the transition wouldn't be easy," Aldo muttered. "But I didn't think we'd be facing armed resistance."

Nina nodded grimly. "These groups feel like they've been abandoned. While we were building the future, they were left behind. Some have resorted to violence to get their voices heard. And now they're organizing globally, spreading misinformation, attacking infrastructure, and creating chaos in cities where we've made the most progress."

Aldo rubbed his temples, the weight of their mission growing heavier with each passing moment. They were caught between two worlds: one where progress was unstoppable, and another where the past clung to power through fear and destruction.

"We can't allow this to spiral out of control," Aldo said finally, his voice firm. "We've seen how fragile society is in the face of change. We need to act quickly, but with care. This isn't just a fight for the future of the planet, it's a fight for the hearts and minds of people who have been left in the dark. We can't afford to alienate them any further."

The room was silent for a moment as his words sank in. The rebellion wasn't just about rejecting new technology or sustainability, it was a rejection of being left behind, of feeling powerless. Aldo knew that their path forward could not ignore the suffering of those who had been displaced by the green revolution. If they were to succeed, they had to find a way to address the root of the problem, displacement, fear, and inequality, before they could hope to maintain peace and stability.

Nina broke the silence. "We need to find a way to make the transition smoother. Not just for the environment, but for the people who are being left behind. They need to see that we are building a future for everyone, not just the privileged few who can adapt to the new world."

Aldo nodded in agreement. "I've been thinking about this for a while. It's not enough to just implement the technology and infrastructure, we need to integrate displaced workers into the process. There are thousands of people who know how to build, how to work with machinery, how to grow food. They might not be experts in renewable energy or waste management, but they have the skills we need."

"We need to offer them training," Nina said. "Provide new opportunities for them to be part of the green economy. We can't just tell them to adapt, we have to help them do it."

Aldo stood up, pacing the room. The solution wasn't going to be easy, but it was necessary. If they didn't act fast, they risked losing everything they had worked for.

"Let's set up a global initiative," Aldo said, his mind working quickly. "A program that offers retraining for those affected by the transition. We can provide resources, workshops, and subsidies to help people move into the green economy. In exchange, they can be part of the solution, helping to build renewable energy plants, working in sustainable agriculture, and contributing to waste management systems."

Nina nodded, her expression determined. "We can't forget about the communities that have been left behind. These protests are just the beginning. If we don't act now, we risk seeing full-blown revolutions."

Aldo looked out the window, the city below still reeling from the recent violence. There was no turning back now, but the path forward was murky. He could feel the tension in the air, the fear and anger of the disenfranchised rising like a storm.

"Let's mobilize," Aldo said. "We'll start by reaching out to the leaders in these communities, offer them a way to bring their people back to the table. It's time for a new kind of diplomacy. One that doesn't rely on politics, but on cooperation and mutual benefit."

For the next few days, Aldo, Nina, and their team worked around the clock, preparing the groundwork for their new initiative. They reached out to global leaders, environmental organizations, and union representatives, all while carefully monitoring the escalating protests. The unrest had spread to every corner of the globe, but it was particularly fierce in regions that had relied on industries now deemed unsustainable.

They organized meetings in conflict zones, bringing together local leaders and representatives from grassroots movements. There was a palpable sense of mistrust in the air, many felt that the green revolution had left them behind, and they were unwilling to accept solutions that came from those they considered responsible for their suffering. But Aldo and Nina were determined. They knew that the future of the world rested on their ability to unite divided factions.

"Let's not just talk about solutions," Aldo said at one of the meetings, his voice calm but insistent. "Let's create them together. We can't afford to leave anyone behind. We're all in this together, and only together will we survive."

It was slow work, and the road to reconciliation was fraught with tension. But the more Aldo and Nina listened to the stories of those affected by the revolution, the more they understood the magnitude of the task before them. This wasn't just about environmental solutions, it was about restoring dignity, offering hope, and providing a path forward for those who had been marginalized.

Meanwhile, the violence continued to escalate. Groups of rebels, some supported by powerful corporations, were targeting the newly established green cities, launching cyberattacks, and sabotaging renewable energy facilities. They were desperate to hold onto the old ways, unwilling to accept that their industries, built on fossil fuels and exploitation,vwere now obsolete.

It wasn't just a battle of ideas anymore, it was a battle for survival.

Aldo knew that the real work was just beginning. The rebellion was not just a challenge, it was an opportunity. An opportunity to forge a new kind of society, one that would not only survive but thrive in the face of adversity. They had already proven that change was possible, but now they had to prove that unity was too.

The weeks that followed were intense. The protests continued, but Aldo and his team pressed forward with their initiative. They established training centers across the world, focusing on reskilling displaced workers and giving them the tools they needed to thrive in the green economy. They partnered with local businesses and organizations to create new job opportunities, showing people that the future was not just something to fear, it was something they could build together.

And slowly, very slowly, the tides began to turn.

The protests began to subside as communities saw the benefits of their involvement in the new economy. People who had once been suspicious of the green revolution now became its greatest advocates. The rebellions didn't disappear overnight, but they were replaced by dialogues, discussions about how to build a future that worked for everyone.

The global uprising had been a wake-up call. It had shown Aldo and his team that no change could ever be imposed without understanding the deep, underlying fears that drove resistance. But it had also given them the chance to prove that the path forward was not one of division, but of collective action.

And as Aldo watched the first rays of dawn light up the horizon, he felt a sense of cautious hope. The struggle was far from over, but the world was on the right path. Together, they could rebuild, together, they could heal the Earth.

Chapter 50: The People's Movement

The air hummed with anticipation. What had once been a distant ideal, something abstract and unattainable, was now becoming a tangible force, a global movement, ignited by the passionate voices of ordinary people. It was no longer just the scientists, activists, or politicians pushing for change. Now, every person who had witnessed the devastation, every soul who had suffered the consequences of environmental neglect, was rallying for the future. The time had come for a true revolution, a revolution of the people, by the people, for the planet.

Aldo stood on the balcony of their newly established headquarters in one of the newly rebuilt cities, gazing out at the crowd gathering in the streets below. From all corners of the Earth, people were united by a common goal: to restore the planet and build a sustainable future for all. The movement, once a small coalition of activists, had grown into an unstoppable wave that transcended borders and barriers.

"We're witnessing the beginning of something extraordinary," Nina said, her voice filled with awe as she joined him at the balcony. She, too, could feel the shift in the air, the palpable energy that surged through the crowds below. "People are no longer just protesting. They're organizing. They're taking ownership of the future."

It had been years since the great disaster had devastated the world, but now the signs of hope were everywhere. The cities that had once been on the brink of collapse were slowly rebuilding. New technologies were being integrated into every facet of life, and renewable energy had become the norm. The global movement Aldo and Nina had fought so hard to nurture was gaining momentum, and it was clear that the foundation for a new world had been laid.

But it wasn't just the technology or the solutions they had developed that was driving this change. It was the people. People who had witnessed the horrors of the old world, people who had been left behind in the wake of technological advancements, people who had once felt powerless were now standing up, demanding a voice.

"This isn't just about us anymore," Aldo said, his tone resolute. "This is about the collective will of humanity. The change isn't top-down, it's grassroots, organic, and it's everywhere."

The movement had taken on many forms. In every major city, people had formed local chapters to spread the message of sustainability, environmental consciousness, and social equity. The digital platforms that had once been used to spread misinformation and fear were now being used to share knowledge, strategies, and success stories. From community gardens to solar-powered neighborhoods, local action was transforming the world, one small step at a time.

The heart of the movement was a call for justice—not just environmental justice, but economic and social justice as well. People were recognizing that the same systems that had caused environmental collapse were also responsible for inequality, exploitation, and division. The people who had been most affected by the environmental crisis were now the ones leading the charge for change.

In Africa, communities that had long been dependent on deforestation for fuel were now learning how to cultivate sustainable energy sources. In Latin America, indigenous groups who had been on the frontlines of environmental preservation for centuries were now forging alliances with global environmental activists. In Asia, former factory workers who had lost their jobs to the collapsing industries of the old world were now leading the way in sustainable farming and green technology.

MOUNT OF WASTE

"People are realizing that we can't keep living the way we did before," Nina continued, her gaze fixed on the masses below. "The world they want is one where they're not just surviving, but thriving. And it's not just for them, it's for their children, their communities, the Earth."

Aldo nodded, his eyes scanning the crowd. He could see it in their faces, the hope, the determination, the knowledge that change was possible, that it was happening. The people who had once been the victims of a broken system were now the architects of the new world.

"We've created something powerful," Aldo said. "But this is just the beginning. If we're going to truly change the world, we need to do more than just offer solutions. We need to empower these communities. They need to see that they have the tools, the knowledge, and the ability to create the world they want to live in."

As the movement grew, so did the challenges. There were still those who resisted change, corporations clinging to old methods, political leaders afraid of losing power, and communities who felt alienated by the rapid changes. But the people's movement was not a fleeting wave, it was a sustained, coordinated effort that refused to be silenced.

The media, once a tool of manipulation for the powerful, had become an ally to the people. Grassroots journalists and independent news outlets now covered the stories of those who were succeeding with sustainable practices. It wasn't just about technological innovation anymore, it was about the human element, the stories of real people working together to create something better.

"The media has become a weapon for the people," Nina remarked one evening, as they watched a documentary on the success of a local community in the Andes, who had transformed their arid land into a thriving hub of greenhouses and sustainable agriculture. "This is more than just a story, it's a movement that's spreading across the world. And the best part is, it's not just about one place, it's happening everywhere."

Aldo leaned back in his chair, a tired but contented smile on his face. "When I first started, I never imagined something like this. I thought we'd be fighting against corporations and governments forever. But now, the people are the ones fighting for change. And they're winning."

The movement had grown into a global force, but Aldo and Nina knew that they couldn't let up. The old systems of power would not go down without a fight. The corporations that had once controlled the world's resources, the governments that had been complicit in environmental destruction, were now seeing their power wane. They would try to regain control, to discredit the people's movement, to tear apart the progress that had been made.

But Aldo had confidence in the people. He knew that when ordinary people came together with a common purpose, they could overcome any challenge.

"These people will not be silenced," he said, his voice firm. "The power is with them now. We've shown them that it's possible to change the world. And together, we will build a future that's sustainable, just, and equal for all."

As the movement gained ground, Aldo and Nina traveled the world, visiting cities, communities, and organizations that were leading the charge. They spoke at conferences, organized workshops, and participated in global summits. They met with leaders, activists, and everyday people who were making a difference.

One day, as they visited a rural village in Southeast Asia, they were greeted by a group of farmers who had turned their once barren land into a thriving green oasis. The farmers had partnered with local scientists to develop sustainable farming methods that not only provided food for their community but also regenerated the soil and protected the local ecosystem.

"We used to depend on chemicals and fertilizers," one of the farmers said, his face beaming with pride. "But now, we use compost, we work with nature, not against it. And our crops are healthier, our soil is richer, and our water is cleaner."

The success stories like these were spreading like wildfire, and they were changing the narrative. They were showing the world that sustainability wasn't just a lofty ideal, it was achievable, practical, and essential for the survival of humanity.

"This is what it's all about," Nina said, her voice filled with emotion as she watched the farmers work. "These are the people who are making the change happen. Not politicians, not corporations, just people like them, working together to restore the Earth."

Back in the cities, the movement was reaching its peak. Large-scale protests had turned into peaceful demonstrations, with millions of people taking to the streets not to demand change but to celebrate the progress that had been made. The streets were filled with signs that read, "Our Future, Our Planet," "We Are the Change," and "Together for the Earth."

It was a moment of unprecedented unity, a global acknowledgment that the world was heading in a new direction. The challenges were far from over, but the people had shown that they could not be stopped. Together, they had risen from the ashes of environmental collapse to build a future where sustainability, equality, and justice were the cornerstones of society.

Aldo and Nina stood once again on the balcony, watching the crowds below. They had been at the forefront of this revolution, but it was the people who had truly made it happen. And as they looked out at the sea of faces, old and young, rich and poor, from every corner of the Earth, they knew that the work was far from over.

But the movement was unstoppable now. The people had spoken, and their voices would echo through history.

"Together, we can rebuild," Aldo said softly, his voice full of hope. "Together, we will save this planet."

And with that, the movement that had begun as a whisper in the dark was now a roaring wave of change, a force that would reshape the world for generations to come.

Chapter 51: A New Dawn in the Western World

The world had turned a corner. What had once seemed like an insurmountable crisis was now becoming the catalyst for an unprecedented transformation. The environmental movement, sparked by disaster and the relentless work of activists like Aldo and Nina, was no longer a fringe cause. It had reached the hearts and minds of billions. The global south had led the charge, but now, the Western world, long entrenched in industrial and consumer-driven paradigms, was beginning to confront its own complicity in the planet's collapse.

The shift was palpable. The United States, the European Union, and other industrial giants had been slow to acknowledge the urgency of the crisis. For decades, they had prospered by exploiting resources, polluting the oceans, and fostering a culture of unchecked consumption. But the global movement, the pressure from the people, and the undeniable reality of environmental degradation had forced their hand. A new day was dawning in the West, one in which sustainability was no longer optional but an absolute necessity for survival.

Aldo and Nina had been traveling non-stop, attending conferences, meeting with world leaders, and witnessing firsthand the shift taking place. In the United States, where the conversation had long been dominated by corporate interests and political gridlock, something remarkable was unfolding. Across the country, state governments, local communities, and even large corporations were making public commitments to sustainability. Renewable energy projects were being fast-tracked. Waste-to-energy technologies were being implemented on a scale previously thought impossible. And, most importantly, the people had found their voice.

It all started in Washington D.C., where a summit was being held to address the new climate reality. The summit, called "The Green Pact," was the first of its kind, an event in which world leaders, environmental experts, business tycoons, and everyday citizens gathered to discuss the future of the planet. Aldo had been invited to speak, as had Nina, who had become a prominent activist and spokesperson for the movement.

The mood in the room was tense, but optimistic. Aldo could sense the weight of history in the air. The decisions made here would shape the world for generations. As the keynote speakers took their turns, it was clear that the Western world, once reluctant to take bold action, was beginning to acknowledge the profound changes needed.

During his speech, Aldo outlined the breakthroughs that had been made, including the revolutionary waste-to-energy technologies and the successful implementation of sustainable agricultural practices. He spoke passionately about the importance of a global commitment to reduce waste, protect biodiversity, and make a shift towards renewable energy.

"The future of our planet depends not on the actions of a few powerful nations," Aldo said, his voice steady and unwavering, "but on the collective will of humanity. The time for half-measures is over. If we are to ensure the survival of our species and the Earth's ecosystems, we must act decisively. We must come together, not just as nations, but as stewards of this planet."

The room was silent as Aldo's words hung in the air. For the first time, it seemed that the audience wasn't just listening, they were considering the possibilities. The urgency of Aldo's message was being heard, and it was clear that something had shifted.

MOUNT OF WASTE

Nina spoke next, reminding the leaders of the consequences of inaction. "We've seen what the world looks like when we prioritize profit over people," she said, her voice strong and clear. "We've seen the destruction of ecosystems, the exploitation of communities, and the erosion of hope. But we've also seen what happens when people come together, when they put the Earth before their own interests. Look at the communities around the world who have embraced sustainable practices, who have reimagined how we can live with the planet, not against it. This is not a distant dream. This is a reality we can achieve, if we commit to it."

The applause that followed Nina's speech was the loudest of the day, a sign that something was beginning to shift in the hearts of those gathered. Even the most skeptical leaders seemed to be considering the implications of the ideas presented. The Green Pact summit wasn't just a discussion, it was a turning point.

Across the Atlantic, in Europe, the momentum was just as powerful. The European Union, long a leader in environmental policy, had seen its resolve tested by years of economic stagnation, political infighting, and corporate resistance. But the devastation caused by the global waste crisis had left no room for denial. European leaders, particularly those from the Nordic countries, were pushing for bold policies to reduce waste, increase recycling efforts, and embrace renewable energy.

The EU's Green New Deal, which had previously been a concept in the background of political debates, was now gaining traction. Countries like Germany, Denmark, and Sweden were already leading the way in renewable energy production, having transitioned to wind, solar, and geothermal power. But now, the focus was expanding beyond energy. The issue of waste management had moved to the forefront of the discussion, with nations committing to phasing out single-use plastics, incentivizing the development of biodegradable materials, and investing heavily in circular economies.

"Change is not just possible," said Ursula von der Leyen, the President of the European Commission, in a speech to the summit. "It is already happening. The European Union is committed to achieving carbon neutrality by 2050, and we will not stop there. We will ensure that sustainability becomes the foundation of our future economy, one that respects both our environment and our people."

For Aldo and Nina, this shift in Europe was encouraging. It was clear that the urgency of the environmental crisis was being recognized by Western powers. But they knew that the work was far from finished. The challenge now was to maintain momentum and ensure that these new commitments translated into meaningful, long-term action.

Back in the United States, the momentum continued to build. Several major cities, once notoriously wasteful and reliant on fossil fuels, had become leaders in sustainable living. Cities like San Francisco, Seattle, and Portland had adopted zero-waste policies, working tirelessly to divert waste from landfills by increasing recycling efforts, composting, and creating sustainable urban environments. The adoption of green technologies was being fast-tracked, with solar panels and wind turbines sprouting on rooftops and fields once dedicated to industrial agriculture now being repurposed for organic farming.

But the real success stories were coming from small towns and communities that had embraced the ideals of sustainability and regeneration. Aldo and Nina had visited several of these places in their travels, seeing firsthand the positive impact of waste-to-energy technologies, sustainable farming practices, and community-driven environmental initiatives.

MOUNT OF WASTE

In a small town in the Midwest, Aldo stood at the edge of a vast solar farm that stretched for miles. The town had once been dependent on coal mining, and the local economy had been devastated when the mines closed. But now, with the help of local governments and private investors, the town had become a model for renewable energy. The solar farm provided power for the town, while the once-polluted soil had been regenerated with sustainable farming practices.

"It's not just about survival," said Marisol, a local community leader, as she guided Aldo and Nina through the fields. "It's about thriving. We've rebuilt our economy, and we've done it by working with the Earth, not against it. We've learned that when we take care of the land, the land takes care of us."

Marisol's words echoed a growing sentiment across the West: sustainability was not a sacrifice, it was an opportunity for growth. By embracing renewable energy, waste management, and regenerative agriculture, the Western world had the chance to not only heal the planet but also build stronger, more resilient economies.

Back in Washington D.C., the Green Pact summit had concluded, but the work was just beginning. Aldo and Nina had been invited to meet with several key policymakers to discuss the next steps in the implementation of their solutions. There was a new urgency in the air as governments realized that the crisis was not a temporary challenge, it was a new way of life. The survival of humanity depended on how quickly the Western world could transition to a sustainable future.

"It's time for a new kind of economy," Aldo said during the meeting with policymakers. "One that's built on renewable energy, circular economies, and sustainable living. We must move beyond the old paradigms and invest in the future."

The room fell silent as everyone considered the weight of his words. It was clear that the conversation had shifted. The once-polarizing issues of sustainability and climate action were now seen as essential to the future of humanity. The Western world had opened its eyes, and the momentum for change was unstoppable.

As Aldo and Nina left the meeting, they looked out over the Capitol building. They knew that the road ahead would not be easy, but they also knew that the spark of change had been lit. The people had risen, and the Western world had finally joined the fight for the planet.

"The revolution is not over," Nina said, a smile creeping onto her face. "But today, it feels like we've won something big."

Aldo nodded, his eyes reflecting the same hope. "The real work begins now. Together, we'll build a future that's sustainable, equitable, and just, for everyone."

And with that, the dawn of a new world had truly begun.

Chapter 52: A Shift in the Eastern World

The winds of change were sweeping across the globe, from the bustling cities of the West to the burgeoning economies of the East. While the Western world had been the first to realize the importance of sustainability and environmental responsibility, the Eastern and Southern hemispheres had long been skeptical. Their industrial growth had been built on the same paradigms of unchecked development and overconsumption. But the evidence was clear: the environmental collapse was not something confined to the West, and the dire consequences of neglect could not be ignored any longer.

In Asia and Africa, the struggle to balance development with environmental conservation was taking center stage. It was no longer enough to simply grow economically; the cost of that growth had become too apparent, and there was no way to ignore the toll it was taking on the planet. Now, nations across Asia and Africa were looking for answers, and many were turning to the lessons learned from the global movement that had begun with Aldo, Nina, and their team.

In China, the world's most populous country and a manufacturing powerhouse, the shift began in the most unlikely of places: the industrial heartland of Hebei Province. Hebei, home to some of the country's most polluting factories, had been ground zero for the environmental crisis in China. Smog-choked skies, rivers clogged with waste, and the relentless mining of coal for energy had defined the region's industrial era.

But now, Hebei had become a beacon of change. The government, faced with mounting pressure from both citizens and the international community, had rolled out a series of sweeping green initiatives. Huge investments in renewable energy, waste-to-energy technologies, and electric vehicles were making Hebei one of the largest green energy hubs in the world. The region's factories were being retrofitted with cutting-edge technologies to reduce emissions, and large-scale solar farms were rising in the same places where coal mines had once dominated the landscape.

Aldo and Nina, having spent the past few years working with governments around the world, found themselves on a flight to China to witness the transformation firsthand. They arrived in the heart of Hebei Province and were met by a local government official, Li Wei, who had become an advocate for green development. As they drove through the province, Aldo couldn't help but marvel at the sight of solar panels and wind turbines dotting the landscape.

"The shift here has been nothing short of remarkable," Li Wei said as they passed an enormous solar farm stretching across the hills. "We were once known for our pollution, but now, we're leading the way in renewable energy. We've seen the data, and we know that investing in clean technologies isn't just good for the planet, it's good for business. It's creating jobs, driving innovation, and building a more resilient future."

Aldo nodded, impressed by the scale of the change. "I never thought I'd see this day come so quickly. You've done more than just adopt new technologies, you've completely reimagined your future."

Li Wei smiled. "It wasn't easy. It took a lot of political will, but we knew we had no choice. Our people were suffering. The air quality was unbearable. We were on the brink of a collapse that would have been irreversible. But now, we're not just talking about clean energy; we're talking about a clean future."

MOUNT OF WASTE

As the car continued through the countryside, Aldo and Nina observed more of the same. Fields that once housed industrial waste were now home to organic farms. Old coal-burning plants had been converted into biomass power stations. In just a few short years, Hebei had gone from one of China's most polluted regions to one of its greenest.

Across Asia, other nations were also following suit. India, often seen as a country grappling with rapid industrialization and deep poverty, had taken major steps toward embracing renewable energy. The Indian government had committed to installing over 500 gigawatts of solar energy by 2030, and solar panels were now a common sight in villages and cities alike. India, with its abundant sunlight and vast deserts, had become a leader in solar energy development.

In Bangladesh, a country ravaged by flooding, rising sea levels, and environmental degradation, the government had started to invest heavily in sustainable farming techniques and flood management systems. The country was working with international organizations to bring green infrastructure into the heart of its cities, developing vertical farms and renewable energy projects to address both food insecurity and the challenges posed by climate change.

Meanwhile, in Southeast Asia, countries like Vietnam and Thailand were making significant strides in sustainable tourism. These nations, long dependent on industries like fishing and logging, were turning their attention to ecotourism as a way to protect their ecosystems while providing economic opportunities for local communities. The government of Thailand had implemented a national strategy to restore its coral reefs, a key part of the nation's marine biodiversity, by promoting sustainable fishing practices and reducing coastal development.

The shift wasn't limited to Asia. Across Africa, the environmental movement was gaining momentum, with countries like Kenya, Ghana, and South Africa leading the charge. In Kenya, a massive reforestation initiative had been launched, with millions of trees being planted each year to combat deforestation and protect biodiversity. South Africa, once dependent on coal mining, had begun to invest heavily in wind and solar energy, and its government had committed to reaching net-zero emissions by 2050.

Ghana had taken bold steps to address waste management, implementing a nationwide recycling program and investing in technologies to convert plastic waste into clean energy. It was clear that the entire African continent, once dismissed as a passive player in global environmental efforts, was now becoming an active participant in the green revolution.

Aldo and Nina's visit to China had been an eye-opener. The transformation they saw in Hebei was not just a localized success; it was a testament to the power of change when governments, businesses, and people united for a common cause. The shift in the Eastern world was gaining momentum, and it was clear that the global transition to a sustainable future was no longer a matter of if, it was a matter of when.

Back in their hotel room, Aldo sat by the window overlooking the city of Beijing, his mind racing. The challenges had been immense, and the road to sustainability had been anything but easy. But as he looked out at the sprawling metropolis, now powered by renewable energy, he felt a sense of optimism. The impossible was becoming possible.

Nina, ever the optimist, was equally hopeful. She had been speaking with local activists who were working tirelessly to push for greener policies and practices. "I think the tide has really turned," she said, sitting down beside him. "People here are more willing to embrace the future now. And it's not just the government. It's the people, too. They're pushing for change, and they're ready to fight for it."

Aldo smiled. "It's incredible, isn't it? I never imagined we'd be here, seeing this kind of transformation on such a massive scale. It's proof that change is possible. And it's proof that when we work together, when we push for sustainable solutions, we can make a difference."

Nina nodded. "The work's not over. There's still so much to be done. But this is the kind of progress we need to see everywhere."

The global shift toward sustainability was no longer a Western-led movement; it had become a truly global effort. As Aldo and Nina returned to their base of operations, they reflected on the incredible progress they had witnessed. It was clear that the solutions they had worked so hard to develop were not just ideas on paper, they were being put into action on a global scale.

The transformation was happening in every corner of the world. Governments, businesses, and individuals were realizing that the future they had been living in was unsustainable, and that a new era was beginning, one built on sustainability, cooperation, and innovation. The world, once divided by economic and political interests, was now united by the shared understanding that the survival of the planet depended on their collective action.

As the sun set on the horizon, casting its golden light over the sprawling cities of the East, Aldo and Nina knew that the road ahead was still long. There would be setbacks, resistance, and unforeseen challenges. But they also knew that, with each step forward, they were building a better, more sustainable future for generations to come.

Together, they would continue the fight. The East, like the West before it, had begun to see the light, and it was shining brighter than ever.

Chapter 53: Digging Deeper

Aldo sat in the quiet of the research facility's conference room, his fingers tapping rhythmically on the table. He had just returned from a series of global meetings where the world's leaders were more open than ever to embracing the technologies and solutions his team had been developing. The work was far from over, but the momentum was undeniable. However, for all their progress, Aldo knew that they had only scratched the surface of the problems plaguing the planet. The task of reversing the damage caused by decades of unchecked waste and environmental destruction still loomed large.

Aldo had always been driven by a sense of curiosity, a deep need to uncover the solutions that could change the course of humanity's future. And now, with the support of nations rallying behind their efforts, he and his team were beginning to explore new frontiers in waste management, looking for ways to tackle the growing waste crisis on a scale that matched the urgency of the problem.

Across from him, Nina was skimming through a stack of reports, her face lighting up as she uncovered new insights. "Aldo, this is it," she said, her voice laced with excitement. "We've been focusing on recycling and waste-to-energy technologies, but there's a breakthrough here that could take everything to the next level."

Aldo raised an eyebrow. "What do you have?"

"It's a new biocatalytic process," Nina continued, "One that could break down plastics and other non-biodegradable materials faster and more efficiently. This could potentially solve our biggest challenge, the slow pace of recycling and the fact that many plastics still don't break down easily."

Aldo leaned forward. The idea of using biocatalysts to accelerate the decomposition of plastic had been an ongoing theory among environmental scientists, but no one had found a way to make it both scalable and commercially viable. If Nina's discovery was real, it could be a game-changer.

"What's the catch?" Aldo asked, skeptical yet intrigued.

"There's no catch, at least, not yet," Nina replied, flipping through the pages. "This is a process developed by a small biotech company in Europe. They've managed to identify enzymes that can break down specific types of plastics, turning them into harmless by-products. The technology is still in its early stages, but it's showing real promise. They're getting results in laboratory conditions, and they're even working on industrial applications."

Aldo's mind raced as he processed the information. He knew that plastics, the scourge of modern waste, were responsible for a significant portion of the global pollution problem. If this biocatalytic process could be perfected and scaled, it could revolutionize waste management on a global scale. But there was always a catch in technologies like this. They were expensive, untested, and often lacked the flexibility needed to work on the vast variety of materials the world produced.

"We need to connect with this company," Aldo said decisively. "We need to bring them on board and see if we can fast-track their development. This could be the missing link we've been looking for."

Nina nodded in agreement. "I'll reach out to them immediately."

The team's days quickly became filled with research and collaboration. Aldo and Nina, along with their top engineers and scientists, worked tirelessly to refine the biocatalytic process, ensuring that it could be adapted to a range of different plastic types. At the same time, they continued to focus on scaling their waste-to-energy systems, hoping to integrate the new technology into their existing infrastructure.

Months of testing followed, with the team operating around the clock to perfect the solution. They faced numerous setbacks, issues with the enzymes breaking down too slowly in real-world conditions, complications with industrial-scale deployment, and challenges in integrating the technology into existing waste management systems. Yet, despite the obstacles, the team pushed forward, motivated by the knowledge that this breakthrough could hold the key to addressing one of the planet's most pressing environmental crises.

And then, one day, it happened. A breakthrough in their testing.

The biocatalytic enzymes, when combined with a new type of synthetic bio-organic material developed in their labs, began to break down plastics not only faster but also in a way that produced minimal byproducts. The rate of decomposition was exponentially higher than anything they had previously achieved with traditional recycling methods.

"This is it," Aldo said, barely able to contain his excitement. "This could change everything."

Nina grinned, her eyes wide. "We're on the verge of something huge. We're not just dealing with plastics anymore; we're solving the entire waste management issue. This can scale globally."

Aldo looked around the room at his team, seeing the same spark of hope in their eyes. The relentless hard work had paid off. They had taken a massive step toward the world they had always envisioned, a world where waste could be dealt with in a sustainable, efficient manner, without the environmental burden that had come to define modern life.

But Aldo was not one to rest on his laurels. This breakthrough, though monumental, was just one piece of the puzzle. The technology had to be tested on a global scale, implemented in a wide variety of settings, and refined to ensure that it would work under the most challenging conditions. For all their excitement, Aldo knew that the road to fully integrating this technology into global waste management systems would be long and fraught with challenges.

"Now we scale," Aldo said, his voice firm. "This isn't just about a single solution. This is about changing the entire way the world handles waste. We're not just solving a problem, we're creating a new paradigm for the future."

As Aldo's team began the process of scaling the biocatalytic technology, they focused on several key areas. First, they needed to develop large-scale reactors capable of processing waste at a rate fast enough to keep up with the world's growing piles of plastic. This required significant investment in infrastructure, as well as collaboration with governments and international organizations to ensure that the technology would be implemented globally.

Second, they had to address the issue of public and corporate buy-in. Many industries were hesitant to embrace new waste management technologies due to the cost of transitioning from traditional methods and the uncertainty of new systems. Aldo knew that they needed to demonstrate the efficiency and cost-effectiveness of their solution on a global scale to win over the skeptics.

And third, they had to confront the environmental challenges that were still deeply embedded in the world's existing systems. While their new technology had the potential to revolutionize waste management, it was clear that the issue went beyond just plastics. E-waste, hazardous materials, and organic waste all presented their own challenges, and Aldo was determined to find ways to address each of these problems.

The next step in their journey was to conduct a large-scale pilot program. They decided to launch the program in a city that had been devastated by waste buildup, a city that had experienced the worst of the environmental collapse.

The city of Jakarta, Indonesia, had long been plagued by overflowing landfills, toxic air, and water pollution. The streets were often clogged with waste, and much of the city's infrastructure had crumbled under the weight of its garbage crisis. Jakarta had become a symbol of the world's waste problem. Aldo believed that by launching their pilot program here, they could demonstrate the effectiveness of their technology and provide a model for other cities to follow.

Months of planning went into the pilot program. Aldo's team worked with local authorities, community organizations, and environmental activists to prepare the city for the large-scale deployment of their technology. Jakarta's waste management system would be revamped, and the biocatalytic technology would be integrated into the city's infrastructure to break down plastic waste and convert it into useful products, such as clean energy.

As the pilot program was rolled out, Aldo watched as the first signs of progress began to take shape. Landfills that had once been a dangerous health hazard were transformed into green energy hubs, producing power from the very waste that had once been a source of pollution. Streets that had been clogged with plastic waste were cleaned and rehabilitated. Local communities rallied behind the initiative, eager to see the positive changes taking root in their city.

Despite the success of the pilot program in Jakarta, Aldo knew that the real challenge lay ahead. Scaling this technology to the global level would require international cooperation, massive investment, and the willingness of governments, corporations, and individuals to embrace change. There would be resistance, of course. But Aldo had witnessed firsthand the power of innovation, collaboration, and resilience in the face of global challenges.

MOUNT OF WASTE

The world was not going to be saved by a single breakthrough, but by a collective effort to dig deeper, to push the boundaries of what was possible, and to continue striving for a more sustainable and equitable future. And Aldo, alongside Nina and his dedicated team, was ready to face whatever challenges lay ahead.

The journey was just beginning, but the hope for a cleaner, more sustainable world was shining brighter than ever.

Chapter 54: Innovations in Waste Management

Aldo stared out of the large windows of the new research facility, his mind swirling with excitement and anticipation. The progress they had made in the past few months was nothing short of remarkable, but the road ahead was still long. His team had just completed the prototype for a new waste management system that could revolutionize the way the world handled its trash. They were on the cusp of something big, something that could change everything.

The new system, which Aldo had dubbed EcoCycle, wasn't just about recycling or converting waste into energy. It was an entirely new approach to the problem, one that treated waste as a resource rather than a burden. By using a combination of advanced sorting technologies, biocatalytic processes, and automated manufacturing systems, EcoCycle would take waste, particularly plastics and organic matter, and convert it into useful products, everything from biodegradable packaging to construction materials, energy, and even food.

"Are we ready?" Nina asked as she walked into the room, her voice filled with equal parts excitement and trepidation. She had been working closely with the engineering team to refine the system, and her expertise in environmental science had been invaluable.

Aldo turned to face her, a smile playing on his lips. "Ready as we'll ever be. The pilot cities are lined up, the systems are in place. Now, we just need to see it work in real-world conditions."

Nina nodded, her face serious but hopeful. "It's going to be a game-changer, Aldo. If this works, we're not just solving the waste crisis, we're turning waste into something valuable. We can transform the entire global economy in the process."

"Exactly," Aldo replied. "But it's not just about the technology, it's about the mindset. This is a new way of thinking, a paradigm shift. We need the world to see that waste isn't just a problem, it's an opportunity."

The EcoCycle system wasn't just a mechanical marvel. It represented the culmination of years of research, testing, and hard work. The system used an innovative combination of AI-driven sorting mechanisms, biodegradable chemical catalysts, and automated processing plants to turn waste into valuable materials. The beauty of the system lay in its versatility: it could handle all kinds of waste, from household garbage to industrial by-products, and transform it into products that were either reusable or environmentally neutral.

The AI sorting system was the first component of the EcoCycle system. It used advanced algorithms to identify and separate different types of waste, plastics, metals, organics, and more, before feeding them into the next phase of the system. From there, the biocatalysts went to work, breaking down the waste at a molecular level, converting it into raw materials that could be used for various applications.

One of the most exciting aspects of EcoCycle was its ability to take organic waste, food scraps, agricultural waste, and even sewage, and turn it into usable products like bioplastics, fertilizers, and clean energy. The system's decentralized approach allowed it to be deployed in cities, towns, and even rural areas, offering a scalable solution that could be tailored to different regions' needs.

The first test city for the EcoCycle system was New York, one of the world's largest and most waste-stricken urban centers. For years, New York had struggled with the overwhelming problem of waste disposal. The city's landfills were overflowing, and the waste management system was barely keeping up with the demand. Local authorities had long been searching for a solution that could help reduce waste while generating useful byproducts, and they saw EcoCycle as their last hope.

Aldo and his team arrived in the city to oversee the implementation of the pilot program. The streets of New York were lined with trash, as usual. But Aldo saw beyond the heaps of waste, imagining a future where every piece of discarded material was put to good use. This vision was the foundation of EcoCycle, a future where cities weren't defined by pollution but by their ability to transform waste into wealth.

Over the next several weeks, the team worked closely with city officials, local businesses, and community organizations to implement the new system. First, they set up the AI-driven waste sorting machines at key waste collection points across the city. Then, they installed the processing units, which would convert the sorted waste into useful materials. The most challenging part was ensuring that the technology could handle the vast amount of waste that New York generated every day. It wasn't just about making the system work; it was about making it work at a scale that matched the city's needs.

As the system went online, the team anxiously awaited the first results. It was a huge risk, launching a project of this magnitude in one of the most populous and waste-ridden cities in the world. But Aldo was confident that the technology would perform as expected.

Two weeks later, the first reports came in. The waste sorting systems were operating at near 100% efficiency, accurately identifying and sorting different types of waste with minimal error. The biocatalytic reactors were breaking down plastics and organic materials faster than anticipated, and the energy produced by the system was already being fed back into the city's grid.

MOUNT OF WASTE

But it wasn't just the energy that impressed the team—it was the byproducts. The system had successfully converted organic waste into high-quality fertilizer, which was being distributed to local farms. The plastics were being transformed into biodegradable packaging material, and the construction materials produced by the system were being used to repair buildings and infrastructure that had been damaged by the waste crisis.

The residents of New York were beginning to see the tangible benefits of the system. The streets were cleaner, the air was fresher, and the once-overwhelming mountain of garbage was now being transformed into valuable resources. The city, once a symbol of waste and decay, was beginning to experience a revival.

The success of New York's pilot program set the stage for other cities to follow. Aldo and his team were inundated with requests from around the world, cities like Tokyo, Paris, and São Paulo all expressed interest in implementing the EcoCycle system in their own waste management operations. Aldo knew that this was the moment they had been waiting for. The world was finally ready to embrace a new way of thinking about waste, and EcoCycle was at the forefront of that change.

But as they expanded to other cities, Aldo was mindful of the challenges ahead. Scaling the system was no small feat. It required not just advanced technology but also careful coordination with local governments, businesses, and citizens. And perhaps most importantly, it required a shift in the way people thought about waste. For centuries, waste had been something to get rid of, something that went into landfills or incinerators. But now, with EcoCycle, waste was being redefined as a resource.

One of the key challenges Aldo faced in scaling the system was ensuring that the products produced by EcoCycle were of the highest quality and could compete with traditional materials in terms of price and performance. The biodegradable packaging materials, for example, had to meet the same standards as conventional plastics if they were going to be widely adopted. The bioplastics had to be durable, flexible, and cost-effective. And the construction materials had to be strong enough to meet the demands of modern infrastructure.

To address these challenges, Aldo and his team worked closely with engineers and manufacturers to refine the system's output. They tested and retested the materials, making adjustments to the processing methods and the chemical catalysts used in the system. Over time, the quality of the products improved, and they were able to scale up production to meet the demands of the global market.

One of the most promising developments was the use of EcoCycle's waste-to-energy technology to power entire cities. The system's energy generation capabilities were not only helping to power homes and businesses but were also being used to replace fossil fuels in industrial processes. Aldo saw this as a critical step toward achieving true sustainability, moving away from the reliance on nonrenewable resources and embracing a future powered by waste.

By the end of the year, EcoCycle was operating in dozens of cities around the world. The technology had proven itself in diverse environments, from the bustling streets of New York to the rural villages of Sub-Saharan Africa. It was clear that the system had the potential to revolutionize waste management on a global scale.

Aldo stood before the gathered crowd at a global sustainability conference, ready to share the success of EcoCycle with the world. The audience included scientists, environmental activists, corporate leaders, and government representatives from all corners of the globe. He had spent his life working toward this moment, the moment when the world would finally begin to treat waste as a resource, not a burden.

MOUNT OF WASTE

"We have proven," Aldo said, his voice firm with conviction, "that waste is not something to be discarded. It is not a problem to be buried or burned. Waste is a resource. It is the key to building a sustainable future, one where we can power our cities, feed our people, and protect our planet."

The applause was deafening.

As Aldo looked out at the crowd, he realized that they had not just created a new technology. They had ignited a movement, a movement that was changing the way the world viewed its most pressing environmental challenge. The future was no longer a world of waste. It was a world of possibility.

And Aldo knew that this was only the beginning.

Chapter 55: Success Amid Despair

The air was thick with tension as Aldo walked down the sterile white hallways of the research facility. His thoughts were a whirlwind of emotions, each one competing for dominance. The world was slowly beginning to notice the results of their work, yet the road to success had been anything but smooth. Everywhere he turned, there was resistance, political, economic, and social obstacles that seemed insurmountable at times. Yet, the progress was undeniable. It was a beacon of hope, cutting through the fog of uncertainty that surrounded them.

Aldo glanced at the screens showing the live data feeds from the various cities where the EcoCycle system had been implemented. The numbers were encouraging, even astonishing. In New York, waste levels had dropped by nearly 40% in just six months. The EcoCycle system was proving that it could do what no other technology had been able to do on such a grand scale: tackle the waste crisis head-on, while also producing clean energy, construction materials, and sustainable products.

But despite the success, Aldo couldn't help but feel the weight of the world on his shoulders. The environmental crises had only worsened in the wake of the waste catastrophe. Global temperatures were still rising, storms were becoming more violent, and ecosystems that had been decimated by the disaster were struggling to recover. It was as if nature itself was fighting back against the damage humanity had inflicted upon it.

As Aldo sat down at his desk, he thought back to the early days of the project, the days when it seemed like nothing would ever work, when every idea was met with skepticism, when it felt like they were fighting an uphill battle. Even now, there were moments when he doubted whether they could truly turn things around. But then, he remembered something Nina had told him at the beginning of their journey: "Hope is the most powerful tool we have, Aldo. It's what drives us to keep going, even when everything seems impossible."

A soft knock on the door interrupted his thoughts.

"Come in," Aldo called, and Nina stepped into the room, her face illuminated with a rare smile.

"Got a minute?" she asked, closing the door behind her.

Aldo nodded, gesturing to the chair across from his desk. "Of course. What's on your mind?"

Nina took a seat, leaning forward with a spark of excitement in her eyes. "You should see the data from the field tests in São Paulo. The EcoCycle system is outperforming our expectations. The reduction in waste is significant, but the real kicker is the energy production. We've generated more than 30 megawatts in the last month alone, and it's all going straight back into the city's power grid."

Aldo's heart lifted at the news. "That's incredible. But what about the pushback? Are the corporations still trying to shut us down?"

Nina's face darkened. "You can say that again. There's been more sabotage, more misinformation campaigns. We've had incidents of our equipment being tampered with in several locations. They're scared, Aldo, scared that their profits will plummet when people start to realize that EcoCycle isn't just a solution for waste management, it's a whole new way of thinking about resource consumption."

Aldo leaned back in his chair, rubbing his temples. "It's frustrating. Every time we make a breakthrough, they find new ways to undermine us. But we can't stop. We're at a tipping point now, and if we can show the world that this system works on a global scale, we'll have the momentum we need."

Nina nodded in agreement. "Exactly. But there's more good news. We're getting interest from several governments, including countries in Africa and Southeast Asia. They're eager to implement the system, especially in areas that were hardest hit by the environmental collapse. These regions don't have the infrastructure to handle the amount of waste they generate, and EcoCycle could be the solution they need."

Aldo felt a glimmer of hope rising in his chest. "That's promising. We need to focus on scaling up the system and getting it into as many cities as possible. We've proven that it works in the field, but now we need to make sure it's sustainable, both environmentally and economically."

Nina's eyes softened. "You know, Aldo, there are days when it feels like we're fighting a losing battle. The world is in chaos, the effects of the storm are still devastating, and the corporations are pulling every dirty trick in the book. But then, I look at these numbers, at the people we've helped, and I see that we're making a difference. It's not just about technology, it's about people's lives."

Aldo smiled, a wave of gratitude washing over him. "You're right. It's always been about people. This isn't just about solving a problem, it's about giving hope to people who thought they were beyond help. We can't let the setbacks stop us from moving forward. Not now, not when we're so close."

The next few days were a whirlwind of activity. Aldo and Nina worked with the international team to refine the EcoCycle technology further. They were tweaking the biocatalytic processes, improving the waste-to-energy conversion rates, and ensuring that the materials being produced were of the highest quality. They were also building relationships with new governments and private sector partners, seeking to expand their reach and increase the adoption of the system.

MOUNT OF WASTE

Meanwhile, the political landscape was shifting. Several large nations had begun to acknowledge the reality of the climate crisis and the need for drastic action. The economic and environmental costs of inaction were becoming too high to ignore. The United Nations held an emergency summit to discuss the global waste crisis and the urgent need for sustainable solutions. Aldo was invited to speak at the summit, along with other leading environmental experts and activists.

The summit was a pivotal moment. As Aldo stood before the assembly of world leaders, he felt the weight of history pressing down on him. This was the moment he had been preparing for, the moment when he could show the world that it was not too late to turn things around. The room was silent as he began to speak, his voice steady and filled with purpose.

"The time for talk is over," Aldo said, his gaze sweeping across the room. "The waste crisis, the environmental collapse, it's all part of a larger problem, one that we've ignored for too long. We've pushed the planet to its breaking point, and now, we're faced with a choice: we can continue down the path of destruction, or we can choose to innovate, to change, and to rebuild. The EcoCycle system is not just a solution, it's a way forward. It's a way to turn waste into wealth, pollution into productivity, and crisis into opportunity."

He paused for a moment, letting his words sink in. "But this will only work if we come together. If we stop fighting each other and start working toward a common goal. If we stop prioritizing profit over the planet. The world is watching us. Our children are watching us. And we cannot afford to fail."

As Aldo finished his speech, the room erupted into applause. For the first time in years, there was a sense of unity among the world's leaders. They understood that the time for incremental change was over. The world needed bold action, and Aldo's vision for a sustainable, waste-free future was the blueprint for that change.

In the weeks that followed, EcoCycle systems were deployed in cities around the world. From Tokyo to São Paulo, from Lagos to Sydney, the technology was helping to transform urban landscapes. Waste management became more efficient, energy production grew cleaner, and the environment began to show signs of recovery. People began to believe that change was possible, that the crisis they had lived through was not the end of the world but the beginning of a new one.

Yet, even as the successes mounted, Aldo knew there was still much work to be done. The EcoCycle system was just one piece of the puzzle. To truly heal the planet, humanity needed to rethink its relationship with nature, to embrace sustainability at every level of society. The work was far from over, but for the first time in years, Aldo felt a sense of optimism. They had made it this far. And if they could keep going, if they could keep pushing for change, maybe, just maybe, the world would survive.

The EcoCycle project was more than just a technological breakthrough, it was a symbol of what was possible when humanity refused to give up. And as Aldo looked out over the city, he knew that they had not only found a way to fight back against the chaos. They had found a way to build a better world.

Chapter 56: Exploring Sustainability

The laboratory buzzed with activity as Aldo and his team gathered around the workstations, their minds focused on the next big breakthrough. It was no longer just about implementing solutions for the waste crisis; now, it was about maximizing the potential of what had once been seen as garbage. After months of fine-tuning the EcoCycle system, Aldo was convinced that they had only scratched the surface of what could be achieved. The materials that had been discarded in landfills for decades, plastic, paper, metal, and organic waste, had the potential to fuel entire industries. It was time to dig deeper.

"Alright, team," Aldo said as he addressed the group gathered around the sleek table in the center of the room. "We've made great strides with the EcoCycle technology, but now we need to go beyond just waste management. We need to focus on the sustainability of the systems we're building. The next phase of our work isn't just about reducing the waste. It's about transforming it into something useful."

Nina, ever the optimist, leaned forward, her eyes alight with curiosity. "What do you have in mind, Aldo?"

"We're going to explore the possibility of turning waste materials into building materials, energy sources, and even agricultural products. There's a huge untapped potential here, and if we can harness it, we could reshape entire industries."

Aldo's words resonated with the team. They had already seen how EcoCycle was capable of transforming waste into energy, but this new direction would push the boundaries of what they had believed possible.

1. Waste to Energy

The first area of focus was energy. As the world's demand for sustainable energy solutions continued to grow, the team began investigating how they could use waste materials to produce more clean energy. Aldo and his team knew that burning waste for fuel wasn't a new idea, many countries had already started using waste-to-energy (WTE) plants, but their approach would be different. They weren't simply going to burn the waste; they would extract its intrinsic value by using cutting-edge technologies to break down waste at a molecular level, releasing energy without the harmful emissions that typically came with combustion.

"We need to rethink how we're using waste for energy," Aldo said during one of their brainstorming sessions. "Rather than incinerating everything, we'll develop a technology that converts waste into biofuels and gases in a controlled environment, without the toxic byproducts."

One of the team members, Maria, a chemist specializing in bioenergy, suggested exploring the potential of anaerobic digestion, a process that could be used to turn organic waste into methane. "If we can enhance the efficiency of methane production, we could provide clean and renewable energy to areas that still rely on coal and natural gas."

Aldo nodded. "Exactly. Anaerobic digestion could be the perfect solution for areas with high organic waste. By optimizing the process, we could make this a sustainable energy source on a global scale."

The team worked tirelessly over the next few months, experimenting with different methods of energy extraction. They developed a new reactor system that used waste as a feedstock, producing biofuels that could be used in everything from power plants to vehicles. Their findings were groundbreaking, revealing that waste was not a burden but a resource. And with this technology, they could harness its potential to meet the growing global demand for energy.

2. Waste to Building Materials

MOUNT OF WASTE

While the energy revolution was underway, Aldo's team also turned their attention to building materials. The demand for construction materials was skyrocketing as cities rebuilt from the devastation of the environmental disaster. Aldo saw an opportunity to turn the mountains of plastic waste into something valuable, something that could be used to create sustainable and durable building materials.

"We know that plastic takes centuries to decompose," Aldo said during a discussion about the next stage of their project. "But if we can find a way to break it down and repurpose it for construction, we'll reduce waste and create something useful at the same time."

Sophia, a materials scientist on the team, suggested looking into the creation of composite materials. "Plastic, when combined with other materials like recycled glass or organic fibers, could be transformed into strong, lightweight building products like insulation, flooring, and even structural components."

Aldo's eyes lit up. "That's it! If we can make these composites both affordable and durable, we can help solve the housing crisis in the wake of the disaster while simultaneously addressing the plastic waste problem."

The team set to work on developing new composite materials that could replace conventional construction materials like concrete, wood, and steel. They experimented with different blends of plastics, natural fibers, and recycled materials. Their goal was to create materials that were not only environmentally friendly but also economically viable for large-scale production.

By the end of their research, they had successfully created several prototype materials that were lighter, stronger, and more insulating than traditional building products. The materials could be used to build homes, schools, hospitals, and other structures. They were fire-resistant, weather-resistant, and could be produced with minimal energy consumption. The possibilities were endless.

3. Waste to Agriculture

While Aldo and his team were revolutionizing energy and construction, they also recognized another pressing issue: food security. In the wake of the global disaster, agricultural systems had collapsed in many regions, leaving millions hungry. The land was contaminated, and traditional farming methods were no longer viable. The team turned to waste once again to help solve this crisis.

"We know that organic waste is abundant and can be a rich source of nutrients," Aldo said. "What if we could use composting and waste-to-soil technologies to restore agricultural lands that have been ravaged by the storm?"

Nina, who had been studying permaculture and regenerative agriculture for years, proposed a method for converting organic waste into rich, fertile compost that could be used to replenish degraded soils. "By using the EcoCycle technology to process organic waste and turn it into nutrient-dense compost, we can regenerate the soil and make it possible for communities to grow food again."

The team worked alongside agricultural scientists to develop techniques for using waste products to restore and enhance the productivity of soil. Their research focused on how to compost organic waste in a way that was both efficient and scalable. They also worked on developing a system for producing organic fertilizers that could be applied directly to farmland, increasing crop yields and improving food security.

The results were remarkable. In several test farms in Africa and Southeast Asia, they were able to regenerate depleted soil and increase crop yields by as much as 60%. Local farmers were able to grow more food with fewer resources, and food prices began to stabilize in regions that had previously been struggling with shortages.

4. A New Era of Circular Economy

MOUNT OF WASTE

The breakthroughs Aldo and his team achieved in energy, construction, and agriculture were more than just technological innovations, they were the foundation of a new economic paradigm. The world was moving toward a circular economy, where waste no longer existed as a problem to be discarded but as a valuable resource to be reused, recycled, and repurposed.

As Aldo sat in his office, looking out at the city below, he realized that their work was no longer just about saving the planet. It was about creating a new way of life, a way where people respected the environment, where resources were used efficiently, and where sustainability was woven into the fabric of every industry.

But there was still much work to be done. Governments, corporations, and citizens around the world needed to understand the importance of the circular economy and how they could play a part in this transformation. Aldo knew that if they were going to make this vision a reality, they would need to work together with every sector of society.

"True sustainability isn't just about technology," Aldo said as he looked at Nina, who had just entered his office. "It's about a shift in consciousness, a recognition that we are all connected to the planet and to each other. If we can get people to see that, then we'll have a future worth fighting for."

Nina smiled. "And that's exactly why we're doing this."

Aldo stood up and walked over to the window, gazing at the horizon. He could see the first signs of change in the world around him, the rise of a new economy, a new way of living. The journey was far from over, but for the first time, he felt that there was real hope for the future.

They had turned waste into a resource. Now, they would help the world do the same. The future was, at last, within reach.

Chapter 57: Growing Trust

The world had come a long way from the days when the environment seemed on the brink of collapse. Aldo stood in the middle of the bustling conference hall, his eyes scanning the sea of faces, scientists, government officials, environmental activists, business leaders, and representatives from countries across the globe. It had been a year since they had first introduced their breakthrough technologies, and the results were undeniable. What had once been viewed with skepticism was now becoming the beacon of hope for a planet teetering on the edge of disaster.

Aldo had always believed that change started with one step, but now, it felt like they were running, full speed ahead, towards a sustainable future. Every successful implementation of the EcoCycle system in cities around the world, every energy plant powered by recycled waste, every home built from composite materials made from plastic waste, these were all tangible victories. They were proof that Aldo's vision for a cleaner, more sustainable planet was possible. But more importantly, they were proof that it was happening.

As he took the stage to address the audience at the annual Global Sustainability Forum, Aldo felt a weight of responsibility. This moment was bigger than just presenting their latest technology, it was about inspiring global action. He knew that in order to bring about real, lasting change, trust was the most important currency.

1. From Skepticism to Belief

When Aldo and his team had first presented their solutions to the international community, they had faced intense resistance. Many world leaders were hesitant to embrace their vision, fearful of disrupting the status quo, of the costs associated with the new technologies, or simply unwilling to acknowledge the magnitude of the environmental crisis. The more established industries, including fossil fuel and manufacturing giants, had viewed the waste-to-energy and sustainable building materials with suspicion. After all, these innovations threatened their lucrative business models.

The first year of implementation had been tough. Some countries had hesitated to invest in the technologies, unsure of their efficacy. However, as cities began to rebuild, powered by clean energy, and as rural communities revived their farmlands using organic waste compost, the tide began to turn. The results were too substantial to ignore.

Now, as Aldo stood before the world's leaders, he could see how much had changed. The atmosphere in the room was different. There were no longer whispers of doubt, only eager conversations about how they could implement the EcoCycle system and other sustainable technologies in their own countries. Governments that had previously been reluctant to engage in the movement were now eager to collaborate.

2. Showcasing Success Stories

Aldo began his presentation by showing a series of images. The first was of a devastated city, rubble strewn across the streets, buildings reduced to charred remains. "This," he began, "is what we inherited. A world left in ruins, struggling to survive after the great disaster. But we didn't give up. We fought, not just for survival, but for something greater, a future."

The slides changed to show the same city, now rebuilt using sustainable methods. Waste that had once been an eyesore and an environmental burden was now an asset. "This," Aldo continued, "is the power of innovation, collaboration, and trust. This is the future we are building."

He showcased more examples, communities in Africa using waste to regenerate the soil and produce crops, small towns in the

Americas powered by biofuels derived from organic waste, and entire urban centers in Europe constructing homes using plastic composites that had been sourced from oceans and landfills.

"These are not isolated cases. These are the new realities of our world. The EcoCycle technology is changing lives, reducing pollution, and rebuilding ecosystems," Aldo said, his voice steady and confident. "This is not just about technology. This is about the people, the farmers, the engineers, the workers, the families who have embraced these solutions and are thriving because of them."

Aldo paused and looked out at the audience. His words had clearly resonated, and the energy in the room had shifted. The room that had once been filled with uncertainty was now charged with excitement. He knew that the trust they had fought so hard to build was beginning to take root.

3. A Global Commitment

As Aldo finished his presentation, a round of applause erupted in the hall. It wasn't just polite clapping; it was a genuine expression of admiration for what had been achieved. But it wasn't the applause that mattered most, it was the pledges that began to come in from the countries and organizations present.

Representatives from nations that had previously held back, China, India, the United States, and Russia, now stood up and pledged their commitment to implementing the sustainable technologies on a global scale. These were countries that, for years, had been major contributors to environmental degradation. Yet here they were, committing not just to adopting the technology, but to sharing the knowledge with others, helping to build infrastructure, and leading the charge for a greener future.

Aldo felt the weight of history on his shoulders. This was the moment he had been working toward, an international alliance of nations, united by a common cause, all committed to a sustainable future. It was no longer just about one man's vision; it was about the collective vision of the planet.

4. Overcoming the Challenges

Despite the overwhelming support, Aldo knew that the path forward would still be challenging. There were political complexities to navigate, some countries were more progressive, while others were slower to change. There were industries that felt threatened by the shift to renewable energy and sustainable materials, and they wouldn't go down without a fight.

But Aldo was confident. The technology was sound, the evidence was irrefutable, and now, more than ever, the world was on their side. He turned to Nina, who had been sitting in the front row, her gaze locked on him with quiet determination.

"We've come a long way," Aldo said quietly. "But this is just the beginning. The real work starts now."

Nina smiled and nodded. "Let's make sure the world never looks back."

5. Bridging the Gap

One of the most profound outcomes of this conference was the emergence of a new global framework for sustainability. The nations that had pledged their support agreed to form a global coalition that would focus on the research, development, and implementation of sustainable technologies. This coalition would not just focus on the EcoCycle system but would work on other critical environmental challenges such as water scarcity, deforestation, and biodiversity conservation.

Aldo and his team were asked to be part of a newly formed advisory board that would guide the coalition in shaping policies and providing technical expertise. It was a significant responsibility, but Aldo knew that it was also an incredible opportunity to ensure that the solutions they had pioneered would be scaled and maintained.

Over the next few months, Aldo and his team traveled the world, meeting with leaders and policymakers, helping to craft national plans for sustainability. They worked on training programs for local governments and businesses, sharing their knowledge about waste management, energy solutions, and sustainable construction. In every country they visited, they encountered people who were ready to take action, eager to implement the solutions that had worked so well in other regions.

6. The Growing Movement

As Aldo and Nina returned home after the conference, they reflected on how far they had come. The days of skepticism and resistance felt like a distant memory. Now, they were part of a growing movement, one that was not just about technology but about the collective will of humanity to save the planet.

More and more grassroots organizations were forming around the world, uniting citizens, activists, and local businesses to push for sustainable practices. Aldo and Nina saw firsthand how communities were coming together to support one another and implement the changes that would help heal the Earth.

Even in the face of ongoing challenges, there was a palpable sense of optimism in the air. Aldo knew that the road ahead would not be without obstacles, but he also knew that there was no turning back. The trust they had earned, the commitment from world leaders, and the growing momentum of the global movement were all signs that they were on the right path.

As Aldo looked out over the horizon, he felt a deep sense of hope. The world was changing, and it was changing for the better. With trust now firmly established, there was nothing they couldn't accomplish.

Chapter 58: Fighting the Giants

The morning after the historic Global Sustainability Forum, Aldo awoke to an unsettling realization. The overwhelming support for the sustainable technologies they had developed had not gone unnoticed by the world's most powerful corporations. While governments were pledging their support, the corporate giants that had profited for decades from polluting industries saw their hold on the global economy slipping. And they weren't about to let it go without a fight.

Aldo had known that the road to a sustainable future would not be smooth. He had anticipated resistance from the fossil fuel sector, manufacturing conglomerates, and multinational corporations whose business models were built on exploiting natural resources and creating vast amounts of waste. What he hadn't anticipated was the sheer scale of their response.

The first signs of trouble appeared within days of the conference. At first, it was subtle, whispers in the media, the planting of negative stories in newspapers, and online articles claiming that the EcoCycle technology was unreliable, too expensive, or unproven. But it wasn't long before the attacks became more direct. By the time Aldo and his team arrived at their next meeting with government leaders, they knew that the fight would be far more complicated than they had anticipated.

1. The Corporate Machine Strikes Back

It began with a series of high-profile press releases. Corporate behemoths, many of whom had previously ignored the emerging sustainability movement, now openly criticized the technologies that Aldo had pioneered. They raised doubts about the efficacy of EcoCycle, claiming that it would disrupt global supply chains and put millions of jobs at risk.

These companies, some of the largest in the world, controlled vast swathes of the global economy. They were embedded in every major industry, energy, agriculture, manufacturing, and logistics, and their influence extended into every corner of political power. They understood that Aldo's innovations threatened their very existence.

Their primary tactic was a multi-pronged attack on the credibility of the technology and its creators. First, they launched a massive disinformation campaign. Coordinating with think tanks and industry lobbyists, they flooded the media with articles casting doubt on the safety, efficiency, and scalability of the EcoCycle technology. They played on fears of job losses, instability in energy markets, and the risk of widespread economic collapse if the world were to make the transition to sustainable technologies.

In parallel, they manipulated the stock markets, shorting shares of companies involved in renewable energy and waste-to-energy technologies. By creating a volatile financial environment, they aimed to sow doubt in the minds of investors and slow the flow of capital into the very industries that Aldo's team had worked so hard to nurture.

Their campaign also targeted politicians. Using their vast networks of influence, they pressured governments to slow down or even reverse their commitments to sustainable policies. In some cases, they used financial incentives to encourage politicians to publicly denounce the transition to green technologies. Aldo and Nina quickly realized that their battle wasn't just against outdated technologies, it was against an entire economic system that had thrived on the destruction of the environment.

2. The Personal Attacks

But it wasn't just business as usual. The attacks on Aldo and his team became personal. Social media platforms, once the tools of environmental activists and advocates, were hijacked by corporate interests to launch vicious smear campaigns. Aldo's private life was scrutinized, and false rumors were spread about his involvement in scandals and corruption. His image was manipulated, making him appear greedy and self-serving.

Nina, too, found herself at the center of a media storm. As a prominent environmental activist, she had long been a target for those who believed that her push for global change threatened their established ways of doing business. The attacks were swift, personal, and cruel. They questioned her motivations, painted her as an idealist who didn't understand the realities of the global economy, and accused her of promoting "radical" ideas that would lead to economic ruin.

Aldo and Nina were both heartbroken by the tactics employed against them, but they knew this was part of the larger battle. The corporations were scared, and they would stop at nothing to protect their profits. They had the resources to shape public opinion, manipulate markets, and wield political power.

Yet, Aldo refused to back down. He had fought for a world where the environment came first, where sustainable practices became the norm, and where humanity could thrive without destroying the planet. He wasn't about to let a few powerful corporations derail the progress that had already begun.

3. The Battle for Public Opinion

Aldo and Nina spent countless hours strategizing how they could turn the tide against the corporate giants. They knew that the media had become a powerful weapon in this battle, and they needed to fight back by amplifying their message. With the support of scientists, environmental organizations, and grassroots movements, they launched a counter-campaign that highlighted the successes of their technology. They showcased the real-world examples of cities and communities that had embraced sustainable practices and were thriving because of them.

Nina took the lead in speaking at global events, holding interviews with international news outlets, and attending protests organized by environmental activists. She used her platform to expose the corporate sabotage and to rally people around the cause of environmental justice. She highlighted how the corporations' greed had driven the world to the brink of destruction and how Aldo's solutions could offer a way out.

At the same time, Aldo worked behind the scenes to form new alliances with smaller, more ethical companies that had already embraced green technologies. They formed a coalition of businesses that were committed to sustainability, using their collective influence to fight back against the corporate giants. Through this coalition, Aldo and his team also gained access to investors who were willing to put their money into truly transformative technologies, ones that would benefit people and the planet rather than perpetuating environmental harm.

Despite the corporations' financial power, Aldo knew that the real battleground was in the hearts and minds of the people. And if they could win over public opinion, they could shift the balance of power.

4. The Turning Point

The breakthrough came when a series of investigative reports exposed the corrupt practices of the corporations leading the smear campaigns. It turned out that some of the largest companies involved in the disinformation campaign had been using their influence to block the development of clean technologies for years. These revelations were a game-changer. The media, once complicit in amplifying the corporations' message, now found themselves unable to ignore the truth.

As the public began to demand accountability, Aldo and Nina's credibility grew. The media turned its focus toward the environmental movement, and the corporations' tactics were laid bare for the world to see. It was no longer possible for the public to ignore the corporate greed that had been driving the environmental crisis for so long. People everywhere began to demand that their governments stand up to the corporate giants and protect the future of the planet.

Aldo and his team doubled down on their efforts. They worked tirelessly to implement EcoCycle in more cities, proving once again that their technology could restore the planet and empower communities. They expanded their outreach programs, helping people understand that the future could be different, that there was another way.

5. The Final Showdown

The battle was far from over. The corporations, realizing they were losing the war for public opinion, began to escalate their tactics. They attempted to co-opt some of the smaller companies in Aldo's coalition, offering them lucrative deals in exchange for abandoning their commitment to sustainability. In some cases, they tried to sabotage the EcoCycle installations, sending agents to destroy equipment or infiltrate the research teams.

But Aldo and his team were ready. They fortified their infrastructure, enhanced security, and continued to expose the truth to the world. The support for sustainable technologies only grew stronger as the corporate giants were increasingly seen for what they were: profiteers who had placed their own interests above the well-being of the planet.

In the end, it was a battle not just for the future of technology, but for the soul of humanity. Would the world continue down the destructive path of greed and exploitation, or would they choose a future where innovation worked hand-in-hand with the planet?

Aldo knew the answer. The world was ready for change.

Chapter 59: Revolution in Energy

The world was on the edge of a new epoch—a transition from the destructive past into a sustainable, renewable future. Aldo and his team had long believed that the key to saving the planet was not just in reducing waste or recycling, but in transforming waste into a powerful resource. For years, they had worked tirelessly to develop technologies that could harness the untapped energy potential of waste. Now, they stood at the threshold of a breakthrough that could change the course of history.

It had all started as a modest experiment. When Aldo first envisioned turning trash into energy, it seemed like a far-fetched dream. But now, after years of research, trial and error, and countless late nights in the lab, they had finally cracked the code. The EcoCycle system, which had already proven to be a revolutionary waste management solution, was now about to be integrated with a game-changing new energy source.

1. The Breakthrough

It was early one autumn morning when Aldo received the call that would forever alter the future of energy. The test results from their latest energy extraction experiment were in, and the numbers were staggering.

The new system was based on a unique process that transformed organic and inorganic waste into a high-efficiency fuel. The team had managed to develop a process that not only converted waste into clean energy but did so with minimal emissions and a much higher energy output than anyone had previously thought possible. The energy yield per ton of waste was enough to power entire cities for weeks. The breakthrough wasn't just theoretical; it was real, and it was happening.

Aldo's heart raced as he read through the test results. The technology had passed every trial with flying colors. They had

MOUNT OF WASTE

found a way to extract energy from waste in a manner that was more efficient than any of the existing methods for burning fossil fuels or harnessing renewable energy. This wasn't just a small victory for their team—it was the key to ending humanity's dependence on fossil fuels.

The implications were immense. If this technology could be scaled globally, it would drastically reduce the need for coal, oil, and natural gas. It would eliminate the vast carbon footprints left by traditional energy extraction methods. And most importantly, it would solve the twin crises of waste management and energy scarcity in one fell swoop.

2. Scaling the Technology

The next step was to scale up the technology for real-world use. This was where Aldo's team faced their biggest challenge yet. Although their tests had been successful on a small scale, integrating the technology into cities and industries that had relied on fossil fuels for centuries was no small feat.

Aldo, Nina, and the rest of the team began working with government officials, scientists, and business leaders from around the world to create a global rollout plan. The first step was to implement pilot programs in cities with severe waste and energy crises. They selected urban centers that had large amounts of waste and unreliable energy infrastructure. These cities would serve as testing grounds for the new energy solution.

The pilot projects quickly gained momentum. Cities that had once been drowning in waste now saw their mountains of trash being transformed into clean, renewable energy. Energy grids powered by the waste-to-energy systems began to light up entire neighborhoods. Factories, homes, and transportation networks were powered by the same waste that had previously polluted the environment.

Within months, Aldo's technology became a global sensation. Countries that had once been skeptical of the technology, especially those heavily reliant on fossil fuels, now saw the potential for economic growth, energy security, and environmental protection. International collaborations were established, and large-scale investments began pouring into the new energy infrastructure. The media hailed it as a revolution in energy—an innovation that could finally end the age of fossil fuels.

3. The Economic and Environmental Impact

The impact of the waste-to-energy technology was not just technological, it was economic and environmental. On a global scale, the project had the potential to create millions of jobs. New industries would be born, ranging from waste collection and sorting to energy production and distribution. The world was beginning to see that investing in sustainability was not just a moral imperative, it was a financial opportunity.

In addition to job creation, the economic savings were substantial. Governments that had spent billions on waste management and fossil fuel imports now had the chance to redirect those funds into green energy initiatives. The efficiency of the new system also meant that energy costs would decrease over time, helping both individuals and businesses. With this, Aldo and his team could prove that environmental responsibility didn't have to come at the expense of economic prosperity.

The environmental benefits were equally staggering. The world's landfills, once overflowing with plastic, food waste, and discarded electronics, were now being repurposed as energy hubs. Oceans that had been plagued by plastic debris saw a dramatic reduction in pollution, as waste products were converted into fuel rather than being dumped into the water. Carbon emissions from burning fossil fuels dropped sharply, contributing to a cleaner atmosphere. In just a few short years, cities that had been suffocating under the weight of pollution and waste now had the potential to become green energy havens.

Aldo and Nina traveled the world, speaking at conferences and meeting with policymakers to help further the cause. They worked tirelessly to convince nations that the waste-to-energy technology could become the backbone of a new, sustainable global economy. As their message spread, more and more countries signed on to the project, eager to move away from their reliance on fossil fuels and embrace the new, sustainable future that Aldo had helped to create.

4. Challenges from the Past

However, despite the widespread enthusiasm, the project was far from easy. As Aldo and his team expanded the technology's reach, they began to encounter resistance from some of the very industries that had benefited from the fossil fuel economy. Coal, oil, and natural gas companies, who saw their profits plummeting as waste-to-energy technology gained traction, lobbied governments to slow down or even halt the transition.

The oil industry, in particular, fought tooth and nail to maintain its grip on the global energy market. Corporate leaders, some of whom had been at the forefront of the disinformation campaigns against Aldo's earlier work, began to target the waste-to-energy revolution with renewed ferocity. They attempted to discredit the technology by claiming that it was too expensive to implement on a global scale, that it would result in job losses in traditional energy sectors, and that the long-term environmental impact was still uncertain.

Despite these challenges, Aldo remained resolute. He knew that the road ahead would be difficult, but he also knew that the people, who had already seen the benefits of sustainable technology in their own cities, would rise up to support the change. And in the end, it was the people who were his greatest allies.

5. Global Transformation

As more and more countries adopted the waste-to-energy technology, the world began to witness a profound shift. The fossil fuel industry slowly began to lose its influence as nations, empowered by Aldo's solutions, embraced renewable energy on a massive scale. Coal plants were decommissioned, oil rigs left unused, and natural gas pipelines were abandoned in favor of cleaner, more efficient energy sources.

The success of the waste-to-energy revolution became a symbol of global collaboration. Nations that had once been divided by political and economic differences came together in the shared pursuit of a healthier, more sustainable world. They recognized that energy was not just a resource, it was the key to unlocking a future free from the environmental destruction of the past.

Cities that had once been struggling with waste management problems now boasted advanced, self-sustaining energy systems. Rural areas that had been without reliable access to power now thrived on clean, locally generated energy. The world had entered an age of energy abundance, one that was powered not by the exploitation of the Earth's resources, but by the Earth's own waste.

Aldo and his team were finally seeing the fruition of their vision, a world no longer dependent on fossil fuels, where waste was no longer a burden, but a resource. The revolution in energy was more than just a technological breakthrough; it was a revolution in thinking, one that would transform the way humanity viewed its relationship with the planet.

The work was far from over. As the world moved toward full adoption of the waste-to-energy technology, Aldo knew that new challenges would arise. But for the first time in a long while, there was hope. A hope born of ingenuity, collaboration, and the unrelenting desire to build a better world.

Chapter 60: Challenges in the Remote Regions

As the world began to embrace the revolutionary waste-to-energy technology that Aldo and his team had developed, the transformation seemed almost unstoppable. Cities and industrial hubs were becoming beacons of sustainability, powered by clean, renewable energy sourced from their very own waste. The global movement to end dependence on fossil fuels was gaining traction at an unprecedented rate. However, in the midst of this growing global success, Aldo and his team encountered an obstacle they had not fully anticipated: the challenge of bringing their technology to the world's most remote and isolated regions.

While major metropolitan areas were rapidly adapting to the new system, there were vast swaths of the planet that remained untouched by the progress sweeping across the globe. These regions, often found in the heart of jungles, high in the mountains, or in the desolate corners of deserts, were far removed from the bustling cities where the revolution had started. For many of these communities, the very idea of modern energy infrastructure seemed like a distant dream, let alone the cutting-edge waste-to-energy systems Aldo's team had pioneered.

1. The Struggles of Isolation

One of the first challenges Aldo and his team encountered in these remote regions was the sheer difficulty of access. Many of the most isolated communities had little to no infrastructure, no roads, no electricity, and in some cases, no form of communication with the outside world. The waste-to-energy technology required a complex setup involving large machinery, power grids, and skilled workers. Even the most basic components, like the transport vehicles to deliver equipment or the communication tools to coordinate efforts, were in short supply in these places.

Aldo and Nina sat in the operations room of the central command in the main headquarters, discussing the logistics of delivering the technology to these remote communities. The situation was more complicated than they had originally anticipated. The team had already succeeded in implementing their systems in urban areas and had even been successful in scaling up production for larger cities. But now, they had to find a way to address the needs of regions that were not only geographically isolated but also struggling with a lack of basic necessities.

"There are areas in the highlands of South America, parts of sub-Saharan Africa, and the remote villages in Southeast Asia that are still entirely off the grid," Nina said, flipping through a report. "Their infrastructure is either completely destroyed by natural disasters or never existed in the first place."

Aldo nodded, his fingers tapping nervously on the table. "We can't allow this to be a problem that leaves people out. These areas are the hardest hit by the waste crisis and the energy shortages. If we can't reach them, then we've failed."

The reality of the situation was harsh. The people in these remote areas were already living on the margins of society, struggling to survive with limited resources. They had no access to reliable energy, and in many cases, they had no means to deal with the overwhelming waste that had accumulated in their environments. While the rest of the world moved forward, these isolated communities remained stuck in the past, suffering from the same problems that had once plagued the entire planet.

2. A Glimmer of Hope

Despite the challenges, Aldo and his team were determined to make a difference. They knew that if they could bring the waste-to-energy technology to these remote areas, it would not only provide much-needed power but also help to clean up the environment that had been devastated by waste. But how could they achieve this in places that lacked even the most basic infrastructure?

The team spent weeks brainstorming solutions. They came up with a plan that involved building small, mobile units that could be easily transported to remote regions. These units would be self-contained, requiring minimal infrastructure to operate. They could be powered by solar energy and wind, providing an additional source of clean energy to help run the systems. The waste-to-energy technology would be incorporated into these units in a modular fashion, allowing for easy installation and maintenance even in the most isolated areas.

The design of these mobile units was groundbreaking. They were compact, durable, and designed to be adaptable to a variety of environments. Each unit was equipped with advanced technology that allowed it to process waste and convert it into energy with minimal human intervention. The units could be transported on the backs of trucks, boats, or even mules, depending on the terrain.

Aldo was excited by the possibilities. "This could be the key to reaching the world's most isolated communities," he said, standing before the team. "We don't need to rely on existing infrastructure. We can create a new, decentralized system that allows these communities to become self-sustaining. It's about giving them the tools to take control of their own futures."

3. Overcoming the Logistics Nightmare

Despite the team's optimism, the logistics of getting these mobile units into remote areas proved to be a massive undertaking. Transportation was one of the biggest hurdles. Many of the regions Aldo's team was targeting were located in areas that were nearly impossible to reach by traditional means. High mountain passes, dense forests, and vast deserts stood between them and their goal.

To tackle this, Aldo and Nina enlisted the help of local communities, as well as global organizations that specialized in providing aid to remote areas. They worked closely with local governments, NGOs, and grassroots organizations that had experience navigating the challenges of working in isolated regions.

"We need to think about this as a community effort," Nina said, stressing the importance of collaboration. "These people have been living without proper energy for years. We're not just going to drop these units off and walk away. We need to train local workers, create local jobs, and build long-term partnerships."

The team focused on developing a training program that would equip local workers with the skills needed to operate and maintain the new energy systems. They collaborated with universities, international organizations, and local experts to create comprehensive training materials. They also formed partnerships with local businesses that could help with ongoing support and maintenance.

As Aldo and his team worked to implement the mobile units, they faced additional challenges. Natural disasters, like floods, droughts, and earthquakes, had wreaked havoc on some of the most isolated regions, leaving entire villages cut off from the outside world. It was a race against time, as the team worked to get the necessary equipment into these areas before another disaster struck.

But through sheer determination and a willingness to work alongside local communities, Aldo's team slowly began to make progress. The first successful installation of a mobile unit took place in a remote village in the Andes Mountains. The village had been devastated by a combination of waste accumulation and energy scarcity, and the installation of the waste-to-energy system brought hope to a place that had been struggling for years.

4. Building a New Future

MOUNT OF WASTE

The success of the first installation in the Andes provided a blueprint for future projects. As more units were shipped to other remote regions, the team encountered different challenges, some of which were even more severe than anticipated. But with each new success, Aldo and his team gained valuable knowledge and insight, adapting their approach to better meet the needs of each community.

The key to success was not just in delivering the technology, it was in building trust and forging lasting relationships with the people who lived in these remote regions. By involving local communities in every step of the process, from planning to installation to ongoing maintenance, Aldo's team was able to create a sense of ownership and pride. The waste-to-energy systems were not just foreign technologies; they were part of the solution, owned and operated by the very people who had once been marginalized and left behind.

In one village in sub-Saharan Africa, the introduction of the technology sparked a revolution. The community, which had long been plagued by waste, now had access to a reliable source of energy. Local farmers were able to use the energy to power irrigation systems, allowing them to grow crops year-round. Small businesses thrived as they gained access to electricity, and the community's overall quality of life improved dramatically.

5. A World Transformed

As Aldo and his team continued to push forward with their mission, they began to see a glimmer of hope in the most unexpected places. Remote regions that had once been written off as too difficult to reach were now at the forefront of the global sustainability movement. The waste-to-energy technology was spreading, slowly but surely, to every corner of the Earth.

What started as a solution to one of the world's biggest problems had now become a movement for global change. The isolated communities that had once been forgotten were now leading the charge toward a cleaner, more sustainable world.

The road had been long and filled with obstacles, but Aldo knew that this was only the beginning. The work was far from over, but every success brought the world one step closer to the sustainable future they all envisioned.

Chapter 61: Global Dissemination of Technology

As the first rays of dawn broke over the horizon, casting their golden light across the gleaming, futuristic cityscapes, Aldo and his team stood before a map of the world that was slowly but steadily changing. It wasn't just the geography they were concerned with, but the intricate web of partnerships, logistics, and strategies that had brought them to this pivotal moment. Their revolutionary waste-to-energy technology was now on the brink of being adopted on a global scale.

Aldo had always believed that the key to saving the planet lay not in individual, isolated solutions but in the collective power of global cooperation. It wasn't enough for a few regions or nations to embrace the change; for the world to truly heal, the technology had to spread, igniting a fire of innovation and action across every corner of the Earth. And now, with the help of powerful international alliances and organizations, Aldo and his team were about to witness the realization of that dream.

1. The Power of Alliances

The global collaboration that had been so crucial to the success of Aldo's technology had finally matured. Years of negotiation, mutual compromise, and the building of trust between governments, non-governmental organizations, and multinational corporations had laid the groundwork for a massive, coordinated effort to introduce the waste-to-energy systems worldwide. International treaties, global summits, and grassroots movements had converged to create a perfect storm of support.

At the heart of this movement was the United Nations Sustainability Initiative (UNSI), which had quickly recognized the profound potential of Aldo's technology to address multiple global crises, waste accumulation, energy scarcity, and climate change. Under the auspices of the UNSI, a coalition of nations had formed to implement the technology across continents, beginning with the nations most severely affected by waste pollution and energy deficits.

For Aldo and Nina, the road to this moment had been long and fraught with obstacles, but now it was clear that the effort had been worth every sleepless night. Countries that had once been hesitant to embrace change were now eagerly signing agreements to integrate the waste-to-energy technology into their national strategies.

2. A Step Toward Global Implementation

Aldo stood at the helm of the United Nations Sustainability Initiative's headquarters, addressing a room filled with representatives from various countries. The mood was one of cautious optimism, but there was a palpable sense of excitement in the air. The walls of the conference room were adorned with digital screens showcasing the progress of the new waste management systems in different parts of the world, images of lush green fields in India, clean urban streets in the United States, and thriving coastal communities in Africa, all benefiting from the technology.

"Aldo, your technology is changing the world," the UN Secretary-General, Maria Delgado, said warmly as she looked around the room. "We've seen its success in the pilot projects. It's time for the world to see what we can achieve when we all work together."

Aldo's heart swelled with pride, but he knew that the task at hand was monumental. The next phase of their work would be critical: scaling up production, managing international logistics, and ensuring the technology was accessible to even the most remote areas of the planet.

"What we've achieved here," Aldo began, addressing the room, "is nothing short of a miracle. But this is just the beginning. We must now focus on bringing these systems to every country, every city, every village. We need to ensure that no one is left behind, no matter their geography, no matter their economic status."

His words were met with applause, and the global collaboration began in earnest.

3. Navigating Political Landscapes

Even as the world celebrated the widespread adoption of Aldo's technology, challenges continued to emerge. Each country had its own set of political dynamics, and in many cases, entrenched interests were determined to slow or even derail the progress.

In the United States, corporate lobbyists from the oil and gas industry fought tooth and nail to protect their dominance in the energy sector. They spread misinformation about the waste-to-energy systems, claiming they were inefficient or too expensive. The fight in the U.S. was heated, but Aldo's team had prepared for this moment. They had worked tirelessly to gather data, conduct studies, and develop pilot programs that demonstrated the efficiency and cost-effectiveness of their technology.

"We need to counter their narrative," Nina said during a strategy session in New York. "The data is on our side. We have to show the world that the future of energy isn't dependent on the old guard. It's here, and it's happening."

Aldo nodded. "We're not just fighting against corporations, we're fighting for the future of our planet. And the truth is on our side. The more people see the benefits, the harder it will be for them to ignore the truth."

By strategically partnering with advocacy groups and influential political figures who understood the urgency of the climate crisis, Aldo and his team were able to break through the corporate resistance. It wasn't easy, and there were setbacks along the way, but the tide was turning.

4. Scaling Up Operations

The true challenge in scaling the technology was not just political, it was logistical. Each installation of the waste-to-energy systems required careful planning and execution. The team needed to produce millions of modular waste-to-energy units, each capable of processing vast amounts of waste and converting it into usable energy. The production facilities had to be expanded, and the necessary raw materials, plastics, metals, and other recyclable materials,vhad to be sourced at a scale that was unprecedented.

Aldo and Nina worked closely with manufacturers across the globe to create a network of production hubs. By sourcing raw materials locally and utilizing advanced robotics and automation, the team was able to reduce production costs and increase efficiency. As a result, the technology began to reach countries that had once been unable to afford such solutions.

"Now, the technology can be deployed everywhere," Aldo said during a meeting with his team. "We can provide nations, even smaller ones, with the tools they need to solve their energy and waste problems. We've democratized the solution."

One of the first success stories came from Indonesia. The archipelago, once overwhelmed by the mountain of plastic waste that had plagued its shores for years, had begun to see dramatic improvements. The government had signed on to the global initiative and worked with Aldo's team to roll out the new waste-to-energy systems in key areas. Coastal cities saw reduced pollution, cleaner beaches, and a surge in renewable energy production.

5. The Ripple Effect

As the technology spread across the globe, its impact became undeniable. The systems installed in cities, rural areas, and remote communities began to make a tangible difference. In India, the use of waste-to-energy technology allowed farmers in the rural north to produce more food, while in Brazil, cities with previously unreliable power grids now enjoyed a constant, sustainable energy supply.

In Africa, waste that had once been discarded or left to accumulate in landfills was now being converted into power to support schools, hospitals, and factories. In Europe, the move away from fossil fuels accelerated, with countries like Germany and France leading the charge by integrating the technology into their green energy portfolios.

"We're seeing a global shift, and it's happening faster than we imagined," Nina said with a smile during a video call with Aldo. "This is more than a technology, it's a movement."

The ripple effect was now being felt worldwide. Communities that had been on the frontlines of the climate crisis, those that had been bearing the brunt of environmental degradation, were the ones leading the way in adopting the technology. They were no longer victims of the waste crisis; they were the innovators, the trailblazers.

6. The Road Ahead

Despite the overwhelming success of the global rollout, Aldo knew that the work was far from finished. There were still challenges to overcome, new technologies to develop, old systems to dismantle, and old habits to break. But with the world now united in the pursuit of a cleaner, more sustainable future, Aldo and his team felt a renewed sense of purpose.

The future was bright, and for the first time in a long while, Aldo felt the weight of the world lift from his shoulders. They had done it. Together, they had turned the tide. They had shown that change was possible, and now, there was no turning back.

Chapter 62: Political Tensions

The global community was standing on the edge of a new era. With the waste-to-energy technology implemented across the world, the effects were already visible, cleaner cities, reduced reliance on fossil fuels, and a gradual reversal of the environmental damage caused by decades of neglect. The message was clear: humanity could change its course, and it could do so quickly and efficiently. But, as with every significant transformation, challenges remained, particularly in the realm of politics.

1. The Divide Between Developed and Developing Nations

Despite the overwhelming success of the new technology, the world was far from united. The long-standing divide between the developed and developing nations, a gap that had always been a source of friction, was now more pronounced than ever.

Developed countries, such as those in North America and Europe, had been early adopters of the waste-to-energy systems. They had the infrastructure, the financial resources, and the political stability to implement the technology efficiently. They were also leading the charge in renewable energy initiatives, driven by both economic incentives and climate goals.

In contrast, many developing nations in Africa, Asia, and parts of Latin America had struggled with the financial burden of adopting the new technologies. While the waste-to-energy systems were a game-changer for these regions, their implementation was not without complications. Many of these nations still lacked the necessary infrastructure to support large-scale technological rollouts, and the economic disparities between them and their wealthier counterparts remained a constant point of contention.

Aldo sat at his desk in the sleek headquarters of the United Nations Sustainability Initiative (UNSI), staring at the map on his screen. The countries in green represented those that had successfully adopted the technology, while the countries in yellow and red indicated areas where the deployment had been slow or had encountered significant challenges. The disparity was glaring.

Nina walked into his office, her face a mixture of determination and concern. "Aldo, we need to talk. The political tensions are growing. There's a real risk that the rift between the developed and developing world could derail everything we've worked for."

Aldo leaned back in his chair. "I know. I've been monitoring the situation. There's a lot of frustration on both sides. The developed nations are getting frustrated because they feel they've done their part, but the developing nations are struggling to meet the financial demands of this transition. It's a vicious cycle."

2. The Diplomacy Dilemma

The United Nations had called for a summit to address these tensions. The world's leaders were convening in Geneva, with Aldo and Nina invited to attend as special guests. The atmosphere at the summit was charged with political maneuvering, as delegates from various countries presented their cases.

On one side, the developed nations argued that they had already provided significant aid and support to the developing world and that they could not continue to bear the financial burden of global change alone. They pointed to the economic growth that had been spurred by the waste-to-energy technology in their own regions and how they had transitioned away from fossil fuels, helping to reduce global emissions.

On the other side, the developing countries voiced their frustration. For many of them, the transition to greener technology had been costly, and without significant support, they would not be able to make the necessary changes to sustain their populations. They argued that the developed world, which had contributed most to the environmental crisis, should provide more substantial financial backing to help them meet their obligations under the global climate accords.

Aldo stood at the front of the room, the weight of the moment pressing on him. This summit could either be a turning point or a breaking point for the future of the planet. He knew that if he could find a way to bridge the divide, it could change the trajectory of the global effort. But if the tensions continued to escalate, it could lead to economic isolation, trade wars, and, worst of all, a reversal of the progress they had made in the fight against climate change.

"We must recognize that these are not just political differences," Aldo began, his voice steady but filled with urgency. "This is a matter of survival for the future of our children, for the future of all life on this planet. The technology we have developed has the potential to change the world. But it is only effective if every nation has access to it, and every nation is able to participate in this global transformation."

Nina joined him on stage, addressing the room. "What we have accomplished is unprecedented. But we can't afford to leave anyone behind. The disparity between the developed and developing nations must be addressed, not through blame or competition, but through cooperation. We must come together and share both the risks and the rewards of this transition."

3. The Economic Equation

One of the key arguments from the developed nations was the economic burden of continuing to provide financial support to the developing world. Many of these nations had already faced severe economic hardship as a result of the climate crisis, and while they were on the path to recovery, the costs of maintaining the technology infrastructure were not insignificant.

"Let's be clear," said Maria Delgado, the UN Secretary-General, as she stepped to the podium. "We all acknowledge the economic disparities. However, this is not a time for finger-pointing. This is a time for new thinking. The financial support we provide to developing countries must come with shared responsibility. We have the resources, but we must make sure they are used efficiently, for the good of all. It is time for a global fund, an initiative in which all nations, rich and poor, contribute to the shared cost of sustainability."

Aldo nodded in agreement. "This is a crucial point. We can't continue to expect one group of countries to carry the entire burden. We must create a global sustainability fund, one that brings together governments, private sector partners, and international financial institutions to create a shared pool of resources."

Several representatives from developing nations voiced their support for the idea, but others were more skeptical, fearing that such a fund would be mismanaged or that it would become a tool for further exploitation.

"The key will be transparency," Aldo said. "The fund must be managed in a way that prioritizes the needs of the most vulnerable countries. Every nation, no matter its size, must be able to contribute, but we must also ensure that the benefits are distributed equitably."

4. Building Trust

As the summit wore on, the tension in the room began to dissipate. Aldo and Nina worked tirelessly to keep the discussions focused on solutions, rather than the differences that had kept the world apart for so long. Slowly but surely, they managed to build a consensus that embraced both the technological and financial challenges of the transition.

By the end of the summit, a new agreement was in the works, a framework for a global sustainability fund that would support the adoption of waste-to-energy systems in developing nations. The fund would be supplemented by private-sector investments and matched with technical assistance from the wealthier nations.

The delegates from both sides of the divide had made compromises, but the resulting agreement marked a victory for the global community. For Aldo, the work was far from over. The next step would be to ensure that the fund was established and that it functioned efficiently, without the bureaucracy and inefficiency that often plagued international aid programs.

5. The Road Ahead

As Aldo and Nina left the summit, they felt a sense of accomplishment. The political tensions that had once threatened to derail their progress had been addressed, but they knew that the real work was just beginning. The true challenge lay in maintaining the momentum, ensuring that the global community would continue to work together to build a sustainable future.

Aldo turned to Nina as they walked toward the exit. "We've taken a big step forward. But we still have a long road ahead. The political landscape will continue to shift, and we'll face new challenges. But we've built a foundation of cooperation, and that gives me hope."

Nina smiled, her determination unwavering. "We've started something that can't be stopped. We've planted the seeds of change. Now it's time to watch them grow."

Chapter 63: The Fall of the Anti-Development Groups

The world was shifting. The dawn of a new era, where sustainability was at the forefront, was no longer a distant dream, it was a living reality. Global cooperation, technological innovations, and the unified push towards a cleaner, more sustainable future had gained remarkable momentum. What had once seemed impossible was now achievable, and humanity was embracing it, slowly but surely.

But with every revolution, there are those who resist. While the world celebrated the advancements in waste-to-energy technology, renewable energy, and ecological recovery, a series of well-established anti-development groups began to face an unprecedented downfall. Once powerful organizations, these groups had built their ideologies on fear, misinformation, and the rejection of modern technological advancements. As the truth of the sustainability movement became undeniable, these groups found themselves losing the battle, not only against the global community but also against their own supporters.

1. The Rise and Fall of Resistance

In the early years of Aldo's journey, the anti-development movement had been loud and influential. These groups had preached a message of fear and caution, warning the public of the dangers of technological progress and global cooperation. They painted the world's transition to a sustainable future as a threat to individual freedoms, to economic stability, and to the very fabric of society.

Some of these groups had garnered significant political support. Their leaders, often charismatic and well-spoken, framed the issue as a fight for sovereignty, against the alleged "globalist" agenda and for the preservation of traditional ways of life. They tapped into the public's anxieties about rapid change and the uncertain future, playing on the fears of job losses, economic dislocation, and the erosion of national identity.

But as the years passed, and the positive effects of sustainable development became more evident, the tide began to turn. The mounting evidence was undeniable. Cities had transformed. Carbon emissions had dropped. Clean energy was no longer a luxury, it was a necessity. As countries around the world adopted waste-to-energy systems and sustainable agricultural practices, the opposition's once-strong foundation began to crumble.

2. Public Perception Shifts

One of the pivotal moments that contributed to the fall of the anti-development groups came with the international media coverage of the environmental recovery. In the aftermath of the disasters that had ravaged cities and ecosystems, a new narrative began to emerge: the restoration of the planet was not only possible but was happening.

Documentaries, news reports, and social media posts highlighted communities around the world that had embraced sustainable technologies. They showcased the clean, thriving cities built from the very waste that had once been their downfall. People saw for themselves how renewable energy projects were revitalizing economies, creating jobs, and reducing poverty. The message was clear: sustainability was not a threat, it was a chance for a better world.

With each success story, the once-glamorous anti-development groups began to lose their grip. People started questioning the fear-mongering tactics of these organizations. In countries where the groups had been most vocal, public support for their agendas began to erode.

"We can't deny it any longer," said Maria Delgado, the UN Secretary-General, during a press conference. "The future is here, and it's sustainable. The fear that we would lose everything to a greener world was just a tactic used by those who sought to maintain control. What we see now is a future in which we thrive, not only as nations but as a global community."

It wasn't just the political landscape that was shifting. People from all walks of life were beginning to understand that change was not something to fear, but something to embrace. Local communities, once skeptical of global initiatives, were seeing firsthand the benefits of sustainable practices. Agriculture was thriving without the overuse of harmful chemicals. Oceans, once choked with plastic, were slowly returning to life.

And as public awareness grew, the anti-development groups found themselves facing a severe loss of support. Their messages of doom and gloom fell on deaf ears, as people began to see that the world was not falling apart, it was coming together in a way they had never imagined.

3. The Collapse of Key Leaders

In a world where influence was often tied to charismatic leaders, the downfall of the anti-development groups was accelerated by the disillusionment of their key figures. These leaders had built their reputations on resistance to change, but when the evidence of the success of sustainable technologies became irrefutable, many of them were forced to either adjust their stances or face public outrage.

One such leader, Jonathan Blackwell, once the face of the anti-development movement, found himself in the eye of a public storm. Blackwell had led the most influential anti-sustainability organization, "Save Our Way," which had rallied against the global push for green technologies, calling it an assault on personal freedom. He had positioned himself as the voice of reason in an increasingly chaotic world, warning of the dangers of economic ruin and social collapse if technology went unchecked.

But as more cities implemented Aldo's waste-to-energy systems and saw tangible benefits, reduced waste, cleaner air, and new economic opportunities, Blackwell's message started to falter. His once-loyal followers began to question the very basis of his arguments. His latest media campaign to discredit renewable energy was met with ridicule when a viral video showed how much cleaner the skies were in cities that had adopted green technologies.

Blackwell's response was to double down, but the backlash was swift. A former supporter turned whistleblower revealed internal communications that suggested the organization had been secretly funded by industries with vested interests in maintaining fossil fuel dominance. The truth was clear: Blackwell's movement had been more about protecting outdated industries than protecting the people.

The final blow came when Blackwell, unable to face the growing wave of evidence, retreated from the public eye. The movement he had built, once a powerful force, was now in disarray. His resignation marked the end of an era for the anti-development groups.

4. The Collapse of the Global Movement

As Blackwell and other leaders of the anti-development factions fell, the larger movement began to crumble. With their influence waning, smaller, more extreme factions tried to keep the resistance alive. But as time passed, their messages became increasingly fringe. Some attempted to stage protests or sabotage key infrastructure, but their efforts were met with little public support. The global community had moved on.

At the heart of the movement's downfall was the undeniable success of Aldo's waste-to-energy technology. In every major city around the world, there were visible improvements: reduced landfill sites, cleaner air, and a reduction in waste that had once been an overwhelming problem. People were seeing the results, and they no longer had patience for those who were attempting to stop progress.

The international community, once divided over issues of sustainability, was now united. It was no longer about whether the technology worked, it was about how quickly the world could adopt it. Every major nation, from the United States to China to Brazil, had embraced the new systems, and the global economic agenda had shifted towards green technologies. The old guard of the anti-development groups had been left behind.

5. The Aftermath: A New World Emerging

The fall of the anti-development groups was not without its lessons. The world had learned a valuable lesson about the dangers of fear-based politics and the power of misinformation. While it was tempting to resist change in the face of uncertainty, the truth was that humanity had to evolve or face irreparable destruction. And Aldo's team had proven that it was possible to innovate and create a better, more sustainable world.

The lessons of the past were not lost on the global community. Governments, industries, and citizens alike understood that this was just the beginning. The fight for a sustainable future was ongoing, and while the anti-development groups had been silenced, the work was far from over.

As Aldo stood at the United Nations, delivering his speech about the success of the global transition to renewable energy and waste management, he couldn't help but feel a sense of pride. The work had been hard. The road had been long. But the world was now on a path to healing.

"I have always believed that the human spirit has the power to adapt, to change, and to create a future we can all be proud of," Aldo said, his voice ringing out across the hall. "Today, we see the fruits of that belief. Together, we have proved that change is not only possible but inevitable. And in this new world, there is no place for fear or resistance to progress. There is only the opportunity to thrive, together."

The room erupted in applause, a symbol of the collective will to build a brighter, more sustainable future.

Chapter 64: Technology That Touches Daily Life

The world had changed, and with it, the rhythm of daily life. The progress that Aldo and his team had made in revolutionizing waste management and sustainable living had reached a crucial point: it was no longer just an abstract concept or an ambitious initiative. It was now embedded into the very fabric of everyday existence. From bustling urban centers to quiet rural villages, people everywhere were beginning to feel the profound effects of these new technologies.

1. Waste Management at Home

One of the most visible changes had been in the homes of ordinary citizens. Aldo's waste-to-energy technology, which had once been the focal point of his groundbreaking research, had now been adapted for residential use. The small, compact machines that could convert household waste into clean energy were installed in homes across the globe, offering a solution to both the mounting waste problem and the growing energy crisis.

Families no longer had to rely on traditional garbage collection services, which had become increasingly overwhelmed as the global population swelled and the volumes of waste multiplied. Instead, each household could manage its own waste efficiently. Food scraps, packaging materials, and even the plastic waste that had once threatened to choke entire ecosystems could now be processed and transformed into usable energy. The technology was simple enough for anyone to use, and it was designed to be intuitive.

The impact was immediate. Waste disposal no longer required large, polluting trucks to cart trash across cities. Landfills, once growing out of control and emitting harmful gases, were now a thing of the past. Each home had become an active participant in solving the waste crisis.

"Look at this," remarked Sofia, a mother of three in a small suburban neighborhood. "Every night, we just throw our waste into this little machine, and it not only turns it into energy but also gives us electricity for a few hours. The kids are excited about it. They think it's magic, but it's just our way of doing our part."

The machine itself was an elegant marvel of engineering. Small but efficient, it fit into any kitchen or utility space and processed everything from vegetable peels to packaging material. As it converted waste into clean energy, it released minimal emissions, nothing like the harmful, toxic fumes of previous methods of waste disposal.

Local governments had quickly recognized the potential for this technology to dramatically improve both urban and rural waste management systems. The rise of home-based waste-to-energy systems, in turn, led to a decrease in the burden placed on municipal waste services and helped prevent further environmental damage. People were living in cleaner homes, with cleaner air and water,vand they were more self-sufficient than ever before.

2. The Rise of Eco-Friendly Manufacturing

Beyond the home, Aldo's technology had begun to permeate the industrial world. The waste-to-energy systems initially designed for small-scale applications had evolved to serve as the backbone of eco-friendly manufacturing plants. The transition to these sustainable systems didn't happen overnight, but over time, more and more factories replaced their outdated, polluting operations with state-of-the-art, eco-friendly production lines.

One of the major success stories was the transformation of the textile industry, which had long been notorious for its waste production. As fashion trends became more rapid and consumption spiked, the environmental toll of textile production became unsustainable. The introduction of waste-to-energy solutions allowed manufacturers to reduce, recycle, and reuse a vast portion of the materials used in the creation of clothes and fabrics. By converting waste fibers, packaging, and even dye waste into clean energy, factories were able to lower their carbon footprints and drastically cut down on waste.

These factories were not just minimizing waste but were turning it into a powerful asset. The closed-loop systems in place ensured that nothing went to waste. The byproducts of one part of the production line fed directly into the next, creating a harmonious, efficient process.

At the same time, large-scale waste-to-energy plants began to emerge in places that were once seen as environmental hotspots. In these plants, waste from industrial sectors like food production, construction, and electronics recycling was processed and transformed into usable energy. In places like China, India, and the European Union, such plants had become standard, ushering in a new era of responsible production.

"Today, our factory is almost entirely self-sustaining," said Rajesh Patel, CEO of a large textile manufacturer in India. "We use our own waste to power the entire plant. This new system has not only saved us money on energy but has improved our image. We're no longer a polluter; we're part of the solution. The fashion industry has always been in the spotlight for all the wrong reasons, but now we can proudly say we're contributing to a more sustainable future."

3. Agricultural Transformation

The changes Aldo and his team brought were not limited to cities and factories. Rural communities, where the majority of people lived in close connection to the land, also found themselves deeply affected by the new technologies. Agricultural systems that once relied heavily on chemical fertilizers and non-renewable resources were now powered by sustainable practices and technology.

Using waste materials to fertilize the soil became a core practice. The introduction of organic waste composting machines allowed farmers to recycle their agricultural waste, such as crop residue and animal manure, into valuable organic fertilizers that enriched the soil. This not only reduced reliance on synthetic chemicals but also helped maintain the health of the soil and the surrounding ecosystem.

In addition, the creation of small biogas digesters allowed farmers to convert agricultural waste, including animal dung, into biogas that could be used as cooking fuel. These digesters were a game-changer for rural communities, particularly in developing countries, where access to clean and affordable energy had once been scarce. With a simple but effective design, biogas digesters began providing millions of families with a renewable source of cooking energy, reducing indoor air pollution and improving health outcomes.

"I no longer have to worry about the cost of fuel for cooking," said Nia Moyo, a farmer in rural Tanzania. "The biogas digester provides us with all the energy we need, and it's made from waste that would have just rotted away. We use our cow dung and crop leftovers to power our home and our farm."

Increased agricultural productivity was also a direct result of the technology Aldo's team had developed. Crops were healthier, as the soil was treated with organic fertilizers rather than harmful chemicals. Communities that had once struggled with food security were now producing more than enough to feed themselves and even export their surplus.

4. Energy Independence

MOUNT OF WASTE

One of the most profound impacts of Aldo's technology on daily life was the shift towards energy independence. For centuries, human society had been tethered to large, centralized power grids, reliant on fossil fuels, coal, and nuclear energy. But as waste-to-energy systems expanded across homes and industries, people began to sever their dependency on traditional energy sources.

By tapping into their own waste streams, citizens were generating their own power. Solar and wind energy also complemented these systems, allowing individuals, neighborhoods, and even entire cities to take charge of their energy needs.

In places like rural Africa, where power lines were sparse and unreliable, small, decentralized energy systems allowed entire villages to become self-sustaining. The ability to generate energy from local waste eliminated the need for large, expensive energy infrastructure projects that had often left underserved communities in the dark.

"I never thought this would happen," said Eniola, a village elder in Nigeria. "We used to rely on diesel generators, and it was always a struggle. Now we have solar panels and a waste-to-energy system that powers our homes. It's given us the ability to be more independent and sustainable."

5. The Urban Renaissance

Cities, once choking on their own pollution, were undergoing a renaissance. Buildings were now designed to be energy-efficient, with green roofs, rainwater collection systems, and solar panels on every surface. Public transportation was electric, reducing the need for gasoline-powered cars. Urban agriculture flourished in every corner of the city, from rooftop gardens to vertical farms in old warehouses. People no longer saw waste as a nuisance, they saw it as a resource.

The once-vibrant chaos of city life had found a new rhythm, one where every decision, every action, every process contributed to a cleaner, greener world. People embraced their role as active participants in the healing of the planet.

6. A Global Community

The most heartwarming aspect of these changes was the newfound sense of global solidarity. Communities, once isolated by geography or economic status, now shared knowledge and resources. The technologies that had changed Aldo's world were being shared across borders.

"We are no longer fighting this fight alone," Aldo said during a global summit on sustainable development. "This is a movement. A global movement, where every person has the power to make a difference."

And make a difference they did. Through grassroots organizations, local governments, and global initiatives, the transformation was well underway. Every step forward was a step closer to the world Aldo had envisioned, a world where technology didn't just serve humanity but helped restore the Earth itself.

The impact of Aldo's work was far-reaching. From homes to industries, from farmers to urban dwellers, the change was real. And it was only just beginning.

Chapter 65: Building the Green City

The sun had barely risen over the horizon, casting a warm golden glow over the sprawling landscape that had once been an industrial wasteland. Today, it was the site of something extraordinary, a green city, a beacon of hope, and a tangible proof that humanity could rebuild its future in harmony with the Earth.

Aldo stood on the edge of the construction site, his eyes scanning the vast project ahead. For years, this moment had seemed like a distant dream, a world where technology not only solved the problems of the present but created a thriving ecosystem for future generations. And now, standing before the rising walls of the Green City, it was clear that this dream was becoming reality.

"This is more than just a city," Aldo murmured to Nina, who stood beside him, her eyes reflecting the same mix of excitement and determination. "It's a living organism. A place where everything is interconnected, where technology, nature, and humanity work together to create something truly sustainable."

1. Laying the Foundations of the Green City

The first step in creating the Green City had been selecting the perfect location. Aldo and his team scoured the globe, searching for a place that was not only suited for sustainable construction but also offered a blank slate, an area that had been damaged by previous industrial activities or disasters and needed revitalization. They found their location in a region once known for its heavy industrial use, which had left behind scars on the land and a polluted environment.

This site, however, offered unique advantages. The land was relatively inexpensive, and the surrounding areas had been neglected for years, providing the perfect opportunity to reshape it into something new, something better.

The design of the city itself was unlike any other. Unlike the sprawling, chaotic urban landscapes that had dominated the world for centuries, the Green City was built with purpose, efficiency, and nature at its core. Each aspect of the city was designed to minimize waste, maximize energy efficiency, and foster an environment where people could live in harmony with nature.

The foundations were laid with sustainable materials, recycled plastics, biodegradable concrete, and locally sourced timber. The city's infrastructure was carefully planned to integrate renewable energy sources from the start. Solar panels covered rooftops, wind turbines dotted the horizon, and the roads were lined with green spaces, promoting biodiversity.

Aldo's vision for the Green City was clear: it would be a self-sustaining ecosystem. Waste would be collected and processed to generate energy, while green roofs, rainwater harvesting systems, and vertical gardens would ensure that every building contributed to environmental well-being.

2. Smart Waste Management and Clean Energy Systems

One of the most revolutionary aspects of the Green City was its waste management system. Drawing from the success of Aldo's waste-to-energy technology, the city was designed to function on a closed-loop waste management system. All organic waste, food scraps, yard trimmings, and agricultural by-products, would be processed into biogas and used to power the city's infrastructure.

However, it wasn't just the organic waste that was put to good use. Plastics, metals, and other materials would be collected, sorted, and sent to recycling centers, where they would be broken down and transformed into useful products. In this way, the city would have no need for landfills, and waste production would be reduced to a minimum.

The city's energy needs were met through a combination of solar, wind, and waste-to-energy solutions. Solar panels lined the rooftops of every building, providing renewable energy to power homes, businesses, and public spaces. Wind turbines, strategically placed in open areas, supplemented the energy grid, while biogas plants converted organic waste into clean energy, ensuring that the city operated with minimal reliance on fossil fuels.

"The entire city is an ecosystem," said Aldo as he walked through the streets, taking in the various energy systems that powered the city. "Every building, every park, every streetlight, it all contributes to the energy cycle. No more dependence on external resources. We've made ourselves self-sufficient."

As the city grew, so too did its ability to generate energy. The residents of the Green City weren't just consumers of energy, they were part of the energy-producing process. Even homes were equipped with small energy-producing devices that turned waste into usable power, and energy surplus could be stored in community batteries or fed back into the grid.

3. Green Spaces and Urban Farming

The Green City was more than just an efficient machine for waste management and energy production; it was a place where people could reconnect with nature. One of the key features of the city was its integration of green spaces, urban farms, and natural landscapes into the urban fabric.

Green parks, community gardens, and forests were interwoven into the city's design. These green spaces served multiple purposes: they provided recreational areas for residents, helped regulate the local climate, and played a critical role in maintaining biodiversity within the city. By incorporating nature into the city, Aldo and his team created an environment where humans could live more closely with the natural world, rather than apart from it.

Vertical farming became a central feature of urban life. On the rooftops of apartment buildings and office complexes, residents could grow their own food in soil-free systems that used hydroponics or aquaponics. These rooftop farms not only provided fresh, local produce but also helped reduce the city's carbon footprint by minimizing the need for transportation and refrigeration.

As the city expanded, large-scale agricultural zones were established on the outskirts, where crops were grown using sustainable, regenerative farming practices. These farms were powered by renewable energy, and waste from the farms was cycled back into the system to fuel biogas plants or compost for new crops.

"Food security is no longer a distant goal for us," said Nina, walking through one of the vertical farms. "Every home in the Green City has access to fresh produce, and we've reduced the distance between the farm and the table. Our food is grown right here, by the people who live here."

4. Housing and Transportation Innovations

The housing in the Green City was designed to be energy-efficient, sustainable, and adaptable to the needs of future generations. Buildings were constructed with materials that minimized heat loss, reducing the need for heating and cooling. Walls were made from biodegradable, eco-friendly materials, and each home was equipped with smart technologies that optimized energy usage.

Transportation in the city was equally innovative. The Green City was designed to be a pedestrian-friendly environment, with car traffic reduced to a minimum. Instead, the streets were lined with electric buses, bicycles, and autonomous electric vehicles that operated on clean energy. Public transportation was free for residents, reducing the need for private cars and cutting down on air pollution.

The city's transportation infrastructure was integrated with the waste management system. For example, electric buses were powered by biogas produced from organic waste, and electric vehicles charged their batteries using solar energy. This interconnected system ensured that the city remained sustainable without relying on external energy sources.

"Imagine a city where you can walk, bike, or take an electric bus anywhere you need to go," said Aldo, a smile on his face as he watched people moving through the streets, free from the noise and pollution of traditional transportation. "This is what a future city should look like, clean, efficient, and full of life."

5. Community Involvement and Education

The Green City was not just a technological marvel, it was a community-driven project. From the beginning, Aldo and his team made sure that the residents played an active role in shaping the city's development. They were not just inhabitants of a futuristic utopia; they were integral to its success.

Education was a cornerstone of the Green City. Schools, universities, and community centers were established to teach residents about sustainability, renewable energy, waste management, and regenerative agriculture. Workshops, training programs, and sustainability courses were offered to everyone, from children to adults, ensuring that the next generation of leaders and innovators would continue the work that had started with Aldo's vision.

"We can't just build a city and expect change to happen on its own," Aldo explained during a community event. "We need to teach the people who live here the value of sustainability. We need to make sure that the next generation grows up with the mindset that the planet comes first."

As the city flourished, the residents took pride in their role as caretakers of the environment. From composting organic waste to reducing water consumption, they embraced sustainable practices as part of their daily lives. They understood that the success of the Green City wasn't just about the technology, it was about a collective shift in mindset.

6. The Ripple Effect

As the Green City continued to grow and thrive, its success began to inspire other cities around the world. Leaders from all corners of the globe visited to witness firsthand how sustainability could be integrated into urban life. The Green City became a model for future cities, showing that it was possible to create urban environments that didn't just exist alongside nature but worked in harmony with it.

Aldo, Nina, and the entire team had achieved what many had once thought impossible. They had built more than just a city, they had built a vision of the future. A future where technology didn't harm the planet but instead helped it heal. A future where humanity could thrive in balance with the Earth, creating a world of abundance, sustainability, and shared prosperity.

And as Aldo stood at the heart of the Green City, watching it come to life, he knew that this was just the beginning. The Green City was the first step—a prototype for a future where every city, every community, and every person could be a part of the global effort to restore the planet.

Chapter 66: Forging Global Cooperation

The world had reached a critical point. The consequences of years of neglect had become too stark to ignore, pollution, climate change, environmental degradation, and the ongoing struggles of communities trying to recover from the aftermath of disaster. But with the Green City standing as a beacon of hope, Aldo realized that the solutions to these challenges were no longer theoretical, they were here, waiting to be implemented. Now, it was time to unite the world's leaders, harness collective action, and set the stage for a global transformation.

For years, Aldo had worked tirelessly to develop groundbreaking technologies and foster local efforts to combat waste, restore ecosystems, and create sustainable living solutions. But he knew that true change would require a worldwide commitment, a collective effort that transcended national borders. It was no longer just about local success, it was about transforming the entire planet.

The idea of hosting a global summit on waste management and environmental recovery had been brewing in Aldo's mind for months. He had seen the resistance from certain political and economic groups, but he also saw growing momentum from communities and nations that understood the importance of sustainability. The question was: Could the world's leaders set aside their differences long enough to commit to meaningful action? Could they agree to sign a treaty that would change the course of human history?

And so, Aldo made a bold decision. He would host a conference, a gathering of minds and a meeting of political will. The goal was clear: to establish a global framework for waste management, sustainability, and environmental restoration, one that would involve every country, every organization, and every community.

1. Organizing the Conference

The planning process was grueling. Aldo knew that bringing together the world's most powerful leaders, along with environmentalists, scientists, business executives, and activists, would require meticulous preparation. He assembled a team of organizers, each with their own expertise in diplomacy, logistics, and sustainability, and together, they set the stage for what would be the most ambitious conference of its kind.

The venue was to be in Geneva, Switzerland, a city that had long been a center of diplomacy and international cooperation. It was fitting that the world's leaders would gather here, where global treaties and agreements had been forged in the past. The conference would be held at a state-of-the-art facility equipped with cutting-edge technology to allow for real-time communication, presentations, and interactive workshops.

The invitation list was carefully curated, ensuring that representatives from every corner of the globe would be present. Heads of state, ministers of the environment, CEOs of multinational corporations, influential philanthropists, and prominent environmental scientists, all were invited to attend. But Aldo was clear about one thing: this would not be a one-sided affair. For the conference to succeed, every participant needed to be ready to listen, collaborate, and commit to actionable goals.

"We are at a crossroads," Aldo said during one of his preparation meetings. "This conference is about setting a new path forward, one where waste is no longer a burden, but a resource. A world where sustainability isn't a buzzword, but a way of life. We have the technology, we have the knowledge, and we have the will.

MOUNT OF WASTE

Now we need the world's leaders to come together and make this happen."

The weeks leading up to the event were filled with intense discussions, behind-the-scenes negotiations, and coordination with various international bodies. Aldo knew that if they were to succeed, they had to find common ground between the various interests at play: the economic powers that prioritized profit, the developing nations that sought assistance and investment, and the environmental groups pushing for radical change.

Aldo and his team worked tirelessly to ensure that the summit would provide a platform for open dialogue, constructive solutions, and, above all, action.

2. The Opening Day

The day of the conference arrived, and the energy in Geneva was electric. The streets were lined with flags representing countries from every continent. The world's media was present in full force, ready to cover what was expected to be a historic moment in global cooperation. This was no ordinary summit, this was the opportunity for the world to reset its relationship with the planet.

Inside the conference hall, the atmosphere was charged with anticipation. Leaders from various nations filed in, taking their seats at the large round table. Aldo looked around the room and felt a wave of gratitude mixed with nervous excitement. This was it, the culmination of years of hard work, research, and struggle. Now, it was time to take the next step.

As the conference began, Aldo took the stage as the keynote speaker. He looked out at the assembled leaders, his heart racing. This was the moment he had been working toward for so long. He cleared his throat and began to speak, his voice steady but full of passion.

"Honored leaders, esteemed colleagues, and citizens of the world," Aldo began. "We stand on the edge of a new era. A time when we can no longer ignore the consequences of our actions on this planet. Climate change, pollution, resource depletion, these are not just distant threats; they are realities we face today. But we are also standing at the precipice of a solution. We have the technology, the knowledge, and the will to change the course of history."

He paused, letting the words sink in. The room was silent, the weight of his message hanging in the air.

"For too long, we have treated our planet as a resource to be exploited, rather than a partner in our survival. But the time has come for a new approach. An approach that sees waste as a resource, that sees sustainability not as a luxury, but as a necessity for our survival. This summit is our opportunity to come together and create a global framework for managing waste, restoring ecosystems, and creating a sustainable future for all."

The room erupted into applause. Aldo felt a surge of hope. The words had been heard. Now, it was time for the leaders of the world to step forward and make their commitments.

3. Bridging the Divide

Throughout the next few days, the conference was a whirlwind of discussions, debates, and negotiations. The leaders of the world had differing views on how best to proceed, each representing the unique challenges and opportunities within their own nations. Some countries, particularly those that had been hit hardest by climate change, were eager for action and committed resources to support large-scale environmental initiatives. Others, especially those with strong economic interests in fossil fuels and industries that generated significant waste, were more hesitant.

But despite these differences, Aldo remained steadfast. He knew that compromise was necessary for progress, and he was determined to find common ground. Behind closed doors, Aldo met with key leaders, listening to their concerns and presenting innovative solutions that could address their needs while ensuring long-term sustainability.

One of the most difficult moments came when a powerful coalition of industrialized nations expressed skepticism about the cost of implementing waste management systems globally. They were worried about the economic impact, especially on industries that relied on traditional models of resource extraction and waste disposal. Aldo and his team responded with a detailed plan, demonstrating that the transition to a circular economy, where waste is reused and repurposed, would not only be environmentally beneficial but also economically advantageous in the long run.

"We must look beyond short-term profits and focus on the long-term health of our planet," Aldo argued in a private meeting with the skeptical leaders. "The cost of inaction is far greater than the cost of change. Every dollar we invest in sustainability today is a dollar invested in a stable, prosperous future for all."

Gradually, the tide began to turn. More and more countries expressed their willingness to sign on to the treaty, and the tone of the conference shifted from one of skepticism to one of hope. The leaders of developing nations, many of whom had been hit hardest by environmental disasters, pushed for support in implementing the technology and infrastructure needed to transition to a green economy. Aldo's team worked with international organizations to ensure that funding and resources would be allocated to these nations, empowering them to build sustainable futures.

4. The Signing of the Treaty

On the final day of the conference, the leaders of the world gathered once again in the grand hall. There was a palpable sense of optimism in the air. After days of heated debate and negotiation, Aldo knew that they were on the brink of something extraordinary.

One by one, the heads of state and representatives of various nations stood before the gathered audience and signed the historic treaty. The agreement outlined a global framework for waste management, a commitment to renewable energy, and a pledge to invest in sustainable technologies that would protect the planet for future generations. It was a promise to not only reduce waste but to redefine the relationship between humanity and the Earth.

As Aldo signed his own copy of the treaty, he felt a profound sense of accomplishment. This was the culmination of everything he had worked for, the start of a new global movement, one that would not just heal the planet but set the stage for a future where sustainability was the foundation of all human progress.

As the conference came to a close, the world watched in awe as leaders from every nation stood united, ready to embrace a future built on collaboration, innovation, and shared responsibility.

5. A New Era

The signing of the treaty marked the beginning of a new era in global cooperation. In the years that followed, Aldo's vision for a sustainable world became a reality. Countries worked together to implement waste management systems, invest in renewable energy, and restore damaged ecosystems. The world had finally turned the page on a chapter of exploitation and unsustainable growth, and had begun writing a new one, one where the planet and its people thrived together. For Aldo, the journey was far from over. But as he looked out over the world, now united in its efforts to build a sustainable future, he knew that the road ahead was filled with promise. The planet was healing, and together, humanity would see it through.

Chapter 67: Facing an Attack from Within

The world had taken a monumental step forward. The treaty signed at the international summit marked a new beginning for global cooperation in environmental sustainability. The promise of a greener future was no longer a distant dream but a tangible reality. With the signing of the agreement, Aldo and his team had become global leaders in the fight for a sustainable world. But in the blink of an eye, their world was shattered.

The attack came without warning.

It was a cold morning when the news broke. An armed group of radical extremists had infiltrated Pusat Riset Alfa, the heart of Aldo's revolutionary work. The team had been busy preparing to implement their next series of global solutions when the attack occurred. The group, known as The Coalition of the Pure, had been growing in influence over the past months, fueled by a fear of globalism and a belief in self-sufficiency. They believed that the rise of global governance and collective environmental efforts posed a direct threat to individual freedoms and national sovereignty.

Their primary aim was clear—to dismantle everything Aldo and his team had worked for, to send a message to the world that their ideology would not be silenced. The radicals struck at the core of the research hub, targeting the most sensitive and cutting-edge technologies developed by Aldo's team. It wasn't just a physical attack, it was an ideological war.

The damage was devastating.

Key infrastructure was destroyed, crucial servers containing years of research were obliterated, and many of the team's most innovative projects were lost in a matter of hours. The research that had propelled them to the forefront of the environmental movement now lay in ruins. The attack was well-planned, a calculated strike against the heart of the movement for global sustainability.

As the news spread, the world watched in horror. For many, this was a turning point. The attack represented more than just an assault on a building, it was an attack on the future of the planet itself. If the radicals could disrupt the most promising efforts for global change, they might derail the entire movement. The consequences were dire, but Aldo and his team refused to let this setback stop them.

1. The Immediate Aftermath

In the immediate aftermath of the attack, Aldo and his team were in shock. The scale of the destruction was incomprehensible, and there was a sense of disbelief hanging in the air. How could something like this happen? How could a group so radical, so determined to halt progress, inflict such devastation?

But there was no time for mourning. Aldo quickly gathered his team in what was left of the operations center. The building was partially in ruins, with debris scattered across the once pristine halls. They were facing a colossal challenge, but Aldo knew that giving in was not an option.

"We can't let them win," Aldo said, his voice steady despite the emotions swirling within him. "This attack is an attempt to set us back, but we've come too far. We have the knowledge, and we have the support of the world. We will rebuild, and we will move forward."

His words resonated deeply with the team. They had seen the destruction firsthand, and they had felt the weight of this assault. But they knew that their work was far from over. They had to act quickly to mitigate the damage, salvage what they could, and ensure that the work could continue. Every minute counted. The stakes were too high.

MOUNT OF WASTE

2. Assessing the Damage

The first priority was to assess the damage. Aldo, Nina, and the rest of the team worked tirelessly to determine the extent of the destruction. The building's core structure remained intact, but the laboratories, storage rooms, and data centers had been heavily damaged. It was clear that the extremists had been focused on destroying the key assets, research papers, blueprints, and prototypes, things that could not be replaced easily.

As they combed through the debris, Aldo found himself grappling with a sense of despair. Much of the research was gone, but then something caught his eye. A small, charred device, one of the key innovations they had developed for waste-to-energy conversion, was still intact. It wasn't much, but it was a sign of hope. Amid the chaos, there was something left to work with.

"We can rebuild," Aldo said, picking up the device. "It won't be easy, but we've faced adversity before. This is just another challenge we'll overcome."

The team rallied around Aldo's words. They were no strangers to setbacks. They had encountered challenges at every stage of their work, but they had always found a way to move forward. Now, they had to do it again. They had to rebuild from the ground up, not just the physical infrastructure, but the very trust and belief in their mission.

3. Rebuilding the Research

In the days that followed, Aldo's team worked around the clock. They pooled together their resources, their knowledge, and their unwavering commitment to their cause. The first task was to restore their data systems. With the loss of the main servers, they had to rely on backup systems stored in remote locations across the globe. Thankfully, the team had anticipated the possibility of a cyberattack and had stored critical data in multiple, secure locations.

The real challenge, however, was rebuilding the physical research and prototypes. Many of the technologies, advanced waste-to-energy systems, water purification units, and eco-friendly building materials, had been in the final stages of testing. They had been so close to rolling them out on a global scale. Now, they would have to start over.

But the team was determined. Aldo put out a call to researchers and scientists from all over the world, asking for their help in rebuilding the lost technologies. In response, a wave of solidarity poured in. Teams of engineers, environmental experts, and innovators volunteered to support Aldo's efforts. The global network that had supported the Green Revolution began to mobilize. They weren't just rebuilding a building, they were rebuilding the future.

The process was grueling. Every day brought new challenges, limited resources, broken equipment, and the looming fear that the attack could be a sign of something larger. But the team pushed forward. They knew that the stakes were too high to back down now. Their mission was too important, and the world was watching.

4. The Global Response

The attack on Pusat Riset Alfa reverberated across the world. Political leaders, business magnates, and environmental activists all condemned the assault. But more than just outrage, the attack sparked a wave of solidarity. The global community came together to support Aldo and his team, pledging resources, expertise, and financial support to rebuild the center and continue the work.

Governments from every corner of the world rallied behind the cause. Many countries offered to send financial aid, while others provided technical support, helping to recreate the lost technologies. Environmental organizations launched global fundraising campaigns to ensure that the recovery process was swift and effective.

In a show of unity, the world's most influential leaders sent messages of support, condemning the violence and reaffirming their commitment to the global sustainability agenda. It was clear that the radicals had underestimated the strength of the global movement. The world had not been divided, it had been galvanized.

"We will not be intimidated by extremists," said the United Nations Secretary-General in a public address. "This attack is a sign of fear, not strength. Aldo and his team have shown us the way forward. We will stand with them and continue our work to heal the planet."

5. The Fight Continues

Despite the challenges, Aldo's team was undeterred. They knew that the road ahead would be long and difficult, but they had faced adversity before. They had learned to rise above challenges, to innovate in the face of limitations. This attack would not be the end of their work, it would be the catalyst for a new phase in their journey.

In the weeks that followed, the rebuilding process gained momentum. The world's collective effort to restore Pusat Riset Alfa was nothing short of extraordinary. Researchers and scientists from across the globe volunteered to contribute, and within a few months, the center was operational once again. Aldo and his team worked tirelessly to bring the lost technologies back to life, and soon, their research was back on track.

The radicals had made a mistake. They had thought that by attacking the heart of the movement, they could stop the global shift toward sustainability. But they had underestimated the resilience of those who believed in the cause. The attack on Pusat

Riset Alfa had only strengthened the resolve of Aldo and his team, and the world's commitment to a better future.

As the work progressed, Aldo reflected on the journey that had brought them here. He had seen the world come together in ways he had never imagined. The Green Revolution had sparked a wave of innovation, cooperation, and hope. And even in the face of extreme opposition, the world was moving forward.

"We will not be stopped," Aldo said, as he stood in front of the rebuilt research center, looking at the team around him. "Together, we will continue to fight for a better world. This is just the beginning."

And as they moved forward, the team knew one thing for certain: the struggle for the planet's future was far from over, but with unity, resilience, and innovation, they would see it through.

Chapter 68: The Impact on Marine Ecosystems

The air was thick with optimism, but Aldo knew that the battle for the future was far from won. His team's groundbreaking advances in waste management, renewable energy, and sustainable technologies had brought the world closer to healing. Yet, amid the successes, one glaring issue loomed larger than ever, the oceans.

The oceans, vast and mysterious, had long been the lifeblood of the planet. They were the primary source of oxygen, regulating climate, and supporting an incredible diversity of life. But they were also the dumping ground for humanity's waste. Plastic, chemicals, and other pollutants had infiltrated the waters, creating a toxic legacy that threatened not only marine ecosystems but the very fabric of life on Earth.

The oceans were suffocating.

Despite the significant strides made on land, the effects of oceanic pollution were catastrophic. Coral reefs, often called the "rainforests of the sea," were dying at an alarming rate, suffocated by toxic waste and climate change. Marine life, from the smallest plankton to the largest whales, was being decimated by plastic debris and chemical pollutants. And, perhaps most disturbingly, the ocean's ability to absorb carbon dioxide was being compromised, further accelerating climate change.

Aldo stood at the edge of the research center overlooking the vast expanse of the ocean. He had always felt a deep connection to the sea, having spent much of his childhood by the coast. The beauty of the ocean was undeniable, but the damage it had sustained was impossible to ignore.

"Something needs to be done," Aldo murmured to himself, watching the gentle waves crash against the shore.

Nina, his steadfast partner, stood next to him, sharing the same somber gaze. She, too, knew that their work wasn't done yet. They had cleaned up the land, but the oceans, which covered over 70% of the Earth's surface, remained a gaping wound in the planet's health.

"It's not just the land anymore, Aldo," Nina said softly. "The oceans are crying for help. If we don't act now, we risk losing everything we've worked for."

Aldo nodded solemnly. The thought of failing to restore the oceans weighed heavily on him. But he knew they couldn't ignore it any longer.

And so, with renewed determination, Aldo and his team launched their most ambitious project yet: The Ocean Restoration Initiative.

1. Understanding the Crisis

Before they could begin their mission to save the oceans, Aldo and his team knew they had to understand the full extent of the problem. They partnered with marine biologists, environmental scientists, and oceanographers to conduct a comprehensive study on the health of the world's oceans.

The findings were disturbing.

Plastic pollution had reached unprecedented levels. It was estimated that over 8 million tons of plastic entered the oceans every year. The Great Pacific Garbage Patch, a vast accumulation of debris in the Pacific Ocean, was now twice the size of Texas. Microplastics had infiltrated every part of the ocean, from the deepest trenches to the surface waters. Marine life, including fish, sea turtles, and seabirds, were consuming these toxic particles, causing untold harm to ecosystems.

Meanwhile, coral reefs were experiencing widespread bleaching events due to rising sea temperatures and acidification caused by excess carbon dioxide. The delicate symbiotic relationships between coral and algae were collapsing, causing massive die-offs of coral ecosystems. Without healthy coral reefs, entire marine food chains were at risk.

The ocean's ability to absorb carbon was also severely compromised. The rapid rise in atmospheric carbon levels, combined with the destruction of marine ecosystems, was accelerating climate change in ways that could be irreversible.

It was clear that the oceans were at a tipping point.

2. The Ocean Restoration Initiative

The Ocean Restoration Initiative was Aldo's response to this crisis. It was a multifaceted approach that aimed not only to remove the existing waste from the oceans but also to restore the ecosystems that had been devastated by years of neglect. The project would tackle the root causes of marine pollution while offering sustainable solutions to reverse the damage.

The initiative had three main pillars: cleanup, conservation, and regeneration.

A. Cleanup

The first step in the initiative was to tackle the vast amounts of waste that had accumulated in the oceans. The team designed a series of innovative technologies to remove plastics, chemicals, and other pollutants from the water.

One of the key technologies developed was a fleet of autonomous, solar-powered vessels that could skim the surface of the ocean and collect plastic debris. These vessels were equipped with state-of-the-art filtration systems that could capture even the smallest microplastics, preventing them from entering the marine food chain. Aldo's team also developed a network of drones that could track and map the locations of floating debris, allowing for more efficient cleanup operations.

The project also included large-scale operations to clean up the most polluted areas of the ocean, including the Great Pacific Garbage Patch. These cleanup efforts were coordinated with local governments, environmental NGOs, and private companies, creating a global network of collaboration.

B. Conservation

Conservation efforts were equally vital. Aldo and his team recognized that protecting what remained of the oceans' ecosystems was just as important as cleaning up the pollution. They focused on creating marine protected areas (MPAs) that would safeguard critical habitats, such as coral reefs, mangrove forests, and seagrass beds.

MPAs were established along the most vulnerable coasts and seas, where biodiversity was under severe threat. These areas were designed to limit human activity and allow ecosystems to recover naturally. By restricting harmful practices such as overfishing, bottom trawling, and oil drilling, Aldo and his team could give marine life the space it needed to regenerate.

They also worked to implement sustainable fishing practices that would protect endangered species and ensure that the oceans' resources were used responsibly. By promoting eco-friendly fishing methods and developing new, sustainable alternatives, Aldo aimed to reduce the pressure on marine ecosystems.

C. Regeneration

Finally, Aldo's team focused on regenerating the damaged ecosystems. One of the most critical aspects of this was coral reef restoration. The team worked with marine biologists to develop innovative methods for growing and transplanting coral in areas where reefs had been severely damaged.

Using cutting-edge technologies, such as 3D printing, Aldo's team created artificial coral structures that could support coral growth. These structures were placed in areas that had been impacted by bleaching and other environmental stressors. Over time, the artificial reefs would serve as a foundation for coral to grow and restore the health of the ecosystem.

In addition to coral restoration, Aldo and his team worked on restoring other vital marine ecosystems, such as mangroves and seagrass beds. Mangrove forests, which serve as natural barriers against coastal erosion and provide crucial habitat for marine life, were being cleared at alarming rates. By replanting mangroves in vulnerable coastal areas, Aldo's team could help protect coastlines and rebuild habitats for marine species.

Seagrass beds, which are essential for carbon sequestration, were also a focus. Aldo's team developed new methods for growing and transplanting seagrasses in areas where they had been lost. By restoring these vital ecosystems, Aldo hoped to not only help marine life thrive but also increase the ocean's ability to absorb carbon and mitigate climate change.

3. Global Collaboration

The success of the Ocean Restoration Initiative depended on global collaboration. Aldo knew that no single nation or organization could solve the ocean crisis alone. It required a unified, coordinated effort from governments, corporations, and communities around the world.

To facilitate this, Aldo organized a series of global summits, bringing together stakeholders from all sectors. Governments committed to strengthening marine protection laws, companies pledged to reduce their plastic footprints, and local communities volunteered to assist with cleanup efforts.

The initiative also gained significant support from the public. People around the world were becoming increasingly aware of the ocean's plight and were eager to take action. Schools, universities, and grassroots organizations began organizing beach cleanups and advocating for ocean protection policies.

Aldo's team also partnered with the world's leading tech companies to develop advanced monitoring and tracking systems that could track the health of marine ecosystems in real-time. Using satellite imagery, drones, and AI-powered analytics, they could assess the condition of coral reefs, monitor fish populations, and track the movement of ocean currents.

4. The Road Ahead

As the initiative gained momentum, Aldo felt a sense of hope he had not experienced in years. The world was waking up to the importance of protecting the oceans, and there was a genuine commitment to change. But Aldo knew that this was only the beginning. The oceans were vast, and the damage was deep. The work ahead would take decades, if not longer, to complete.

But the tide was beginning to turn.

The cleanup operations were yielding results. The amount of plastic in the Great Pacific Garbage Patch was decreasing, and new technologies were emerging to help reduce plastic production and consumption globally. The restoration of coral reefs was showing signs of success, and fish populations were beginning to recover in protected marine areas.

And for the first time in decades, there was a glimmer of hope that the oceans could heal.

As Aldo looked out over the ocean once more, he knew that their work was far from over. The challenges were immense, but the possibilities were endless. The oceans, like the planet itself, were resilient. With time, dedication, and global collaboration, they could be restored.

The battle for the oceans had begun, but Aldo was determined to see it through.

Chapter 69: Collaboration Between Scientists and Activists

The world had changed, but Aldo knew it was only the beginning. Despite their numerous successes, cleaner cities, healthier ecosystems, and more sustainable energy solutions, the planet still had a long road ahead. Now, the time had come to confront the greatest challenge of all: the intertwining of science and activism in a way that would accelerate the global healing process.

Aldo had always believed in the power of collaboration. Over the years, he had witnessed the remarkable results of working with like-minded individuals, from engineers to environmentalists. But the true magic, he realized, lay in the fusion of two powerful forces that, for too long, had been separate: the rigorous world of science and the passionate advocacy of activists. Both had the same goal in mind, preserving the Earth, but their approaches often felt worlds apart. It was time to bring them together.

1. Bridging the Divide

Aldo sat in his office, surrounded by a jumble of blueprints, data charts, and environmental reports. He had just come back from a major international summit where leaders from around the world had signed a pact to reduce global waste and accelerate the transition to renewable energy. Yet, despite the monumental significance of the event, he felt a nagging emptiness. There was still a disconnect, a gap between those who had the resources and expertise to make real change, and those who were directly affected by environmental issues and fighting tirelessly on the front lines.

Activists were doing incredible work on the ground. From organizing protests to lobbying governments, they were the loud voices pushing for real change. But too often, their efforts were misunderstood by the scientific community. On the other hand, while scientists had the technical know-how to create solutions, their work often lacked the urgency or emotional appeal needed to drive mass action.

Aldo knew something had to change. He believed that the power of science could fuel the passion of activists, and the energy of activism could drive science forward with an urgency never seen before.

To make that happen, Aldo needed to build a bridge.

2. The Scientist-Activist Summit

With this vision in mind, Aldo proposed a bold idea: a global summit that would bring together scientists and activists from across the world. The goal? To foster a collaboration that would result in actionable solutions for environmental recovery, utilizing both the rigor of scientific innovation and the passion of grassroots movements.

It wasn't going to be easy. There was a certain skepticism between the two camps. Activists often viewed scientists as detached from the struggles of real people, while some scientists believed that activists lacked the data-driven approach necessary for real change. But Aldo was determined to prove them wrong.

He began by reaching out to key figures from both worlds. Environmental scientists, renewable energy innovators, conservationists, and climate change specialists were all invited to participate. On the activist side, he contacted leaders from environmental groups, indigenous rights movements, and local grassroots organizations. Their task was clear: come together and create solutions that would not only heal the planet but also inspire people to take action.

3. The First Day of the Summit

The day of the summit arrived, and Aldo stood on the stage in front of a packed auditorium. Scientists, activists, policymakers, and journalists filled the seats. There was an air of anticipation mixed with skepticism. Would the two sides be able to set aside their differences and collaborate? Or would this be just another failed attempt to reconcile two worlds that seemed to operate in parallel universes?

Aldo stepped up to the podium, his heart pounding, but his voice steady. "We are here today not as scientists and activists, but as people who are united by one simple truth: the planet is in crisis, and it's up to all of us to fix it. This summit is not just about debating facts or pointing fingers at who's to blame. It's about creating solutions, solutions that draw on the expertise of both worlds. We need both the knowledge of science and the energy of activism to succeed."

The room fell silent.

"The future of our planet doesn't belong to any one group," Aldo continued. "It belongs to all of us. Together, we can find the answers. Together, we can change the world."

4. The Breakthrough: Collaborative Projects

After Aldo's speech, the summit dove into a series of working sessions. The room buzzed with discussion, ideas flowing between the tables as participants from all backgrounds shared their thoughts. What emerged was nothing short of revolutionary.

The activists brought their real-world experience, how communities were struggling with environmental destruction, how climate change was already affecting vulnerable populations, how waste and pollution were destroying livelihoods. They didn't just speak of statistics; they spoke of lives impacted, of entire ecosystems lost, of futures threatened.

The scientists brought their deep knowledge of the environment, energy systems, and technological innovation. They presented research that showed how technological advances, such as the use of algae for biofuel production, or AI-powered systems for monitoring deforestation, could be scaled to make a real difference. They also discussed the need for large-scale policy changes to address systemic environmental issues, emphasizing the importance of international cooperation.

As the discussions unfolded, it became clear that both sides needed each other. The scientists needed the activists to help raise awareness and drive grassroots support for the solutions they were developing. The activists needed the scientists to back their demands with evidence, to create feasible, long-term solutions that could be implemented at scale.

From these conversations came a series of collaborative projects, initiatives that would see scientists and activists working side-by-side to tackle key environmental challenges.

5. Building a Circular Economy Together

One of the most exciting collaborations to come out of the summit was the development of a circular economy model that could be adopted by cities around the world. The idea was simple: instead of extracting raw materials, manufacturing products, and discarding them as waste, everything would be designed to be reused, recycled, or regenerated.

The activists brought their deep understanding of community-based solutions, showing how local systems could be adapted to fit into a circular economy. They proposed models that could reduce waste at the grassroots level, including community-based composting programs, zero-waste shops, and local recycling hubs. The scientists, on the other hand, provided the data and technological innovations needed to support these initiatives. They developed AI systems to track the flow of materials, ensuring that nothing was wasted. They worked on creating new materials that could be fully recycled and biodegraded without causing harm to the environment.

Together, they created a blueprint for circular cities, where everything, from energy to food to waste, would be part of a closed-loop system, reducing the strain on natural resources and minimizing pollution.

6. A New Approach to Conservation

Another successful collaboration was in the field of conservation. Aldo had long been an advocate for protecting ecosystems, but the challenge had always been finding a way to balance human development with environmental preservation.

During the summit, scientists and activists came together to create a new model of conservation, one that incorporated both scientific research and the local knowledge of indigenous communities. The scientists used cutting-edge technology, such as drones and satellite imaging, to monitor ecosystems, track endangered species, and prevent illegal activities like poaching. The activists worked with local communities to help them protect their land, advocate for policy changes, and develop sustainable livelihoods that didn't depend on exploiting natural resources.

They called it Community-Led Conservation, and it quickly gained traction among governments, NGOs, and local communities. The model allowed for better stewardship of natural resources while also promoting economic development and social justice for those most affected by environmental destruction.

7. Shaping the Future Together

The summit marked the beginning of something much bigger, a new era of collaboration between scientists and activists. Over the following years, Aldo's vision became a reality. The lines between the two worlds began to blur, with both sides working together to implement groundbreaking solutions for environmental recovery.

Scientists and activists worked together on a variety of projects: from regenerating degraded land with sustainable farming practices to developing renewable energy technologies that could be deployed in remote communities. They tackled issues like plastic pollution, biodiversity loss, and deforestation, all while ensuring that local communities were central to the solution.

As the collaborations grew stronger, so did the results. Pollution levels dropped, biodiversity began to recover, and new, sustainable economies were formed. People everywhere, scientists, activists, and ordinary citizens, came together to fight for a better, more sustainable future.

8. The Legacy of Collaboration

Years later, when Aldo looked back on the summit, he realized that it wasn't just the projects that had succeeded, it was the spirit of collaboration that had taken root. The summit had proven that when science and activism worked together, they could achieve the unimaginable.

And it all started with a simple idea: to bring together two worlds that had too often been at odds, to remind everyone that they shared one common goal, saving the planet.

In the end, it was this unity, this collaboration, that would define the future of humanity. A future where people didn't just talk about saving the Earth, but actively worked together to make it happen.

Chapter 70: Building a Green Economic System

The world was on the precipice of a monumental shift, and Aldo knew that the next step was crucial. They had succeeded in developing groundbreaking technologies and launching global initiatives to combat climate change and pollution. Yet, there was one more, more fundamental challenge that remained: the very foundation of the global economy itself. For centuries, the world had relied on an economic system built on resource extraction, consumerism, and unsustainable growth. This system had caused irreparable damage to the planet, depleting natural resources, increasing pollution, and driving species to extinction. It was time for something radically different.

Aldo, with his team of innovators, environmentalists, and economists, began the daunting task of designing a new economic system, one that would be based on sustainability, equity, and the careful stewardship of the Earth's resources. The vision was ambitious: to replace the old system, which had driven much of the environmental destruction, with a green economic system that could sustain both the planet and its inhabitants for generations to come.

1. Rethinking the Current System

Before they could design the new economic model, Aldo and his team had to understand the flaws of the existing system. It was clear that the old model was built on a foundation of infinite growth. Economic success was often measured in terms of GDP, a number that failed to account for environmental damage or resource depletion. Businesses pursued profit at any cost, using cheap, non-renewable resources and generating massive amounts of waste. Governments, in turn, supported this growth through policies that encouraged consumption and disregarded environmental impact.

Aldo understood that they needed a model where success wasn't measured by the number of products consumed or the volume of resources extracted. Instead, the new economic system needed to value the planet's health, the well-being of its people, and the sustainable management of natural resources. They would need to fundamentally change how wealth was created and distributed.

This new system would have to take into account ecological limits, ensuring that the economy operated within the carrying capacity of the Earth. It would focus on regeneration, not just extraction. And it would prioritize equity, ensuring that the benefits of this new system were shared fairly among all people.

2. Designing the Green Economic System

The team's first task was to lay out the core principles of the green economic system. These principles would guide every decision made, from resource management to trade policies, ensuring that the economy could thrive while remaining sustainable.

a. Sustainable Resource Management

The first core principle of the new system was the sustainable management of resources. Aldo and his team developed a model that focused on circular economy principles. In a circular economy, products were designed to be reused, repaired, and recycled, rather than discarded after a single use. Materials such as plastics, metals, and textiles would be kept in circulation, reducing the need to extract new resources from the Earth.

This new approach would eliminate the concept of "waste" altogether. Rather than discarding materials, industries would work together to repurpose and recycle, creating a closed-loop system where everything had value. Products would be made to last, and manufacturers would be held accountable for the full lifecycle of their products.

The green economy would also prioritize renewable resources over non-renewable ones. Solar, wind, and hydropower would replace fossil fuels, and plant-based materials would be used instead of harmful chemicals and plastics. The team worked with engineers to develop technologies that could harness the power of nature to create clean energy and sustainable materials.

b. Economic Decoupling from Growth

One of the most difficult concepts to introduce into the new economic system was the idea of decoupling growth from resource consumption. Traditional economics had always focused on increasing production and consumption as a measure of progress. But Aldo and his team argued that true prosperity should not be dependent on the exploitation of finite resources.

Instead, they proposed a model where economic success was tied to well-being and quality of life, not the sheer quantity of goods produced or consumed. This model would prioritize human health, happiness, education, and community over material accumulation. To achieve this, they looked to the well-being economy model, which focused on the flourishing of individuals, societies, and ecosystems, rather than the maximization of wealth.

c. Environmental Justice and Equity

The new economic system would also prioritize equity and environmental justice. Aldo understood that environmental degradation disproportionately affected marginalized communities, those living in poverty, indigenous populations, and developing nations. The current economic system had left these communities vulnerable to climate change, pollution, and resource depletion.

To address this imbalance, the new system would provide fair compensation for communities most affected by environmental harm. It would also create mechanisms for social safety nets, ensuring that all people had access to basic needs, such as food, water, healthcare, and education. The green economy would ensure that economic development did not come at the expense of social justice.

d. Biodiversity and Ecosystem Restoration

A critical component of the green economy was the restoration and preservation of biodiversity. The team worked closely with conservationists to integrate ecosystem services into the economic model. This meant placing a monetary value on the services provided by nature, such as clean air, water, and fertile soil, and ensuring that these services were protected.

The team also proposed the establishment of green corridors, protected areas where wildlife could roam freely and ecosystems could regenerate. By restoring ecosystems that had been damaged by industrialization and deforestation, the green economy would help reverse some of the most devastating impacts of human activity on the planet.

3. The Green Currency and Investment System

To make the green economy a reality, Aldo and his team understood that they needed to reshape the global financial system. They proposed the creation of a green currency, which would be used to incentivize sustainable business practices and investments. This currency would function alongside traditional currencies but would be tied to environmental goals.

Investments in renewable energy, sustainable agriculture, and ecosystem restoration would be encouraged through tax breaks and subsidies, while companies that engaged in unsustainable practices, such as pollution, deforestation, and resource depletion, would face penalties. The idea was to create a financial ecosystem that rewarded positive environmental and social outcomes and penalized negative ones.

They also worked on creating new impact investment channels that focused not only on financial returns but also on the impact of investments on the planet. Investors would be able to directly contribute to projects that were addressing environmental degradation, poverty, and climate change, with the assurance that their investments were making a positive difference.

4. A Global Transition: Implementing the Green Economy

While Aldo and his team had designed a robust green economic system, the challenge now lay in scaling it globally. They knew that the world's largest economies would be resistant to change, especially those that profited from the current system. However, Aldo was determined to show that the green economy was not just a moral imperative, it was also economically viable.

The team started by working with smaller nations and regions that were already committed to environmental sustainability. They partnered with countries that had been hit hardest by climate change, helping them rebuild their economies with the green system in place. These countries became test beds for the green economy, allowing Aldo and his team to fine-tune the model.

Simultaneously, they engaged with global organizations such as the United Nations, the World Bank, and the World Trade Organization to promote the green economic system as the new standard. They organized conferences, workshops, and forums to educate governments, businesses, and the public about the benefits of this new model.

5. The First Successes

As the green economic system began to take shape, the results were undeniable. Countries that had adopted the system saw increases in green jobs, economic stability, and social equity. Renewable energy projects boomed, with solar and wind farms replacing coal and oil plants. Circular economy initiatives took hold in major industries, and new sustainable supply chains were established.

Perhaps the most significant outcome was the growing momentum for systemic change. As more countries embraced the green economy, others began to follow suit. The new system started to spread across borders, creating a global movement for sustainability.

6. A New Dawn for the Planet

Aldo watched as the green economy began to change the world in ways he had never imagined. Cities became greener, businesses adopted sustainable practices, and people's relationship with the environment shifted. The Earth, once on the brink of collapse, began to heal. Forests were regenerated, oceans were cleaned, and wildlife populations began to recover.

The green economy was no longer a dream—it was a reality.

And as Aldo looked out over the world, he felt a deep sense of pride. The future of the planet was no longer defined by endless growth and exploitation. It was now defined by balance, sustainability, and respect for the natural world. And it was all thanks to the vision of a new economic system, one that would sustain humanity and the planet for generations to come.

Chapter 71: Nurturing the Next Generation

The world had undergone remarkable changes over the past few years. From environmental breakthroughs to the creation of sustainable cities, Aldo and his team had been at the forefront of these transformations. But despite the progress, Aldo knew that the battle for the future of the planet was far from over. There was still much work to be done. While the systems they had created were sustainable, the mindset that drove destructive behavior had not disappeared. For Aldo, the key to long-term success lay in the hearts and minds of the next generation.

He had seen firsthand how the youth of today were more environmentally conscious than ever before, but Aldo also realized that simply caring about the environment wasn't enough. To create lasting change, young people needed to be equipped with the knowledge and skills necessary to act, skills that would allow them to become stewards of the Earth. They needed to understand the science of sustainability, the importance of resource conservation, and, most importantly, how to lead by example. The task before Aldo was clear: he had to empower the next generation to not only care for the planet but also act to preserve it.

1. A Vision for Environmental Education

Aldo knew that for the transformation to be lasting, it had to start with education. Education was the foundation on which everything else rested. If the younger generation was not taught how to live sustainably, how could they possibly lead the world into a better future?

He began by establishing green schools, educational institutions that would serve as incubators for environmental stewardship. These schools would go beyond traditional curricula, offering a hands-on approach to environmental education. Students would not only learn about climate change, pollution, and sustainability in the classroom, but they would also engage in real-world projects that focused on solving these issues.

Aldo's green schools would teach students how to reduce their carbon footprints, how to recycle and compost efficiently, and how to engage with their local communities to drive change. By involving students in active environmental projects, Aldo believed that they would gain a deeper understanding of the challenges at hand and the solutions they could offer.

But Aldo didn't stop there. He knew that education had to go beyond just the classroom. He envisioned a global movement where young people, empowered with knowledge, would go out into their communities and begin to change the world. They would become leaders who advocated for sustainable practices in their homes, schools, and neighborhoods.

2. Incorporating Sustainability into the Curriculum

The first step was to collaborate with educational authorities, curriculum developers, and environmental experts to redesign the school system's curriculum. Aldo and his team worked tirelessly with educators to incorporate sustainability into every aspect of learning, from science and geography to economics and history.

At the heart of this transformation was a shift from theory to practice. While students would learn about the importance of biodiversity, carbon cycles, and ecosystems in science class, they would also have opportunities to participate in practical activities, such as planting trees, cleaning up local rivers, and building sustainable urban gardens. Students would understand that sustainability wasn't just something discussed in books, it was something they could practice every day.

In the economics class, Aldo envisioned a new approach to teaching students about the economy. Instead of focusing solely on profit and growth, the curriculum would teach the principles of the circular economy, emphasizing resource efficiency, waste reduction, and the importance of keeping materials in use for as long as possible. Students would also learn about the environmental cost of traditional economic practices, helping them understand why a green economy was not just a moral choice but a necessary one for the future.

3. Empowering Students with Practical Skills

One of Aldo's key initiatives was to equip students with practical skills that would help them manage waste more effectively. Waste management, after all, was one of the most pressing environmental challenges facing the world today. Aldo understood that to solve this issue, people had to be more aware of the types of waste they produced, how to reduce it, and how to dispose of it responsibly.

In every green school, students were taught the art of waste segregation, learning how to separate organic and non-organic waste properly. They also learned how to compost food scraps and recycle everyday materials such as plastics, paper, and glass. The schools even had zero-waste programs, where students took on the challenge of producing as little waste as possible over the course of a year. This exercise taught them how small actions, like avoiding single-use plastics, repairing broken items, and choosing reusable products, could make a huge difference in reducing waste.

But it wasn't just about managing waste. Aldo also focused on giving students the tools to design and implement waste reduction strategies. They would learn how to conduct waste audits in their schools and communities, identify areas where waste could be reduced, and then create action plans to improve waste management practices. These skills would not only benefit the students in their future careers but also empower them to be advocates for sustainability wherever they went.

4. Promoting Global Awareness and Action

Aldo understood that the challenges of climate change and environmental degradation were not confined to a single country or region, they were global problems that required a collective effort. To foster a sense of global solidarity, he introduced programs that connected young people from around the world.

Through virtual classrooms, students from different countries could collaborate on environmental projects, exchange ideas, and learn about the sustainability challenges faced by other regions. This cross-cultural exchange was not only educational but also promoted empathy and understanding, as students learned about the interconnectedness of their actions and the impact they had on the planet as a whole.

Aldo also partnered with international organizations and youth movements to amplify the voices of young people in global conversations about the environment. He encouraged students to participate in global climate strikes, where millions of young people around the world gathered to demand urgent action on climate change. Through these movements, students were able to make their voices heard and advocate for policies that would protect their futures.

In every classroom, students were reminded that they were not alone in their efforts. They were part of a growing movement of young people dedicated to creating a sustainable future. They could take inspiration from environmental activists, young and old, who had fought for a greener, more just world.

5. Fostering Leadership and Entrepreneurship

Aldo believed that the next generation of environmental leaders would come not only from governments and environmental organizations but also from the private sector. Entrepreneurs and business leaders had the power to shape the future of the planet by creating sustainable products and services that would revolutionize industries.

In his green schools, Aldo emphasized the importance of green entrepreneurship, teaching students how to start their own businesses with environmental goals in mind. They learned how to design sustainable products, create green supply chains, and use business strategies that prioritized long-term environmental and social impacts over short-term profits.

Aldo also encouraged students to think about the broader implications of their work. How could they use technology to address environmental issues? What kind of innovations could reduce waste, promote clean energy, or improve food security? He invited industry leaders and successful green entrepreneurs to speak to the students, offering them valuable mentorship and guidance.

By nurturing this spirit of entrepreneurship, Aldo knew he was empowering the next generation of environmental innovators. These young leaders would drive change in industries ranging from agriculture to manufacturing to tech, creating businesses that put the planet first.

6. A Movement for Global Change

As the green schools flourished, Aldo began to see the ripple effect of his efforts. Students who graduated from the program didn't just leave with knowledge, they left with a deep sense of responsibility and a commitment to act. They carried the principles of sustainability with them, applying them in every aspect of their lives, whether they were designing green buildings, leading conservation projects, or running eco-friendly businesses.

The movement Aldo had started began to spread across the world, creating a network of young people who were united by their desire to protect the Earth. They were no longer passive recipients of education, they were active agents of change, working to create a better future for all.

7. The Long-Term Vision

Aldo knew that the work he was doing today would have a profound impact on the planet, but it was the work of the next generation that would truly shape the future. The young people he was educating today would grow up to become the leaders, innovators, and activists of tomorrow. They would be the ones to implement the solutions, to advocate for policies that protect the planet, and to inspire the next wave of environmental stewardship.

As Aldo stood before a new generation of students, he felt a sense of hope and determination. The world was on the brink of a new era, one in which sustainability, equity, and environmental stewardship were not just ideals, they were the foundation upon which the future would be built.

And in the hands of these young people, Aldo knew that the Earth had a future worth fighting for.

Chapter 72: Overcoming the Global Financial Crisis

The world was now at a crossroads. The environmental disasters of the past decade had taken a heavy toll on the global economy, and the financial crisis that followed seemed insurmountable. What began as a series of localized environmental catastrophes had spiraled into a full-blown global crisis, one that affected every country, every industry, and every individual. Economic systems were teetering on the edge of collapse, and the burden of an overwhelmed planet seemed almost too much to bear.

Aldo and his team had dedicated their lives to solving the world's environmental problems, but they knew that the true test of their work had only just begun. The effects of the waste crises and the collapse of ecosystems were reverberating through global financial markets. Governments were struggling to balance their budgets, industries were suffering from unsustainable practices, and entire sectors of the economy were shifting toward more environmentally friendly practices, leaving massive gaps and economic disruption in their wake. Aldo knew that to truly address the world's environmental crisis, they would also need to tackle its economic implications.

1. The Global Financial Collapse

It all started with the collapse of the waste management systems in the most industrialized nations. Cities were inundated with unsorted waste, and the infrastructure that had once processed the world's garbage was no longer capable of handling the deluge. As landfills reached capacity, incinerators were overwhelmed, and the oceans became vast repositories of plastic and other pollutants, the economic impacts began to trickle down.

It wasn't just the environmental toll that was taking a toll on the global economy, it was the cost of cleaning up the mess. Governments around the world were forced to divert vast sums of money into waste management and environmental restoration, all the while their economies were already reeling from the effects of climate change. Storms, floods, and droughts had wreaked havoc on agricultural production, displacing millions of people and creating mass migrations. The energy sector, which had long been reliant on fossil fuels, was in flux as renewable energy sources began to take center stage.

The stock market, once a symbol of stability and growth, now fluctuated wildly as investors pulled out of traditional industries and sought refuge in more sustainable ventures. However, even these new industries, though promising, could not fill the economic vacuum left behind. Governments were scrambling to find ways to keep their economies afloat while also addressing the mounting environmental costs.

2. The Economic Cost of Environmental Damage

Aldo and his team recognized that this crisis was not just about pollution, it was about the entire structure of the global economy, one built on unsustainable practices and an ever-increasing consumption of resources. He understood that addressing the financial collapse would require addressing the deep-rooted flaws in the economic system itself.

The first step was to bring together the world's leading economists, environmentalists, and business leaders to start developing a roadmap for an economic transformation. Aldo reached out to his network of partners, including the brilliant economists who had been collaborating with him on sustainability issues, and invited them to a special summit. The mission of the summit was clear: create solutions that could not only help mitigate the financial fallout from the global environmental crisis but also lay the foundation for a new economic system that was sustainable and resilient in the face of environmental challenges.

The summit would focus on three key areas: sustainable investment, new financial mechanisms for environmental restoration, and the transition to a circular economy.

3. Sustainable Investment: Redirecting Capital

One of the most pressing issues was the need for massive investment in sustainable industries. Traditional sectors, such as fossil fuels and unsustainable agriculture, were increasingly being seen as risks by investors, and their decline was pushing the global economy into further turmoil. To counter this, Aldo and his team sought to redirect global capital into industries that would support long-term environmental sustainability.

Aldo knew that financial systems could no longer ignore the environmental costs of the business practices they supported. He proposed the creation of a Global Green Investment Fund, a financial institution that would pool resources from governments, corporations, and private investors to fund projects related to renewable energy, sustainable agriculture, waste management, and ecosystem restoration.

The idea was simple yet ambitious: channel financial capital into sectors that were not only environmentally responsible but also economically viable in the long term. Instead of continuing to invest in the short-term profits of industries that were damaging the planet, the fund would support businesses that were developing clean technologies, sustainable infrastructure, and green jobs.

Aldo partnered with a team of financial experts to draft the blueprint for the fund, which would be governed by a council made up of international stakeholders, including environmental organizations, government representatives, and financial institutions. The goal was to create a financial ecosystem that rewarded sustainable development rather than penalized it.

4. New Financial Mechanisms for Environmental Restoration

As the summit discussions progressed, Aldo realized that addressing the financial costs of environmental damage could not simply rely on redirecting existing funds—it also required creating new financial tools that could leverage the power of the global economy to fund large-scale environmental restoration projects.

One such tool was the Green Recovery Bond, a new type of bond that would be issued by governments and financial institutions to raise funds for environmental recovery efforts. These bonds would be backed by long-term environmental goals and would provide investors with returns tied to the success of sustainable projects.

The proceeds from these bonds would be used to fund global reforestation efforts, ocean cleanup projects, and the development of green infrastructure in cities. Aldo and his team worked with international financial experts to structure these bonds in a way that would make them attractive to both private and institutional investors. By creating a sustainable financial vehicle, they hoped to address the immediate need for environmental restoration while ensuring that investors would be incentivized to support the planet's future.

5. Transitioning to a Circular Economy

Aldo and his team also recognized that the key to resolving the global financial crisis lay in rethinking the very nature of economic production and consumption. The old linear economy, which relied on the extraction, use, and disposal of natural resources, was simply no longer viable. To create long-term stability, Aldo proposed a radical shift to a circular economy, where resources were used more efficiently, waste was minimized, and products were designed for reuse.

The transition to a circular economy would require businesses to rethink their production methods, focusing on designing products that could be recycled, repaired, or repurposed. This would reduce the reliance on raw materials and create new industries centered around the repair, reuse, and recycling of goods. Aldo knew that this would not be an easy task, businesses, governments, and individuals would need to change their mindset, viewing waste not as something to discard but as a valuable resource to be reintegrated into the economy.

To encourage businesses to adopt circular economy practices, Aldo and his team proposed tax incentives and subsidies for companies that adopted green technologies and sustainable business models. They also worked with governments to create global standards for recycling, waste management, and sustainable manufacturing, ensuring that the transition to a circular economy was not only economically feasible but also globally coordinated.

6. Overcoming Political and Economic Resistance

Despite the progress made in developing solutions to the global financial crisis, Aldo knew that they would face significant resistance from powerful political and economic forces. Large corporations, entrenched in traditional business models, would be reluctant to change. Governments that relied on fossil fuels for revenue would resist transitioning to renewable energy sources. Even some economists were wary of the radical changes Aldo proposed, fearing that the economic shift would destabilize markets even further.

Aldo and his team had to navigate these challenges carefully. They spent months meeting with political leaders, business executives, and financial regulators to explain the benefits of a green economy and the need for urgent action. They argued that the longer the world delayed transitioning to sustainability, the greater the economic damage would be in the long term. Through patience, persistence, and clear economic reasoning, Aldo and his team were able to convince many influential leaders to support the green investment fund and circular economy transition.

7. The Road Ahead

The financial crisis, while devastating, also presented an opportunity, a chance to rebuild the global economy on a foundation that would support the well-being of both people and the planet. Aldo and his team knew that the road ahead would not be easy. It would require coordination between nations, industries, and individuals. But they also knew that the crisis could be overcome, not just by managing the immediate fallout but by fundamentally rethinking the economic systems that had led the world to this point.

As Aldo stood before the summit's closing session, he felt a sense of cautious optimism. The world had taken the first steps toward healing both its environmental and economic wounds. The solutions they had developed would take time, but they had laid the groundwork for a brighter, more sustainable future.

The true challenge now lay in making those solutions a reality, one step at a time, with every decision made in service of the planet and its people.

Chapter 73: Spreading Technology in the Third World

The world had shifted. What once seemed like a distant dream of a cleaner, greener future had now become a reality. Aldo and his team had managed to innovate sustainable technologies that not only addressed the environmental crisis but also created economic opportunities. The road ahead was not just about preserving the planet for future generations; it was also about ensuring that the solutions could reach those who needed them the most, the people living in the world's most underdeveloped regions.

In these areas, known as the Third World, poverty, and environmental degradation had been intertwined for generations. Access to clean water, reliable energy, and proper waste management had long been out of reach. Many communities relied on outdated and polluting technologies to meet their basic needs. The air was thick with smoke from inefficient cooking methods, and rivers were choked with untreated waste. For the people in these regions, change had often seemed impossible. But now, with Aldo's groundbreaking technology, there was hope.

1. The Opportunity for Change

The first step was awareness. Aldo and his team understood that introducing their innovations to developing nations meant more than just sending equipment and resources. It required educating people, building trust, and ensuring that the technology was adapted to the unique challenges faced by these communities. The goal was not just to alleviate poverty but to empower local communities, making them self-sufficient and environmentally conscious in the process.

The potential for change in the Third World was immense. With limited infrastructure and resources, many countries had been bypassing the most polluting stages of industrial development. This meant they had a unique opportunity to skip over the damaging processes that had led wealthier nations to environmental ruin. The transition to sustainable technologies could be faster and more cost-effective in these areas, providing a path to economic stability while also benefiting the planet.

Aldo's solution to this challenge was multi-faceted. First, they focused on creating scalable, low-cost technologies that could be easily integrated into these regions. Then, they worked to build partnerships with local governments, NGOs, and grassroots organizations to ensure that the technology would be accepted and properly maintained. The mission was clear: to give developing countries the tools they needed to create a sustainable future for themselves.

2. The Technology of Hope

Aldo's team had developed several key innovations that could dramatically impact life in the Third World. The first and most important was the Waste-to-Energy System, which could turn organic waste into clean energy. In many rural areas, people still relied on firewood or charcoal for cooking, a practice that contributed to deforestation and severe air pollution. With the waste-to-energy system, waste from food scraps, agricultural leftovers, and even discarded plastics could be converted into electricity or cooking fuel. This not only solved the issue of waste disposal but also provided an affordable and sustainable energy source for communities that had little to no access to electricity.

Another crucial technology was the Solar Water Purification System. In regions where clean drinking water was scarce, this system used solar energy to purify contaminated water, making it safe to drink. Solar-powered desalination units were also introduced in coastal areas, providing fresh water from seawater.

For many villages that had relied on dangerous and unreliable sources of water, this technology was a game-changer.

Then, there was the Eco-Friendly Agriculture System. Traditional farming methods in the Third World often led to soil degradation and deforestation. Aldo's new approach focused on regenerative agriculture techniques that used organic waste, crop rotation, and sustainable irrigation to restore the land. This not only helped to feed local populations but also provided them with the tools to manage their own food production in a way that was both environmentally and economically sustainable.

Lastly, Aldo introduced Green Housing Technologies. With rapid urbanization occurring in many developing nations, there was a pressing need for affordable housing solutions. Aldo's team developed construction methods using recycled materials and energy-efficient designs that were not only cost-effective but also reduced carbon emissions. These homes were powered by solar energy and were built to withstand extreme weather conditions, making them ideal for regions that were frequently affected by natural disasters.

3. The Challenge of Implementation

While the technologies were groundbreaking, their implementation in the Third World was not without challenges. Many of these countries had limited infrastructure, and even the best solutions could fail if they were not adapted to the local context. Aldo knew that it would take more than just technology, it would take a complete shift in mindset, as well as careful planning and coordination.

One of the biggest obstacles was the lack of education and training in many regions. Local communities often lacked the technical know-how to operate, maintain, and repair the new systems. To address this, Aldo and his team partnered with local organizations to set up training programs. They trained local technicians and engineers to install and maintain the new systems, ensuring that the technology could continue to thrive long after the initial deployment.

Additionally, there was resistance from some local leaders and communities who were skeptical of new technologies. In many areas, there was distrust toward foreign solutions, especially ones that came with high costs or that required significant lifestyle changes. To overcome this, Aldo and his team focused on creating relationships with trusted community leaders and influencers who could help promote the new technologies. They also involved local communities in the design and implementation process, ensuring that the solutions were culturally appropriate and aligned with local values.

Aldo's team was also aware that they could not do this alone. They formed partnerships with international NGOs, local governments, and even global corporations to ensure that resources and expertise were available. By working with local stakeholders, they were able to create tailored solutions that met the specific needs of each region.

4. The Success Stories

Despite the challenges, the results were promising. In Kenya, for example, the introduction of the Waste-to-Energy System in rural communities had an immediate impact. Local farmers who had once struggled to dispose of their agricultural waste now had a reliable source of energy for their homes and farms. The system also helped to reduce the widespread deforestation caused by the overharvesting of wood for fuel. With the new technology, communities were able to harness their own waste as a resource, turning it into electricity for lighting, cooking, and irrigation.

In Bangladesh, the Solar Water Purification System was implemented in several coastal villages that had previously relied on contaminated river water. The solar-powered devices provided safe drinking water to thousands of people, significantly reducing waterborne diseases. In areas affected by flooding, the system's portability meant that it could be moved to different locations as needed, ensuring that communities always had access to clean water.

The Eco-Friendly Agriculture System had a profound impact in rural areas of India. Farmers who had once relied on harmful chemicals and unsustainable practices were introduced to regenerative farming techniques. With the help of Aldo's team, they learned how to use organic waste and crop rotation to restore the health of their soil. As a result, crop yields improved, deforestation was reduced, and farmers were able to generate income while improving the environment around them.

In Peru, the Green Housing Technologies were introduced in the aftermath of a devastating earthquake that left thousands of people homeless. The new homes, made from recycled materials and powered by solar energy, were not only affordable but also built to withstand future natural disasters. The project became a model for sustainable housing in other regions of South America, showing that it was possible to rebuild communities with both resilience and sustainability in mind.

5. Overcoming Global Inequality

One of the most powerful aspects of Aldo's work was the ability to create solutions that helped lift people out of poverty without causing further harm to the environment. These technologies were designed to be affordable, accessible, and adaptable to the realities of life in the developing world. They provided a unique opportunity for countries in the Third World to break free from the cycle of poverty and environmental degradation that had held them back for so long.

However, Aldo knew that the success of these initiatives required continued support. He worked tirelessly to secure funding and resources to expand the deployment of these technologies, reaching more and more communities every day. He also lobbied for global policies that would incentivize the adoption of sustainable practices in developing countries, recognizing that true progress would require a coordinated effort from both governments and private sectors.

6. The Future of Sustainable Development

Looking to the future, Aldo saw endless possibilities. The technologies his team had created were not just solutions to the current environmental crisis, they were tools for long-term, sustainable development. By providing the Third World with the resources they needed to prosper in a way that was both environmentally responsible and economically viable, Aldo believed that a new era of global prosperity could emerge.

He envisioned a world where no matter where a person lived, they could access the same sustainable technologies that had helped so many others. A world where the economic divide between the rich and the poor was narrowed by the shared goal of a greener, more equitable future. The work of Aldo and his team had shown that sustainability and development could go hand in hand, creating opportunities for everyone to thrive, regardless of their location or circumstances. As Aldo looked toward the horizon, he knew that their work was far from over. But he also knew that the seed had been planted, an idea that would continue to grow and spread, one community at a time.

Chapter 74: The Rise of Terrestrial Ecosystems

The world was beginning to heal. After years of tireless effort, Aldo and his team had made remarkable strides in their quest to restore not only the planet's oceans but also its vital terrestrial ecosystems. The earth, scarred by centuries of human exploitation, had been pushed to the brink. From deforestation to soil erosion, the land had suffered under the weight of unchecked industrialization and unsustainable agricultural practices. Yet, now, a new chapter was unfolding. The promise of revitalizing the planet's terrestrial ecosystems was no longer a mere dream—it was becoming a tangible reality.

This transformation was driven by the combination of cutting-edge technology and Aldo's unyielding dedication to sustainability. Armed with innovations that could reverse the damage done to the land, Aldo's team began a global effort to rejuvenate the earth's ecosystems, one step at a time. The ultimate goal was to create a future where the land was not just sustainable but thriving, a vital source of life for all the species that called it home.

1. The Challenge of Soil Degradation

The journey to restoring terrestrial ecosystems started with an urgent focus on one of the planet's most pressing issues: soil degradation. Over the decades, industrial farming practices had depleted the earth's soil, leaving it barren, compacted, and incapable of supporting new plant life. This loss of soil fertility had led to a decline in agricultural productivity, deforestation, and the desertification of large swaths of land. In some parts of the world, entire landscapes had been turned into wastelands.

Aldo and his team knew that reversing soil degradation would be the first step in creating healthier ecosystems. Their solution came in the form of bio-enhanced soil regeneration technology. This breakthrough technology involved using microbes, fungi, and other natural organisms to restore soil health. By reintroducing vital microorganisms that had been lost due to industrial farming, Aldo's team could reinvigorate the soil, making it fertile once more.

The team used a combination of composting techniques, natural fertilizers, and soil-building practices to enhance the soil's ability to retain moisture, increase its nutrient content, and reduce erosion. The results were astounding. In areas that had once been barren, the land began to show signs of life. Seeds sprouted where they had never been able to grow before, and vegetation quickly flourished. With time, the soil's capacity to support diverse plant life returned.

2. Reforestation: Bringing Back the Green

Once the soil was restored, Aldo's team turned their attention to reforestation, the process of bringing back the forests that had once covered the land. Forests were the lungs of the planet, vital for maintaining the balance of oxygen and carbon dioxide in the atmosphere. They provided habitats for countless species, helped regulate water cycles, and prevented soil erosion.

However, deforestation had taken a heavy toll. Industrial logging, agricultural expansion, and urbanization had cleared vast swaths of forest, leaving ecosystems fragmented and vulnerable. To combat this, Aldo's team developed a reforestation strategy that was both innovative and environmentally sustainable.

Rather than simply planting trees, they used advanced tree planting drones that could plant large quantities of native species at a time. These drones were equipped with artificial intelligence that allowed them to analyze the land and determine the optimal locations for planting. This method drastically reduced the cost of reforestation efforts and allowed for large-scale planting operations in areas that were otherwise difficult to access.

The team also integrated agroforestry, a practice that combined trees with crops and livestock. This not only helped to restore forests but also provided local communities with sustainable sources of food and income. The interdependence between crops, trees, and animals created a balanced ecosystem that promoted biodiversity while providing practical benefits.

In the years that followed, forests began to reclaim vast tracts of land. The once barren hillsides were now covered in vibrant green canopies, and species that had long been absent began to return. Aldo and his team knew that this was just the beginning, but they had taken the first crucial steps toward reversing the damage done by centuries of exploitation.

3. Biodiversity Restoration: Bringing Species Back

One of the most pressing concerns in the restoration of terrestrial ecosystems was biodiversity loss. As ecosystems were destroyed, countless species were driven to extinction, and many others were pushed to the brink. Aldo and his team recognized that the recovery of terrestrial ecosystems could not happen in isolation. It had to go hand in hand with efforts to bring back the species that had once thrived in these habitats.

To achieve this, the team focused on habitat restoration. In addition to reforesting areas, they worked to restore wetlands, grasslands, and other crucial ecosystems that provided homes for a wide range of species. The creation of wildlife corridors that connected fragmented habitats allowed animals to migrate freely and safely, ensuring genetic diversity and the health of populations.

Aldo's team also worked closely with global conservation organizations to reintroduce species that had been extirpated from certain regions. Using state-of-the-art breeding programs and genetic research, they carefully reintroduced animals such as wolves, bison, and various species of birds to areas where they had once lived. This was a delicate process, as the reintroduced species had to be carefully monitored and integrated into their new environments.

For example, in areas of North America, the reintroduction of wolves had a profound impact on the ecosystem. Wolves are apex predators, and their presence helped regulate the populations of other species, such as deer, which had become overabundant and had been damaging the vegetation. With the wolves back in the ecosystem, the balance was restored, and the biodiversity of the entire region flourished.

4. Sustainable Agriculture: A New Model

As reforestation and biodiversity efforts progressed, Aldo's team worked on a model of sustainable agriculture that could coexist with these restored ecosystems. Traditional farming practices had been a major contributor to deforestation, soil erosion, and biodiversity loss. To break this cycle, Aldo's team introduced agroecology, an approach to farming that emphasized working with nature rather than against it.

Agroecology involved a variety of techniques, including crop rotation, reduced tillage, and the use of organic fertilizers. These practices not only restored the health of the soil but also supported the biodiversity of the region. By diversifying the types of crops grown, farmers were able to create a more resilient agricultural system that was less vulnerable to pests, diseases, and extreme weather events.

Additionally, Aldo and his team developed precision farming technologies that helped farmers use water, nutrients, and energy more efficiently. Drones, sensors, and AI-powered systems enabled farmers to monitor their fields in real-time and make data-driven decisions about irrigation, fertilization, and pest control. This reduced the environmental impact of farming while increasing yields and improving food security.

One of the most successful projects was in sub-Saharan Africa, where Aldo's team worked with local farmers to implement agroecological principles. The results were transformative. The land that had once been degraded and unproductive was now supporting thriving crops, and farmers who had once struggled with food insecurity were now able to grow enough to feed their communities.

5. The Role of Technology in Restoration

The success of the restoration efforts could not have been achieved without the advanced technologies developed by Aldo and his team. From soil regeneration microbes to drone-powered reforestation, the use of technology allowed them to scale their efforts and reach places that were once inaccessible. The integration of AI, machine learning, and data analytics enabled Aldo's team to monitor progress, predict outcomes, and adjust strategies in real time.

But Aldo knew that technology alone wasn't enough. The true key to success lay in collaboration. He had always believed that restoring the earth's ecosystems would require a global effort, and now, with the backing of governments, NGOs, local communities, and the private sector, the movement was gaining momentum.

Aldo's focus was now on scaling these technologies to every corner of the globe. From the deserts of Africa to the rainforests of South America, the tools to restore the earth were being put into action. The vision of a healthy planet, once thought to be unattainable, was now becoming a reality.

6. Looking Ahead: A Sustainable Future

As Aldo stood on the edge of a newly restored forest, watching the sun filter through the canopy, he couldn't help but feel a sense of accomplishment. The land that had once been barren was now teeming with life. Birds chirped from the trees, and the air was thick with the smell of fresh, earthy growth. It was a testament to the power of innovation, collaboration, and a relentless pursuit of a sustainable future.

But Aldo knew that the journey was far from over. The earth was vast, and the challenges ahead were immense. Climate change, rising populations, and shifting political landscapes all presented obstacles that would require continued effort. Yet, as he looked at the rejuvenated land around him, Aldo felt a renewed sense of hope.

The work to restore the earth's terrestrial ecosystems was a long-term endeavor, but it was one that held the promise of a brighter, more sustainable future for all. And with each success, Aldo knew that they were one step closer to a world where nature and humanity thrived together in harmony.

Chapter 75: Accelerating Global Transformation

The world had changed in ways that Aldo had never imagined possible when he first embarked on his mission to reverse the damage inflicted on the planet. What began as a solitary effort to innovate and implement sustainable technologies had evolved into a global movement, a movement that was beginning to pick up speed with each passing day. The collective momentum was undeniable. Across continents, nations, and cultures, the world was awakening to the reality of its environmental crisis, and more importantly, to the solutions that Aldo and his team had so tirelessly worked to create. The transformation that Aldo had hoped for was no longer a distant dream; it was happening now.

But this was just the beginning. The challenge that lay before Aldo and his team was how to accelerate the progress. The stakes were higher than ever, and they knew that time was of the essence. As the impacts of climate change became more severe, the need for swift action was paramount. It was no longer enough to make slow, incremental improvements. The global community had to move faster, work smarter, and collaborate on a scale never before seen in history.

1. A Global Network of Change

The first step in accelerating the transformation was building a global network of like-minded individuals and organizations. Aldo and his team knew that no single nation, company, or individual could solve the world's environmental problems alone. The key to success was collaboration, on a massive scale.

To facilitate this collaboration, Aldo initiated the creation of a Global Sustainability Network. This network would bring together governments, corporations, scientists, activists, and citizens from around the world to share knowledge, resources, and best practices for sustainability. The network would also serve as a platform for coordinating joint initiatives, sharing technological advancements, and supporting efforts to scale up solutions in the most affected regions.

One of the most significant successes of the network was the Global Innovation Summit, a conference that Aldo and his team organized to bring together the world's foremost experts in sustainability and environmental science. The summit was a turning point. Leaders from every sector, from finance to agriculture to technology, gathered to discuss solutions and formulate plans for rapid deployment. The summit set the tone for what would become a new era of global cooperation.

During the summit, Aldo presented his team's latest innovation: the Global Environmental Restoration Plan (GERP). This comprehensive strategy outlined how the world could restore ecosystems, mitigate climate change, and transition to a green economy. The plan included detailed frameworks for urban planning, reforestation, ocean cleanup, sustainable agriculture, and waste management. It was bold, ambitious, and exactly what the world needed to hear.

As the summit concluded, the world's attention shifted. More and more countries committed to the principles of GERP, pledging to integrate the plan into their national policies and work together to share knowledge, technology, and resources. The momentum had officially shifted into high gear.

2. The Role of Technology in Scaling Up

Technology had always been at the heart of Aldo's mission, and it was clear that in order to accelerate the transformation, the team had to scale up their technological innovations. Over the years, Aldo and his team had developed groundbreaking solutions in waste management, energy generation, and environmental restoration. Now, the goal was to expand these solutions to the scale of entire countries, continents, and eventually the planet.

One of the key areas of focus was clean energy. With fossil fuel consumption still dominating global energy production, Aldo knew that transitioning to renewable energy sources was critical. His team had already developed highly efficient energy systems that utilized waste as a resource, but now they needed to spread these solutions worldwide.

To do this, Aldo and his team launched a series of global energy initiatives in collaboration with major energy providers, governments, and renewable energy companies. The goal was to rapidly deploy clean energy technologies, such as solar panels, wind turbines, and waste-to-energy plants, in regions most affected by pollution and energy shortages. By tapping into the collective power of international partners, they were able to scale up production and infrastructure quickly, reducing costs and increasing the availability of green energy to millions of people.

In addition to energy, Aldo focused on sustainable transportation. The global transportation sector was one of the largest contributors to greenhouse gas emissions. With this in mind, Aldo's team worked alongside automotive manufacturers, tech companies, and governments to accelerate the development and deployment of electric vehicles (EVs), public transportation systems, and high-speed rail networks. By making transportation more sustainable, they could drastically reduce carbon emissions, improve air quality, and create more resilient urban infrastructure.

3. The Power of Collaboration with Corporations

One of the key obstacles to achieving global sustainability was the reluctance of large corporations to change their business models. Many industries were heavily invested in practices that contributed to environmental degradation, and the idea of shifting to more sustainable methods was often seen as a financial risk. Aldo knew that changing the hearts and minds of powerful corporations would take time, but he also understood that the scale of the problem required their involvement.

To address this challenge, Aldo and his team developed a new framework for corporate sustainability, which they presented to some of the world's largest companies. The framework provided a roadmap for businesses to reduce their environmental footprint, increase efficiency, and invest in sustainable technologies. Aldo's team also partnered with major corporations to co-create innovative solutions that could help scale up sustainable practices in industries like manufacturing, fashion, and food production.

The breakthrough came when several major corporations, ranging from tech giants to retail conglomerates, signed on to the Global Corporate Sustainability Pact. This agreement pledged to reduce corporate emissions, adopt sustainable supply chain practices, and invest in green technologies. By leveraging the influence of these companies, Aldo's team was able to drive significant progress in industries that had previously been resistant to change.

This corporate shift was instrumental in accelerating the spread of sustainable practices across the globe. Companies were no longer just paying lip service to sustainability, they were integrating it into their core business strategies. As a result, the demand for green technologies skyrocketed, and the world began to move toward a low-carbon economy at an unprecedented pace.

4. Overcoming Political Barriers

Despite the overwhelming support for global sustainability, Aldo and his team faced significant political challenges. Not all nations were eager to embrace the changes necessary to combat climate change and environmental degradation. Some governments, particularly those with economies deeply tied to fossil fuels or deforestation, were resistant to the changes Aldo's team proposed. There were also political factions that denied the reality of climate change, further complicating the situation.

Aldo recognized that political change was crucial for the success of the global transformation. He worked tirelessly to engage with leaders from all corners of the globe, including both developed and developing countries. Through diplomacy and negotiation, Aldo was able to find common ground, emphasizing that sustainability was not just a moral imperative, but an economic one. He argued that investing in green technologies, renewable energy, and sustainable industries would create millions of jobs and help future-proof economies against the impacts of climate change.

Slowly but surely, Aldo's efforts began to pay off. Governments started to pass green policies, enacting laws that incentivized renewable energy production, green building practices, and waste reduction. In addition, international agreements, such as the Global Climate Accord, were signed, committing countries to ambitious carbon reduction targets. The political landscape was shifting, and the world was beginning to come together in support of a shared, sustainable future.

5. The Role of Education and Advocacy

In addition to the technical, corporate, and political aspects of the transformation, Aldo and his team knew that education and advocacy were critical components of the global movement. In order to create lasting change, they had to inspire people of all ages to take action.

Aldo launched an educational campaign aimed at raising awareness about the importance of sustainability and environmental stewardship. The campaign targeted schools, universities, and communities, empowering the next generation to think critically about the environment and the role they could play in shaping the future. Through documentaries, interactive learning platforms, and public service announcements, Aldo and his team reached millions of people around the world, instilling a sense of urgency and responsibility.

Additionally, Aldo worked with activist organizations to amplify the voices of those who had been advocating for environmental change for decades. These grassroots organizations became powerful allies in the fight for a sustainable future, mobilizing communities and holding governments accountable for their commitments to sustainability.

6. The Path Forward: A Unified World

As Aldo stood before the assembly at the Global Sustainability Network summit, he could sense the growing energy in the room. The work that lay ahead was immense, but for the first time, Aldo felt a deep sense of hope. The world was changing, and the collective effort to restore the planet had gained undeniable momentum. The transformation was underway, and it was only going to accelerate from here.

The acceleration of global transformation was no longer just an idea, it was a movement in full motion. By harnessing the power of technology, collaboration, and collective action, Aldo and his team had set the stage for a world that was not just recovering but thriving. The path forward was clear: together, humanity could overcome the challenges of the past and create a future that was sustainable, equitable, and prosperous for all.

Chapter 76: The City that Became a Model

The world was watching. After decades of environmental degradation, inequality, and unsustainable growth, humanity had reached a pivotal moment in history. The transformation was no longer a far-off dream; it was unfolding before their eyes. And in the heart of this transformation stood one shining example, a city that embodied the principles of sustainability, innovation, and harmony with nature. This city had become a beacon of hope for a world that desperately needed it, offering a vision for the future of urban living.

The city was called Gaia, named after the ancient Greek goddess of the Earth, a fitting tribute to its commitment to the planet. It was the first city to be fully designed, developed, and built with the guiding principles of sustainability at its core. Every aspect of Gaia's infrastructure, economy, and culture was focused on minimizing its environmental impact and maximizing its positive contributions to the Earth. It was a city that proved it was possible to live harmoniously with nature while maintaining a high standard of living.

1. The Birth of Gaia

Gaia was conceived years earlier as an ambitious project to demonstrate that a sustainable city was not just possible but desirable. Aldo and his team had long recognized the urgent need to rethink urban living, especially as the world's cities became increasingly overcrowded and polluted. Traditional cities were built with a mindset of exploitation, exploiting resources, land, and people for economic growth. But Gaia was designed with a completely different ethos: to restore, regenerate, and balance.

The development of Gaia began with the selection of its location. Aldo and his team carefully chose a site that was once an industrial wasteland, a place where ecosystems had been devastated and the land had been scarred by years of mining and pollution. The vision for Gaia was clear: to rehabilitate the land, restore the natural environment, and create a thriving urban ecosystem that could sustain future generations.

The planning phase of Gaia was unlike any city project before. Aldo and his team worked closely with architects, urban planners, environmental scientists, and community leaders to create a blueprint that would serve as a model for cities worldwide. The design incorporated green spaces, renewable energy systems, zero-waste infrastructure, and closed-loop water and energy cycles. From the beginning, the goal was not just to create a sustainable city but a living, breathing example of what was possible when technology, nature, and people worked together.

2. The Heart of Gaia: Sustainable Infrastructure

Gaia was built on the foundation of green infrastructure—systems that worked with nature, rather than against it. The city's energy grid was powered entirely by renewable sources. Solar panels covered rooftops, wind turbines dotted the outskirts, and waste-to-energy plants provided a steady supply of power. The city's commitment to clean energy was reflected in its smart grid, which optimized energy use in real-time, reducing waste and ensuring that every kilowatt of power was used efficiently.

The transportation system in Gaia was entirely electric. There were no gas-guzzling cars clogging the streets or spewing pollutants into the air. Instead, the city was equipped with a network of electric buses, self-driving vehicles, bike-sharing programs, and pedestrian-friendly streets. The use of private cars was discouraged, and residents were encouraged to walk, cycle, or use public transportation, reducing traffic congestion and air pollution. The city's streets were lined with green corridors, making it easy and pleasant to travel from one area to another while surrounded by nature.

Gaia also implemented zero-waste principles in its waste management system. Every piece of waste, whether organic, plastic, or electronic, was sorted, recycled, or repurposed. There were no landfills in Gaia. Instead, the city had state-of-the-art composting systems, upcycling facilities, and waste-to-material plants. In fact, much of the city's construction materials, furniture, and products were made from recycled materials, reducing the need for virgin resources and minimizing environmental harm.

3. Nature Integrated Into Every Corner

One of the most striking features of Gaia was how nature was integrated into the fabric of the city. Unlike traditional cities where green spaces were limited to parks or gardens, Gaia took a holistic approach to nature. Urban farming was a central part of the city's design. Rooftops were transformed into community gardens, where residents grew their own food, reducing their reliance on external food supply chains and cutting down on the carbon footprint associated with food transportation.

In addition to urban farming, Gaia also had biophilic design principles integrated into every building. Every structure, from homes to businesses to public buildings, was designed to promote a connection with the natural world. Buildings were constructed with living walls, vertical gardens that not only provided insulation but also contributed to biodiversity. Green roofs were common, and natural ventilation systems reduced the need for artificial heating and cooling. The use of sustainable materials such as recycled wood, reclaimed steel, and locally sourced stone minimized the environmental impact of construction.

The city's commitment to biodiversity was evident in its extensive network of green corridors, pathways that connected urban areas with natural ecosystems. These corridors allowed for the movement of wildlife, creating a healthier environment for both humans and animals. Rewilding efforts were undertaken in the surrounding areas, where previously damaged ecosystems were restored to their natural state, providing a safe haven for endangered species.

4. A Culture of Sustainability

Gaia wasn't just a city of technological marvels; it was also a city that had fostered a culture of sustainability. The citizens of Gaia were deeply committed to living in harmony with the planet, and this mindset was embedded in every aspect of their daily lives.

The education system in Gaia played a crucial role in shaping this culture. From an early age, children were taught about environmental stewardship, resource management, and the importance of living sustainably. Schools incorporated outdoor classrooms, where students learned about ecosystems, biodiversity, and agriculture, and they were encouraged to participate in community-based sustainability projects. Every student graduated with a deep understanding of how their actions impacted the environment and how they could contribute to its preservation.

In addition to education, Gaia had a local economy that was based on sustainable practices. Local businesses thrived on the principles of fairness, sustainability, and circularity. Many of the city's restaurants, for example, sourced their ingredients from nearby urban farms, reducing food waste and minimizing the carbon footprint of transportation. Clothing stores sold only eco-friendly garments made from recycled materials and sustainable fabrics. Businesses were incentivized to adopt green practices through tax breaks and support from the city's

MOUNT OF WASTE

sustainability fund, which helped small enterprises transition to more eco-friendly models.

5. The Global Impact of Gaia

As Gaia began to flourish, it quickly became clear that this city was not just a model for other cities in its region, it was a model for the entire world. The city's success was a living testament to the idea that urban spaces could be sustainable, prosperous, and livable, without compromising the health of the planet.

Governments and cities from around the world began to take notice. Delegations from countries as diverse as Brazil, Japan, Nigeria, and Germany visited Gaia to study its success and learn how they could replicate its achievements. The city became a hub for international collaboration, where architects, urban planners, and environmentalists exchanged ideas and strategies. Gaia hosted global sustainability conferences, where experts and leaders from all sectors, government, business, academia, and civil society, came together to share their knowledge and create a shared vision for the future.

As a result of Gaia's success, similar projects were launched in cities across the globe. The principles that had guided Gaia's development were adapted to suit different climates, cultures, and economic contexts. From Copenhagen to Cape Town, from Singapore to Buenos Aires, cities around the world began to implement the lessons learned from Gaia, accelerating the global transition to sustainable urban living.

6. A Legacy of Hope

In the years following Gaia's completion, the city had evolved into a living symbol of what humanity could achieve when it embraced sustainability at every level. The city had not only reduced its own environmental impact but had sparked a global movement, a movement that had the power to reshape the future of urban life.

The success of Gaia was a testament to the power of collaboration, innovation, and perseverance. It showed that it was possible to build a better world, a world where cities were not just places to live but places to thrive. And as Gaia continued to inspire cities around the world, it became clear that this was only the beginning. The transformation had already begun, and Gaia was leading the way.

As Aldo stood at the city's edge, gazing out over the lush greenery and the shining solar panels, he couldn't help but feel a sense of pride. Gaia was not just a city, it was a legacy, a blueprint for the future, and a beacon of hope for a world that still had a long way to go.

And in that moment, Aldo knew that the true transformation was just beginning.

Chapter 77: Tensions Between Nations

The world had witnessed an unprecedented transformation in recent years. Cities that were once choking on pollution were now being reborn as models of sustainability. Technology that had once been seen as a threat to the environment was now a tool for healing the planet. Yet, despite the progress, the path forward was not as smooth as Aldo had hoped. A new challenge was emerging, one that could derail everything they had worked for—the growing tension between nations that were struggling to keep up with the pace of change.

Some countries had embraced the sustainable revolution, quickly adopting new technologies and adjusting their policies to promote a greener, more equitable future. But others, particularly those that had built their economies on traditional industries such as fossil fuels, mining, and manufacturing, found themselves lagging behind. These nations were grappling with the economic and social consequences of the global transformation, and many felt left behind in the rush toward sustainability. It was this feeling of being left out that was beginning to spark tension on the international stage.

In boardrooms, legislative chambers, and diplomatic halls across the globe, leaders were questioning whether the shift to a green economy was happening too quickly. They feared that their economies would suffer irreparably if they were forced to abandon established industries. More than that, some feared the loss of political power as the balance of global influence shifted toward those who had successfully embraced the green revolution.

The stage was set for a new kind of geopolitical struggle, a struggle not over land or resources, but over the very future of the global economy.

1. The Rising Tensions

It started slowly. At first, there were whispers in the corridors of power, quiet concerns about the pace of the global transition. Then, those concerns began to turn into public statements. Leaders of several powerful nations began to publicly question the need for drastic changes in their economies. These countries, whose industrial sectors had long relied on fossil fuels, argued that the rapid pace of transformation was unfair to those who had not had the same resources or opportunities to invest in new technologies.

In a meeting of the United Nations, one of the most vocal critics, a leader from a major oil-producing country, addressed the assembly with growing frustration. "We have been told time and again that we must abandon our economic models to save the planet," he said, his voice tinged with anger. "But what of the livelihoods of our people? What of the millions who depend on traditional industries for their survival?"

The words struck a chord with many. Nations that were still struggling with poverty, political instability, or economic fragility began to raise similar concerns. Some of the world's poorest nations argued that they had no choice but to prioritize economic development over environmental preservation. They pointed to the fact that wealthier nations had long reaped the benefits of industrialization without considering its environmental costs. Why should they be forced to adopt green technologies when the developed world had already benefited from the same resources without any constraints?

Aldo and his team watched with growing concern as the diplomatic community became increasingly divided. It was clear that some nations were beginning to question the very foundation of the global green movement. Their voices, once isolated, were now growing louder and more insistent. Aldo knew that if the growing dissatisfaction was not addressed, it could lead to a global rift, one that would undermine everything they had achieved.

2. A Call for Dialogue

Understanding the gravity of the situation, Aldo called for an emergency meeting with his core team. In the sleek, glass-walled conference room of the Alpha Research Center, the team gathered around a large table, their faces serious and focused. Aldo stood at the head of the room, his mind racing through the options before him.

"We need to address the growing tensions between nations," he began, his voice steady but tinged with concern. "If we don't find a way to bring people together, this divide will threaten everything we've worked for. Our mission has always been about collaboration, not division."

His words resonated with the group, each member aware of the delicate nature of the situation. But Aldo was determined to find a solution, even if it meant pushing through diplomatic challenges that seemed insurmountable.

After hours of intense discussion, the team came to a consensus. They would initiate a global dialogue—a summit that would bring together world leaders, diplomats, business leaders, and activists to discuss the future of the global green revolution. The goal would be to foster a sense of cooperation rather than competition and to address the concerns of nations that felt left behind. Aldo knew that the transition to a sustainable world couldn't be forced on anyone; it had to be a shared journey, one that recognized the unique challenges and needs of different countries.

"We'll need to be transparent, inclusive, and, above all, empathetic," Aldo concluded. "This is not just about technology or policy; it's about rebuilding trust."

3. The Summit: A Meeting of Minds

Months later, the summit was set to take place in a neutral location: Geneva, Switzerland. The world's eyes were fixed on the event, eager to see how the leaders of the world would navigate the delicate balance between sustainability and economic development. The summit promised to be a historic moment, one that could either propel the world closer to unity or deepen the rift that had already begun to form.

The conference hall was packed with delegates from nearly every country. Aldo and his team stood at the forefront of the event, ready to lead the discussions. As the opening session began, Aldo took the stage to deliver his address.

"Ladies and gentlemen," Aldo began, his voice calm yet firm, "We are here today not just to discuss the future of our planet, but to discuss the future of our shared humanity. The world is facing challenges that transcend borders, and the only way we will succeed is together. Our journey toward sustainability is not a path of division, but one of collaboration."

He paused, allowing his words to settle. "It is true that some nations have had the privilege of industrialization, while others have yet to reap the benefits. It is also true that those nations who have led the charge toward sustainability must recognize the challenges faced by those who are still transitioning. Today, we come together not as opponents, but as partners in the effort to heal the planet, not just for some, but for all."

Aldo's words set the tone for the summit. Over the following days, intense discussions unfolded. The leaders of countries with growing economies, particularly those in the developing world, expressed their concerns. They were worried that their economic growth would be stifled by the rapid shift toward green technologies. Some feared that they would be left behind in the race for global power, as wealthier nations dominated the new green economy.

At the same time, the countries that had embraced sustainability pushed for stronger action, arguing that the stakes were too high to wait. "If we don't act now," one European delegate said, "we will condemn future generations to live in a world ravaged by climate change, biodiversity loss, and resource depletion."

The debates were heated, but Aldo's team worked tirelessly behind the scenes to facilitate dialogue. It wasn't about pushing a single agenda but finding common ground. They focused on crafting shared goals, goals that would ensure sustainable development for all nations, regardless of their current economic standing.

4. The Breakthrough: A New Global Framework

After days of tense negotiations, a breakthrough finally came. The summit resulted in the creation of a global framework for sustainable development, one that would address the concerns of both developed and developing nations. This new framework included several key provisions:

1. Fair Transition Mechanisms: Developed nations committed to providing financial and technological support to developing nations, helping them to transition to sustainable energy sources without sacrificing economic growth. This included investments in renewable energy infrastructure, capacity building, and knowledge sharing.

2. Technology Transfer Programs: A global partnership would be established to facilitate the transfer of green technologies to nations that needed them most. This would ensure that the benefits of innovation were shared equitably, and that no nation would be left behind in the global green revolution.

3. Economic Diversification Plans: Countries that were heavily dependent on traditional industries like fossil fuels would be given assistance in diversifying their economies. This would involve creating new industries centered around renewable energy, sustainable agriculture, and eco-tourism, providing opportunities for job creation and economic stability.

4. Global Green Investment Fund: A global fund was created to support sustainable projects in the developing world. This fund would be supported by both public and private sectors and would be used to finance large-scale environmental projects such as reforestation, renewable energy initiatives, and sustainable agriculture.

5. Inclusive Policy Frameworks: All countries, regardless of their economic status, would be encouraged to develop national policies that prioritized sustainable development while taking into account their unique challenges and needs. These policies would be reviewed and updated regularly to ensure they were achieving the desired outcomes.

5. A New Era of Cooperation

As the summit came to a close, there was a palpable sense of relief and hope in the air. The world had not only avoided a potential geopolitical crisis but had forged a new path forward, one of cooperation and shared responsibility. Aldo and his team felt a deep sense of accomplishment, knowing that they had helped to bridge the gap between nations and create a framework that would guide the world toward a more sustainable future.

For Aldo, this moment marked a new beginning. The journey to save the planet was far from over, but the creation of a new global framework for sustainable development was a turning point. It was a reminder that even in the face of division and tension, dialogue, understanding, and collaboration could bring people together for the common good.

As he left the summit, Aldo reflected on the long road ahead. The world had taken a significant step forward, but there was still much work to be done. Still, for the first time in a long while, he felt a renewed sense of optimism. The global community had come together, and together, they would move forward, toward a sustainable and united future.

Chapter 78: Overcoming Water Scarcity

The climate crisis was not only about rising temperatures, extreme weather events, and polluted air; it also had devastating consequences for one of the most vital resources for human survival: water. As temperatures rose and freshwater supplies dwindled, water scarcity became one of the most pressing challenges Aldo and his team had to tackle. The world's growing population, combined with changing weather patterns and poor water management practices, had left many regions of the planet struggling to secure adequate supplies of clean water.

Aldo had seen the devastating impact of water shortages firsthand. During his travels to regions already facing severe droughts, he had witnessed the suffering of communities that had to rely on contaminated water sources, often resulting in devastating health crises. In some areas, people were forced to travel long distances just to collect water, and the quality of water available was often far below what was needed to sustain life.

The situation was dire, and Aldo knew that finding a solution was critical, not just for the survival of communities, but for the success of the global sustainability movement. Water scarcity threatened agriculture, health, industry, and entire ecosystems. Without enough water, the planet's ability to recover from environmental degradation would be severely limited. If they could solve this problem, it would be a major step forward in ensuring the survival of humanity and the natural world.

1. The Challenge of Water Scarcity

Aldo and his team began by analyzing the global water crisis from every angle. They studied the regions most affected by water scarcity, many of them located in arid and semi-arid regions of the world, including parts of Africa, the Middle East, and South Asia. The statistics were alarming: nearly two billion people lived in water-scarce regions, and by 2030, half of the world's population could face severe water shortages.

The issue was not only a lack of freshwater sources but also poor infrastructure and inefficient water management. Many countries had inadequate systems for water storage, filtration, and distribution. In areas where water was available, it was often polluted by industrial waste, agricultural runoff, and human activity, making it unsafe to drink.

The team quickly realized that there was no single solution to this problem. Addressing water scarcity required a multi-faceted approach, one that combined technology, policy, and community engagement. They would need to focus on developing new technologies for water purification, improving water management practices, and promoting water conservation worldwide.

Aldo knew that their goal was not just to develop a solution for the short-term, but to create systems that could be sustained over the long term, ensuring access to clean water for generations to come.

2. Research and Development: A Technological Approach

Aldo's team set to work, focusing on finding technological solutions that could address the issue of water scarcity in a scalable and sustainable way. They began by researching existing water treatment and desalination technologies, assessing their efficiency and the resources required to implement them. However, Aldo quickly realized that traditional methods, such as large-scale desalination plants, were not feasible for many of the world's most water-scarce regions. These plants required vast amounts of energy and infrastructure, and many of the regions that needed clean water the most lacked the resources to support such operations.

Instead, Aldo and his team began to focus on developing decentralized solutions, small, portable systems that could provide clean water at the local level. They looked into a variety of technologies, including solar-powered water purification systems, atmospheric water generators that extracted water from the air, and advanced filtration methods that could purify even the most contaminated water sources.

One of the most promising solutions came from a partnership with a leading innovator in water technology. The team began developing a solar-powered desalination unit designed to extract freshwater from seawater using minimal energy. This technology used a highly efficient solar still, coupled with a multi-stage filtration process, to purify water quickly and with minimal environmental impact. The system was small enough to be deployed in rural communities, where access to centralized infrastructure was limited.

Another breakthrough came when they refined atmospheric water generation (AWG) technology. These devices could extract water from the air, even in arid environments where the humidity was low. By using advanced filtration and condensation techniques, AWG units could produce potable water from thin air, making them an ideal solution for regions with no nearby freshwater sources.

These new technologies were not only efficient but also sustainable. Powered by renewable energy sources like solar and wind, they would not contribute to the depletion of the Earth's resources.

3. Deploying Solutions in Water-Scarce Regions

As the research and development phase progressed, Aldo and his team began preparing to deploy their solutions in the field. They knew that technology alone would not solve the problem.

MOUNT OF WASTE

Community engagement and proper infrastructure would be just as important for the success of their efforts.

They decided to pilot their solutions in some of the most water-stressed regions of the world. They partnered with local governments, NGOs, and community organizations to bring the technologies directly to the people who needed them most. In collaboration with these partners, they began installing solar-powered desalination units and atmospheric water generators in rural villages, small towns, and urban slums that were suffering from chronic water shortages.

One of the first deployments took place in a remote village in sub-Saharan Africa, where a severe drought had left the local population without access to clean drinking water. The village relied on a small, polluted river for water, which led to frequent outbreaks of waterborne diseases. Aldo's team installed a solar-powered desalination unit that could provide the community with enough clean water to meet their needs. In addition, they set up several atmospheric water generators in the village, ensuring that there was a backup system in case of equipment failure.

The results were remarkable. Within weeks, the community began to see improvements in their health, with fewer people suffering from waterborne illnesses. Children no longer had to walk long distances to collect water, and families had access to clean water for cooking, cleaning, and drinking.

The success of this project served as a model for other communities. Over the next few months, Aldo and his team began deploying similar systems in other water-scarce regions, including parts of the Middle East and South Asia. In each case, the results were overwhelmingly positive. The communities were able to regain control over their water supply, and local economies began to stabilize as people had access to water for agriculture, industry, and daily life.

4. Water Conservation and Management

While the technology was making a significant impact, Aldo knew that it was only part of the solution. For water scarcity to truly be alleviated, people had to change the way they used and managed water. Education and policy reforms were crucial to ensuring that the world's water resources were used wisely and sustainably.

Aldo's team worked with local governments and NGOs to promote water conservation efforts, including the implementation of rainwater harvesting systems, more efficient irrigation practices, and public awareness campaigns about the importance of reducing water waste. They helped train farmers to use water more efficiently and supported local governments in implementing policies to protect water sources from pollution and overuse.

One of the most impactful programs was the promotion of smart irrigation systems. These systems used sensors and data analytics to monitor soil moisture levels and adjust irrigation schedules accordingly, minimizing water waste and ensuring that crops received the precise amount of water they needed to grow. In areas where agriculture was heavily dependent on irrigation, these systems proved to be a game-changer, dramatically reducing water consumption and improving crop yields.

5. Overcoming Political and Economic Hurdles

Despite the success of the technology and the widespread benefits it offered, there were still significant political and economic challenges that Aldo and his team had to overcome. Many governments, particularly in developing countries, lacked the infrastructure or financial resources to implement the technologies at scale. Additionally, some countries were reluctant to embrace the new technologies because they perceived them as a threat to their existing water policies or economic models.

To address these concerns, Aldo worked closely with international development organizations, donors, and financial institutions to create a funding model that would make the technology accessible to all. They established a global water fund to support large-scale deployments of water technologies in the most vulnerable regions. This fund was designed to provide grants, loans, and technical assistance to countries and communities that needed it most, ensuring that no one was left behind.

Through these efforts, Aldo was able to secure the support of international governments and corporations that had the resources to make a real difference. He also worked to ensure that the technology was affordable and scalable, making it accessible even in the most economically challenged regions.

6. A New Era of Water Security

As the years passed, Aldo's vision for a world free from water scarcity began to take shape. The combination of innovative technologies, community engagement, and effective water management policies had begun to reverse the tide of the global water crisis. More and more communities were gaining access to clean, sustainable water sources, and the world was starting to realize that water scarcity was not an inevitable fate but a challenge that could be overcome with determination and collaboration.

In cities once plagued by water shortages, people began to see a brighter future. Families no longer had to worry about the next drought or the next waterborne disease outbreak. Industries that once relied on the destruction of water sources could now operate in harmony with the environment. And, most importantly, the world had come together to solve one of humanity's most pressing crises.

Aldo stood at the forefront of this change, knowing that the battle was not over but that they had achieved something extraordinary. Water scarcity was no longer an insurmountable problem, it was a challenge that had been met with ingenuity, compassion, and a commitment to a sustainable future.

Chapter 79: Coral Reef Restoration

The ocean was alive, full of color, movement, and sound. But beneath the surface, in the hidden depths of the world's oceans, the reefs were dying. Once teeming with life, coral reefs around the globe had become victims of the very crisis that Aldo and his team were working to solve: the world's growing pollution problem. The delicate ecosystems that had supported marine life for millennia were now struggling to survive, choked by plastic waste, chemical runoff, and the devastating effects of climate change.

Coral reefs are often called the "rainforests of the sea," as they provide a habitat for around 25% of all marine species. They also protect coastlines from erosion, support fishing industries, and are a vital part of the ocean's carbon cycle. But as pollution and climate change intensified, coral reefs were dying at an alarming rate. In some parts of the world, entire reef systems had been reduced to bleached, barren landscapes devoid of life. The loss of coral reefs meant the loss of biodiversity and the collapse of ecosystems that humans depended on for food, livelihoods, and coastal protection.

Aldo had always been an advocate for the preservation of nature, and he knew that saving the planet meant saving its oceans. But the task before him and his team seemed insurmountable—could they really restore entire ecosystems that had been ravaged by decades of pollution and climate change? Yet, Aldo was determined. If humanity could clean up its mess, then perhaps there was hope to reverse some of the damage and give the oceans a chance to heal.

1. Understanding the Problem

Before Aldo and his team could act, they needed to understand the scale of the problem. Coral reefs were dying from a combination of factors: rising sea temperatures, ocean acidification, pollution, overfishing, and coastal development. Of these, pollution, particularly plastic waste and agricultural runoff, had become one of the most pressing threats to the health of coral reefs.

Plastic waste, in particular, had become ubiquitous in the world's oceans. Floating islands of plastic garbage, including bottles, bags, and microplastics, were choking the marine environment. The corals, already stressed from the rising temperatures and acidity, were unable to thrive in these polluted waters. And as the coral reefs died, so did the intricate web of marine life that depended on them.

Aldo's team began by working with marine scientists, ecologists, and oceanographers to map out the most affected coral reef regions. They studied the dynamics of coral bleaching, a phenomenon in which corals expel the algae that live within them, turning them white and leaving them vulnerable to disease. Coral bleaching was exacerbated by the rising ocean temperatures linked to global warming.

The next step was to develop an understanding of how pollution affected the health of these ecosystems. They worked with environmental groups, local governments, and community organizations to assess the damage caused by plastic waste, chemicals, and untreated sewage that were being discharged into the oceans.

It was clear that the problem required a multi-pronged solution. Aldo knew that they needed to focus not only on the restoration of coral reefs but also on reducing the pollution that was killing them. They had to clean up the oceans, reduce carbon emissions, and protect marine biodiversity, no small task, but one that was essential to the future of the planet.

2. Partnering with Marine Scientists

Aldo knew that his team couldn't solve this problem alone. To tackle such a complex and delicate issue, they needed the expertise of marine scientists who specialized in coral reef restoration. He reached out to some of the world's leading marine biologists and coral reef experts, assembling a coalition of top minds in the field.

Together, they began brainstorming solutions to restore coral reefs on a global scale. The scientists pointed to innovative techniques that had already shown promise in isolated areas, but Aldo was determined to take these approaches and scale them up to address the crisis at a global level.

One of the most promising solutions was coral restoration farming. By cultivating coral species in controlled environments, such as coral nurseries, scientists could grow healthy coral fragments that could later be transplanted into damaged reef systems. The idea was to grow corals in these nurseries, where they could be protected from the stresses of the open ocean, and then replant them on degraded reefs to encourage natural regrowth.

Another innovative method being explored was assisted evolution. By selectively breeding coral species that were more resistant to heat and acidification, scientists could create coral strains that were more resilient in the face of climate change. These "super corals" could be used to repopulate damaged reefs, giving them a better chance of surviving in the warming oceans.

Finally, Aldo and his team worked on an experimental project that involved microbe-assisted restoration. By introducing beneficial microbes into the coral environment, they hoped to enhance the natural healing processes of the reefs. These microbes could help corals better tolerate environmental stresses, such as higher temperatures and increased acidity.

3. Reducing Pollution: Cleaning the Oceans

While coral restoration was important, Aldo knew that they couldn't just restore the reefs and leave the pollution problem unsolved. In fact, the continued pollution of the oceans was one of the biggest threats to the success of their restoration efforts. To address this, Aldo and his team launched a global ocean cleanup initiative.

The first step in the cleanup was to address the problem of plastic waste. Using the latest waste collection technologies, the team began developing large-scale systems to collect floating plastic debris from the oceans. These systems were designed to be efficient, low-energy, and capable of removing massive amounts of plastic waste from the sea.

Aldo's team also worked on creating more sustainable alternatives to plastic. By collaborating with innovators in the field of biodegradable materials and circular economy solutions, they began promoting the use of materials that could safely break down in the ocean. This initiative also included public education campaigns to reduce single-use plastics and promote recycling.

To complement these efforts, Aldo focused on improving wastewater treatment and agricultural runoff management. In many regions, untreated sewage and agricultural chemicals were being discharged into the ocean, creating toxic environments for marine life. Working with local governments and international organizations, Aldo's team developed technologies to improve wastewater filtration systems and reduce nutrient pollution from agricultural runoff. These measures would help to keep the oceans cleaner and reduce the stress on coral reefs.

4. Large-Scale Coral Restoration Projects

With the science and technology in place, Aldo's team began launching large-scale coral restoration projects in regions where coral reefs were most threatened. The first project took place in the Great Barrier Reef, the world's largest coral reef system, located off the coast of Australia. The reef had experienced severe bleaching and coral loss in recent years, and Aldo's team was determined to help restore it to its former glory.

The project involved setting up several coral nurseries in areas that were less affected by pollution and climate change. These nurseries acted as safe havens for young corals, allowing them to grow in a protected environment before being transplanted onto the reef. In addition, the team employed assisted evolution techniques to grow heat-resistant coral species that would be better able to cope with the rising sea temperatures.

In the Maldives, another major project was launched to restore the island nation's coral reefs, which were threatened by both rising ocean temperatures and pollution. This project focused on growing coral fragments in underwater nurseries and transplanting them onto degraded reefs. The team also worked to reduce pollution around the reefs by installing wastewater filtration systems and collaborating with local communities to reduce plastic waste.

As the success of these projects spread, Aldo and his team began replicating their efforts in other regions around the world. They worked with local governments, environmental organizations, and communities to implement coral restoration projects in the Caribbean, Southeast Asia, and the Pacific Islands. The goal was not just to restore coral reefs but to create a global movement for the protection and recovery of marine ecosystems.

5. The Global Impact of Coral Restoration

The impact of Aldo's coral restoration efforts was profound. As coral reefs began to heal and thrive again, marine biodiversity started to recover. Fish populations rebounded, and the health of the entire ecosystem improved. Coastal communities that relied on the reefs for food, income, and protection from storms saw a significant improvement in their livelihoods. The restored reefs began acting as natural barriers, protecting coastlines from erosion and reducing the damage caused by storms and rising sea levels.

At the same time, the global efforts to clean the oceans were paying off. Large-scale ocean cleanup projects successfully removed billions of tons of plastic waste from the sea, and the push for biodegradable alternatives to plastics began to reduce the amount of plastic entering the oceans in the first place. The combination of these efforts led to cleaner, healthier oceans, providing the foundation for coral reefs to recover.

In the end, Aldo's vision for restoring coral reefs was not only about bringing these ecosystems back to life but about creating a model for global environmental cooperation. The success of these projects showed that, with the right technology, policy, and global collaboration, it was possible to restore and protect the planet's most vital ecosystems.

Aldo looked out over the crystal-clear waters of a newly restored coral reef, watching the vibrant fish swim amongst the colorful corals. He knew that this was just one part of the larger battle for the planet's future, but it was a significant victory. It was proof that change was possible. If the world could restore its oceans, perhaps there was hope for the planet after all.

Chapter 80: The Zero-Waste Movement

The global shift toward sustainability had ignited a massive wave of change. What had once been an ambitious idea, barely considered by the mainstream, was now becoming a global movement. The concept of "zero-waste" was taking hold, spreading across continents, industries, and communities with an energy that could no longer be ignored. As the world grappled with the staggering environmental costs of waste, Aldo and his team saw this as an opportunity, an opportunity not just to push for change but to help the world build a future where waste was not a burden but a resource.

Zero-waste was more than just a movement; it was a philosophy, a way of life that rejected the linear economy that had dominated global trade and production for decades. Instead of following a "take, make, dispose" model, zero-waste focused on rethinking how products were made, used, and disposed of. The goal was to move towards a circular economy, where resources were reused, recycled, and repurposed, and waste was minimized or eliminated entirely.

But implementing zero-waste on a global scale would not be easy. It required the cooperation of businesses, governments, and individuals. It would take innovation, dedication, and a profound shift in the way societies thought about consumption. For Aldo, it was the next logical step in his mission to heal the planet.

1. The Rise of Zero-Waste Lifestyle

As Aldo watched the momentum of the zero-waste movement grow, he realized that the greatest potential for lasting change lay in the hands of the people. Individuals, empowered by the idea that they could make a difference in their own lives, were beginning to make conscious choices about their consumption habits. Reusable shopping bags, metal straws, bulk buying, composting, and reducing single-use plastics were becoming part of daily life. The impact was not just felt on a personal level but also within communities, where people were forming local zero-waste groups to exchange ideas and support one another.

The movement had gained an influential following, especially in urban centers across the world. Major cities in Europe, North America, and Asia were embracing the idea of zero-waste living. From small eco-conscious startups to large multinational corporations, the message was clear: people were ready for change. As they saw the environmental toll of plastic pollution and the unsustainable nature of consumerism, they began demanding more responsible practices from businesses and governments.

Aldo understood the power of grassroots movements, and he believed that if enough people took action, the corporate world would have no choice but to follow. He also knew that to truly change the world, he needed to help guide this movement, to provide the resources and the infrastructure necessary to bring zero-waste from a grassroots idea to a global reality.

2. Reaching Out to the Business Sector

Aldo and his team recognized that while individual action was crucial, large-scale change would only come with the full support of industries. It was the businesses, the manufacturers, retailers, and big corporations, that were responsible for much of the waste that was generated worldwide. From packaging to production processes, the waste created by businesses was staggering. Aldo had worked with businesses before, but this time the challenge was different. The zero-waste movement wasn't just about reducing waste in production; it was about transforming entire supply chains.

Aldo began meeting with key business leaders, explaining the philosophy of zero-waste and its potential for long-term sustainability. He spoke about the economic benefits of adopting circular economy principles, such as cost savings from reduced resource consumption, the potential for new business opportunities through recycling and upcycling, and the growing consumer demand for eco-friendly products. His message was clear: zero-waste wasn't just an ethical choice, it was a smart business decision.

While many businesses had already made moves toward more sustainable practices, few were fully committed to the zero-waste model. Aldo knew that the corporate world needed a nudge. He created a series of incentives, working with international regulatory bodies to set clear standards for waste reduction and offering support for businesses that took the leap toward circular economies.

Aldo's team helped companies develop waste-reducing technologies, such as advanced sorting systems that allowed companies to reuse raw materials, or compostable packaging alternatives to single-use plastics. They also encouraged businesses to embrace a "design for disassembly" mindset, where products were made with the intention that they could be easily taken apart and reused at the end of their lifecycle. This would help ensure that resources would not be lost in landfills but instead would be reincorporated into the supply chain.

3. Zero-Waste Policies and Government Action

Aldo was not only focused on engaging businesses but also worked tirelessly to encourage governments to adopt zero-waste policies. In his mind, for the zero-waste movement to truly flourish, governments would need to lead the way by setting legislative frameworks that encouraged responsible consumption and production practices.

He reached out to international organizations, lobbying for stronger regulations on waste management, extended producer responsibility, and improved recycling infrastructure. Aldo also worked with national governments to implement extended producer responsibility (EPR) laws that held manufacturers accountable for the lifecycle of their products, from design to disposal. EPR laws required companies to take responsibility for the end-of-life management of their products, encouraging them to create products that could be reused or recycled rather than discarded.

In many countries, Aldo and his team helped governments create incentives for businesses to invest in waste reduction and recycling technologies. They also worked to establish policies that would promote public-private partnerships, bringing together governments, businesses, and local communities to build comprehensive waste management systems.

4. Educating the Public

The success of the zero-waste movement depended on widespread public engagement. People needed to understand the environmental and economic importance of reducing waste, and they needed to be equipped with the knowledge and tools to make lasting changes in their everyday lives.

Aldo and his team launched a global public awareness campaign, focusing on the benefits of zero-waste living and providing practical steps for individuals to take. They created educational content that was accessible to people of all ages and backgrounds, explaining how simple actions like reducing plastic use, composting, and supporting sustainable brands could have a significant impact on the planet.

The campaign also emphasized the importance of community-level action. Aldo believed that when people worked together, they could amplify their efforts and create lasting change.

His team organized events, such as zero-waste fairs and community clean-up days, where people could come together to learn, share ideas, and get involved in local projects. These events were designed to foster a sense of belonging, empowering individuals to make a difference and build momentum for the movement.

Aldo also worked with schools and universities, helping educators incorporate sustainability into their curricula. By teaching the next generation about zero-waste principles, he believed they would grow up with a deeper understanding of the importance of waste reduction and resource conservation. This education would form the foundation of a more sustainable future.

5. Scaling the Zero-Waste Movement Globally

As the zero-waste movement gained momentum, Aldo knew that it was crucial to scale these efforts globally. Waste management systems varied widely around the world, with some countries having advanced recycling systems, while others struggled with basic waste disposal issues. Aldo's team worked with governments in developing countries to help them build infrastructure that would support the zero-waste transition, focusing on community-based solutions and leveraging local knowledge.

One of the most successful initiatives was the creation of "waste-to-resource" projects, where communities were encouraged to convert waste materials into valuable products, such as compost, biofuels, or building materials. This not only reduced waste but also created economic opportunities for local communities, especially in regions with high unemployment.

Through international partnerships, Aldo helped to create a network of zero-waste advocates and organizations that could share knowledge, resources, and best practices. These networks connected people from different parts of the world, helping them collaborate on innovative waste reduction projects and spread the message of zero-waste living far and wide.

6. The Results of a Global Movement

The impact of the zero-waste movement was felt on a global scale. Cities that embraced zero-waste principles began to see significant reductions in waste sent to landfills and incinerators. Businesses that adopted circular economy practices not only reduced their waste but also saved money and attracted environmentally conscious consumers. Communities that committed to reducing waste saw improvements in public health, cleaner streets, and a more engaged, eco-conscious population.

As the movement continued to grow, Aldo realized that the true power of zero-waste was not in the technologies or policies but in the people—the individuals who had embraced the idea that waste was not inevitable, but something that could be reduced, reused, and repurposed. The movement had empowered them to take action in their own lives, and together, they were changing the world.

Aldo stood at the forefront of this global shift, knowing that the path ahead was long, but the foundation for a more sustainable future had been laid. The zero-waste movement was no longer just a dream; it was a reality, and it was spreading.

Chapter 81: Infrastructure Renewal

The world had reached a pivotal moment, a point at which the old ways of doing things could no longer sustain the future. As Aldo looked around, it was clear that the true measure of progress would lie not just in technological advancements or policies but in the very infrastructure that supported society. The outdated, unsustainable systems that had once served human civilization were now exposed as a liability. The challenge was enormous, but so was the opportunity: to rebuild the global infrastructure with sustainability as the core principle.

For years, Aldo and his team had pushed for a world powered by clean energy, designed for zero waste, and capable of supporting future generations without compromising the planet's health. The road to this vision had been difficult, but with the groundwork laid through the success of their initiatives and growing support from both governments and the public, they were now poised for something larger: the full-scale renovation of global infrastructure. It wasn't just about creating new systems but transforming the ones already in place into something far more resilient, sustainable, and efficient.

1. Rebuilding Energy Systems

One of the most significant challenges in the infrastructure renewal process was the transformation of the global energy grid. Fossil fuels, coal, oil, and natural gas, had powered civilization for centuries. However, their environmental cost was undeniable. The world had become increasingly reliant on fossil fuels, and the systems designed to extract, refine, and distribute them were deeply entrenched in the global economy.

Aldo knew that the only way to address climate change and ensure long-term sustainability was to shift from fossil fuels to renewable energy sources. Solar, wind, hydro, and geothermal energy had already proven their potential. The technology existed; the challenge lay in creating infrastructure capable of supporting their widespread adoption.

With the global commitment to reducing carbon emissions, governments began to set ambitious goals for renewable energy integration. Aldo's team worked alongside energy experts and national leaders to modernize energy grids, incorporating smart technologies that could efficiently distribute renewable energy from diverse sources to urban and rural areas alike. They designed a new, decentralized energy system that would allow communities to generate and store their own clean energy through local solar farms, wind turbines, and microgrids.

In cities, traditional power plants began to give way to solar panels and wind turbines on rooftops, while large-scale solar farms and offshore wind farms were built in rural areas and coastal regions. These installations generated clean, renewable energy that was then transmitted through a highly efficient, interconnected grid. This system utilized advanced smart grid technology that could adjust energy distribution in real-time, optimizing usage and ensuring a constant, stable supply of power.

Renewable energy storage also became a major focus. The variability of renewable energy sources like wind and solar posed a challenge, as they were not always available when demand was highest. Aldo and his team championed the development of advanced battery technologies and energy storage systems to mitigate this problem. By using large-scale battery storage systems, renewable energy could be stored during times of abundance and distributed during periods of low production, creating a reliable and continuous energy supply.

In addition to large-scale solutions, Aldo's team focused on integrating microgrids into isolated and underserved regions. These microgrids allowed remote areas to become self-sufficient in terms of energy, generating their own electricity from local renewable sources. It was a transformative development for rural communities, as they no longer had to rely on costly and inefficient energy imports.

2. A New Approach to Waste Management

Alongside the energy revolution, Aldo's team worked on overhauling the global waste management systems. A major part of this overhaul was the integration of cutting-edge waste recycling technologies and waste-to-energy processes. With the world now embracing the zero-waste philosophy, it was no longer acceptable to continue dumping billions of tons of waste into landfills, nor was it feasible to burn waste without addressing the pollution it caused.

Aldo's vision was to create a circular waste economy, one in which every product, whether plastic, metal, glass, or organic material, could be fully reused or recycled. The key to achieving this was the development of automated waste sorting systems, which used artificial intelligence, robotics, and advanced sensors to separate recyclable materials with unparalleled precision.

These systems were deployed in cities and towns worldwide, allowing for the efficient collection and processing of waste. Plastics, metals, and paper were separated and sent to recycling plants, while organic waste was composted and returned to the soil. But the most innovative development was the waste-to-energy technology, which allowed non-recyclable materials to be converted into renewable energy.

Using cutting-edge pyrolysis and gasification methods, Aldo's team pioneered the creation of energy from otherwise non-recyclable waste materials. These systems broke down waste into its elemental components, converting it into biofuels, electricity, or even synthetic natural gas. The result was a highly efficient, environmentally friendly way of managing waste that also produced useful energy.

Cities began to see the benefits of these systems. Landfills, once a blight on the landscape, were reduced to a fraction of their former size. Municipal waste processing plants, once antiquated and inefficient, became advanced centers of sustainability, where materials were sorted, recycled, and transformed into valuable resources. With the integration of smart waste management systems, Aldo's vision of a circular economy was gradually becoming a reality.

3. Green Transportation Networks

Another critical piece of infrastructure renewal was the transformation of transportation systems. The global reliance on gasoline and diesel-powered vehicles had created a transportation sector that was one of the largest sources of carbon emissions. If cities and countries were to meet their carbon neutrality targets, transportation would need to change dramatically.

Aldo's team pushed for the electrification of transportation, advocating for a global shift toward electric vehicles (EVs) and public transportation systems. Governments responded by offering incentives for EV adoption, including tax breaks, rebates, and subsidies. Cities began investing in the infrastructure necessary to support electric vehicles, including charging stations, battery swapping networks, and EV-friendly road systems.

Public transportation also underwent a significant transformation. Cities that had relied on buses and trains powered by fossil fuels shifted to electric buses, trams, and light rail systems. These public transit networks were not only more environmentally friendly but also more cost-efficient, reducing long-term operating expenses for municipalities. Moreover, they helped reduce congestion and improve air quality, which was especially important in densely populated urban centers.

Aldo also recognized the importance of sustainable freight transport, particularly in the context of global supply chains. He worked with logistics companies to transition to electric trucks and autonomous cargo systems that could move goods with minimal environmental impact. These innovations revolutionized the way goods were transported, reducing the reliance on diesel and contributing to the overall reduction in global carbon emissions.

4. Smart Water Management Systems

Water scarcity had long been a major issue in many parts of the world, exacerbated by climate change and unsustainable consumption patterns. Aldo's team worked alongside environmental engineers to create advanced water management systems designed to preserve and optimize the world's water resources.

Through the use of smart water technology, Aldo's team helped communities monitor water use in real time, ensuring that every drop was accounted for. They introduced water-saving devices in homes, businesses, and factories, which significantly reduced water consumption without sacrificing quality or comfort. These systems included low-flow faucets, advanced irrigation techniques, and leak detection sensors.

In addition to water conservation efforts, Aldo's team worked to address water pollution by developing advanced filtration and desalination technologies. These systems allowed communities to safely treat and reuse wastewater, ensuring that every drop of water was used as efficiently as possible.

The most ambitious project was the construction of large-scale desalination plants in coastal regions, which converted seawater into fresh water. These plants utilized renewable energy sources, such as solar and wind power, to minimize their environmental impact while providing clean water to areas suffering from droughts or unreliable freshwater supplies.

5. Building Resilient Infrastructure

Perhaps the most significant aspect of infrastructure renewal was the creation of systems that were resilient to the challenges posed by climate change. Rising sea levels, extreme weather events, and shifting environmental conditions were becoming an ever-greater threat to cities and infrastructure around the world.

Aldo's team partnered with architects and engineers to design buildings and cities that could withstand these challenges. Green roofs, which not only provided insulation but also supported biodiversity, became a common feature in urban areas. Flood barriers and permeable pavements were installed in flood-prone regions to help manage stormwater runoff and prevent flooding. Coastal cities built sea walls and raised buildings to protect against rising ocean levels.

The new infrastructure was also designed to be energy-efficient, with buildings constructed using sustainable materials such as bamboo, reclaimed wood, and recycled steel. Solar panels and wind turbines were integrated into building designs, ensuring that every structure contributed to a sustainable energy future.

6. The Impact of Infrastructure Renewal

The results of these global infrastructure renovations were nothing short of transformative. Cities were cleaner, healthier, and more resilient to the impacts of climate change. Energy systems were cleaner, more efficient, and more equitable. Waste was no longer a burden on the environment but a resource that fueled the economy. Water resources were preserved, and transportation networks were sustainable and accessible.

Aldo had envisioned a future where technology and nature worked in harmony, where human progress didn't come at the expense of the planet. Through the renewal of global infrastructure, that vision was beginning to take shape. The world had started to rebuild itself, and though the path ahead remained long, the foundation for a sustainable future had been firmly established.

Chapter 82: Forest Restoration

The world had come to realize that nature was not just a backdrop to human existence but an essential partner in the survival of all life. Forests, which once covered vast swaths of the earth, were now dwindling, victims of deforestation driven by urbanization, agriculture, and industrial expansion. They had been the lungs of the planet, absorbing carbon dioxide and releasing oxygen, maintaining the delicate balance that life needed to thrive. But as the world had begun to recognize the interconnectedness of life on Earth, it also understood that if it hoped to mitigate the impacts of climate change, it would have to restore the forests that had been lost.

Aldo and his team had already accomplished great strides in global sustainability efforts. They had revolutionized energy production, waste management, and urban infrastructure. But they knew that none of these achievements would be truly transformative if the natural ecosystems that sustained life were not restored. The loss of forests, especially tropical rainforests, had caused irreparable damage to biodiversity, climate regulation, and the livelihoods of millions of people. The time had come for a global reforestation initiative, a massive, coordinated effort to heal the planet's forests and, in doing so, secure the future of all life on Earth.

Aldo, with his ability to rally both individuals and nations to a common cause, took it upon himself to lead this initiative. His vision was simple: bring back the trees that had been lost, protect the ones still standing, and restore the balance between nature and humanity. With the growing support for environmental sustainability, Aldo was optimistic that the world was ready for this next, crucial step.

1. The Scope of the Problem

The numbers were staggering. Over the last century, the world had lost nearly 50% of its forests, with tropical rainforests, the most biodiverse ecosystems on the planet, being particularly affected. According to the UN Food and Agriculture Organization (FAO), around 10 million hectares of forest were being lost every year due to logging, agriculture, and urbanization. This deforestation not only contributed to the loss of biodiversity but also exacerbated climate change, as trees played a critical role in absorbing carbon dioxide and regulating the planet's temperature.

The situation was dire. Aldo and his team understood that simply halting deforestation would not be enough. They needed to embark on a grand-scale restoration project that would not only stop the loss of forests but actively work to restore those that had already been decimated. This would require collaboration across borders, coordination among governments, non-governmental organizations (NGOs), businesses, and local communities. It would demand significant investments in both technology and manpower.

But Aldo believed that reforesting the planet was not just an environmental issue, it was a moral imperative. Forests were home to millions of species, many of which had never been studied and some of which might already be on the brink of extinction. They also provided crucial services to humanity, from regulating the water cycle to providing food, medicine, and livelihoods for billions of people.

2. The Global Reforestation Initiative

Aldo's first step in the reforestation effort was to launch the Global Reforestation Initiative (GRI), an ambitious program that aimed to restore the planet's forests within the next few decades. The GRI was built around three core principles: scale, speed, and sustainability.

Scale: The goal of the GRI was to restore a staggering 1 billion hectares of forest worldwide. This included replanting trees in areas that had been deforested, as well as creating new green corridors in urban areas, deserts, and degraded lands. The scale of the initiative was necessary to offset the damage already done and to ensure that future generations could inherit a planet capable of supporting life.

Speed: Reforestation could not be a slow, piecemeal effort. The urgency of the climate crisis meant that Aldo needed to fast-track the restoration process. In the early stages, the focus was on planting trees at an unprecedented rate, using new technologies to optimize planting methods, and accelerating reforestation efforts in regions most vulnerable to environmental degradation, such as tropical rainforests.

Sustainability: While the goal was to plant billions of trees, Aldo knew that planting alone would not solve the problem. Sustainability had to be at the heart of the GRI. Reforestation efforts needed to involve local communities, creating jobs, improving livelihoods, and ensuring that these restored forests would remain protected long after the initial planting efforts were completed. This meant addressing the root causes of deforestation, such as illegal logging, agricultural expansion, and lack of land tenure for indigenous people.

Aldo and his team also partnered with environmental organizations, local governments, and international bodies like the United Nations to create a coordinated global approach to reforestation. They reached out to nations with the greatest deforestation challenges, such as Brazil, Indonesia, and parts of Africa, and worked to align their efforts with local development goals, ensuring that reforestation would be integrated into each country's broader economic and environmental strategy.

3. Innovations in Reforestation Technology

While the idea of planting trees was not new, Aldo and his team recognized that to meet their ambitious goals, they needed to embrace technology. Traditional reforestation efforts had often been slow, labor-intensive, and limited by the availability of resources. The key to scaling up the reforestation effort was to utilize innovative technologies that could speed up the process and make it more efficient.

One of the breakthrough technologies Aldo championed was drone-assisted reforestation. These drones could fly over large areas, mapping out the land and analyzing soil quality, moisture levels, and other factors that would affect tree growth. They were then equipped with seed pods containing a variety of native tree species and released over vast areas in need of restoration. The drones could cover thousands of hectares in a fraction of the time it would take human workers to plant trees manually.

The seed pods themselves were designed to protect the young trees from environmental challenges, such as drought or poor soil quality. They were coated with a mixture of nutrients and hydrogels that helped them germinate and thrive in even the most challenging environments. This technology allowed Aldo's team to plant trees in areas that were previously considered too difficult or remote to reach by traditional means.

In addition to drones, Aldo's team worked with biotechnology companies to develop genetically modified tree species that could better withstand the impacts of climate change. These trees were designed to be more resilient to drought, pests, and disease, and were able to grow faster than their natural counterparts, allowing for quicker restoration of degraded ecosystems.

4. Involving Local Communities

Aldo knew that the success of the reforestation initiative would depend on the involvement of local communities. In many parts of the world, particularly in developing countries, deforestation had been driven by poverty and the need for agricultural land. The solution to this problem was not just to plant trees, but to ensure that the local populations had a stake in the project's success.

In collaboration with local governments, Aldo's team worked to create programs that would provide employment opportunities for local communities. They trained people in tree planting, forest management, and eco-tourism, creating jobs that would help sustain the reforestation efforts. These programs also included education on the importance of preserving forests and the long-term benefits of healthy ecosystems.

Aldo's team focused on restoring indigenous lands, many of which had been cleared for agriculture or development. By working with indigenous communities to restore their ancestral forests, they not only contributed to the preservation of cultural heritage but also created a sense of ownership and stewardship that would help ensure the success of the reforestation efforts.

In some regions, reforestation efforts were tied to the creation of carbon credits, providing a financial incentive for local communities to engage in sustainable land management practices. By preserving and restoring forests, communities could sell these credits on the global carbon market, generating revenue that could be reinvested into local development.

5. Benefits of Forest Restoration

The benefits of forest restoration were manifold and far-reaching. Restoring forests helped to mitigate climate change by absorbing vast amounts of carbon dioxide from the atmosphere. Healthy forests also played a crucial role in regulating the water cycle, preventing floods, and maintaining soil fertility. By replenishing degraded ecosystems, Aldo's team helped to restore biodiversity, providing habitats for countless species of plants and animals, many of which had been pushed to the brink of extinction.

Perhaps one of the most tangible benefits of reforestation was the improvement in air quality. Forests act as natural air purifiers, filtering pollutants from the atmosphere and providing fresh, clean oxygen. In urban areas, where air pollution was a growing concern, Aldo's team worked to integrate green spaces, such as parks and urban forests, into city planning. These green spaces not only improved air quality but also provided recreational areas for communities to reconnect with nature.

For communities living in or near forests, the benefits were also economic. Reforestation brought new opportunities for sustainable livelihoods, from eco-tourism to forest-based products like medicinal plants and sustainable timber. By restoring forests, Aldo's team helped to create a sustainable economy that was both environmentally and socially responsible.

6. A New Vision for the Future

As the reforestation efforts gained momentum, Aldo saw a new world emerging, one in which human civilization lived in harmony with the natural world. Forests were no longer just resources to be exploited but vital partners in the survival of the planet. The forests that had once been lost were being returned to their former glory, and with them, the hope of a brighter, more sustainable future.

The success of the reforestation initiative was a testament to the power of collective action. It showed that when people from all walks of life, from local communities to world leaders, came together for a common cause, they could achieve extraordinary things. Aldo's dream of a world where forests flourished, biodiversity thrived, and humanity lived in harmony with nature was beginning to take shape. The collective effort to restore the planet's forests had sparked a broader environmental renaissance, a movement that not only focused on reforestation but also included other vital efforts such as soil regeneration, the protection of wetlands, and the restoration of oceans.

In the years to come, the world would begin to see the real, lasting effects of Aldo's vision. As the trees took root and the forests grew back, ecosystems began to heal, and the earth started to recover from centuries of environmental neglect. The air became cleaner, the soil more fertile, and the wildlife returned to their rightful habitats.

7. The Ripple Effect

The success of the forest restoration initiative reverberated far beyond just the environmental sector. As countries came together to meet the reforestation targets, they realized that the true cost of environmental degradation was not just financial but also social and cultural. Communities began to recognize the long-term value of a healthy, thriving environment in terms of not only the economy but also quality of life.

Many regions that had previously been in economic decline began to experience revitalization. Indigenous groups whose land had been cleared for agriculture or development found new opportunities through forest-based livelihoods, from sustainable timber harvesting to eco-tourism ventures. In fact, a new generation of entrepreneurs emerged, focusing on environmentally sustainable practices that created both jobs and a cleaner environment.

Cities also began to evolve, taking inspiration from the restoration efforts in rural areas. Urban planners started to design cities with the goal of incorporating green spaces, reforestation, and renewable energy systems into the very fabric of urban life. Green roofs, vertical forests, and urban wetlands became commonplace, and cities began to reclaim areas once filled with pollution and industrial waste.

Even the corporate sector, once a staunch opponent of environmental regulations, began to change. Many companies had been forced to recognize that their long-term viability depended on a healthy environment. The same companies that had once promoted unsustainable practices began to invest in green technologies and sustainable supply chains. Businesses around the world began to develop new, eco-friendly products, using renewable materials and reducing waste.

8. A Global Legacy

Aldo's reforestation initiative became a symbol of the global transformation that was taking place. The forests that had been brought back to life were not just trees, they were a testament to what humanity could accomplish when it set aside its differences and worked toward a common goal. Aldo's success in leading the restoration of the world's forests was recognized globally, not only in environmental circles but also in political, economic, and social arenas.

As the forests flourished, Aldo and his team saw the beginning of what would become the planet's greatest ecological revival. It was a movement that transcended borders, ideologies, and industries. It was a reminder that the future of the planet depended on the choices that individuals, communities, businesses, and governments made today. It was a reminder that everything was interconnected, and only through collective action could humanity hope to restore the planet to its former glory.

In the years that followed, Aldo's efforts would inspire generations to come, serving as a model for future generations who would face even greater challenges in preserving the delicate balance of nature. And through it all, Aldo continued to stress one simple, powerful message: the restoration of the Earth was not just about saving the environment, it was about ensuring a better future for every living being on the planet.

As the planet healed, it began to thrive once again. The Earth was no longer on the brink of disaster, and the restoration of the forests marked the beginning of a new chapter in the story of humanity, a chapter of hope, healing, and harmony between people and the planet.

Chapter 83: Global Cultural Shift

The world had undergone an extraordinary transformation. The environmental crises that once seemed insurmountable had sparked a revolution, not just in technology, but in the hearts and minds of millions. As the planet slowly began to heal, so too did the culture of consumption and waste that had dominated the global landscape for centuries. A new era was dawning, one in which simplicity, sustainability, and respect for nature were no longer just ideals but fundamental aspects of everyday life.

1. A Changing Mindset

The cultural shift that had taken place was not an overnight occurrence. It was a gradual, collective awakening that had unfolded over years. People across the globe began to realize that the planet could no longer bear the burden of excessive consumption. The pursuit of more, more possessions, more wealth, more convenience, had reached a breaking point. It was a culture of excess, one that had strained the Earth's resources, polluted its waters, and poisoned its air.

The environmental disasters of the past decade, from massive wildfires to devastating hurricanes and melting glaciers, had provided a wake-up call. What followed was not just a change in policies or technologies, but a fundamental shift in how people viewed their relationship with the planet. This shift had not been led by governments, corporations, or scientists alone, but by ordinary people, activists, educators, and passionate citizens who had come together to demand change.

Sustainability had become the new currency. It was not about being the biggest or the richest, but about being the most responsible. It was a change that began with the individual and rippled out to communities, nations, and, eventually, the entire world. People began to embrace the idea that less was more, and that living in harmony with nature was not only necessary but deeply fulfilling.

2. The Rise of Minimalism

Minimalism, once seen as a fringe movement, had become mainstream. People were no longer striving for more possessions or trying to outdo one another with the latest gadgets and luxury items. Instead, they were choosing simplicity, quality over quantity, and functionality over excess. The concept of "enough" had taken root in the global psyche.

In homes, the era of clutter and unnecessary items had come to an end. Instead of purchasing new products every season, people focused on owning fewer, more meaningful things. Clothing was no longer seen as disposable. The fast fashion industry had fallen into decline, replaced by slow fashion, a movement that celebrated durability, sustainability, and timeless style. People were more likely to buy secondhand clothes, repair what they had, or swap items with others.

Technology, too, had shifted toward sustainability. Devices were designed to last longer and be repaired rather than replaced. The emphasis was on creating fewer but better products, eliminating planned obsolescence, and reducing electronic waste.

Minimalism also spread to the way people consumed resources. More individuals adopted a zero-waste lifestyle, carefully considering what they bought and how it would affect the environment. The idea of "buying less, but better" resonated with people in all walks of life, especially in cities where overconsumption had been most prevalent. Public awareness campaigns, combined with grassroots movements, had turned sustainable living into a global trend. People were no longer willing to ignore the waste they generated or the impact their consumption had on the planet.

3. Embracing Nature in Everyday Life

One of the most profound changes was the way people began to reconnect with nature. Urbanization, which had once driven people further away from the natural world, started to reverse. Cities, once dominated by concrete and steel, became hubs of green space. Parks and community gardens flourished, and urban farms became a common sight on rooftops and vacant lots. The beauty of nature was no longer something to be experienced on a vacation but was embedded into everyday life.

Sustainable agriculture practices gained prominence, and local food production became a central part of many communities. People were growing their own vegetables, fruits, and herbs in their backyards or on small plots of land in their cities. Farmers' markets thrived, bringing fresh, local produce directly to urban residents. The concept of "food miles" became an important factor in how people chose their food, with many prioritizing locally sourced ingredients that were grown with minimal environmental impact.

Additionally, nature-based solutions were implemented in urban planning. Cities adopted green roofs, permeable pavement, and natural water management systems to reduce their ecological footprint. The idea of living in harmony with the natural world had become integral to urban design.

4. A Return to Craftsmanship

As mass production had declined, craftsmanship had been reborn. People once again began to appreciate the value of handmade, locally sourced goods. Artisans and craftspeople were in high demand, as people sought quality and uniqueness over mass-produced items. Furniture, clothing, jewelry, and even food were made with care and skill, often in small, independent workshops.

This revival of craftsmanship also helped preserve cultural traditions and skills that had been passed down through generations. Ancient techniques of weaving, pottery, and woodworking were once again embraced, not just for their beauty but for their sustainability. The appreciation for handmade goods also led to a resurgence of interest in slow food and traditional culinary practices. People were rediscovering the joy of preparing meals from scratch, using seasonal ingredients, and sharing food with friends and family in a communal setting.

5. The Transformation of Consumption Patterns

The way people consumed goods had undergone a profound change. Instead of focusing on acquiring more things, people began to place value on experiences over possessions. Travel, leisure activities, and time spent with loved ones became more meaningful than accumulating material goods. Sharing, rather than owning, became the norm. Communities thrived on collaborative consumption, where people shared everything from tools and appliances to cars and clothing.

In the global economy, businesses that promoted a circular economy model flourished. These companies focused on reducing waste by designing products that could be repaired, reused, and recycled. "Renting" instead of owning became a popular trend, whether it was clothing, vehicles, or even electronics. People no longer saw ownership as a status symbol but instead valued the benefits of a sharing economy.

Additionally, eco-conscious companies were now the most successful, as consumers increasingly chose brands that aligned with their environmental values. Businesses were held accountable for their supply chains, waste management, and carbon footprints. Corporate social responsibility became a key factor in brand loyalty, and companies that did not adhere to sustainable practices were quickly phased out.

6. A New Era of Education and Awareness

Education played a crucial role in the cultural shift. Children were taught from an early age to respect the environment and practice sustainability. Schools had become centers of environmental learning, where students not only learned about the planet's challenges but also how to actively participate in creating solutions.

Environmental education extended beyond schools, with programs and workshops offered to adults as well. Media, once focused solely on entertainment and consumerism, now also played a vital role in spreading awareness about sustainability. Documentaries, social media campaigns, and books inspired people to take action in their own lives.

7. Global Solidarity and Collective Action

The cultural shift was not just a series of isolated changes but a global movement. People around the world came together, united by a shared desire to create a better future for the planet. Climate action, sustainability, and social responsibility were no longer fringe concerns but were at the forefront of global discourse.

At the same time, the recognition of environmental justice became more prominent. The most vulnerable communities, those that had suffered the most from environmental degradation, were now leading the charge for change. People recognized that the impacts of environmental harm were not distributed equally, and they worked together to ensure that the benefits of the green economy were shared fairly across the world.

8. The Path Forward

As the cultural shift continued to take root, the world began to move toward a more balanced and sustainable future. What had started as a small movement had now become a global force for change. The new culture, one that valued sustainability, simplicity, and respect for the planet, had become the guiding principle for future generations.

The transformation was not perfect, and challenges remained. But with each passing year, the cultural shift deepened, and the

MOUNT OF WASTE

world moved closer to the ideal of living in harmony with nature. And through it all, Aldo and his team watched with pride, knowing that the seeds of change they had planted had grown into something far greater than they could have ever imagined, a future where humanity no longer took the planet for granted but worked in partnership with it to create a world that would thrive for generations to come.

Chapter 84: Sustainable Economy

In the early decades of the 21st century, the world had been plunged into a relentless cycle of environmental degradation and economic inequality. Rising levels of carbon emissions, deforestation, pollution, and resource depletion had led to an alarming decline in the planet's health, threatening the livelihoods of millions and the very future of human civilization. But amidst this turmoil, a new paradigm was beginning to emerge, one that sought to balance economic growth with the health of the planet.

This new economic framework, known as the sustainable economy, was built on principles of ecological stewardship, social responsibility, and long-term viability. It was based on the understanding that economic prosperity could no longer be separated from environmental sustainability. As Aldo and his team had demonstrated through their groundbreaking work in waste management, clean energy, and resource efficiency, the future of the global economy depended on shifting from a model of extraction and consumption to one of regeneration and resilience.

The transition to a sustainable economy was no small feat. It required an overhaul of decades, if not centuries, of economic thinking and a fundamental rethinking of the values that had driven the global market. But as governments, businesses, and individuals began to embrace this new reality, the world was witnessing the birth of an economy that would prioritize the well-being of both people and the planet.

1. The Foundations of the Sustainable Economy

At the core of the sustainable economy was the recognition that the Earth's resources were finite, and that its ecosystems provided vital services that were essential for human survival. The exploitation of natural resources for profit, while temporarily benefiting a few, was ultimately harmful to the global population and future generations. It was clear that this extractive economic model needed to change if the planet was to survive and thrive.

The sustainable economy was rooted in a circular economic model, where resources were not simply extracted, used, and discarded, but were continuously reused, recycled, and regenerated. This shift from a linear to a circular system fundamentally changed the way people viewed products, services, and the resources they consumed. Companies and consumers alike were encouraged to rethink waste, viewing it not as an inevitable byproduct of consumption, but as a valuable resource to be reused or repurposed.

In addition to the principles of circularity, the sustainable economy was also founded on the idea of renewable energy. Fossil fuels, which had long been the cornerstone of the global economy, were now seen as a thing of the past. The fossil fuel industry, once a source of immense wealth and power, was slowly being phased out in favor of renewable energy sources, wind, solar, hydro, and geothermal. These sources were not only sustainable and abundant but also cleaner, reducing the harmful emissions that had caused global warming and environmental destruction.

2. The Role of Governments in Shaping the Sustainable Economy

Governments played a crucial role in guiding the transition to a sustainable economy. While the shift was driven by a growing public demand for environmental accountability, it was through policy and legislation that the changes truly gained traction. The importance of political leadership in this transition could not be overstated.

One of the most significant steps taken by governments around the world was the implementation of carbon pricing mechanisms. These included carbon taxes and cap-and-trade systems, which placed a price on carbon emissions, creating financial incentives for businesses to reduce their carbon footprint. Such policies were designed to internalize the environmental costs of carbon emissions, ensuring that polluting industries would bear the true cost of their actions.

In addition to carbon pricing, many countries also implemented regulations to curb pollution, limit the use of harmful chemicals, and protect biodiversity. National governments were also increasingly investing in green infrastructure, such as renewable energy projects, sustainable transportation systems, and energy-efficient buildings. In the global marketplace, governments that embraced sustainability were often rewarded with foreign investment, as companies and investors sought to align their operations with growing environmental standards.

International cooperation also played a key role in the transition. Countries that were once divided by political ideologies or economic interests were finding common ground in the pursuit of environmental sustainability. The signing of global agreements such as the Paris Agreement on climate change marked a historic moment in the collective effort to reduce global emissions and limit global warming.

3. The Rise of Green Businesses

While governments set the stage, it was the private sector that played a pivotal role in driving innovation within the sustainable economy. Across industries, businesses began to recognize that sustainability was not just a moral imperative but also a strategic advantage. The emerging demand for eco-friendly products and services created new opportunities for businesses to grow while doing good for the planet.

Green businesses were no longer just niche startups—they were becoming mainstream. From renewable energy companies to electric vehicle manufacturers, businesses that embraced sustainable practices were seeing significant growth. For example, companies in the renewable energy sector were benefiting from falling production costs for solar panels, wind turbines, and batteries, making green energy more accessible and affordable for consumers.

Other industries were adopting circular economy principles, designing products with longer lifespans and reducing the amount of waste generated. Large multinational corporations, once notorious for their environmental harm, were increasingly adopting sustainability-focused business models. Many companies were committing to carbon neutrality, setting ambitious goals to reduce their greenhouse gas emissions and invest in carbon offset projects. These initiatives were often driven by consumer demand, as more people were becoming conscious of the environmental impact of their purchasing decisions.

Furthermore, the rise of green businesses was supported by the financial sector. Investment funds that focused on sustainable companies, known as Environmental, Social, and Governance (ESG) funds, had become an essential part of the global investment landscape. Investors, both individual and institutional, were increasingly looking to fund companies that aligned with their values and contributed to the health of the planet.

4. The Transition to Sustainable Agriculture

Another critical aspect of the sustainable economy was agriculture. For centuries, industrial farming practices had contributed to soil degradation, deforestation, and the depletion of water resources. The transition to a sustainable economy required a reimagining of food production, one that would prioritize the health of the land, animals, and consumers.

Agroecology, a farming approach that emphasized biodiversity, soil health, and the reduction of synthetic chemicals, was gaining traction as a viable alternative to industrial agriculture. Small-scale farmers, once marginalized by the global agribusiness industry, were now at the forefront of this movement. By working with nature rather than against it, agroecology promoted farming practices that could regenerate soil, conserve water, and protect ecosystems.

In addition to agroecology, sustainable agriculture also embraced innovations in food production, such as vertical farming, aquaponics, and lab-grown meat. These technologies promised to reduce the environmental impact of food production while providing enough food to meet the demands of a growing global population.

As demand for sustainable food grew, consumers were increasingly choosing organic, locally sourced, and plant-based options. Meat consumption, once considered a symbol of affluence, was on the decline as more people embraced plant-based diets. Governments supported this shift by offering subsidies and incentives to farmers who adopted sustainable farming practices, while also implementing policies to reduce food waste throughout the supply chain.

5. The Social Dimensions of the Sustainable Economy

The sustainable economy was not just about the environment, it was also about people. At its core, the transition to sustainability was a movement that sought to create a more equitable world. As the global economy evolved, it was crucial that the benefits of this transformation were shared by all, particularly marginalized communities that had long borne the brunt of environmental harm.

Social equity and inclusion became central themes in the sustainable economy. Green jobs, such as those in renewable energy, sustainable agriculture, and green construction, provided new opportunities for workers around the world. Efforts were made to ensure that these jobs were accessible to people from all backgrounds, and that they paid fair wages and offered safe working conditions.

Moreover, the shift to sustainability also meant tackling issues such as poverty, access to education, and gender inequality. Governments, businesses, and civil society organizations worked together to create policies and programs that addressed these interconnected challenges. In the global south, countries that had long struggled with poverty and underdevelopment were now benefiting from investments in clean energy, sustainable agriculture, and green technologies, helping them leapfrog over traditional industrial models and create more resilient economies.

6. Looking Ahead: A Bright Future

As the sustainable economy continued to grow, the world was beginning to see the fruits of its labor. Emissions were down, ecosystems were recovering, and poverty rates were beginning to decline. But this was just the beginning. The transition to a sustainable economy was an ongoing process, one that would continue to evolve and adapt to the challenges of the future.

The lessons learned from this transformation would shape future generations, ensuring that the mistakes of the past were not repeated. The shift to sustainability was no longer a choice, it was a necessity. But as governments, businesses, and individuals embraced this new economic model, they were proving that a better, more sustainable world was not only possible, it was already happening.

Chapter 85: The Rise of the Green Generation

The world was undergoing a profound transformation. The environmental crises that had once seemed insurmountable, the rising levels of carbon emissions, the depletion of natural resources, and the destruction of ecosystems, were now being met with a different kind of energy. A new wave of young people, inspired by the knowledge of what had been lost and empowered by the tools of innovation, were coming into leadership positions around the globe. This was the rise of the Green Generation.

The Green Generation wasn't just a demographic shift. It was a cultural movement, an era marked by a fundamental reorientation of values. It was an era where technology, education, and industry converged to create a world that no longer prioritized short-term profit over long-term planetary health. The Green Generation was not content with the status quo. They were determined to revolutionize how the world thought about growth, consumption, and progress.

1. The Mindset of the Green Generation

What set the Green Generation apart was not just their commitment to sustainability; it was their vision for the future. They had grown up in a world that was waking up to the urgent reality of environmental collapse. They had watched as their parents and grandparents struggled with the consequences of industrialization, and they had inherited the lessons of the past.

From a young age, the Green Generation had been taught to value nature, not as a resource to be extracted but as a partner in their collective survival. They were taught that everything was interconnected. They were encouraged to think critically, challenge outdated systems, and build a world that was rooted in justice, equality, and ecological balance.

This mindset was not limited to a small group of activists. It became widespread, cultivated by a combination of environmental education, social media, and the ever-growing awareness of climate change. Schools began to teach environmental responsibility as a core part of their curricula, with young people learning about climate science, sustainable practices, and the importance of biodiversity. As a result, the Green Generation was not only well-versed in the challenges facing the planet but also in the innovative solutions needed to address them.

2. Technology and Innovation at the Forefront

Technology had long been a double-edged sword. On one hand, technological advancement had contributed to the environmental crises, industrialization, pollution, and the overuse of resources. On the other hand, technology was now emerging as the key to solving many of the issues that had been created.

The Green Generation embraced technology as a tool for positive change. They did not shy away from technological innovation but rather sought to leverage it to create solutions that were both environmentally responsible and economically viable. The entrepreneurs, engineers, and scientists of this generation understood that to change the world, they had to harness the power of cutting-edge technology.

One of the most significant technological advances brought forward by the Green Generation was the development of energy storage systems. With the rise of renewable energy, such as solar and wind, the challenge of energy storage became more pronounced. But young innovators began to develop more efficient and affordable battery technologies that could store energy for later use, ensuring a stable and reliable supply of clean energy.

Another major breakthrough came in the field of sustainable agriculture. The Green Generation was at the forefront of developing vertical farming technologies, which allowed food to be grown in urban environments with minimal land use. By utilizing hydroponics, aeroponics, and other soil-free methods, these young innovators were able to produce food efficiently and sustainably while minimizing water and energy consumption. They were also leading the charge in creating lab-grown meat, a sustainable alternative to traditional livestock farming, which had long been a major contributor to environmental destruction.

But it wasn't just technological innovation that defined the Green Generation, it was their ability to think holistically. They were not focused on quick fixes but on systemic solutions. They knew that in order to create a truly sustainable world, they needed to rethink entire industries and societal structures.

3. The Role of Education in Shaping the Green Generation

Education played a critical role in the rise of the Green Generation. As the world faced increasingly severe environmental crises, the educational system began to change in response. Sustainability was no longer an optional subject, it became integrated into every aspect of education, from elementary schools to universities.

Young people were taught not only the science behind climate change and ecological destruction but also the importance of empathy, community building, and resilience. They learned how to be informed consumers, how to advocate for policy changes, and how to take individual responsibility for their impact on the planet. Most importantly, they were taught that their generation had the power to shape the future.

Universities and research institutions were at the forefront of this educational revolution. They became hubs for sustainable innovation, where young minds worked alongside experienced researchers and industry leaders to develop new technologies, policies, and business models that could address the challenges of climate change. The Green Generation wasn't just passive learners, they were active participants in the search for solutions.

This shift in education also gave rise to a new wave of environmental activism. The Green Generation didn't just accept the status quo, they were organizing, protesting, and demanding change from their governments and institutions. Whether it was through global movements like Fridays for Future, spearheaded by young climate activist Greta Thunberg, or local grassroots campaigns, young people across the world were making their voices heard and pushing for bold action on climate change.

4. Green Businesses and the Circular Economy

The Green Generation understood that the future of the economy had to be sustainable. In a world where traditional industries were rapidly depleting resources and polluting the environment, they turned to the concept of the circular economy, a model that focuses on reducing waste, reusing materials, and recycling as much as possible.

The rise of green businesses was one of the defining features of the Green Generation. They understood that profit could coexist with sustainability, and they began to build companies that prioritized environmental responsibility. From startups focused on renewable energy to fashion companies producing clothes made from recycled materials, young entrepreneurs were proving that a business model based on sustainability could be both profitable and planet-friendly.

The circular economy became the backbone of this new wave of business. Products were designed for longevity, and waste was minimized by creating systems of reuse and recycling. Companies started to adopt strategies that reduced their carbon footprint and helped mitigate the damage caused by centuries of unsustainable practices. They were not just responding to consumer demand, they were shaping it.

5. A Green Workforce and Jobs for the Future

One of the most significant impacts of the Green Generation was the creation of green jobs. As renewable energy projects, sustainable agriculture, and eco-friendly industries grew, the demand for workers with skills in these fields skyrocketed. The Green Generation was ready and eager to meet this demand, and the workforce became increasingly skilled in the areas of sustainable technology, environmental science, and green business practices.

The creation of green jobs didn't just benefit the environment, it also helped alleviate social inequality. Many young people, particularly in developing countries, found new opportunities in the emerging green economy. In rural areas, sustainable agriculture initiatives provided jobs and boosted local economies. In urban centers, green construction projects were revitalizing neighborhoods while reducing energy consumption.

This transformation wasn't just about saving the planet—it was about creating an economy that worked for everyone. The Green Generation was determined to make sure that the benefits of sustainability were shared across society. They knew that the future of work had to be green, and they were working hard to ensure that their generation had the tools and resources to lead this transition.

6. The Green Generation and Global Collaboration

One of the hallmarks of the Green Generation was their ability to collaborate across borders, cultures, and disciplines. The environmental crisis was a global problem, and it required a global solution. Young people from all corners of the earth were coming together, united by a common cause: to protect the planet.

Global collaborations were taking place at every level. Governments were working together to create international climate agreements. Non-governmental organizations, activists, and businesses were forming partnerships to share knowledge, resources, and technologies. And young people were leading the charge, using social media to organize and advocate for bold climate action.

This global spirit of cooperation was a testament to the power of youth. The Green Generation understood that the environmental challenges facing the world were not isolated, they were interconnected. Whether it was tackling deforestation in the Amazon, cleaning up oceans, or reducing emissions from industrialized nations, young people were working together across borders to create real change.

7. A Bright Future for the Green Generation

As the Green Generation took on leadership roles in the world, the future began to look brighter. They were creating a world where the health of the planet was prioritized, where technology was used for the good of society, and where every person had a stake in the future of the Earth. But the journey was far from over. The Green Generation knew that the challenges ahead were immense, and that they would require even greater innovation, collaboration, and determination. Yet, for the first time in history, there was hope that the world could truly change. And it was the Green Generation leading the way, with their passion, creativity, and unshakable belief in a better future.

Chapter 86: Healing the World

The world, once teetering on the brink of irreversible collapse, was slowly beginning to breathe again. The relentless cycle of pollution, waste, and exploitation that had choked the planet for centuries was beginning to reverse. It had taken years of tireless work, innovation, and collaboration, but the signs of healing were undeniable. Aldo sat at the window of his newly established lab, gazing out over the city that had transformed from a wasteland into a thriving hub of sustainability.

The Recovery of Ecosystems

One of the most tangible signs of the Earth's recovery was the revival of ecosystems once thought to be beyond saving. Forests that had been reduced to barren land by deforestation and industrialization were now alive with new growth. Aldo had spearheaded global reforestation efforts that not only replenished lost forests but introduced new, climate-resilient trees and plants that could thrive in the changing environment. The air was cleaner, the waters clearer, and wildlife was slowly returning to areas that had once been void of life. Aldo's heart swelled with pride as he thought back to the times when they'd first started these programs.

Through innovations in waste management, the vast piles of garbage that once littered cities and towns had been converted into compost or recycled materials, fueling the growth of plants and trees. The soil, which had been tainted with chemicals and plastic waste, was now rich again, allowing crops to grow and forests to thrive.

Marine ecosystems, which had once been suffocated by the immense volumes of plastic waste, were also showing signs of life. Aldo and his team had been part of groundbreaking underwater reclamation projects that utilized biodegradable materials to remove plastics from the oceans, while promoting coral restoration. Entire regions of coral reefs were coming back to life, vibrant and bustling with marine life. The oceans, once on the verge of collapse, were now being rejuvenated by collective human effort.

The progress they had made wasn't just about undoing the damage; it was about creating a new world, one in which nature and human society existed in harmony, where the environment was not something to be conquered, but something to be nurtured.

Climate Stabilization

The planet's climate was another aspect of healing that was finally taking shape. The relentless heatwaves and extreme weather events that had ravaged the world just a decade ago had become less frequent. While it was clear that climate change would not be reversed overnight, global efforts to reduce carbon emissions and shift toward renewable energy had made a significant impact. Solar farms stretched across the once-barren deserts, wind turbines dotted coastal cliffs, and geothermal energy stations provided power to entire regions. The global transition from fossil fuels to renewable energy was a success story that had been driven by leaders like Aldo, who had advocated for large-scale investments in green energy solutions.

Aldo and his colleagues had worked tirelessly with governments and private sector companies to eliminate dependence on fossil fuels. They had successfully deployed carbon capture technologies and were now beginning to repurpose the captured carbon to produce materials like building blocks and fuel. This innovation reduced the carbon footprint while generating valuable resources for the new economy.

The atmosphere was less polluted, and the effects were being felt by communities around the world. Cities, once shrouded in smog, were now breathing freely. Air quality had drastically improved in major metropolitan areas, giving rise to healthier, more vibrant communities. People no longer suffered from the chronic respiratory issues that had once been the norm.

A Shift in Society's Mindset

More than anything, the change was visible in the people. It had taken years of education, grassroots movements, and a cultural shift for the global community to embrace a sustainable way of living, but that change had finally arrived. The "throwaway" culture that had defined much of the 20th and early 21st centuries was a thing of the past. People no longer saw consumption as a status symbol but as a potential threat to their very existence.

Cities were designed around the idea of sustainability. Buildings were made from materials that had been sustainably sourced or even recycled. Food was grown locally, reducing the carbon footprint of transportation and eliminating the need for unsustainable industrial agriculture. The concept of "zero waste" had become a standard in both private and public life. Individuals no longer saw the planet as an unlimited resource but as a shared space that required collective responsibility.

Aldo had been instrumental in pushing for policy changes that incentivized businesses to adopt sustainable practices. Corporations were no longer motivated solely by profit but by the understanding that the survival of their industries depended on the health of the planet. There was a widespread push for sustainable production, with circular economies replacing the traditional linear models of consumption. This cultural shift was not just confined to the wealthier nations, either. Developing countries, empowered by green technologies, had been able to leapfrog traditional industrial models and build sustainable futures from the ground up.

The Struggles That Remained

However, Aldo knew that the work wasn't finished. There were still millions of people living in regions that had not yet felt the full benefits of this new world order. Climate change had left indelible marks on many nations, and some countries had struggled to implement green technologies as quickly as others. Poverty and inequality remained pressing issues, even in the wake of environmental recovery. Aldo knew that true sustainability had to encompass not just the planet, but the people living on it.

Although the Earth had made great strides in recovering from the brink of disaster, human suffering, exacerbated by past exploitation, still lingered. There were still parts of the world where clean drinking water was a luxury and where food scarcity remained an ever-present threat. For these areas, Aldo had partnered with international aid organizations to ensure that the technology and knowledge for sustainability were shared equitably. The mission was clear: no one would be left behind in the journey to heal the world.

A Sense of Accomplishment

As Aldo sat by the window, reflecting on the journey that had brought them here, he felt a deep sense of accomplishment. It had been a long, difficult road filled with setbacks, resistance, and moments of doubt. But every hardship had been worth it. The planet was healing, the people were starting to live in balance with nature, and the next generation was more committed than ever to carrying the torch forward.

"Are we done?" Nina asked as she entered the room, interrupting his thoughts.

Aldo turned and smiled, his heart full. "No, not yet. But we're getting there. The world is healing. And that's something we can all be proud of."

Nina nodded, joining him by the window. Together, they watched the horizon, where the sun was beginning to set over a city transformed. It was a symbol of the world they had worked so hard to create, a world that, though scarred by the past, was now well on its way to healing.

The future was no longer uncertain. It was bright. And it was theirs to shape.

Chapter 87: Keeping the Awareness Alive

The world had made unprecedented strides toward environmental recovery. Cities were cleaner, ecosystems were being restored, and the global commitment to sustainability was palpable. Yet, as Aldo stood on the balcony of his newly constructed, sustainable headquarters, watching the vibrant world below, he couldn't help but feel a deep sense of urgency. The battle for a sustainable future wasn't won through technology alone; it was won in the hearts and minds of every individual on Earth. And this, Aldo knew, was the true challenge. The momentum that had been built could easily fade if the collective awareness was not maintained.

For decades, Aldo had seen how easily people's attention shifted. When immediate crises faded and solutions became routine, there was always a risk of complacency. That's why he had made the decision to launch a global awareness campaign, a movement not just about facts and figures, but one that sparked a deep, emotional connection to the planet itself.

A World at a Crossroads

The Earth had been given a second chance. And yet, Aldo knew that sustainability was not something that could be taken for granted. There was a very real possibility that, as the scars of environmental destruction began to fade, the urgency behind the green revolution might start to dull. It was critical, Aldo believed, to embed sustainability into the very fabric of society, so that future generations would never forget the lessons of the past.

He had seen firsthand how easy it was to fall back into old habits. When technology solved one problem, the temptation to grow complacent was always present. The world could no longer rely solely on technological innovation to address environmental issues; it needed a society-wide commitment to continue evolving sustainably.

It was in this moment of realization that Aldo decided that his next mission would not be another technological breakthrough. Instead, it would be a campaign for the hearts and minds of the people.

The Foundation of the Campaign

The concept behind Aldo's campaign was simple yet profound: sustainability cannot be a trend, but a way of life. He knew that it wasn't enough for people to recycle or switch to solar panels, it needed to be something much deeper. He envisioned a world where every child grew up with an inherent understanding of their place in the ecosystem, where every adult felt personally responsible for the future of the planet, and where every company felt the moral and ethical obligation to leave the earth better than they found it.

Aldo had already taken significant steps toward this with education systems across the globe. Schools had adopted green curriculums, teaching children how to live sustainably, use resources wisely, and advocate for the environment. But what Aldo realized was that the roots of lasting change had to be stronger than just what was taught in classrooms, they had to be instilled into the collective consciousness of the entire population.

His plan was to initiate a campaign that would reach every corner of the world, from bustling cities to rural villages. It would transcend social classes, cultures, and languages, uniting humanity under the banner of environmental stewardship.

He titled the campaign "The Green Promise."

The Green Promise

The campaign, which Aldo envisioned as both a rallying cry and a call to action, would revolve around the idea of promise. The Green Promise would be a pact made by individuals, communities, governments, and corporations to ensure that the work of the last few decades was not undone. It would emphasize the importance of respecting the Earth, of making conscious decisions that would ensure the planet's future for generations to come.

It was not just about reducing waste or using renewable energy, it was about living in harmony with the planet. Aldo knew that human behavior could not be changed overnight, but by framing sustainability as a moral responsibility, as something deeply personal, the world could be moved to action. People had to be made to feel as if the very fate of their grandchildren and great-grandchildren rested in their hands.

The first part of the campaign was to tell a story. It would remind people of what had been lost in the past, forests that were cleared, rivers that were poisoned, ecosystems that had been destroyed. But more importantly, it would show them the future that was possible, a future where sustainability wasn't a choice but a lifestyle.

Using the Power of Media

Aldo had always been a proponent of leveraging media and technology to drive social change, and this campaign would be no different. He partnered with influential filmmakers, documentarians, and influencers to create powerful visual content that could spread across the globe. These short films would tell the stories of individuals, families, and communities who had embraced sustainability in every aspect of their lives, showcasing the tangible benefits of their actions.

The key to these media campaigns was storytelling. Aldo believed that it wasn't enough to present dry statistics or to show people the consequences of their actions. Instead, the campaign would highlight personal stories, stories of farmers who had adopted regenerative agricultural practices, of young people starting eco-conscious businesses, of communities that had rebuilt themselves after environmental devastation. These stories were compelling because they were real, they were hopeful, and they showed that anyone, anywhere, could make a difference.

Aldo also understood that social media would be a vital tool. By creating viral challenges and encouraging people to share their personal sustainability journeys, the campaign would turn individual actions into a global movement. People were already embracing sustainable practices, and Aldo knew that by amplifying those voices, he could create a snowball effect, one that would take on a life of its own.

Engaging Governments and Corporations

The next step in the campaign was to engage governments and corporations. Aldo had learned over the years that policy change and business practices were just as crucial to sustainability as individual actions. He knew that governments played a key role in shaping the future, and companies had the power to influence consumer behavior. It was time to bring them on board.

Aldo worked tirelessly to encourage world leaders to commit to further environmental protection policies. The Green Promise campaign would serve as a reminder to these leaders that the future was in their hands, that they were the stewards of a planet that had been pushed to its limits. He helped broker international agreements that further expanded renewable energy initiatives, strengthened environmental regulations, and ensured that the progress already made would continue.

Meanwhile, the corporate sector, which had been a crucial partner in many of Aldo's previous projects, would also play a central role. The Green Promise would be a way for companies to show their commitment to sustainable practices. Aldo's team worked with business leaders to create guidelines for reducing their environmental footprints, making sure that they adhered to the highest standards of sustainability. The goal was to create a world where sustainable business practices became the norm, not the exception.

Engaging the Youth

Aldo knew that to ensure the sustainability movement would continue for generations to come, he needed to engage the youth. Young people were already the driving force behind many environmental movements, and they had the potential to shape the future in ways that could not be ignored.

He made sure to connect with schools, universities, and young activists, ensuring that the next generation had the resources and support they needed to lead the world toward a better future. The Green Promise would be integrated into educational curricula worldwide, with students encouraged to take part in sustainability projects, form eco-clubs, and use their voices to advocate for a greener planet.

In addition, Aldo created a platform for young innovators to showcase their green technologies and business ideas. Whether it was through competitions, grant opportunities, or mentorship programs, he wanted to make sure that the leaders of tomorrow had the tools they needed to keep the sustainability movement alive.

A Global Movement

As the Green Promise campaign gained traction, Aldo began to see the ripple effects of his efforts. People from every continent, from every background, embraced the idea that their actions mattered, that their commitment to sustainability could shape the future. Small towns in Africa, rural villages in South America, and sprawling cities in Asia and Europe all saw the campaign as a chance to make a difference.

Aldo had successfully turned awareness into action. It wasn't just about putting out fires anymore; it was about building a future where the flames of environmental destruction could never burn again. The world had learned, had adapted, and had committed to making sure that the mistakes of the past were never repeated.

As Aldo reflected on this new phase of the journey, he knew that the future was still fragile. But for the first time, he felt that the world was truly on the right path, a path forged by the Green Promise.

Chapter 88: Global Victory

It had taken decades of tireless work, countless setbacks, and moments of doubt, but the day had finally arrived. Aldo stood at the center of a bustling global conference hall, his heart swelling with both pride and relief. The world had come together, transcending borders, politics, and ideologies, to achieve what many thought was impossible. An international alliance, forged by mutual commitment and collective responsibility, had reached a historic global agreement that would change the course of the planet's future.

The agreement, known as the Global Sustainability Pact, was not just a document or a political milestone. It was a promise, a promise to protect the Earth, to ensure that future generations would inherit a planet capable of sustaining life, and to set a precedent for unity in the face of adversity. After decades of relentless campaigning, lobbying, and pushing the boundaries of global cooperation, Aldo had witnessed the culmination of his life's work.

The Road to Consensus

The Global Sustainability Pact wasn't born overnight. It had been a long, arduous journey, filled with diplomatic negotiations, compromises, and at times, bitter disagreements. The world's leaders, representing a myriad of cultures and interests, had come together in what was, at its core, a fight for survival. Aldo knew that the stakes had never been higher. Climate change, resource depletion, pollution, and biodiversity loss were no longer theoretical threats, they were very real, and they had reached a tipping point. If something drastic wasn't done, the damage would be irreversible.

The first step in this journey was to recognize the common threat that faced the world. Aldo had worked tirelessly over the years to foster understanding among world leaders, emphasizing that the planet's environmental crises were not confined to any one nation or region. The air pollution in Beijing affected the skies over New York; the deforestation in the Amazon had ripple effects that reached as far as Southeast Asia. The global interconnectedness of environmental issues became undeniable.

Through a combination of scientific evidence, data-driven policy proposals, and the undeniable voice of public support, Aldo and his allies were able to make the case that sustainability was not a choice, it was a necessity. Governments, corporations, and civil societies had to come together to forge a collective path forward, one that would prioritize the planet's health over short-term economic interests.

The negotiations were tense, as the disparity between developed and developing nations was one of the major sticking points. Wealthier nations, with their historically high carbon footprints, were called upon to make deeper commitments to reduce emissions and fund sustainability projects in less developed regions. On the other hand, emerging economies, which were still working to lift their populations out of poverty, demanded greater financial support and access to green technologies to build their economies sustainably.

Aldo had spent countless hours mediating these discussions, finding common ground between these seemingly irreconcilable positions. His experience in bridging the gap between science, technology, and policy made him an invaluable figure in these talks. He pushed for a solution that was fair and equitable, one that recognized the historical responsibilities of developed nations while allowing developing countries to grow without repeating the mistakes of the past.

After years of hard work, dialogue, and compromises, a breakthrough came. The Global Sustainability Pact was born.

MOUNT OF WASTE

The Pact's Core Principles

At the heart of the Global Sustainability Pact were several core principles that would guide the future of the planet's stewardship. These principles not only aimed to tackle the immediate environmental challenges but also set a framework for long-term cooperation between nations, businesses, and communities.

1. Carbon Neutrality by 2050: The pact committed all signatory nations to achieving carbon neutrality by 2050, with intermediate targets along the way. This ambitious goal would require a radical transformation of energy systems, transportation, and industrial practices across the globe.

2. Global Green Fund: Recognizing the economic disparities between nations, the pact established a Global Green Fund to support developing countries in their efforts to transition to sustainable economies. This fund would be used for green infrastructure projects, renewable energy installations, and sustainable agriculture programs, among other initiatives.

3. Biodiversity Restoration: The agreement set specific targets for the restoration of critical ecosystems, such as forests, wetlands, and oceans. These ecosystems would not only help mitigate climate change but also provide vital services like clean water, food security, and natural disaster protection.

4. Circular Economy: The pact embraced the transition from a linear economy, one based on the take-make-dispose model, to a circular economy, where resources are reused, recycled, and regenerated. This shift would reduce waste, conserve resources, and minimize environmental degradation.

5. Global Education and Awareness Campaigns: The pact emphasized the need for a global education and awareness campaign that would teach people of all ages about sustainability, environmental responsibility, and the importance of living in harmony with nature. This campaign would target schools,

communities, businesses, and governments, ensuring that sustainability became a core value in every society.

6. Technological Innovation: The pact committed to accelerating research and development in green technologies, such as renewable energy, carbon capture, and waste management. Countries would collaborate on global initiatives to create and disseminate technologies that could solve the world's most pressing environmental problems.

7. Environmental Justice: Finally, the pact addressed environmental justice, ensuring that vulnerable populations, particularly those in low-income communities and developing nations, would not bear the brunt of environmental destruction. It was vital that the benefits of sustainability were shared equitably across all societies.

The Ripple Effect

The signing of the Global Sustainability Pact was nothing short of a momentous occasion. It was a historic victory not only for Aldo and his team but for the planet itself. As world leaders gathered in a grand ceremony to formally endorse the pact, the global media buzzed with excitement. Headlines proclaimed, "A New Era for Planet Earth" and "The World Comes Together to Save the Earth." But beyond the headlines, something deeper was unfolding.

Around the globe, citizens took to the streets, celebrating the momentous agreement. People of all ages, backgrounds, and nationalities joined in solidarity, knowing that this was the first real step toward ensuring a livable future for their children and grandchildren. Communities, businesses, and governments pledged their support, and the world began to feel the collective power of unity.

For Aldo, the victory was bittersweet. He had seen the destruction firsthand, the smog-choked skies, the barren lands, the disappearing forests. But he also saw the potential for a brighter future. This was not the end of the battle, but the beginning of a new chapter. There was still much work to be done.

The Beginning of a New Era

The impacts of the Global Sustainability Pact began to unfold rapidly. In the months following the signing, world governments moved quickly to implement the pact's provisions. National policies were overhauled to meet carbon neutrality targets, and industries began to transition to more sustainable practices. The demand for clean energy skyrocketed, with solar, wind, and hydroelectric power becoming the dominant sources of energy worldwide.

In developing countries, the Green Fund provided much-needed financial support to kickstart green infrastructure projects. Solar farms and wind turbines sprouted across Africa and Asia, while innovative farming practices began to reverse the environmental degradation caused by years of industrial farming.

Local communities, empowered by education and resources, adopted circular economy practices, transforming waste into valuable resources. Recycling rates soared, and new technologies allowed for the creation of closed-loop systems that reduced the need for raw materials.

Even the oceans began to heal. With greater international collaboration, large-scale projects were launched to clean up plastic pollution, restore coral reefs, and protect marine biodiversity. Aldo's heart swelled with pride as he saw the results of years of effort, species once thought to be on the brink of extinction began to thrive again, and ecosystems that had been degraded for decades started to regenerate.

But Aldo knew that the true measure of success lay in the long-term commitment to sustainability. The real work was in maintaining momentum, ensuring that the promises made in the

Global Sustainability Pact were fulfilled. And so, he continued his work, not as a singular leader, but as part of a global movement, a movement that had, at last, unified the world in the fight for a sustainable future.

The battle for the planet was far from over, but for the first time in human history, Aldo could say with certainty that the world was united in its mission to heal the Earth. The victory was not just in the signing of the pact, but in the unwavering commitment of millions of people around the globe who had made the Green Promise their own.

The Future of Humanity

As Aldo stood on the balcony once more, watching the world evolve beneath him, he knew the journey was just beginning. The challenges ahead were immense, but the world had taken its first steps toward a future that prioritized sustainability, equity, and responsibility. The earth, once thought to be on the brink of destruction, had been given a second chance, and with that, the promise of a future that was not only livable but flourishing.

In the years to come, Aldo would continue his work, but now he knew that he was no longer alone. The world had awakened, and together, humanity had turned the tide.

Chapter 89: The Final Step

The world had shifted. The old paradigms, those that prioritized short-term profit over long-term sustainability, had crumbled under the weight of a global crisis that had pushed humanity to the brink. But from the ashes of environmental collapse had risen a new era, one built on cooperation, innovation, and resilience. Aldo and his team stood at the threshold of the culmination of their work, a moment in history that would be remembered not only for the challenges overcome but for the profound transformation that had reshaped the world.

It had been years since the Global Sustainability Pact had been signed, and since then, the world had changed at a pace that was nothing short of extraordinary. What had once seemed an impossible dream—a world free from the scourge of waste, where every piece of material was valued, recycled, and reused—was now becoming a reality. The breakthrough technologies that Aldo and his team had developed had spread across every continent. Cities that were once choking on their waste now thrived, their air cleaner, their streets free of pollution, and their people healthier. And perhaps most significantly, the global approach to waste management had transformed from a problem to an opportunity. The world had learned how to turn trash into treasure, and in doing so, had healed not only its environment but also its broken systems.

The Path to Global Adoption

When Aldo first embarked on his mission, the road ahead seemed almost insurmountable. The concept of a circular economy, where nothing was wasted and everything had a second life, had been met with skepticism by both governments and corporations. Recycling had existed in some form, but it had always been viewed as a marginal activity, one that was convenient but not transformative. Aldo knew that in order to change the global narrative, he needed to prove that waste could be more than just a problem, it could be a resource.

At the beginning, convincing large corporations to rethink their linear production models had been a battle. Corporations had long operated on the take-make-dispose model, where raw materials were extracted from the Earth, transformed into products, and then discarded once they had served their purpose. This was the most efficient way to run an industrial economy, but it was also the most destructive. The consequences were clear: mountains of plastic, toxic chemicals leaching into water sources, the destruction of ecosystems, and the exacerbation of climate change.

But over time, Aldo's team developed revolutionary technologies, advanced waste sorting, chemical recycling, and bio-based materials, that made it possible to recycle far more than ever before. They proved that waste could be reintroduced into the production cycle, reducing the need for raw materials and cutting emissions in the process. What was once seen as trash could now be transformed into valuable inputs for industries ranging from construction to electronics. The world began to take notice.

Governments, too, had to change their approach. In the beginning, waste management had been fragmented and reactive. Cities, states, and countries each handled their waste independently, with little regard for global coordination. But Aldo's efforts had shifted the conversation. The Global Sustainability Pact had become the framework for international cooperation, with nations agreeing to work together to create efficient, closed-loop systems for waste management. Aldo's groundbreaking research had convinced leaders that the benefits of a circular economy far outweighed the costs of continued inaction. With his team, Aldo had brought together governments, businesses, and nonprofits to create a global movement, a movement that had reached its zenith.

The Global Implementation

The transformation had been a slow process, with hurdles at every step. The initial rollout of waste management technologies had been met with resistance. Some countries were simply unprepared to take on the logistical challenges of implementing advanced recycling systems. In others, entrenched political interests worked against progress, fearing the disruption that new technologies could bring to existing industries. But Aldo and his team were relentless. They knew the stakes were too high to give up.

They launched pilot projects in cities across the globe, from the slums of South Asia to the industrial heartlands of Europe. These pilots showcased the power of the new technologies, proving that large-scale recycling and waste-to-resource initiatives could work even in the most challenging environments. The results were undeniable. Landfills began to shrink, air quality improved, and industries saw the economic potential of adopting circular economy principles.

As Aldo's work expanded, the results began to ripple outward. Countries that had once lagged behind now took on ambitious waste management goals. Advanced sorting technologies, powered by AI, enabled cities to separate organic waste from recyclables with precision. Materials that had once been considered non-recyclable were now being broken down and repurposed, thanks to innovations in chemical recycling and biorefining. Industries were no longer simply producing; they were regenerating. Products were being designed with their lifecycle in mind, and manufacturers were finding creative ways to reuse their own waste. This shift began to foster a new kind of economy, an economy where growth was decoupled from resource consumption.

One of the key moments in the global movement came when Aldo's team rolled out an international standard for waste management that was adopted by over 150 countries. This new framework allowed countries to adopt best practices and technologies that had already been proven successful in various regions. It provided a roadmap for nations to create waste management systems that aligned with the principles of the circular economy and ensured that waste was treated not as a liability but as an opportunity.

The End of Waste as We Know It

The most powerful symbol of the world's transformation was the steady decline of waste generation itself. Cities that had once been overwhelmed by refuse began to emerge as models of sustainability. Aldo stood in awe as he watched firsthand how countries that were once the most wasteful had transformed into leaders of recycling, energy recovery, and sustainable production. What had once seemed like a utopian dream, eliminating waste altogether, was now a tangible reality.

Across the globe, waste was being minimized and diverted from landfills at unprecedented rates. In many places, the last remaining landfills had been transformed into resource recovery facilities that captured methane for energy production or turned organic waste into compost for agriculture. Waste was no longer seen as something to bury or burn but as a resource to be exploited. From the rich soils of the Amazon to the streets of New York, composting programs were flourishing, turning organic waste into valuable inputs for agriculture and carbon sequestration.

Cities like Tokyo, San Francisco, and Copenhagen had become global examples, with nearly all of their waste being diverted from landfills and incinerators. Advanced recycling systems and urban mining techniques had helped reclaim valuable materials from e-waste and construction debris, allowing these materials to be reintroduced into the production cycle.

Meanwhile, the global industrial complex had undergone a dramatic transformation. Corporations, once resistant to change, had now made sustainability a cornerstone of their business models. Their products were designed with the circular economy in mind, and materials were sourced sustainably. Even the fashion industry, notorious for its waste and pollution, had adopted circular practices, from garment recycling to more sustainable textile production. The concept of "zero waste" had moved from niche markets to mainstream businesses, and it was no longer a question of whether sustainability could work, it was a question of how far companies were willing to go to embrace it.

The Legacy of Aldo and His Team

As Aldo reflected on the journey, he realized how far the world had come. The waste crisis that had once seemed insurmountable had been addressed through collective action, technological innovation, and unyielding persistence. What had started as a small team's dream to turn waste into a resource had evolved into a global movement, with Aldo and his colleagues playing a pivotal role.

But as much as Aldo was proud of the tangible changes, cleaner cities, a revitalized planet, and a new global mindset about consumption, he knew that the work was never truly done. The challenges ahead were still great. Climate change continued to threaten the planet, biodiversity loss remained an urgent issue, and waste management was a continual process of improvement. Yet Aldo was confident that humanity had finally turned a corner. The foundation for a sustainable future had been laid, and the world was on track to ensure that future generations inherited a planet that could sustain both them and the diverse forms of life that shared it.

The Final Step

Aldo took a deep breath as he stood at the helm of a new era, an era defined by respect for the planet and its resources. He looked at the team members who had stood beside him for so long. They had worked through exhaustion, overcome personal and professional hurdles, and watched as the world began to heal. Together, they had changed the trajectory of history.

And in that moment, Aldo knew: their work had only just begun, but the world was on its way to becoming what they had always dreamed of, a place where people lived in harmony with nature, a place where waste was no longer a burden but a valuable resource, and a place where the legacy of this moment would echo for generations to come. The final step had been taken, but the journey toward a better world was ongoing.

The victory was not just Aldo's; it was the world's victory. A victory born from unity, perseverance, and the unshakable belief that a better, more sustainable future was possible.

Chapter 90: A New Life

The world had changed in ways that no one could have predicted. What began as a noble endeavor to address the environmental crisis had blossomed into a global movement, one that reshaped society from the ground up. Aldo, who had once stood alone with a vision for a better world, now looked out upon a planet transformed, its cities green, its air clear, and its ecosystems thriving once more. The mission was not over, but the journey had reached a new chapter. The world had entered an era of harmony, a time where the balance between human progress and environmental preservation was no longer a distant dream, but a living reality.

In this new world, people woke up to a different kind of day. The air was fresher, the streets cleaner, and the environment was no longer something to be feared or neglected. Nature, once pushed to the edge of survival, now flourished in the spaces humans occupied. Trees lined the streets of even the busiest cities, parks stretched as far as the eye could see, and the sounds of birds and wildlife could be heard alongside the hum of urban life. It was a world that Aldo and his team had worked tirelessly to build, a world where sustainability was not an afterthought, but the very foundation of society.

A Global Transformation

The transformation was not an accident. It was the product of decades of work, collaboration, and innovation. Aldo's breakthrough technologies in waste management had been the catalyst for change, but they were only one part of a much larger global shift. The circular economy had become the standard, replacing the old linear models that had driven much of human progress for centuries. No longer did industries take from the Earth, manufacture, and discard without a thought for the consequences. Instead, resources were carefully managed, waste was minimized, and every product was designed with its end-of-life in mind.

Cities were no longer the sprawling, chaotic places of pollution and congestion they once were. Instead, they had been redesigned to be sustainable, with energy-efficient buildings, waste-free neighborhoods, and green technologies integrated into every aspect of life. Public transportation systems powered by clean energy connected communities, and renewable energy sources, from wind and solar to cutting-edge advancements in geothermal and tidal power, supplied the electricity that fueled these urban hubs.

Beyond the cities, the rural areas had flourished as well. Agriculture had undergone a revolution, with regenerative farming practices that not only restored the soil but also produced more food with less impact on the environment. The practice of monocropping had been replaced by polyculture, where a diversity of crops supported biodiversity, enhanced soil health, and increased resilience to climate change. Farming communities had once been among the most vulnerable to environmental destruction, but now, they stood as models of sustainability, demonstrating that it was possible to feed the world without destroying it.

In the oceans, Aldo's initiatives had borne fruit. The once-toxic waters were now teeming with life, thanks to the removal of plastics and other pollutants and the restoration of coral reefs. Marine ecosystems had been rehabilitated, and new technologies had been developed to clean the oceans, removing the remnants of humanity's past mistakes. The global effort to protect marine life had led to the creation of vast marine protected areas, where species could thrive without the threat of overfishing, pollution, or climate change.

MOUNT OF WASTE

The energy sector had also seen a monumental shift. Fossil fuels, once the backbone of industrial civilization, had been replaced with clean, renewable energy. Solar panels adorned rooftops, wind turbines dotted the landscapes, and communities had adopted decentralized energy grids that allowed them to generate and manage their own power. The reliance on oil, coal, and gas had evaporated, replaced by a diverse mix of green technologies that not only reduced emissions but also empowered people to take control of their energy needs.

But perhaps the most significant change was in the way people thought. The global awareness that had been cultivated over the past decades had shifted the collective consciousness. Sustainability was no longer a niche concern for environmentalists; it was the guiding principle that informed every decision, from the way products were designed to how food was grown and consumed. The mindset that had once prioritized convenience over consequence had been replaced with a deeper understanding of the interconnectedness of all life. People now recognized that their actions, whether big or small—had an impact on the world around them.

The Role of Education and Awareness

The shift toward sustainability had been driven not just by technological innovation, but by a revolution in education. Aldo and his team had recognized early on that the only way to ensure lasting change was to educate the next generation of leaders, innovators, and citizens about the importance of caring for the planet. Schools and universities had integrated sustainability into their curriculums, teaching students not just the science of environmentalism, but also the ethics of living in balance with nature.

Generations of young people had grown up with a deep sense of responsibility toward the Earth. They understood that their future was inextricably linked to the health of the planet, and they were committed to continuing the work that Aldo and his team had started. Environmental studies were now part of every field of study, from engineering to economics to the arts. The focus on interdisciplinary learning had fostered a generation of individuals who understood the complexity of the world's problems and were equipped with the knowledge and skills to address them.

It was this educated, aware, and passionate generation that would carry the torch forward. Aldo often spoke at universities and community centers, sharing his experiences and inspiring others to continue the work of building a sustainable world. His message was clear: the work was never truly done. Sustainability was a journey, not a destination, and it was the responsibility of everyone, young and old, to ensure that the progress made was not lost but built upon.

Rebuilding Communities and Restoring Harmony

While technology and innovation had played an essential role in the transformation of the planet, Aldo never forgot the importance of human connection. The global effort to protect the Earth had not only improved the environment but had also strengthened communities. People had come together, crossing borders and overcoming differences, to work toward a common goal. It was a reminder that, at its core, sustainability was not just about the Earth—it was about people.

In the early days of the movement, there had been a lot of talk about individual responsibility—reducing waste, conserving resources, and minimizing one's carbon footprint. But over time, Aldo and his team had realized that the real power lay in collaboration. The solutions they were working on needed to be implemented at scale, and that meant building strong partnerships between governments, businesses, communities, and individuals.

MOUNT OF WASTE

The collaborative spirit had led to the creation of sustainable cities, the revitalization of ecosystems, and the establishment of a green economy that provided opportunities for everyone. People had been empowered to make choices that benefitted not just themselves, but also their communities and the planet. Cities had become places of collective action, where individuals and organizations worked together to create sustainable solutions to local problems. In rural areas, farmers and indigenous communities had shared their knowledge of sustainable practices, teaching others how to live in harmony with nature. It was this exchange of ideas and experiences that had truly transformed the world.

A Legacy of Sustainability

As Aldo looked out at the world, he saw a place that had been fundamentally altered. The Earth was healing, its ecosystems were recovering, and its people were living in harmony with the environment. The vision he had once held was no longer a distant dream; it was a living, breathing reality. But even as he marveled at the progress made, Aldo knew that his work was far from over.

The journey toward sustainability was ongoing. New challenges would arise, and new innovations would be required. Climate change, biodiversity loss, and other environmental threats still loomed large on the horizon. But Aldo was confident that the world was better equipped to face these challenges than ever before. The lessons learned, the technologies developed, and the global network of people dedicated to protecting the planet would ensure that the Earth remained on a path to recovery.

And so, as the world entered this new era, Aldo felt a deep sense of fulfillment. The mission he had started was not only changing the course of history, it was inspiring the world to continue the work he and his team had begun. A new life was being built, one rooted in sustainability, harmony, and respect for the planet that gave us life.

Chapter 91: A Promising Future

The world had changed beyond recognition, but for Aldo and his team, this was only the beginning. The earth, once suffocating beneath the weight of pollution and environmental degradation, was now beginning to breathe again. The monumental shifts in how humanity interacted with nature had given rise to cities that once seemed like the stuff of utopian dreams. These green cities were not just an aesthetic improvement, but the very heart of a new era. They were thriving ecosystems where the built environment and nature coexisted in harmony, where renewable energy powered every building, and where the air was clear, and the streets teemed with life.

Aldo had never imagined that the seeds of change he had planted would grow into such a global revolution. When he first started his journey, the problems seemed insurmountable. The pollution, the waste, the climate crises—it felt as though the forces of nature were beyond human control. Yet, here he was, witnessing the emergence of a new world. A world where sustainability wasn't just a political slogan but a way of life. A world where people had learned to live within the planet's means, where the idea of extracting and consuming without regard for consequences had given way to a mindset of care, renewal, and stewardship.

The Rise of Green Cities

Around the world, green cities were sprouting like wildflowers after a long drought. The first truly sustainable urban areas had set the standard for the future. These cities, designed with nature at their core, were now hubs of innovation and ecological balance. Powered by renewable energy sources, solar panels, wind turbines, and even algae-based biofuels, these cities were a far cry from their polluted predecessors.

MOUNT OF WASTE

Each building was a marvel of sustainability, constructed from materials that were not only eco-friendly but also recycled, repurposed, or made from biodegradable substances. The architecture blended seamlessly with nature, with green roofs and vertical gardens that absorbed CO_2 and provided natural cooling. Public spaces were designed to be ecologically diverse, with rain gardens that captured stormwater and green spaces that encouraged biodiversity. The streets were lined with trees that offered shade, oxygen, and habitats for wildlife. The result was not just aesthetically pleasing; it was an environment that was more resilient to climate change, providing natural cooling in the summer and reducing the urban heat island effect.

Public transportation had undergone a transformation, with electric buses and autonomous vehicles that operated on renewable energy. These transport systems had replaced fossil fuel-dependent cars, reducing traffic congestion and air pollution while providing efficient, accessible mobility for everyone. The urban sprawl that had once been a hallmark of industrial cities had been replaced by compact, connected communities where people lived, worked, and played within walking distance of one another. These urban areas had learned to make the most of limited resources, with efficient waste management systems, water recycling plants, and community composting programs.

But these green cities were not just about technology; they were about changing the way people lived. The citizens of these cities were not passive consumers but active participants in their communities. They understood the value of their natural resources, from the water they drank to the food they ate, and they had learned how to reduce, reuse, and recycle to ensure these resources would last for generations to come. In these cities, the ethos of sustainability had become ingrained in everyday life.

Global Acceptance of Green Technologies

The green revolution Aldo had championed had spread far beyond the borders of the cities where it had first taken root. Across the globe, nations had embraced technologies that once seemed like radical ideas. Waste management systems that turned trash into valuable resources had become commonplace. The plastic crisis, which had once threatened marine life and clogged landfills, had been largely addressed through biodegradable alternatives and circular economy practices. People now saw waste not as something to discard, but as something to repurpose.

Energy production, too, had undergone a revolutionary transformation. Solar power, wind energy, and other renewable sources had replaced fossil fuels as the primary source of global electricity. Entire regions of the world were now powered by clean, sustainable energy, reducing humanity's carbon footprint and offering a glimmer of hope for tackling climate change. Even industries that had long been the heavy polluters, like agriculture and manufacturing, had shifted toward more sustainable practices. Regenerative farming techniques had replaced the destructive practices of monoculture, and new innovations in sustainable fashion, construction, and even food production had made their mark.

Cities and rural areas alike had taken up the mantle of sustainability, embracing new technologies that had been developed to make everyday life more efficient and less damaging to the environment. Technologies that once seemed like speculative ideas had become central to the way people lived and worked, from smart grids that optimized energy consumption to desalination plants that turned seawater into fresh drinking water. The world had embraced these innovations with open arms, recognizing that they were not just the future, but the key to a livable, sustainable future.

Living Simply and Sustainably

MOUNT OF WASTE

Perhaps the most profound change was not in the technologies or systems that had been implemented but in the mindset of the people. The lifestyle of overconsumption and waste that had once dominated the modern world had been replaced with one of mindfulness, simplicity, and sustainability. People no longer measured success by the size of their homes or the number of things they owned. Instead, they measured success by the quality of their relationships, the health of their environment, and the contributions they made to the greater good.

Living sustainably had become a way of life for many. People had shifted their consumption habits, prioritizing products that were durable, reusable, and made from sustainable materials. There was a renewed focus on local and organic food, and urban farming had become a widespread practice. In the cities, rooftop gardens, vertical farms, and community-based agriculture projects flourished, providing fresh produce while reducing the environmental footprint of food transportation.

The idea of simplicity had become fashionable. People had learned to embrace a slower, more intentional way of living. With the constant pressure to acquire more now behind them, they had turned their attention to the things that truly mattered: their families, their communities, and their planet. The environmental crises that had once seemed insurmountable were now viewed as challenges to be solved, not only by technology but by a collective effort to shift how humanity interacted with the Earth.

The Work Is Not Over

Though Aldo and his team had accomplished more than they ever could have dreamed, they knew the journey was far from over. The Earth, while on the path to healing, still faced significant challenges. The scars of centuries of industrialization and exploitation would take time to heal completely. Climate change, though mitigated, was still a threat. Species that had been driven to the brink of extinction still needed protection. And poverty, while alleviated in many areas through green technologies and new economic models, remained a serious issue in some parts of the world.

Aldo had always understood that progress is not linear and that true sustainability was not a final destination, but a continuous journey. The advancements made over the past few decades had laid a foundation, but there was still much to be done. Every day brought new challenges, and it was clear to Aldo that the fight to preserve the planet would require constant vigilance, innovation, and collaboration. The Earth was resilient, but it also needed humanity to be its steward, its caretaker, and its partner in healing.

But for now, Aldo could take solace in the progress made. The world was no longer the place it had been when he started his journey. People were living more harmoniously with nature, technology was advancing in ways that supported rather than exploited the environment, and the world's ecosystems were on the mend. The impact of their work was clear, and Aldo's heart swelled with pride.

As he stood before a thriving city built on the principles of sustainability, Aldo knew that the future was not only bright, it was also within their hands. And with this understanding, he and his team prepared to face the next chapter, knowing that as long as there was work to be done, they would continue the fight for a sustainable, harmonious world.

Chapter 92: Global Learning

Aldo stood at the helm of a new world. The years of hardship, struggle, and perseverance had brought him and his team to a pivotal moment: the opportunity to share the lessons they had learned in their fight to restore the planet. Now, it was time to bring together the global community, uniting nations, organizations, and individuals with a shared commitment to sustainability. The time had come to not only celebrate the progress they had made but to learn from the successes and failures along the way and forge a path for the future.

The conference was being held in a city that had become the symbol of what the world could achieve with the right mindset and tools: a city powered entirely by renewable energy, with zero waste, a thriving urban ecosystem, and citizens who had embraced a lifestyle of sustainability. It was here that Aldo had invited thought leaders, activists, scientists, policymakers, business leaders, and even ordinary people who had taken small but significant steps toward protecting the environment. The conference would be a melting pot of ideas, where people from all walks of life could share their experiences, exchange knowledge, and build the foundation for a future where sustainability was the core value of every society.

As the participants began to arrive, Aldo's mind raced with thoughts about what needed to be accomplished during this critical gathering. The stakes had never been higher. While significant progress had been made, the road ahead was still filled with obstacles. It was vital that the global community continued to push forward, learning from the past and developing solutions to emerging challenges. The conference, he knew, would not just be about showcasing achievements, but about fostering collaboration, innovation, and action to ensure the future of the planet.

The Opening Session: A New Era of Learning

Aldo took to the stage as the opening speaker. The crowd, a diverse mix of people from all continents, was eager to hear what he had to say. He looked out at the sea of faces, many of whom had become close allies in the battle for a sustainable future. But there were also new faces, young activists, passionate researchers, and entrepreneurs eager to contribute to the ongoing transformation.

He cleared his throat, his heart swelling with the gravity of the moment.

"Good morning, everyone," Aldo began, his voice steady but filled with emotion. "We are standing at the crossroads of history. The world has changed in ways we never thought possible. We have come together to learn, to share, and most importantly, to chart the path forward. But the work is far from over. If we are to continue on this journey, we must understand the challenges ahead and the solutions that will guide us."

He paused, allowing the weight of his words to settle in.

"We have created cities that are more than just buildings. We've created living systems, thriving ecosystems that work with nature, not against it. We've transformed waste into resources, and we've shifted the global energy grid away from fossil fuels. But we know that progress does not come without challenges. The road we've traveled has been difficult, and the road ahead will require even more from each of us."

The room was silent, captivated by Aldo's words. He continued:

"This conference is about sharing the lessons we've learned along the way. We must reflect on what has worked, what has not, and what more we can do to ensure that the sustainability movement does not falter. We must embrace a mindset of continuous learning, where failure is not a setback but a stepping stone toward greater success. Only then will we be able to tackle

MOUNT OF WASTE

the remaining issues, such as climate change, biodiversity loss, and resource depletion."

Aldo's voice grew stronger with conviction.

"We cannot afford to slow down. This is not just about protecting our way of life; it's about ensuring that future generations inherit a world worth living in. Together, we will continue to learn, adapt, and grow. The future of the planet depends on our collective efforts, and we are just getting started."

The applause that followed was deafening, a resounding affirmation of Aldo's vision for a better world. The stage was set, and the conference was about to begin.

The Learning Sessions: Sharing Knowledge and Insights

Throughout the conference, Aldo and his team organized a series of learning sessions designed to address the most pressing challenges the world still faced in its pursuit of sustainability. These sessions brought together experts from every corner of the globe, each with their unique perspective and knowledge to share. Some spoke about new technological innovations, others about cultural shifts that needed to happen to support sustainable living, and still others about how to adapt to the changing climate.

One of the key sessions focused on the role of technology in achieving sustainability. Scientists and engineers shared groundbreaking innovations in waste management, renewable energy, and carbon capture. New ideas were presented for converting atmospheric CO_2 into usable products, from building materials to biofuels, and the session became a hotbed of ideas for turning environmental challenges into economic opportunities. The conversations ranged from optimizing smart grids to utilizing machine learning in waste sorting, and the energy in the room was palpable.

Another session focused on policy and governance, addressing the need for stronger international agreements and national regulations to support sustainability. Representatives from governments and international organizations discussed the importance of climate treaties, carbon pricing, and the need for a just transition that included marginalized communities in the solutions. The session highlighted the challenges of balancing economic growth with environmental preservation, and the debate over the role of governments versus the private sector in driving change.

The conference also had a dedicated track on cultural transformation. Activists and community leaders shared stories of how they had inspired change in local communities, from grassroots movements to large-scale urban initiatives. They discussed the importance of shifting societal values, from materialism to mindfulness, from consumption to conservation. It was clear that the battle for sustainability was as much a cultural shift as it was a technological one. The need for an interconnected world, where people valued the planet not just as a resource but as a living entity to be nurtured, was at the heart of these discussions.

New Ideas for the Future

As the conference progressed, new ideas began to take shape. One of the most exciting discussions was about the future of food. With global populations continuing to grow, how could the world ensure that everyone had access to nutritious, sustainable food? Several innovative solutions were presented, including vertical farming, lab-grown meat, and precision agriculture techniques that reduced waste and increased yields. Participants also discussed how to create sustainable food systems in developing countries and the role of education in changing dietary habits.

Another key theme was the role of education in sustaining the green revolution. Educators from across the globe spoke about their efforts to teach the next generation about environmental stewardship and sustainable living. They discussed how school curricula had been redesigned to include topics like renewable energy, waste management, and climate change, and how young people were increasingly taking the lead in creating a more sustainable future.

Throughout the conference, Aldo listened attentively, engaging with the experts and activists who were shaping the future. He saw the potential for collaboration across borders, industries, and cultures. The ideas presented were varied and sometimes ambitious, but there was one common thread: the commitment to building a future where people lived in balance with the environment.

The Closing Address: A Call to Action

As the conference neared its end, Aldo took the stage once more for the closing address. The energy in the room was palpable, the discussions from the previous days having sparked a renewed sense of urgency and possibility.

"We have shared incredible ideas, learned from one another, and found common ground," Aldo began. "But the true work starts now. The knowledge we've gained and the insights we've shared must be turned into action. Each one of us has a role to play in this transformation, whether through innovation, advocacy, or education."

He paused, allowing the weight of his words to sink in.

"The future of our planet depends on what we do next. We are not passive observers in this process; we are active participants. We must commit to taking what we've learned here and applying it in our daily lives, our businesses, our governments, and our communities."

Aldo's voice rang with conviction.

"This is not just a moment in time. This is the beginning of an ongoing global effort to create a sustainable future for all. The challenges are great, but they are not insurmountable. Together, we have the power to continue the work we've started. Let us take what we've learned, and let it guide us as we move forward. The world is waiting for us to act."

The applause was deafening, a powerful affirmation of the commitment to continue the fight for a sustainable world.

A Continuing Legacy

As the conference came to a close, Aldo felt a deep sense of pride. The road had been long, and the challenges had been immense, but the future looked brighter than ever. The world was united, not just in its struggle but in its resolve. The lessons shared at the conference would not be forgotten; they would be carried forward, fueling the work that still lay ahead.

Aldo looked out over the crowd, knowing that the next chapter in the story of sustainability was about to unfold. The world had learned from its past, and together, they would continue to shape a future that was not just green, but thriving, for generations to come.

Chapter 93: Protecting What Has Been Achieved

As Aldo stood at the heart of the sustainable city that had been the epicenter of global change, he couldn't help but reflect on the monumental journey the world had undertaken. The technological innovations, the cultural shifts, the international agreements, all had led to a world vastly different from the one he had known before. The atmosphere in many regions was cleaner, the oceans less polluted, and the cities were living examples of sustainability. But despite all the progress, Aldo knew that none of it was guaranteed.

The battle for the future of the planet was not just about creating solutions; it was also about preserving the hard-earned achievements that had already been made. The journey had been long, and at times, the future had seemed uncertain. Yet, here they were: standing on the cusp of a new world. The world had come together, united in its resolve to fight for the planet's future, but Aldo knew the work had to continue. Sustainability wasn't a destination, it was a lifelong commitment, and the planet's recovery could not be taken for granted.

It was time to protect what they had built, to safeguard the future from the forces of greed, ignorance, and neglect that had brought about the environmental crises in the first place. Aldo and his team launched a new initiative, one aimed not at creating new solutions, but at ensuring that what had already been achieved would be sustained, fortified, and safeguarded against future threats.

The New Era of Ecosystem Protection

The concept of ecosystem protection was not new, but it had taken on a deeper and more urgent meaning in this new world. In the past, Aldo had been part of the movement that focused on addressing the immediate environmental crises, such as waste management, pollution, and the energy transition. Now, the challenge was different: it was about protecting the hard-fought gains and ensuring that they could withstand the pressures of time, changing circumstances, and emerging threats.

The first step in their new initiative was to launch a global program focused on preserving ecosystems. It was a broad and ambitious undertaking that aimed to protect forests, oceans, rivers, and all other vital ecosystems that played a role in maintaining the planet's balance. These ecosystems were the lungs of the earth, the purifiers of air and water, and the providers of food and shelter for billions of people and countless species.

Aldo and his team understood that protecting ecosystems was not just about stopping the destruction of natural habitats, it was about creating resilient, self-sustaining ecosystems that could adapt to changing environmental conditions. The new program would focus on restoration, preservation, and protection in equal measure.

1. Restoration of Damaged Ecosystems

The first phase of the program was focused on ecosystem restoration. Despite the immense strides that had been made in restoring the earth's systems, there were still vast areas that had been severely damaged by pollution, deforestation, and climate change. These areas needed urgent attention.

Aldo's team collaborated with environmental scientists, engineers, and ecologists to identify regions that were most in need of restoration. Priority was given to areas that had once been rich in biodiversity but were now barren or degraded. The restoration efforts ranged from reforestation programs to the rehabilitation of wetlands, grasslands, and coral reefs.

In the forests, drones and artificial intelligence were used to monitor the health of the trees, detect early signs of disease or pests, and ensure that the replanting efforts were successful. In coastal areas, Aldo's team worked alongside marine biologists to restore damaged coral reefs and rebuild oyster beds, which were vital for filtering water and providing habitat for marine life.

One of the most significant initiatives in the restoration phase was the rehabilitation of the Amazon Rainforest, which had suffered immense damage due to illegal logging and deforestation. With a combination of satellite monitoring, community engagement, and international cooperation, Aldo's team was able to implement an effective reforestation program, which aimed to restore the forest to its natural state.

2. Preservation of Existing Ecosystems

While restoration was crucial, preserving the ecosystems that remained intact was equally important. Aldo and his team worked with governments, environmental organizations, and local communities to ensure that protected areas were truly protected. This involved strengthening enforcement of laws against illegal activities like poaching, logging, and mining, which continued to threaten fragile ecosystems.

A significant part of the preservation effort was dedicated to ensuring the safety of critical biodiversity hotspots, areas like the Congo Basin, the Great Barrier Reef, and the Arctic tundra. These ecosystems were not only ecologically important but also provided resources and livelihoods to millions of people.

Aldo's team collaborated with indigenous communities who had lived in harmony with the land for generations, ensuring that their knowledge and traditional practices were integrated into conservation efforts. They realized that sustainable development could not be achieved by outsiders alone, it had to be rooted in local culture, values, and ways of life.

3. Building Resilience Against Climate Change

The third pillar of Aldo's ecosystem protection initiative was to build resilience against the impacts of climate change. While the world had made tremendous progress in reducing greenhouse gas emissions, the effects of climate change were still being felt around the world. Rising sea levels, increased frequency of extreme weather events, and changing precipitation patterns were putting ecosystems under increasing pressure.

Aldo's team worked to design climate-adaptive ecosystems, ensuring that they could weather the changes brought about by a warming planet. This meant not just protecting ecosystems, but actively helping them adapt to changing conditions.

In coastal areas, for example, mangrove forests were restored, as they provided natural barriers against storm surges and erosion. In regions affected by droughts, water management systems were put in place to ensure that ecosystems could survive and thrive even in times of water scarcity. The goal was to create ecosystems that were not just surviving but were thriving, even in the face of climate stress.

International Cooperation: A Shared Responsibility

Aldo knew that ecosystem protection was not a task that could be tackled by any single country or organization alone. The world had to come together to share knowledge, resources, and expertise. This was why Aldo and his team focused on strengthening international cooperation.

Through bilateral agreements and multilateral partnerships, countries pledged to work together to protect global ecosystems. There were joint research initiatives, funding for local conservation projects, and commitments to support each other's efforts in tackling environmental challenges.

The United Nations played a key role in coordinating global efforts, organizing summits, and ensuring that commitments were being met. The Paris Agreement, which had originally focused on climate change mitigation, was now broadened to include concrete goals for ecosystem protection and restoration.

The Role of Technology

As in the past, technology played a central role in Aldo's efforts to protect the planet. Advances in satellite imaging, drones, and artificial intelligence allowed for real-time monitoring of ecosystems, identifying areas at risk and ensuring that conservation efforts were effective. Machine learning algorithms helped predict the effects of climate change on ecosystems, allowing for proactive management strategies.

One of the most innovative aspects of the initiative was the development of "smart ecosystems", areas where technology and nature worked in tandem to enhance resilience. In these areas, sensors were used to monitor soil health, water quality, and biodiversity, feeding data into an artificial intelligence system that could provide recommendations for sustainable land and water management.

Aldo was particularly proud of the new bioengineering projects that were designed to enhance the natural ability of ecosystems to recover. Genetic modifications were made to certain plant species to increase their resistance to pests and diseases, while bio-fertilizers were developed to restore soil fertility without harming the environment.

Educating the Next Generation

The final component of Aldo's ecosystem protection program was education. Protecting ecosystems was not just about high-tech solutions or international agreements, it was about inspiring the next generation of environmental stewards. Through global educational campaigns and grassroots efforts, Aldo and his team worked to raise awareness of the importance of ecosystems and biodiversity.

In schools, children were taught about the interconnectedness of all living things and the role they played in protecting the environment. Universities and research institutions were encouraged to develop programs focused on ecosystem management, sustainability, and climate science.

Aldo's vision was clear: the future of the planet depended on people who understood the importance of the natural world and were equipped with the knowledge and tools to protect it. This knowledge would empower future leaders, scientists, and activists to continue the work that he and his team had started.

A Call to Action

As Aldo looked out over the conference room, filled with leaders, scientists, and activists from around the world, he felt a deep sense of hope. The world had changed in profound ways, but the journey was far from over. The planet's future was still at risk, and Aldo knew that protecting what had already been achieved was just as important as making new strides forward.

"Protecting ecosystems is not a one-time effort," Aldo said during the closing session of the conference. "It is a lifelong commitment. We have made incredible progress, but we must remain vigilant. The planet has entrusted us with its care, and it is our responsibility to ensure that the systems we have put in place continue to thrive long into the future."

The applause was loud and sustained, but Aldo knew that this was just the beginning of a new chapter in humanity's relationship with the planet. The future was uncertain, but one thing was clear: the world was ready to protect what had been achieved, and together, they would continue to safeguard the future of the earth.

Chapter 94: New Challenges

The world had transformed in ways Aldo never imagined. The advancements in technology had ushered in an era of sustainability, where green energy powered cities, waste was processed efficiently, and ecosystems were on their way to recovery. Yet, as Aldo and his team stood on the precipice of a new dawn, they were forced to confront a new set of challenges.

While their achievements had brought about a cleaner, more harmonious world, the rapid development of new technologies was beginning to present unintended consequences. Technologies that were initially embraced for their environmental benefits were now causing disruptions in the social and economic fabric of society. The pace of progress was so swift that it sometimes outpaced the ability of governments, businesses, and communities to adapt.

As the world grappled with the positive impacts of these technologies, Aldo realized that the real challenge was not just about creating innovations—it was about integrating those innovations into society in ways that didn't disrupt the balance of human life. It was about ensuring that the benefits of technological progress were distributed equitably and that the new world they had worked so hard to create did not unintentionally create new forms of inequality or environmental harm.

The Rise of Automation and Its Economic Impact

One of the most immediate concerns Aldo and his team faced was the rise of automation and artificial intelligence (AI). While these technologies had revolutionized industries and made processes more efficient, they had also created significant economic disruptions. Entire sectors were being automated, leading to job losses in industries such as manufacturing, transportation, and logistics.

The promise of AI and robotics had always been clear: machines could take over repetitive and dangerous tasks, freeing humans to focus on more creative and intellectual pursuits. However, the reality was more complex. In many cases, automation was leading to large-scale unemployment, as workers who were displaced by machines struggled to find new opportunities in a rapidly changing job market.

Aldo knew that while technology had the potential to solve many of the world's problems, it also risked creating new divides. The benefits of automation were not being felt equally across society. Many communities that relied heavily on traditional industries were now facing economic hardship, and the wealth gap between the tech-savvy elite and the displaced workers was growing.

To address these issues, Aldo and his team worked with economists, sociologists, and political leaders to devise strategies that would ensure that the benefits of technology were shared by all. The solution wasn't to halt progress but to find ways to retrain and reskill workers, to create new jobs in green technologies and sustainability sectors, and to ensure that no one was left behind in the wake of automation.

They developed programs that promoted lifelong learning, focusing on skills that were vital for the future: renewable energy engineering, waste management, environmental science, and sustainable urban planning. These programs were designed to help displaced workers transition into industries that were aligned with the goals of sustainability and the green economy. It was a delicate balance, ensuring that technology could advance while also addressing the economic displacement that came with it.

Social Disruption: The Changing Nature of Work and Identity

Beyond the economic concerns, Aldo and his team also had to consider the broader social implications of technological progress.

MOUNT OF WASTE

The rise of automation and AI was not just changing the way people worked—it was changing the very nature of work itself. In many parts of the world, people had identified their worth and purpose through their jobs. With automation taking over many tasks, some people were left questioning their role in a society that seemed to be moving away from traditional concepts of labor.

People's identities were intertwined with their occupations, and as automation made many jobs obsolete, a sense of purposelessness began to creep into the social fabric. Aldo's team recognized that technological progress had to be paired with efforts to redefine the concept of work, providing people with new ways to contribute to society and find fulfillment outside of traditional employment.

One of the key aspects of Aldo's vision was to create a world where people were not simply defined by the work they did, but by the impact they had on the world around them. In this new society, people were encouraged to engage in community-driven projects, creative endeavors, and environmental conservation efforts. This shift in cultural values was not easy—it required a reevaluation of how people viewed success, fulfillment, and contribution to the greater good.

As part of the solution, Aldo's team introduced a new model of work called "impact-driven employment." In this model, individuals were encouraged to pursue careers that focused on making a tangible, positive impact on society. These careers were not just about economic gain but about contributing to the well-being of the planet and future generations. It was a model that integrated personal fulfillment with environmental responsibility and social justice.

Technological Gaps and the Divide Between Developed and Developing Nations

Another significant challenge Aldo faced was the digital divide between developed and developing nations. While technological progress had improved the lives of people in wealthy countries, many developing nations were still struggling to catch up. The rapid deployment of advanced technologies such as AI, renewable energy infrastructure, and sustainable agriculture methods was largely concentrated in the global north. Meanwhile, the global south was left with limited access to these life-changing innovations.

Aldo knew that for the world to truly be sustainable, all nations needed to have equal access to the technologies that were shaping the future. He worked closely with international organizations to ensure that developing countries had access to the resources and knowledge they needed to benefit from these technological advancements. This included creating partnerships with private companies to build affordable infrastructure, providing grants for sustainable development projects, and facilitating knowledge-sharing initiatives that allowed developing nations to leapfrog traditional, polluting technologies and adopt cleaner, more sustainable alternatives.

This was not just a matter of economic equity but also a matter of global stability. Aldo knew that if the technological gap between developed and developing countries continued to widen, it could create further global tensions and exacerbate existing inequalities. Therefore, his team pushed for the creation of a global technology-sharing initiative that would allow nations to collaborate on developing sustainable technologies and share them equitably across borders.

The Ethical Dilemmas of New Technologies

As technological progress continued, Aldo and his team also found themselves confronting ethical dilemmas that had not been considered in the early days of the movement. While the potential for new technologies to solve environmental problems was vast, there were also risks associated with their use. For example, the proliferation of AI and automation raised concerns about privacy, surveillance, and the potential for misuse of personal data. The implementation of advanced technologies in agriculture, such as genetically modified organisms (GMOs) and CRISPR gene-editing, sparked debates about the ethics of altering the natural world at a genetic level.

Aldo believed that technological progress had to go hand in hand with ethical responsibility. As part of their new initiative, his team created a global ethics council that would monitor the development and use of new technologies, ensuring that they aligned with the principles of sustainability, justice, and human dignity. This council would not only regulate the use of technology but also provide a forum for public dialogue about the ethical implications of new innovations.

The ethical council's work was especially important when it came to issues like data privacy, genetic modification, and AI decision-making. Aldo knew that while these technologies held great promise, they also had the potential to be exploited for malicious purposes. The council worked to create guidelines and standards for the ethical use of technology, balancing innovation with the protection of individual rights and environmental integrity.

The Balance Between Progress and Preservation

Aldo's overarching challenge was finding the right balance between technological progress and the preservation of the world they had worked so hard to create. Technological advancements had brought immense benefits, but they also posed new risks and challenges. The key, Aldo believed, was not to reject progress but to shape it in ways that aligned with the planet's long-term well-being.

The message Aldo and his team sent to the world was clear: technology and sustainability could coexist, but only if the world acted responsibly. It was a message of hope and caution, hope for a future where technology could solve the world's most pressing problems, but caution against the dangers of rushing forward without considering the broader consequences.

The task before Aldo and his team was daunting, but it was not insurmountable. They had already proven that humanity could make a difference when it worked together. Now, the world needed to take the next step, ensuring that technological progress would continue to serve the greater good and be aligned with the values of sustainability, equity, and justice. This was the challenge that lay ahead.

As Aldo sat at his desk, looking out over the city he had helped build, he knew that the work was far from over. The future of the planet was still being written, and it was up to the generations to come to ensure that the technological tools they had been given were used to build a better, more sustainable world. And in that, Aldo saw the true potential for a new world, a world where progress and preservation could live in harmony.

Chapter 96: A Turning Point

The journey had been long and difficult, filled with moments of doubt, hardship, and heartbreak, but as Aldo stood at the top of the hill overlooking a vast expanse of lush, green land, he could hardly believe what he was seeing. The earth, once scarred by the weight of pollution and the suffocating grip of human consumption, now stood strong and vibrant. The skies were clear, the oceans were recovering, and the forests were thriving once again. It was as if the planet itself had taken a deep breath, exhaling the toxic air of the past and inhaling a new, more promising future.

Aldo had spent years of his life working toward this moment, his every waking hour consumed by the desire to reverse the damage that had been done to the environment. Alongside his team, he had fought battles, both political and personal, against powerful forces that sought to maintain the status quo. They had faced setbacks and moments when victory seemed impossible. But through perseverance, innovation, and unity, they had turned the tide.

And now, as he looked out at the green expanses, the flourishing wildlife, and the bustling, sustainable cities below, Aldo realized they had succeeded. They had changed the course of history. The world, once on the brink of collapse, was now a beacon of hope and resilience for the future.

But even as Aldo took in the view of the thriving planet, he knew that this moment was not the end of their journey. It was a turning point, a beginning, not an end. The work they had done was just the foundation, and it was now up to future generations to build upon it.

Aldo stood still for a moment, letting the wind carry his thoughts. He thought about the early days when he had first set out to change the world. He had been just a man with a vision, surrounded by others who shared his passion for the planet. Back then, they were fighting against a world that seemed indifferent to the damage being done to the environment. It had felt like an impossible battle.

But now, as he looked around, he saw the results of that fight. He saw a world where technology and nature had finally learned to coexist, where clean energy powered cities, where waste was almost nonexistent, and where people lived in harmony with the Earth. This wasn't just a dream anymore, it was reality.

The Struggles Along the Way

The road to this point had been fraught with challenges. Aldo and his team had faced immense opposition from industries that were deeply entrenched in practices that harmed the planet. Fossil fuel giants, manufacturers of single-use plastics, and agricultural companies that practiced destructive deforestation had all fought tooth and nail to maintain their hold on the world's economy. Governments were often reluctant to make the changes necessary to move toward a sustainable future, fearing economic collapse or social unrest.

In those early days, Aldo and his team had to battle misinformation and fear. They had faced constant pressure to abandon their ideals, to accept the status quo, to stop fighting for a dream that seemed too big and too audacious. But they never gave up. They couldn't afford to. The Earth was at stake.

One of the hardest moments had been when the first signs of irreversible climate change became clear—melting ice caps, rising sea levels, and increasingly frequent natural disasters. Aldo had felt the weight of the world on his shoulders. How could they convince the world to change when it seemed so much easier to keep living the way they had been? But Aldo had always believed that change was possible. He had faith in humanity's ability to adapt, to innovate, and to come together when faced with a crisis.

And that's exactly what had happened. Slowly, the world had started to wake up. Governments had shifted policies, large corporations had started to adopt sustainable practices, and everyday people had begun to demand more eco-friendly options. A collective effort emerged, and as the years went by, the planet started to heal.

The Role of Future Generations

Standing at the peak of this monumental achievement, Aldo knew that the fight for the planet would never truly be over. While they had made remarkable progress, the task of ensuring that the world remained on a path of sustainability was not something that could be left to one generation. It was a responsibility that would be passed down from one to the next, each generation building upon the foundation laid by those who came before.

Aldo had always been a visionary, but he was also a realist. He understood that there would be setbacks, that new challenges would arise, and that there would always be forces working against the planet's best interests. But he also knew that the momentum they had created was unstoppable. The seeds of change had been planted, and those seeds were now growing into a movement that would be carried forward by the generations to come.

He thought about the young people who had grown up in a world that prioritized sustainability. They had inherited a different worldview, one where environmental stewardship was just as important as economic prosperity. These young people were not only inheriting the Earth, they were also inheriting the tools, knowledge, and technologies necessary to continue the work that had begun.

Aldo had seen this firsthand as he had traveled the world over the years. In communities across the globe, young leaders were stepping up, bringing new ideas and innovations that Aldo and his team could never have imagined. They were developing technologies that Aldo couldn't even begin to comprehend, advances in renewable energy, waste management, and environmental restoration that were pushing the boundaries of what was possible. They were also embracing a way of life that placed the Earth at the center of everything, advocating for simpler, more sustainable living practices that would ensure the planet's health for generations to come.

A World United in Sustainability

As Aldo stood there, reflecting on the monumental transformation that had taken place, he felt a deep sense of gratitude. They had made it. But more importantly, they had proven that the world could change. The concept of a sustainable future, once relegated to the realm of dreamers and idealists, had become a reality.

But it wasn't just the technology or the policies that had brought about this transformation, it was the unity of people from every corner of the globe. Aldo had witnessed firsthand how communities had come together to support the common goal of environmental protection. The collaboration that had taken place, from grassroots organizations to international coalitions, had been the driving force behind this global shift.

In the end, it was not one person, or one team, that had saved the Earth, it was humanity as a whole. It had been the collective will to change, to adapt, and to fight for a future where the Earth and its inhabitants could thrive together. And this was just the beginning.

The End

Don't miss out!

Visit the website below and you can sign up to receive emails whenever Dayat Suryana publishes a new book. There's no charge and no obligation.

https://books2read.com/r/B-A-WJVDD-VKHYF

BOOKS 2 READ

Connecting independent readers to independent writers.

Did you love *Mount of Waste*? Then you should read *The Wise King's Wall*[1] by Dayat Suryana!

Synopsis: In a realm where powerful kingdoms are separated by vast oceans and untamed lands, King Alaric of Eryndor is known not only for his wisdom but also for his insatiable love of adventure. Accompanied by his loyal army, he journeys to the farthest corners of the world, seeking new lands, and discovering ancient tribes and their secrets.

One such expedition leads King Alaric to a remote island, where a peaceful tribe has been suffering under the tyranny of a brutal, war-hungry tribe that seeks to conquer and destroy all in their path. Desperate for help, the peaceful tribe pleads with the

---

1. https://books2read.com/u/bPk50d
2. https://books2read.com/u/bPk50d

king to create a barrier, a massive wall that would divide their lands from the merciless tribe.

1. King Alaric: The wise and adventurous ruler of Eryndor.
2. Princess Selene: The king's daughter, who shares her father's wisdom and sense of justice.
3. General Kaelen: The king's loyal and skilled military commander.
4. Chief Maika: The leader of the peaceful tribe, who seeks the king's help.
5. Zira: A fierce and brave warrior from the peaceful tribe, who aids the king.
6. Orin: The leader of the merciless tribe, ruthless and power-hungry.
7. Eamon: A seasoned engineer and strategist who helps design the massive wall.
8. Thalira: A shaman from the peaceful tribe, offering guidance and mystical knowledge.
9. Galen: A young, idealistic knight in King Alaric's army, eager to prove his worth.
10. Rurik: The king's trusted advisor, wise but mysterious, with a hidden past.

www.ingramcontent.com/pod-product-compliance
Ingram Content Group UK Ltd.
Pitfield, Milton Keynes, MK11 3LW, UK
UKHW030956240225
455493UK00011B/829

9 798230 095293